MW01689192

The Crimson Thread

ISBN: 1-4196-2517-9

Library of Congress Control Number: 2006900502
To order additional copies, please contact us.
BookSurge, LLC
www.booksurge.com
1-866-308-6235
orders@booksurge.com

ROYSTON
POTTER

The Crimson Thread

The Struggle To Become Jesus During The Revolt Against Rome, An Historical Novel

Evanston, Wyoming
2006

The Crimson Thread

TABLE OF CONTENTS

NOTABLE REVIEWS

Royston Potter's novel is the way one should go about approaching history in the First Century in Palestine and he does so in an imaginative, thought-provoking, and historically compelling manner. Since one is largely dealing with fictionalized romance except for Josephus (even at times, Josephus) where the First Century is concerned, fictionalized romance is the way to correct it; and Potter's experience as a Colonel in the U.S. Army gives him an edge over others who are similarly trying to reconstruct the events of this period through the prism of the novel. With a practiced eye, he is able to peer through both the Gospels and Josephus and revive this period with more accuracy than others relying on 'folk' and 'miracle-working wonder tales'. Bringing to bear the precision provided by the Dead Sea Scrolls, he has brought to life a 'Gospel Truth' more incisive than previous more 'wide-eyed', 'Neoplatonic' forays. Choose it for your must-read list."

—Robert Eisenman, author of **James the Brother of Jesus.**

"This book is an excellent window into the true spiritual and religious practices in Israel 2000 years ago, including the impact the Hechalot (latter, Kabbalah) had on events in history. He effectively negates the disinformation, which has surrounded the official origins of what is now called Christianity, and he does so using historical events that he weaves into an exciting story line with a master's touch. A superb and entertaining novel, it clears the air."

—James A. Kirkwood, author of **Jacob's Ladder**, and **Biblical Meditations, 22 Spiritual Gifts of Ancient Israel.**

ACKNOWLEDGMENTS

I wish to thank all those who have assisted me in the completion of this book. Of course, there is my wife, Carol, who encouraged me onward; also, my good friend, Jim Kirkwood, who guided me in the often difficult aspects of Jewish Mysticism, the Hechalot and the Kabbalah. In particular, I would like to express my deep gratitude to Professor Robert Eisenman's encouragement and inspiration. He is one who, as a true patriot, sacrificed himself for the establishment of truth and academic freedom in spite of the odds mounted against him. May we all be so engaged in the battle against tyranny over the mind of man.

PRONUNCIATION GUIDE AND LIST OF PRINCIPLE CHARACTERS

Amelaus (Ă mĕ lay' ŭs) Herodian noble.
Athronges (Ă thrĂn' jŭs) Zealot Leader.
Bethshemesh (Bĕth shĕm' ĕsh) Same place as Emmaus.
Beit Lechem (Bayit Lĕkĕm) Bethlehem.
Caiaphas (Kye' Ă fŭss) High Priest.
Cleophas (Klē ō' phĂs) Miryam's husband.
Elazer (El ā' zĕr) Mystic teacher.
Eleazer (El ē ā' zĕr) Miriam's brother.
Emmaus (Ĕm ā' yŭs) Same place as Bethshemesh but called Emmaus by the Herodians and Romans. The Jews sometimes used this term to disguise their affiliations.
Jacob (YĂ ā' kōv) Miryam's youngest son who was known as James in the New Testament.
Joachanin ben Zechariah (Yō Ăh' kĂ neen ben ZekĕrīyĂ) John the Baptist and the Teacher of Righteousness.
Jochanan (Yō kĂ' nĂn) Martha's son.
Joseph of Arimathea (Ār ĭ mĂ thē' Ă) Cleophas' brother.
Joses (Yō' sŭs) Miryam's oldest son.
Jude (Yū' dĂ) Joses' twin brother.
Kefa (Key fĂ) One of Miryam's sons whose given name was Simon.
Miriam (Mēr' ē yĂm) Benjamin's daughter and wife of Joses .
Miryam (Mēr ē yĂm) Joses' mother.
Nikdimon ben Gurion (Nĭk' dĭ mōn) Member of Sanhedrin.
On (Own) City of mysticism in Egypt.
Reu (Ray' yū) Amelaus' servant.
Sabinus (SĂ bī' nŭs) Roman Procurator.

Sicarii (Sĭ car' ē) Roman term for militant, armed Zealots.
Simon Magus (Sī' mŭn MĂ' gūs) Mystic, healer, and magician.
Zealots (Zĕl' ŏts) Jewish patriots/firm believers.

This Book Is Dedicated To The Memory Of My Loving Parents. And, To My Wife, Carol, Without Whom I Would Have No Inspiration.

"Everything In The Old Testament Is Perverted And Distorted Into Meanings Never Intended By The Writers. The Practice Which The Writers Of The Books Employ Is Not More False Than It Is Absurd. They State Some Trifling Case Of The Person They Call Jesus Christ, And Then Cut Out A Sentence From Some Passage Of The OT And Call It A Prophecy Of That Case. But When The Words Thus Cut Out Are Restored To The Places They Are Taken From, And Read With The Words Before And After Them, They Give The Lie To The New Testament."
-Thomas Paine

"I Have Recently Been Examining All The Known Superstitions Of The World, And Do Not Find In Our Particular Superstition (Christianity) One Redeeming Feature. They Are All Alike, Founded Upon Fables And Mythologies."
-Thomas Jefferson

"Those Who Can Induce You To Believe Absurdities Can Induce You To Commit Atrocities."
-Voltaire

"The All Wise Creator Hath Been Dishonored By Being Made The Author Of Fable And The Human Mind Degraded By Believing It."

-Thomas Paine

"I Have Sworn Upon The Altar Of God, Eternal Hostility Against Every Form Of Tyranny Over The Mind Of Man."

-Thomas Jefferson (Stated By Jefferson During His Campaign For A Second Term As President Of The United States When Christian Ministers And Lobbyists Were Insisting He Support Christianity As The National Religion As A Condition Of His Re-election.)

"Ye Shall Not Add Unto The Word Which I Command You, Neither Shall Ye Diminish Ought From It..."

-Deuteronomy 4:2

INTRODUCTION

The man, legend, or concept known as Jesus can be found in ancient texts long before the New Testament was written, in Old Testament characters, parts and elements found in various so-called Pagan mythologies, principles heralded by Greek philosophers, evidences presented by scholars, new-fangled interpretations, and outright lies. With all the disinformation, sacred cows, and reputations at stake, the whole truth is probably lost forever, corrupted like so many of man's other endeavors. Likewise, my effort cannot be judged as anything less or more than those before me.

But, there is one difference. I wrote this book and its sequels to force me to study the issues in detail and arrive at the most reasonable answer given what facts are available, and try to balance the rest. One does not challenge the fundamental concepts of a world religion without serious reflection, considerations of moral responsibility, a sense of vulnerability, and raw naked awe at the revelation of the magnitude of the project.

This story is based on historical facts and events, which have been ignored or lost to us over the centuries. Academics and researchers have long known of these issues, but I know of few, if any, who have placed them into a readable story. The events of history in the Roman Empire 2000 years ago impact our perceptions and loyalties even today. That fact must be considered when evaluating the actual circumstances of the birth of a new religion around the efforts of Jewish patriots to free themselves from tyranny. The name of the game was liberation from oppression, the independence of Israel and its survival as a nation and people, and the guaranty of individual dignity and liberty.

The revolt against Rome, for that is what it was, was led by a number of aspiring liberators. The greatest of these liberators taught the idea of the freedom of the individual combined with what modern psychiatry identifies as logotherapy,[1] not the prescription of blind acceptance or feel-good spiritualism. He taught that any requirement to obey a dogma, no matter how well meaning, was unrighteous force. While all peoples fashion their gods after the understanding of their own hearts, any attempt to force that image on others upon some pain of retribution or vengeance does not fit in with the need for the right to discover truth for oneself. This is admittedly contrary to the way this story has been handed down through the millennia.

History shows us there were many "saviors" at the time in history we are presenting. From the Pagan god-myths of Mythra and Dionysus, to the historically verifiable Hebrew messiah claimants beginning with Yeishu ben Pandeira (100 BCE) through Judas of Sepphoris, Athronges, Judas the Galilean, and even Simeon Bar Kochba (as late as 135 CE) to name a few, there has hardly ever been a time without someone trying to fit the profile and lay claim to the title. The historian Josephus even named the then soon-to-be Emperor Vespasian as the promised messiah from Judea! The fact is, many peoples, if not all of them, have a legend of some "man-god" who saves mankind from himself. Whether it is a collective subconscious hope, or a teaching of the ancients assimilated into every culture and tongue according to their understandings, the fact is it exists. The extant existence of this hope, especially amongst the so-called pagans, seems to me to be more of a revelation of the validity of this hope, rather than detraction from it.

But, this brings us to a more plausible explanation of the legend, not of a God-man, but a man accepted by God because of his works and faithfulness. Perhaps, it is most likely a blueprint, if you will, for each individual. The truth is not done for you; you do it for yourself. You are the one ultimately responsible. The greatest gift to us is our unquenchable thirst for answers, and no one has the right to inhibit honest inquiry and the experimentation inherent with that as long as we do not interfere with the rights of others. Who really knows the absolute truth? Usually, as history proves, not those who proclaim they do. Often, it is an individual struggle, rewarded with the awe of discovery that brings with it true conversion, not blind obeisance for mere survival. As one of my former teachers put it, the man Jesus was the first to realize the benefits of his religion for himself.

The premise of the story I present here is based on a family that was steeped in Judean and Galilean resistance to the kittim (Hebrew for foreign invaders or usurpers, the time in reference occupied by Rome and the Herodians). This family appears to provide the central figures of the revolt against Rome, and their names are shown not only in the New Testament, but in other references as well. The distortions concerning these individuals resulted from the fog of history as well as the deliberate attempts by those who saw this information as somehow damaging to their theology or political control.

Evidence of this can be seen in the historian Josephus' works, where the period we are discussing basically takes up only four pages in his **Antiquities of the Jews** and little over two in his **Wars of the Jews**. By contrast, a similar period during Herod's reign took fifty-three pages in the **Antiquities** alone! Explanations for this abound, but none are satisfactory. Either someone, hopefully not Josephus, omitted the material concerning the time frame in question, or Josephus was a party to the subterfuge: a possibility given his position with the Roman Flavian Imperial family.

Those who supposedly wrote the Gospels under such names as Matthew, Mark, Luke, and others were likely decades removed from the real events as were many of the historians of the period. The truth of the matter, sadly, is lost. But, one need only see the modern world to recognize what happened. The winners write history. Fortunately, they frequently forget to erase all the details or completely cover the evidence of what they desired to destroy. All one need do is have the courage to look to find the truth. Like a criminal investigation, the truth is only a matter of the evidence left behind. Do we have the courage to reveal it and call it what it is?

Another factor that can partially explain the historical/scriptural discrepancies is the recognition that the major events described in the New Testament actually occurred at least ten to fifteen years prior to the dates traditionally accepted. For instance, the historian Eusebius, and the **Acti Pilati** (Acts of Pilate) mentioned by Epiphanius, place the start of Pontius Pilate's rule in about 19 CE. This is a full seven years earlier than alluded to in Josephus and the Gospel chronologies.

But, the most significant evidence of a calendar discrepancy is in the New Testament. Luke 2:1-2 states "in those days that there went out a decree from Caesar Augustus, that all the world should be taxed. And this taxing was first made when Cyrenius was governor of Syria." It is subsequent to this tax, as explained by Luke, that Jesus was born. But, Matthew 2:2 has Jesus being born during the last days of King Herod. The problem is that King Herod died in 4 BCE. The tax of Cyrenius was not until 6 CE. Here is at least a ten-year difference. It is likely that the person we know as Jesus may actually have been born as early as 15 BCE, and Epiphanius places it even earlier at around 35 BCE with the calculation that James, Jesus' brother, was 96 when he was martyred in 62 CE. Many have tried to explain this discrepancy away with the possibility that Luke was referring to another tax altogether. But, there is no historical evidence of such an event. The end result is that the chronologies of the New Testament are in serious question, as are Josephus', and it could have been an inadvertent error because of the lapse of time, or a deliberate attempt by others to distort the facts for their own purposes.

In fact, what was born amongst the Jews in Judea and Galilee in 6 CE in direct opposition to the tax was what Josephus called the Fourth Philosophy, "innovators", a Zealot Messianic movement that held inviolable the principle of liberty and the right to repel tyranny and oppression. These principles are at the very heart of a leap in consciousness that would enable mankind, despite efforts by the powerful to suppress them, to envision a world where the individuality and freedom of the soul was as important, or more so, than the government or the nation-state. Indeed, as stated in the Gospels, they envisioned a kingdom "not of this world" (meaning the world of Caesar and tyranny in general). The original books depicting the efforts of these people were written for the Jews who lived in those times and knew the Law or Torah where we generally do not. Living under oppressive occupation, they often wrote in symbolism and parable to try and convey ideas, not the history of a real person per se.

What do these recognitions accomplish for us? Historical events of the Messianic Movement that seemed removed from New Testament time periods now are likely simultaneous events with the lives of those people we recognize: Jesus, John the Baptist, James, Jude, etc.... In other words, the characters of the revolt against Rome from 10 BCE to 70 BCE are likely the same people who figure so prominently in the New Testament under another story line that deliberately, and incorrectly, removes them from any political activity.

Regardless, the evidence that survives appears to show that at or around 20 BCE to 35CE there was a real man whose true character and intentions were lost to us through time and history thanks to opportunists and liars who desired, for their own purposes, to build one of the greatest frauds ever perpetrated on the world. The man known to most of us as Jesus of Nazareth was first and foremost a Jew, more appropriately a renewed Israelite, dedicated to the Law of Israel. He worshipped and lived his life in that context. Also, he was not from Nazareth as it is unlikely such a place existed at the time. But, he apparently was a Nazarene or Nazarite, referring to specific oaths he had taken much like the Essenes. And, of course, his name was not "Jesus" which is the Greek rendition of the Hebrew name, "Yeshua." Even the name "Yeshua," in this case, was likely only an appellation or identification of purpose or calling, meaning "one who saves."

His mission took place in the environment and culture of the times, especially those of his national and spiritual roots, and he cannot be understood outside of them. From the subtle evidence available, he attempted to obey what we know as the Old Testament, especially the first five books, called the Pentateuch or Torah. He is credited as saying that with him the Law (Torah) was fulfilled, or in other words, he did it exactly. He did not eradicate it, change it, or modify it, but instead stated that no point of the Law, "not one jot or tittle", could be taken away. If any one did so, and taught others to disobey it, that person would be the least in the Kingdom of Heaven. There are no more authentic words in the New Testament than these.

But, he was not a fanatic, either. He disdained efforts to interpret the law to say more than the scripture intended and he refused to require unswerving devotion to some brand of interpretation of Torah beyond its own framework. Therefore, there is evidence that he found his spiritual path in the mystical Hechalot (meaning "Chambers," and this later became known as Kabbalah, meaning "to receive") and not so much in the literalist philosophy or even the Pharisaic interpretations passed down as the Oral Torah. Also, he undoubtedly rejected the foreign occupation of Palestine. This put him at odds with the Greco-Roman empires and the puppet rulers and collaborators. All the indications show that he did not approve of the Roman system, especially its despotic rule over Judea, Galilee and the Nation of Israel. However, he did not dislike Romans, if the reader will see that difference.

While maintaining a separation (holiness) from those of the world who ate "meat sacrificed to idols," "slept with women in their periods," or otherwise "polluted the temple," he believed, I am certain, in attempting to understand the whole condition of mankind, and offer them a chance to discover the truth on their own even though he recognized his mission was to his own people, Israel.

He took to heart the prayer for the seventy nations of the world offered by the High Priest of Israel. He lived as a man, with all the responsibilities, rights, joys, and concerns that condition brings to any man. He was also confronted with the greatest of contradictions, yet did not turn away from investigating them, nor did he proceed with an invocation to dogma. He studied the heights and depths of every subject, a characteristic that may have branded him a backslider by those closest to him. As a result, he experienced difficulty at the hands of his family and friends (something common in life), all the while trusting in a power superior to his own, and without a great deal more than the hope that what he stood for was not just his own will or a figment of his imagination. And, he did it without falling short of the mark. He lived the Torah exactly, neither adding to it nor diminishing from it.

Since that time, various religions, governments, and sects have tried to structure history from faith and impose it upon us as immutable fact. We must examine, with particular demands on reason, all aspects of the evidence if we are to be honest with ourselves. One point in Christian scripture seems to make sense given our place in the world, and the chance, albeit a small one, to become something greater than we are. If the self-appointed apostle Paul said anything of value, it was that we are to be joint heirs with Christ; meaning we cannot make the Creator anthropomorphic, but it seems obvious that the Creator has provided us a path to achieve a higher level of understanding, to take some of the Creator's attributes to ourselves. A most important aspect of that character is to look for the truth. As one author put it, "To put dogma above truth is no way to honour God."[2]

This is the story of the beginning of that consciousness which would cause the great kingdoms of the Earth to tremble. The empires and governments of the world, the rich and powerful rulers over the common man, saw a vision of their own demise in the rising of the people to new levels of realization. During and beyond the events of this book, the great powers of the world would use highly refined systems of fear and manipulation to hide the truth of these events from subsequent generations, and seek to suppress the swelling of liberty in the hearts of individuals over whom they held power. The Roman Empire, the Inquisition, and even on to the present day, the powerful try to manipulate and control the masses using a potent mixture of religiosity, superstition and fear. But, the truth whispers to our consciousness like the remembrance of a son for a father. Will we listen?

For most of my life, I have studied numerous religions and spiritual paths, particularly Israelite culture and tradition. Most fascinating and enlightening, in my view, are the Torah along with its rabbinical interpretive techniques and the mystical Kabbalah. This story is the result of that most rewarding journey. I must, however, emphasize that this is a story, a novel. It is based on historical and religious research, but it is still a novel. I found it necessary to use some of the esoteric language of the people in this period and that may become awkward for the reader. Where possible, I have defined the terms and conditions. Often, however, I could not. I am not a master of these traditions and techniques; I am merely aware that they exist and played an important part in history. Hopefully, those who find these things of interest or value will search them out on their own.

So, what I can promise here is that I have attempted to keep the story within the framework of historical believability and scriptural law that a most dedicated man, represented in today's world as Jesus Christ, would surely manifest in his life in every way. While this fictionalized account may appear primarily conjecture, it is no more so than the versions handed down through the centuries by theocratic and political leaders. This depiction of the man we know as Jesus does not diminish from his purpose or his contribution to the spiritual advancement of mankind. What it does do is de-Romanize the mission of Jesus, and returns his story to its Jewish origins. The message of his life and his example is that the Kingdom of Heaven is reached, not through the auspices or approval of any man or organization, but only through a personal relationship with the Creator and individual spiritual advancement. Therefore, it is not and cannot be bestowed upon one without warrant. If one only follows in his footsteps and obeys "the law and the testimony," the individual can indeed find his way to the Throne of Glory.

In this book the reader will discover the humanity, and the

true spirituality, of the man called HaMashiach (Hebrew for The Messiah). In his story is the hope of individual freedom, and its cost, along with the realization that our condition is the basic blueprint for approaching the Divine.

PROLOGUE

The world is at war! Any nation or people who will not bow down to the western empire is crushed, destroyed, or absorbed. Under the guise of restoring liberty to the oppressed, a tyrant justifies his expansions and influence. "We know what is best for you, and that we intend to force upon you under the pain of death or economic destruction. You have the right to choose our way; any other is contrary to the will of your people. We are the great republic turned empire, overseen by our beneficent Emperor."

It is the period of 50 BCE to 35 CE and the Roman Empire has swallowed the western world and secured its usurpation of the trade routes to the east. It was all necessary for the national security and the freedoms of the people of Rome. In the wake of the onslaught, millions of people are killed and enslaved, and whole peoples are victims of mass genocide. To ensure control, the Romans have placed their own rulers over the lands they conquer. These rulers are not selected by the local people or by their traditions. The rulers are foreigners and traitors appointed by Caesar. In Caesar's name, these rulers plunder the land, kill or imprison their detractors, and incite the people with contrived disturbances to further justify their presence. They offer a false security in exchange for the people's acquiescence.

Opposing these invaders and usurpers is a group of patriots who do not want to accept the invitation to the Pax Romana. Like all those who want to determine their own course, a number of their brave join ranks and seek to expel the invaders even at the peril of the loss of their fortunes, families, and lives. Their own system of government had worked for them, and if they had had tyrants in their system, well, they were their tyrants and would deal with them accordingly. The rulers put in by the invaders are not of the peoples' choosing, and despite all claims to the contrary, offer no abiding guarantees of good and righteous government. The people conquered by this irresistible force do not lightly accept their fate and know that the real reason for the presence of the invader is robbery of the resources of their own lands and religious treasures.

This is the seedbed of the Jewish resistance against Rome. They do not assent to Roman occupation or rule, and are fierce in the defense of their land. Their leaders are Kefa, Jude the Sicariote, Simon Magus, Eleazer, Jacob, Joses, and even Jesus or Yeshua, the Messianic King. They rise in defiance of the Roman war machine and out of respect for the traditions of their fathers. Their God is the God of their fathers, and they have sworn not to place any man or thing ahead of this deity. To those who listen to the heroes of Judea and Galilee, they hear their plea: "Seek for the truth, and the truth will make you free."

Yet, in the midst of this maelstrom stand two men, brothers, who trace their lineage from King David. They both lay claim to the throne of Israel and neither will surrender to the other. The outcome of this rivalry may decide the fate of Israel and all history. This is their story—and ours.

CHAPTER ONE

The arrow had found its mark in his chest. He had no immediate sense of pain, only of confusion. His compatriots were fleeing towards the rocks in the mountain ravine to the east, knowing they did not have the numbers to stand off an attack by a well-armed and determined Roman Army Century (a unit of infantry of 100 soldiers). They had been caught by surprise while traveling to northern Judea on a recruiting mission to gather converts to the resistance. It was not a normal situation as the Sicarii (the Roman name for a group of Jewish revolutionaries known to carry an Arabic dagger called a sicar) were extremely careful to avoid detection.

But, the haste of the travel had caused them to err in judgment, and now Jude lay helpless on the warm ground watching his life's blood stain the sand a bright, almost iridescent red. He was stunned, but more conscious than he believed he had ever been in his life. The color of the blood reminded him of why he was here, and why his mission was so important. Like King David of old, he had fled to the wilderness to sustain the movement and consolidate his alliances. Though not the recipient of the crimson thread, he still laid claim to the throne of King David, the throne of all Israel, because his twin brother who was the first born, had forfeited his right to the heirship by his refusal to submit to the requirements of the Torah as pronounced by the High Priest.

His small band had fought bravely, fighting the Roman ambush with a fierce counter attack. But, the odds were against them, as were the professional techniques exhibited by the Romans. The Roman Officer had placed his soldiers not in the hills above the path, but in a cleverly concealed depression in the roadside. It was all but invisible until the Sicarii were almost on top of it. Jude himself had killed two Roman soldiers, their corpses now laying not ten feet from his own wounded body. Of his band of 30 warriors, it appeared 20 or more were dead, and several wounded were screaming a short distance from him as the Romans interrogated them, probing the wounds with their blades while demanding answers. The Roman Officer stood above Jude.

"I am impressed with your knowledge of the necessities of close and deadly combat," commented the officer with a broad and victorious smile. "But, then again, a leader of the Sicarii, maybe the chief leader, would understand basic tactics." Jude tried to remain unnerved. How did the Romans know this much about him? Much had been done to cloud the reality of his true identity and the purpose of his mission.

"I think you are the leader of the Sicarii," stated the Roman with an assurance that left Jude unable to contradict. "These men deferred to you during your travels. I believe others have called you, among other names, Simon the Zealot, and Judas the Galilean, is that not true?" asked the officer in a broken Aramaic. But, Jude felt no need to answer the charge. The Roman continued, "Yes, you are in disbelief, I understand. Your god has failed you again. When are you going to admit that all you have stood for is a shepherd god of no consequence?" the officer mused.

Jude remained silent, and the light of day seemed to be fading. Actually, it was near noon, and it was not the rays of the sun that were abating, but Jude's eyesight. He had now lost much blood and the pain was becoming unbearable. He laid his head down on the sand, no longer able to hold it up and look into the eyes of the Roman commander. Was all lost? Would he now never sit on the throne of David?

Kefa, one of Jude's younger brothers and second in command on this mission, was trying to push the remnant of the small band of Zealots up into the hills as fast as he could. The climb, while not high, was difficult for these men as they had just spent much of their energy during the combat. All were weary from the battle, breathing hard and sweating profusely, some wiping sweat from their eyes with hands still dripping with blood that marred their faces and brows. None but Kefa dared look back to take account of the situation they left behind. They could not afford capture, which would prevent a proper message to the revolutionary leadership back in Damascus by the Dead Sea. An heir to the Kingdom of Israel had been wounded and captured, maybe even now dead. There was no thought of rest.

"We must keep moving," Kefa gasped as he pushed one man ahead of him who was particularly slow. "The ambush was only a small part of the Roman force here. See," he pointed to the hilltop across the small valley for anyone who dared to slow down long enough to look, "over there is the main body of the Romans, and they are trying to maneuver around us to stop our retreat." He was pointing to the west where a visible cloud of dust was already rising above the hills, an unmistakable sign of a sizeable Roman force on the move, possibly a century, or even a cohort (300-600 soldiers).

"We have only the hope that HaShem[3] will conceal us from their eyes. We must keep moving and make it across the Jordan before they encircle us to the south." Kefa continued to push them, some stumbling as they headed down the opposite side of the hill and on toward the Jordan River some three furlongs (about 600 meters) to the east. None dared stop until they reached the river.

"There, see? Cross at the widest point so that the water can cover our footprints," Kefa commanded. Two of them men hesitated. "What are you waiting for?" Kefa demanded.

"We are afraid we will drown!" one of the exhausted men replied.

"Go, now!" Kefa yelled, making the men fear him more than the uncertainty of their abilities. As it turned out, the water was also relatively shallow at this point as none of the men's heads went below the surface during the crossing. The water cleansed their skin and clothing, most of the blood and dirt washing off, while it cooled their hot and stressed bodies. Once all were on the other side, the party split up, doing their best to cover their footprints with weeds and other vegetation until they reached a traveled path.

Kefa was nearly a madman when it came to fighting the Romans. But, he was also wise enough to know when to live to fight another day. Large, but not rotund, he could kill silently with a twist of his blade, or his hands. Unkempt hair and soiled clothing marked his constant state of agitation and lack of attention to detail. The men following him did so not out of respect for his ability to make a plan of action, but because they knew he could fight off any small patrol of Roman infantry, as well as help them get across the sometimes swelling waters of the Jordan. And that is precisely what he did. They lost no more men to the Romans that day. What they lost was their hope.

Kefa separated from the last of the band and headed north to the Sea of Galilee, the area where he had taken up residence. Most of the rest of the men had to travel much further south near the Dead Sea to the community named Damascus by their priestly head, the Teacher of Righteousness. But, they were now far from the action of the past day and the likelihood of discovery by Roman soldiers and scouts who would recognize them was remote. Kefa would have accompanied the other men to aid in the report of their captured leader, but his job at the moment was to keep his eyes and ears open in Galilee and notify his oldest brother in Tarichaeae so that the leaders could make decisions based on timely and accurate information. It was to one of the other survivors of the ambush that the responsibility to notify Damascus would fall.

Judea, indeed all of Palestine, was in an uproar. As had been the case for a thousand years or more, Palestine was a primary gateway to the East and to Africa, and as such was always the center of power struggles between major and minor kingdoms. The trade routes through her were prone to raids by robbers and resistance fighters, so those who conquered the area decreed that in the interest of national security, the lands there should be under military control if not also puppet governments. Several times, these puppet governments had been put into place by the predominant power. So it was for Palestine during the last couple of centuries.

The last legitimate Jewish High Priest known to history was

Onias III who died in about 175 BCE. The Greek Seleucid King Antiochus refused to allow Onias' brother to take the office, and Onias' son was still but an infant. The King replaced Onias with men of Onias' family who basically apostatized and became Greeks in all their ways. The faithful Cohanim, priests descended from Aaron, almost vanished from the scene. At about this time, the Maccabean rebellion against the Seleucids began.

The Maccabees, a family of Jews, successfully organized the Jewish people and threw off foreign rule by the Seleucid Kings (Alexander the Great's Generals), but their power had been corrupted as they played politics with Rome, the rising power in the western world. The Maccabees assumed priestly and kingly roles, but had no solid claim by their ancestral descent in either case. Most, if not all, Israelite tribal genealogy had been lost since the Babylonian Captivity several centuries earlier. Anyone claiming specific lineage was usually only adopting it according to legend or family tradition.

In fact, the conduct and claims of the Maccabees caused a rift with those who insisted they were descendants of King David, and these descendants left Jerusalem, presumably followed by the remainder of the legitimate Cohanim/Priests of the line of Aaron. They founded the community by the Dead Sea called Damascus (Qumran) about 152 BCE. Believing they could restore some semblance of the true order of Israel outside of the contested wranglings of the Hasmonaean Maccabees whose spiritual observances had decayed in their placation of Rome, these people who settled Damascus formed a "righteous" or Zadokite community there.

Eventually the Maccabees fell from power and the Romans replaced them with a group of non-lineal Jews (converts) from the Idumean Edomites under the family name eventually known as Herodians. The Maccabean King John Hyrcanus had forcibly converted this family of Idumeans to Judaism around 125 BCE. Force always generates more problems than it solves. The Herodians, as this family and their supporters were called, had submitted to Roman control and presented the Romans favors, for which they were rewarded the rule over the Jews. Indeed, Augustus Caesar had crowned Herod Antipater's son, Herod the Great, as King of the Jews and ruler of Judea, second only to Augustus himself.

This entire arrangement did not set well with Jews. When Herod had the Maccabean Jonathan, his wife Mariamme's (a Maccabean princess) younger brother, drowned after the Jewish people had fondly accepted him as their legitimate High Priest (in fact he was not a Cohanim or of Priestly descent as were none of the other Maccabees), Herod took control of the High Priest vestments and appointed these priestly leaders himself. The Roman Governors who would follow him did the same. This took away any hope of a legitimate birthright high priesthood and gave it to foreigners, a primary cause of the new messianic uprisings against the Roman occupiers and their Herodian puppets.

Herod's jealousy and concern for his throne even caused him to direct the murder of his own sons from the Maccabean women he had married. Such ruthlessness caused Augustus Caesar to comment, "It is better to be Herod's pig, than his son." He executed other family members and friends as time went on. These and other encroachments on the Jewish national identity brought resistance to the new regime. Numerous would-be leaders claiming to be the Jewish Mashiach (in Jewish thought, not a savior of souls as much as a "crown prince," or "anointed king in waiting") would promote themselves as the new King of Israel, only to be quickly and completely destroyed by the Roman war machine aided by Herod's spy apparatus and army.

With the destruction of the Maccabees by Herod and Rome, Herod and his reign further alienated the Jewish bloodlines, inadvertently adding support to the resistance in and out of Damascus. Eventually, several brothers who considered themselves of the lineage of King David of old would make their appearance at Damascus and the new messianic movement would change the course of history. What was known as the "Star Prophecy" (Numbers 24:17), a coming of an Israelite messianic king to rule the world, and the many prophecies of a messianic deliverer in the Book of Daniel, were upon the hearts and lips of most Jews.

The people looked to the royal lineage in hiding as never before. In fact, the name of their city, Damascus, meant the cup of blood, or the vessel holding the royal bloodline. They had built an extensive and well-trained group of followers who supported them in their claims and exhibited a military proficiency in the guerilla warfare tactics of the time. Known as the Zealots (Kanna'im in Hebrew), Nazarenes (those who have taken a Nazarite vow), or Sicarii, they were influential in many of the Jewish sects and divisions, even the Essenes.

Of course, the Herodian rulers and their puppets, though claming to be Jews, or who were Jewish turncoats, considered these Zealots to be criminals. But the true Jewish sects, with all their differences, shared one hope that bound them all, and that was the restoration of the Mashiach ben David or Davidic King who would remove the invaders and usurpers and bring about another, even permanent, golden age under HaShem.

The story of the brothers, four in number, began many years after the rise and fall of the Maccabean dynasty. Sometime before the death of Herod the Great in 4 B.C., a young Jewish woman named Miryam of the tribe of Levi married a man claiming descent from King David. His name was Cleophas. Cleophas, well schooled in the Davidic requirements of succession as practiced at the time, had married Miryam and been sequestered from her for a definitive period. Unlike the methods of older Israelite Kingdoms, these periods of sequester were intended to demonstrate that the children born of the union were of the union and under very pure circumstances, thus producing a pure bloodline.

The first children born to these new parents were a set of twin boys who were born at Beit Lechem in the month of Adar (March/April) during the feast of Purim. For the Davidic dynasty, this month of birth was a problem for anyone who sought to claim the right to the Davidic throne as the Mashiach was supposed to be born during the month of Tishrei (Sep/Oct) around the celebration of Yom Kippur, or Day of Atonement. Yet, this did not deter the family from following all the other requirements. As was the custom, the firstborn was the heir. This was recognized by the attachment of a crimson thread around one of the firstborn's limbs at the moment of birth. That first-born child was named Joses. His twin brother was then born and the parents named him Jude.

Over the next few years the couple bore two more sons, named Jacob and Simon. They eventually nicknamed Simon, Kefa, as the youngster proved to be impetuous, yet predictable and fearless. Also born into the family was a sister named Salome.

During the course of the raising of the family, it was necessary for Cleophas to move to northern Egypt. Herod the Great had been trying to hunt down and destroy all remnants of the Maccabean Dynasty as well as anyone claiming descent from King David, even those in Damascus. While Herod had a respect for the Essenes of Damascus because of the prophecies by Menachem the Essene that seemed favorable to Herod, he could not allow Damascus to shield this potential threat. His insatiable rage and jealousy even necessitated the murder of his Maccabean wife, Mariamme, and his own son by her who would have been the High Priest (popular, but still not of the proper bloodline). It was what he needed to do to ensure that no new threats to his rule would arise. Certainly, he could not afford such an eventuality in his own household, no matter how remote that may be. Herod's ruthlessness had convinced Cleophas to ensure the survival of his family by leaving for the time being.

While in Egypt, Cleophas had the oldest boys schooled at On, where a Hebrew Temple and priesthood were located outside the reaches of Herod and the questionable purity of the priesthood he presided over in Jerusalem. In fact, the temple at On was nearly as well recognized by certain Diaspora (dislocated from Judea into other regions of the world) Jews as was Herod's Temple in Jerusalem, which was basically a renovation and improvement over the older temple structure conceived by King David and begun by his son, Solomon.

The Temple at On, on the other hand, had been built by Onias, the same legitimate High Priest who the Seleucid King Antiochus had deposed. Onias had fled to Egypt and gained the support of the Greek ruler, Ptolemy. Ptolemy allowed him to build the Temple at On at the same ancient site used by the Israelites before the exodus in the previous millennium. In this Temple, Onias established the Torah and all its mysteries for those who desired them and were proven worthy. In addition, known members of the priesthood conducted the sacred rituals, as would those who eventually fled to Damascus.

Here another issue arose that was based on the historical and scriptural "enmity" between the Israelite Tribes of Ephraim and Judah. Shiloh, north of Jerusalem, was the original repository for the Ark of the Covenant, and, therefore, considered by many to be the true location for the Temple[4]. This had been in dispute for centuries. King David had moved the Ark to Jerusalem, a fortified city, for protection, and then planned a Temple, or permanent Tabernacle, to contain it. While David's son, Solomon, originally built the Jerusalem Temple, it was subsequently destroyed and rebuilt several times. The real problem then became the fact that Herod's improvement of it was, by many, considered defiled, partly because he was not a purebred Israelite or descendent of King David. Furthermore, he had brought in other non-Jewish priests to preside over the rites conducted in the temple he built in Jerusalem, and these priests then permitted other activities technically prohibited by the Torah.

In other words, those ruling the Jews who were called Jews at the time may not have been Jews at all, but Herodians or sympathizers of the Herodians. In either case, they were not the legitimate rulers according to Israelite lineage and the purity of the Jerusalem Temple was brought into question. Hence, Cleophas believed the boys could receive an untainted education outside of Judea and Damascus only in On, Egypt. This entire issue of the Temple would eventually become a point of contention between the sons of Cleophas.

Upon Herod's death, Cleophas returned the family to Judea and settled again at the city of the Nazarenes, also called the Wilderness and Damascus. It was here that the sons of Cleophas and Miryam would define their roles in HaShem's Kingdom on Earth.

One of the twins' younger brothers was named Jacob. Even as a child he seemed special, almost angelic. As Jacob grew and matured he accepted a Nazarite vow to devote himself to HaShem and took additional vows to ensure his purity. He maintained a serious piety throughout his life. He never ate meat, not even in childhood, he drank no wine, and he shunned strangers and lived a life of monastic separation and poverty. He treated all men well but maintained a separation from the unholy and impure.

He never associated closely with women and never engaged in sexual intercourse. In this regard to women, he did not entertain distaste for them or a desire to disobey the first commandment to multiply and replenish the earth. To the contrary, his devotion to HaShem brought him to an understanding that he was to join himself only with his female counterpart, his bishirtah or soul mate. In regards to his life's mission, any other was not needful or acceptable. He believed he needed to keep himself separate from the activities of the world so that he could receive direct assistance from HaShem in all matters pertaining to the conduct of his righteous duties.

Furthermore, Jacob entered the Mikvah, a ritual bath, several times a day to maintain his bodily cleanliness and purity. Jacob, like his cousin Joachanin ben Zechariah, was a priest, a high priest. But unlike Joachanin's claims through Levitical lines, Jacob had no claim by birth to the Levitical Priesthood or priesthood of Aaron. Jacob was a High Priest after the order of Melchizedek, a particular priesthood based on righteousness, lineage being a secondary consideration, if at all. He had obtained that priesthood through a process of discipline, piety and absolute righteousness, recognized by the mystics of Emmaus and Damascus, and through the declaration of the Teacher of Righteousness. In fact, Jacob was called the Just, or Righteous One.

Jacob's piety had been taught to him by Chananya ben Menachem, son of Menachem the Essene as Chananya was initiating others, including Joachanin into the sect of the Nazarenes. Chananya, Teacher of Righteousness at the City of the Nazarenes, was the master of the mysteries and the leader of the Community. His principle calling, as he saw it, was to bring about the rise of two mashiachs, a Messianic King from the house of David and a High Priest from the line of Moses' High Priest, Aaron. The first in line for the High Priesthood was Joachanin who was the son of the Priest Zechariah and his wife Elizabeth who was the first cousin to Jacob's mother, Miryam. Joachanin was held as the true High Priest of Israel in opposition to the Herodian hierarchy. As Joachanin matured and began his ministry, he placed Jacob, Jude and Simon into the running Mikvah of the Jordan River and proclaimed them members of HaShem's Kingdom on Earth, soon to be that Kingdom's administrators. Joses, the oldest of the brothers, entered the waters only some years after he was married.

While commendable in many degrees, Jacob's extremism in interpreting the Torah became a point of contention between him and the oldest brother, Joses. In fact, Joses often tried to point out to Jacob that his example was beyond Torah Law, possibly even to the extent of actually defying it. Jacob clung to the Oral Traditions of the Torah as well as the traditions surrounding the Hechalot (early mysticism later to become the Kabbalah). But Joses, seeing the extreme legalities of the Oral Torah as mere commandments of men, clung only to the Torah itself and the Hechalot. As a result of his position and his quests for enlightenment, Joses' efforts were met with ridicule from the entire family and the members of the Community. This brought into question Joses' ability to perform as the kingly mashiach, and all were quick to insist that his younger twin brother, Jude, be recognized as the legitimate heir to the throne.

Joses was born first, before Jude, and received the crimson thread which he wore until the twins were old enough that all could recognize them. Early in his development, it was obvious that Joses was given more to exploration and study, questioning and discovery. This was most evident in his spiritual studies, particularly the mystical Hechalot as taught in On of Egypt and at Emmaus in Judea. While he believed in Torah, his family did not judge him valiant in defending it to their satisfaction, particularly his brothers.

He was somewhat sickly throughout most of his childhood, and developed a slight hunchback as a result of his infirmities, and he did not particularly look the part of a king. Also, he failed to attain to any satisfactory height, being much shorter than his younger brethren.

He was sent away by his mother, Miryam, after his father Cleophas' death, to be with his uncle, Joseph of Arimathea. Joseph was a businessman of considerable wealth and traveled the known world trading goods and raw materials, especially tin. Miryam's motive had more to do with peace in the home than Joses' penchant for discovery. He was in constant contention with his younger brothers over the application of Torah and the rigid interpretation Jacob placed upon it. It was not that Joses did not follow the Torah; it was that he believed its message was summed up in the first two great commandments to love HaShem and to love one's neighbor.

While this teaching of the Torah was also explained and taught extensively in On, Emmaus, and Damascus, Joses felt the leadership of Damascus had added weighty and unnecessary requirements. For one, Joses did not feel it right that Chananya had decreed that any Gentile found discussing Torah should be forced to undergo circumcision and be converted. Yes, the Torah was for Israel, but there could be no harm, in Joses' mind, of people discussing its great lessons and stories. It was done everywhere in the world, anyway, why inflict such regimens on those in Judea? According to the brethren of the Community, these were ostensibly to ensure righteousness, but they went beyond the mark as far as Joses was concerned.

At the same time, Joses had taken the mystical side of the Torah to heart, studying diligently under the tutelage of the priests at On and the mystics of Emmaus. While the mystical side of Judaism was also used and respected by Jacob and Jude, Joses' approach bore what was considered to be some aspects of the eastern religions of India and Persia, along with the Egyptian, where he had traveled with his uncle, Joseph of Arimathea. It made him ever the more suspicious to his siblings and others who thought him lazy in other aspects of his responsibilities. Indeed, even his mother Miryam had decided that Joses was not a serious boy in his preparations to assume any leadership role. That seemed, by default, to fall upon his younger twin brother, Jude.

Almost Joses' direct opposite, Jude kept himself separated from anything but the regimens of Torah as interpreted in Damascus, and he was an active and fierce soldier for the resistance. He fully respected Chananya, Joachanin ben Zechariah and Jacob, in all their interpretations of the Torah and its implications to the chosen people. He considered himself to be, like Jacob the son of the patriarch Isaac, the true heir deserving of the right of the firstborn since Joses did not seem to take the birthright seriously.

Jude was the obvious choice for the leader of the military side of the revolutionary movement, or in simpler terms, to be the Davidic King. Large, quick, agile and even handsome, he could command attention by his mere presence. He was a spectacular orator and could elucidate on the most difficult aspects of the Torah and the Kingdom of HaShem, as well as plan and execute detailed guerilla warfare plans designed with the hope that they could force the Romans to leave Judea. In short, he could perform the duties of a king.

Jude recognized early on that his speeches in public sectors had to be delivered with veiled references and codes, also known as parables. Those who could understand the veiled words were the already chosen members of the movement who understood the codes and took the directed actions. To all others, the speeches were quite benign and even pacifist in orientation. Converts to his brand of Judaism spread quickly as his message became more extant. Converts to the more militant side of the Messianic Movement or Zealots (called by the Romans, Sicarii) were then mined from this group. But, he did not let anyone know his true identity or origins in order to protect the movement. In fact, the Romans and Herodians believed most of the inhabitants in Damascus at the time to be a benign, ascetic and eccentric sect of Jews called Essenes. The cover worked well until the two twins began a competition over the birthright.

The inhabitants of Judea began to see Jude as the kingly mashiach promised to them. After the death of Chananya ben Menachem at the hands of the Romans, the people then recognized Joachanin ben Zechariah's position as Rabbi Tzedeq or Righteous Teacher, the legitimate High Priest in opposition to the Herodian High Priest in Jerusalem. These early leaders of the new messianic movement found followers eager to hear their messages and join in the revolutionary activities against Rome and the Roman puppets, the Herodians.

Particularly in Jude's efforts, he was seen as Yehoshua, the savior of his people. As a result, he was called by another name by his friends and his enemies. He was Yehoshua ha Mashiach, Mashiach ben David, Yeshua ha Mashiach, Jesus the Messiah or Jesus Bar Abbas, Jesus Son of the Father, which can also be Yeshua ben Elohim, interpreted to mean, Jesus, Son of God. He was Barabbas.

As a result of these messianic underpinnings against Roman rule, Rome continually built up the military occupation of Palestine. Roman Procurators and larger army units were sent to Caesarea on the coast of the Mediterranean not far from Galilee. These Roman governors and the military forces under their control were there to ensure that no power would attempt to dislodge the puppets, the Herodians, or threaten Roman national security and control of the trade routes. It was a fierce and violent time, the Roman army slaying thousands at a mere whim. Not a day went by without military action. The Romans sharpened their swords every night.

It is under these conditions that the story unfolds.

CHAPTER TWO

Years before the ambush of Jude and his band of Zealots in northern Judea, his twin brother was sent on one of many journeys.

It was a glorious day! The ocean was relatively calm and swayed the ship gently from side to side as a warm breeze assisted the oarsmen in making headway. The sun shown brightly, warming the wooden planks of the deck as the ocean water glistened and shimmered like diamonds. The crew talked excitedly about their arrival on the shores of India, laughing with the young apprentice of the Master of the Vessel. They had been at sea for nearly two months, dropping off trade goods and tin and picking up spices and other assorted luxuries.

The Master reviewed the scroll of inventory that listed the items soon to be delivered in return for a handsome profit. The laughter and friendship of the crew with his young nephew and apprentice pleased him. He smiled as he thought how the boy was always witty and fun loving, able to hold his own in any company.

The Master had been a businessman all of his life, and had done extremely well. In fact, his family was very wealthy, as were most of the Jewish nobility. He was also a counselor in the prestigious and powerful Sanhedrin in Jerusalem, a legal organization or high court that technically held the highest legal and religious authority over the Jews, even interpreting Torah law. Trading tin with the Roman Empire, as well as much of the rest of the known world, he was well respected. But, there was more about him than just his money.

He was also a man of wisdom, understanding, and vision, which enabled him to hold his faith sacred as he dealt in the world at large. His sister-in-law, Miryam, respected him so much, that she had encouraged him to take her eldest son with him so that the boy might learn more about other places and people. The boy's father, the Master's brother, had died and the ingenuity and creativity of that father was the boy's gift as well. It needed to be channeled properly to allow it to grow. Furthermore, the boy was at constant odds with his siblings, his younger twin brother and two others younger still. He was certainly different from the rest in his habits and interests. While considered lazy by most of his family in regards to certain standards of conduct, the Master of the Vessel felt much differently about him.

As the Master made the final corrections to the scroll, he looked up in time to see the young man of seventeen years leave the workmen and move to the bow of the ship. The boy was of short stature, but had developed his strength by a constant program of physical work and training to try to overcome the infirmities he had experienced from birth. He had, with some effort, overcome the imbalance of a minor spinal deformity that caused a small hunchback just below his shoulders, and had worked to develop a surety in his walk that was almost regal. The Master watched as the young man's long brown hair blew in the wind, his bluish-gray eyes returning the gaze of his uncle as he moved. Neither needed to speak; only smiles of gratitude and respect were exchanged between them. The young man looked again ahead of the ship toward the shore that was now visible in the distance.

When small children, the young lad and his siblings were taken to Jerusalem by their parents, the adept and able Cleophas, a builder who was the area's foremost architect, and his young wife, Miryam, a daughter of a priestly family. Cleophas considered himself to be a descendant of the royal house of King David, and in fact, Cleophas was considered the heir to the throne by those acknowledging his lineage. However, the Herodians had been put into power by the Roman Empire, the Davidic Dynasty shattered by long and brutal wars and intrigue. Cleophas was no threat to Herod, or to Caesar, and paid his due respects like everyone else. His expertise in building was evident throughout the province and the needed skill took second place to any concerns about his rights and claims to royalty.

The oldest son, now with his uncle, the Master of the Vessel, was considered by some to be the next legal heir to the throne of David, although he had been raised in Egypt in the city called in Greek, Heliopolis (On in Egyptian), making him now somewhat foreign to the Jews of Judea. The situation bearing upon his alienation was made even more so after the family had moved to the City of the Nazarenes by the Dead Sea. His particular stand for the Torah and its interpretation would probably cause not only the Judeans, but also even his own family, to reject him in the unlikely event that Herod and Rome relinquished control. But, that did not really matter. The young man was making a name for himself despite the difficulties.

The Master, Joseph the tin trader, also known as Joseph of Arimathea, was at the Temple in Jerusalem at the time the lad's parents took him there when he was about thirteen years of age, and he heard the young man talk with the priests and rabbis for sometime. It was then, more than the genealogy and signs of royalty, that Joseph recognized something intensely different about the young man. Was it his training in On that gave him such power and wisdom in his questions and answers? The priests in On were known for their mystical and speculative ways, although rejected by the Herodian puppets in Jerusalem and most of mainstream Judaism. Yet, how else could one account for the wit of the youngster?

"And what about the flood?" one of the priests asked the boy. "Did it not fill the whole world?"

"More than a flood of water," responded the boy, "it was a loss of the spirituality of the people, the light of HaShem taken from their minds because they did not seek for Him."

"Your Bar Mitzvah is complete, young Joses, but you seem to deny the scripture so soon," retorted the priest.

"Did not our father Abraham place his tent under a tree between Bethel and Ai?" responded the boy.

"Yes," answered the priest.

The boy continued, "Then Abraham was the receding waters, and was the type and shadow for the dry land, placing his tent under a symbol of the Tree of Life. He recognized the balance one must obtain to achieve the notice of Him Who Rules All Things. Therefore, what does it matter if the world was covered by water as long as Abraham's children search for HaShem always in their hearts?"

A Sadducee broke in, "Abraham is our father, but Moses gave us the Torah after he spoke with HaShem on the mountain. Who is greater?"

"For every thing under heaven there is a season," began the boy, "and who is righteous is he who does the will of HaShem. Noah sought HaShem, and built an ark to save the seed of Adam. Abraham sought for HaShem and was HaShem's friend, the father of our people and the most blessed of all nations. Moses sought for HaShem and received the Law that had been lost after Israel's enslavement in Egypt. Mashiach will free us from the kittim, restore Israel, free our spirits, and then present us with the Kingdom. All things are to be done in order, in their time and season. The least in the Kingdom who does the will of HaShem is as great as any of these."

"Will not HaShem free us from Roman rule and restore the Throne of David our King?" interrupted a Pharisee who was not as closely tied to Herod as many who were present. An argument ensued.

"What is this?" demanded a priest sitting close to the boy. "Such talk is sedition and can bring about all our deaths. What good is it to HaShem if we are no more? Quiet this talk of HaMashiach. There are dozens of these crazy ones walking around claiming it and the Romans kill them as soon as they are known. Let us live in peace."

"How can there be peace when Rome dictates our lives, even demanding tribute that should be given as sacrifice in the temple?" responded another.

"You cannot speak against Romans and the Herodian leaders!" exclaimed the first priest. "HaShem has set them above us and it is

His will, or otherwise it would not be so. The Romans leave us to our faith for the most part. They only demand allegiance to their politics. Why do our discussions of the faith always come down to this political debate? Leave it alone and live in the world as HaShem has given it to us."

"You are not truly one of us!" interrupted another priest, "You are an imposter sent by Herod and the Romans! You are the one that should leave us alone!"

Everyone recognized the danger of the moment and a thick air settled upon the assembly. The boy stood so all could see he desired to speak. As was the custom, he waited to be recognized by the senior man present.

"Yes, son of Cleophas, what is your idea on this?" asked the old patriarch.

"It is true," he began, "that we must live in the world as HaShem has delivered it to us. However, Torah requires us to have only one whom we worship and that we must forsake all others, as a bride forsakes all others for her love. The Roman Emperor demands the worship of his subjects, and Torah forbids us to worship any but HaShem. Worshiping other gods, an act similar to adultery, is death under Torah. So does it matter more if Rome kills us or if HaShem kills us?"

No one answered him.

***

Joseph was suddenly reminded of his duties as the ship entered the harbor. Without incident the crew began unloading the slabs of tin under the direction of Joseph's nephew. In perfect order and with expert precision, each slab was taken from the ship and loaded on the dock. On the steps leading from the dock to a warehouse, Joseph moved towards the merchant who was buying the material and handed him the scroll.

"Arimathea!" exclaimed the merchant. "You have delivered on time and I thought there was no possibility. A god of the seas looks after you! How long will you stay this time?"

"I plan on visiting for a period long enough to allow my nephew some time to become acquainted with the area. I will let him finish the unloading of the vessel and will have my next assistant take over loading what you have for us. But, how are you, Rajak?"

"There is much talk of your arrival here," Rajak said excitedly as he looked past Joseph to try and get a look at the boy. "I have tried to keep the time of your arrival a mystery as you requested. Why does he draw that much attention?"

"He attended school in On as a young boy." Joseph looked over toward the ship and took a deep breath. "The priests of On trained him and his twin brother, but he was their brightest student, even teaching his teachers. He may be a person of importance, an heir to the Throne of David, but there is much contention over the matter even in the family. His mother was raised in the temple in Jerusalem. His father, my brother, was a great architect, but had no political ambitions and is now dead. My brother had claims of descent from King David, and this has been a source of notoriety for the family even though he never pursued the claims. So, as for the young lad, his fame precedes him no matter where we go and even if he is unknown, everywhere I have taken him he naturally gravitates to the people, understanding them even when he has not known them. His mystical training was so complete, that I am sure he can even converse with the sages of your land."

"Yes, I have spoken to some who are awaiting the opportunity. Just today, a number of the local mystics asked me if I knew when you might arrive. Of course, I honored your request not to reveal it. But, if they knew you as I do, they would know you would be on time. Can I meet him?"

"Oh, but of course, I am so sorry, my friend," answered Joseph as he motioned for Rajak to follow him.

At that point, the young man looked up and saw the men walking towards him. He smiled and adjusted his clothing which had become somewhat disheveled from the work. He tightened his belt and brushed some ore dust from his shoulder.

"Rajak, this is my nephew, Joses ben Cleophas. Joses, my friend and colleague, Rajak," said Joseph as he proudly placed their right hands together.

"I am pleased to meet you," Rajak announced as he looked deep into the young man's eyes and studied his features, "and I welcome you to India."

"The pleasure is mine, sir," responded Joses, "I trust you and your family are well."

"Yes, I have a wonderful family, and a young son not too far from your own age. He will be most happy to meet you and has traveled some like you. I think you will enjoy his company."

"I am anxious to meet him," said Joses, "What is his name?"

"Rashan," responded Rajak.

"A name of respect, well-deserved I am sure," said Joses. "You are a father who loves him very much."

"We should go now, if you can leave and let our men finish the job," said Rajak. "My wife will have food and it will meet with your approval, prepared carefully according to your requirements."

"We are most happy to go with you now," stated Joseph, and the trio walked towards the city.

"How long have you lived here?" Joses asked Rajak.

"I came here when I saw what the Romans were doing to Judea," he explained. "Things do not look promising there, and I fear that the worst is yet to come. So, I decided to come here where no one will bother me. Besides, my family loves it here and the weather is good all the time. Where else can you see a sea of such exquisite beauty and a land of such wonder? Anyway, I make lots of money," and he heartily laughed.

"You always were good at trade," said Joseph, "I am glad we kept our ties after you left. I am continuing with my business in Gaul and Britain since they provide the tin for me in limitless amounts. My family continues to be the backbone and beneficiary of this enterprise. Rome has made me a citizen because I supply them so well."

"Always the diplomat, eh Joseph?" Rajak said in good humor. "How about you, Joses, how do you like this business? Is your uncle paying you well?"

"It is payment enough just being with my uncle," he replied.

"Well, do not be too humble, nephew, for you are a master in your own right," said Joseph. "Rajak, he was a fine student of his father who was a master architect and builder, may HaShem remember him. Joses can accomplish any engineering feat you require; He is also a master builder, even at his young age. He forgets nothing and requires so little direction."

"You flatter me, uncle, with your praise," interrupted Joses. "I think you should be less illustrative lest Rajak take you up on your words and put me to work here for him."

Everyone laughed, and the noise of the marketplace faded as the group entered the home of Rajak, a comfortable and well-furnished home, deceptively plain from the outside. They were greeted by Rajak's family who waited eagerly to meet the new guests, especially the young Joses they had heard so much about.

"Wash your feet and relax yourselves," Rajak offered, knowing the tradition of his guests' homeland of welcoming visitors with water so they could clean off the dust and refresh their feet. "This is my wife, Havel, my daughter Rachel, and my son, Rashan.

Havel held out several towels for the two men and Joses smiled and nodded his head in gratitude as Joseph dipped his feet in the washbowl. When Joseph was done, Joses handed him a towel and then washed his own feet. The water felt cool and refreshing and the towel mildly massaged his feet as he dried them. He looked over toward Rashan and Rachel and noticed that they had not yet taken their eyes off of him. Rajak had continued talking, as he seemed so used to doing.

"Is the whole family now working with you, Joseph, or are they still assisting Herod?" asked Rajak.

"A little of both," responded Joseph, "but a larger part of the family has taken up the cause of liberation from the Roman occupation. It is a situation I fear may end in great violence. You know, I am old and willing to negotiate, but these younger men..."

"I am glad I left when I did," Rajak commented with a sigh of relief as he reached for a cup from a tray that Havel had just brought in. "I think it unwise to do anything rash...pardon me I should not speak of your family that way."

"No, Rajak, I understand what you are saying. Even Joses and I have had long talks about this dilemma. His brothers, including his twin, are most boisterous about this occupation by the Romans and their Herodian rulers. Being of the royal lineage, they cannot stand the situation. Some are prominent leaders and members of Nazarite societies and advocate acts of violence to overthrow the Roman occupation. Things are becoming more desperate."

"Yes, I understand. But, is not young Joses here the heir apparent, the legitimate successor to the throne of King David?" Rajak was trying to draw in Joses to the conversation.

"It's much more complicated than that," responded Arimathea. "I suppose I can try to explain it to you. You see, Joses is the oldest of the twins, Jude being the younger by moments. However, Jude considers that Joses has turned from the heirship." Joseph looked towards Joses. "That is a long story. It has caused a rift amongst the brothers, especially Jacob, one of Joses' younger brothers. Miryam, the boys' mother, has taken great efforts to ensure that Joses is given the training he needs and has tried to encourage cooperation and understanding among the siblings. But, the weight seems to be slipping to Jude who abides strictly by the Torah interpretations of Jacob and the Community. Joses leaves it all in HaShem's hands, but he is well-versed in the Nazarite discipline, having been raised around it and schooled there as part of his early childhood. His understanding is considered an improper hybrid. The whole problem is similar somewhat to the story of Jacob and Esau, where Esau gives up his birthright to the younger Jacob in the first book of the Torah. The priests at On considered that story of some similitude to our present situation."

He stopped, realizing he had gone too far with his explanation. Rajak stared with wide, anticipating eyes at Joses.

Joses was usually silent around adults out of respect for the elders, and because he knew that listening was the better part of understanding. Looking at Joses and then Joseph, Rajak continued.

"Yes, I see the dilemma. But, let's say you should be the heir, are you going to say something about this violence in Judea, or eventually act?" he asked Joses. "I mean no disrespect, because I truly feel that your current course with your uncle is a much wiser one. Even your father did not pursue his rights because he knew the power of Rome would destroy him."

Joseph looked at Joses as the young man gazed around the room at the expectant faces of Rajak and his family. Joses did not answer at first, but deferred to Joseph who shrugged with slightly upraised hands that signaled to Joses that a response was up to him. Joses decided to address them.

"If I may answer you with respect for your house?" asked Joses. Rajak nodded his head and raised his hand in agreement as Joses continued, "The purpose of Israel is to honor HaShem and keep His commandments that the seventy nations of the world may be blessed. Without the priestly ordinances and the protection of the anointed King of Israel, the world suffers as it does now because the hand of HaShem, our Holy Nation, is stayed. But, I am not ready at all. My understanding is still limited. I desire to learn the ways of all peoples and broaden my experiences, seeking for the will of HaShem not only from the Torah, which is to Israel, but also from the nature of how HaShem works with those of other nations. So, while the Torah is to Israel, I believe that an understanding of it applies to blessing the world through the application of its principles."

"So," noted Rajak, "You again prove your wisdom and foresight. But, this does not sound like the philosophy of your other family members. As I understand it, they seek a strict separation from all others not part of their own."

"Yes, that is correct in strict terms of marriage, eating, close associations, and the like, but they still travel and speak to many people," replied Joses, stopping to gather his thoughts for a moment. He bit his lip, and then continued. "I believe I will take a Nazarite vow for a time, but I will not do so my entire life. The period of the vow would be for specific purposes, and I would then return to normal Torah life, amongst the people."

"How is your mother handling your time away from home?" asked Rajak, seeing that the topic of the Nazarite lifestyle was one of some concern for Joses, and that he was in some discomfort discussing his differences with his family members.

"She expresses her love for me, but knows I must study all things, even outside Israel, to better prepare for my life's work."

"And, what is that?" asked Rajak.

"To allow HaShem to use me to answer the prayers of the fathers," stated Joses.

Rajak and Joseph looked at each other, both wanting to ask the same question of what that may really involve; but neither had the courage to take the conversation any further. Rajak broke the silence.

"Let us dine together on this wonderful day of renewal and celebration to our lasting friendship. The food is prepared and you have traveled far."

A few days later, Joseph of Arimathea decided that it was time for a serious talk with his nephew. Joseph could see that the lad had the maturity and vision to claim his rightful place. Even his infirmities had slowly dissipated because of his attention to his health and his efforts to get well. The only outward sign that the young Joses had ever been ill at all was his slight hunchback. While he had not grown any taller, it was not readily apparent that his lack of stature would be the result of any ailment.

"Joses, it is time for you to return home and begin your life. Your destiny is not in the merchant trade. It is in the footsteps of your fathers. While these travels have served a wonderful purpose in teaching you about the world and giving you time to consider your place in it, you must see the inevitability of the necessity of your leadership in Judea," the Uncle was more serious than Joses had seen him in a long time.

"Uncle, you know my family looks at me as an outsider. I follow Torah, but not their fanatical determinations. And, I do not have the ability to fight as well as they do," said Joses. "Furthermore, HaShem has not given me any light concerning it. Do I step beyond my place?"

"Men are meant to reach further than they believe they have strength, Joses. It is time for you to do so. I believe you have it in you, and your humility will temper ambition. I think you will use good judgment and wisdom. While your family and the community look to Jude, they also know that the issue is not finally decided. If that were so, Jude would be held in a much higher regard. Also, you don't need to embrace the fanaticism. You only need to show your recognition of the rightful leaders, Chananya ben Menachem and Joachanin ben Zechariah in particular. And, I think you have already done that. Just formalize it."

"I have no objection to what you say, Uncle. I just don't desire the contentiousness of it all."

"You will prevail, Joses. You will prevail. And, it is coming closer for the time for you to marry. Your bride-to-be has been waiting patiently for you."

"You know, Uncle," commented Joses with a fondness in his eyes, "I really do miss her. She has always been such a good friend, and I can tell she is so committed to me."

"Miriam bat Benjamin Nikdimon is a jewel," Joseph emphasized, "and she is of the proper lineage, well reared. She will complement you as no other that I can think of. If you are ready to assume your proper place, no matter what the opposition is you face, she will stand by you and the marriage will certainly declare your ultimate right to the throne of David. Your brother, Jude, will finally have to submit. You are much wiser than any of your siblings. Besides, your children will be the heirs of the kingdom, and no one can legitimately challenge them. The observance of the Law you have always kept. The fanaticism of your brothers is not required, despite their vociferous demands. You keep the Law as perfectly as anyone is required. The fences of your brethren are beyond the mark. I question their common sense, although not their devotion. So, back to the issue I am most concerned with. Do you want me to approach Miriam's father and commit to the marriage?"

Joseph had acted as the young Joses' father in all things since the death of Cleophas shortly after the family's return to Palestine from Egypt. Joses recognized his wisdom, and agreed.

"Yes, I am ready to make it formal, Uncle. I have always felt her as if she were constantly at my side. Her spirit is strong and sends comfort to me even at such long distances."

"And, I know she says the same of you," said Joseph, squinting his eyes to further impress the young Joses of his seriousness. "There is your path. Are you ready to walk it?"

"Today, Uncle. Today."

"So be it. We will make sail for Judea tomorrow."

Joses stood up and assisted his Uncle to stand. The elder Joseph looked at him, love swelling in his heart. "You are going to be my King, Joses. I am very proud of that."

The two men embraced.

***

Many miles away back in Judea, the one recognized by the Community at Damascus as the heir to the Throne of David or the legitimate Mashiach ben David was wasting no time. Jude, the younger of the twins, took his training very seriously. He studied Torah and the writings of the leaders of the Way for most of the daylight hours available to him and even late into the night. When not engaged in the concentration of the spiritual regimen, he spent his time training with the various weapons at the disposal of the community. More than this, he consolidated his position with the Teacher of Righteousness and the Teacher's designated successors, Joachanin ben Zechariah and Jude's own brother, Jacob.

Damascus was a small town situated in the desert near the northwestern shore of the Dead Sea. It was also called the Wilderness. Founded by mystics, priests, displaced Jewish nobility, and the self-exiled from Judah many years before, it was the primary gathering place near Jerusalem for those who desired to dedicate their lives to HaShem, or were disaffected with the powerful Herodians and the occupying Roman Empire. While most Judeans and the ruling classes believed the settlement to be populated primarily by the ascetic and apparently pacifist Essenes, it was also the perfect cover for the leaders of the resistance to Rome. It was nearly a no man's land; dry, dusty and rocky, inhospitable in the extreme and out of sight and mind for the Romans who had their hands full controlling the rest of Judea, Galilee, and Jerusalem.

Most of the inhabitants dwelt in caves or tents, the permanent structures of clay brick and stone used primarily for work, social events, study, spiritual rituals, or activities of the governing council. The purpose of this austerity was to shun the riches of the world and cling only to HaShem and His Torah. In this endeavor, the members shared all of their belongings in common, dressed simply, and worked hard.

The people were divided into groups depending upon their length of membership, spiritual progress, and domestic arrangements. These groups were called by various names such as the "Poor," the "Meek," the "Many," the "Living," and the "Dead." The purpose was to identify their spiritual status or their rank in the Community, and was a code for their use when speaking around others who were not initiated in the Way.

While marriage was not prohibited, it was not always encouraged, and often was the deciding factor whether a man could hold a position of importance in the Community Way, the spiritual principles and governing organizations of the society. When a couple engaged in marriage, it was impressed upon them that it was only for procreation, most encouraged to forego the pleasures, and responsibilities, of conjugal contracts. The leaders, claiming to understand and speak for HaShem and the Torah, praised chastity and celibacy almost to the exclusion of the admonishment in the Torah to marry and multiply and replenish the earth. The reason was simple; one could not wholly dedicate himself to HaShem if he had a family.

The most obvious exceptions, of course, were those considered to be part of the royal and priestly bloodlines of Israel, particularly the Davidic kingly and Aaronic priestly families. These, however, were married in situations strictly controlled by what were known as the dynastic marriage rules of the Community, the wife being separated from the husband at various and often extended times, especially when children were planned.

The foods were always simple, approved and prepared according to the strict requirements of the Torah. Most of the people were dedicated vegetarians, especially those who had extended Nazarite vows of separation. Any possibility of ingesting blood or handling something unclean discouraged meat of any kind, even the "clean" animals pronounced by the Torah. Also, the idea of ingesting anything that had resulted from a sexual intercourse made a dietary choice of meat less than desirable.

Men and women often immersed themselves in pools of water called mikvahs. This was not just a bath, but also a ritual symbol of purification of body and spirit. Prior to any special observance, it was common to partake of the mikvah, or the running water of a stream or river. The mikvahs were not stagnant, but were constructed to ensure a constant flow of fresh water. Women, after their periods and after a set time of separation, would use the mikvah before rejoining the company of others. Men used the mikvah as often as occasion permitted, but especially before meditations.

The Torah declared specific days for various observances and these were many and varied. The Sabbaths, one day in seven, were set aside for a day of rest and worship. Others, such as Passover and Yom Kippur, celebrated significant events or demanded specific actions. Passover celebrated the exodus from Egypt after HaShem destroyed the firstborn of all the Egyptians, and Yom Kippur was the Day of Atonement when the sins of Israel were cast away following definitive acts by the people and the priesthood. The life of a dedicated and pious Israelite was one of constant devotion and action, fear and trembling. It was a spirituality reflected in one's works and obedience.

The members of the Community Way in Damascus were exact in all these requirements, usually, with few exceptions, more so than the rest of the people of Israelite descent. In many cases, they went beyond the requirements of the Torah just to ensure their compliance to the letter of the law. Furthermore, the Community kept a calendar based upon esoteric, secret, and Torah calculated dates, as did many mystics, that were different than mainstream

Judaism. Often, observances such as Passover fell on different days for the Community than were observed by the rest of the people.

Jude excelled in this environment, as did his younger brother, Jacob. Their brother, Kefa, followed along as best he could, but did not attain to the same ranks and responsibilities they had. And, of course, they felt their older brother, Joses, was entirely out of the picture with his wanderings around the world and his refusal to submit to proper authority. The regimens of Torah and the additions to it by the twelve men of the Community Council and the Teacher of Righteousness ensured strict compliance and thus helped prepare a righteous people for HaShem. It was everything Jude and Jacob wanted and believed in.

It was now time for Jude to begin the process for his accession to the Throne of David. Jacob was there to support him. The two young men met at Jacob's tent and then proceeded together to the Community Hall, arriving as the early morning sun, still below the hills to the east, illuminated the sky.

"Jude," called the Teacher, Chananya ben Menachem, "Will you come and sit with us?" he asked as he motioned Jude over to the table. The Teacher and several of the elders were reclining around the short table they used to set their food upon. While the meal was over, the men were taking the time to relax and discuss their plans. The Teacher stood as Jude approached and all the men stood as if to recognize not only the authority of the Teacher, but also the rightful heir to the throne of David who now approached them. Jude was tall, strong and well built, with a commanding presence even though he was only seventeen. He came to the table and deferred to the Teacher with a nod of his head. Now that Jude had joined them, the Teacher continued the discussion. "My young Jude, as the rightful heir you have indicated that you are, indeed, going to claim the throne of David?"

Jude, respectfully waiting for any other comments from the elders before proceeding, looked around at the group and then noticed Jacob, his younger brother, standing near the rear door of the smaller room of the Community Hall. The two young men gave each other a faint, approving, smile. "Yes, Teacher, I am preparing myself for my duties. Have I met with your approval?"

Chananya smiled gently. "Only HaShem knows the end from the beginning. Whatever HaShem has designed, that surely shall come to pass. You have been studious and dedicated, a seeker of truth and a noble and valiant defender of our people. You have here before you those who honor your position and defend your place." He then motioned for Joachanin to come closer to him. Jacob watched as Joachanin crossed the floor, his white linen clothing characteristic of the initiated members of the "Way" brushing against Jude as he took to the left side of Chananya who was facing the other men. "Here I have what appear to be the twin pillars of Boaz and Jachin," Chananya said to the assembly. "We have the Mishpat (Kingly Mashiach) and the Tzedeq (Righteous One)," he said motioning to Jude and then to Joachanin respectively. "This is the beginning of our strength. Praise to HaShem, Alleluia."

The assembly bent at the waist and echoed, "Alleluia."

"Jacob," Chananya gestured towards the younger brother of Jude, "has vowed a Nazarite vow to HaShem and will keep his vow all his days, just as he has from birth, of his own choice. He has attained a high degree of piety and purity and is as all of us, the Poor and the Meek in the Way. He has completed his forty days of separation. Yet, he will remain faithful to HaShem, drink no wine, and he will eat no meat to pollute himself and ensure that he ingests nothing sacrificed to idols. In all things when Joachanin is not present, he speaks for him."

Chananya paused as the men all nodded at Jacob. Then, he continued.

"As for Jude, he has completed his responsibilities for the Straight and Narrow Way and is soon to be received into full fellowship after his forty days of separation. Then, it is only HaShem who has the pattern for the rise of David anew." Chananya was partly prophesying the rise of Jude as the new Davidic King, but recognizing the final event was in HaShem's hands. "What does HaShem give you to say, Joachanin?" Chananya continued.

Joachanin spoke easily and forthrightly, holding nothing back, "The time of the end is near at hand, and HaShem, through his chosen ones, will unleash a battle upon the kittim and restore Israel to its rightful place, cleansing our Temple and renewing the daily sacrifice in purity. Death to the kittim, and honor and glory to HaShem!"

All those in the assembly spoke at once, "Blessed are you Oh Lord our God, King of the Universe, Alleluia. Amen."

"Jude will now take his vow, as required by our code, and be received into full fellowship upon its completion and his separation," said Chananya. "Then, he must prepare to marry a pure daughter of Israel, unblemished and properly trained, with which to raise a royal seed." He turned to face Jude. "You are now commanded by HaShem to take your sojourn in this Wilderness and not allow any blade to touch your head, come not near to any dead body, eat nothing but pure plants and water, touch no fruit of the vine, and pray unceasingly to HaShem that you may become acceptable to Him. Now go, and begin the days of your separation."

Jude, who had completed his washings in the mikvahs and sacrificed his youth in the preparation of his mission, looked out the door of the meeting hall. Outside he could see the white desert sands and the barren hills of the area of the Dead Sea that surrounded Damascus, now brightly lit by the sun as it rose over the hills. He placed a portion of his robe over his head and exited the building, feeling the warmth of the sun through his garments. His sandals, already covered with dust, warmed immediately from the heat as he walked purposefully and decisively towards the southern part of the settlement and up into the hills. There he would stay, fasting and praying, for forty days.

***

During this time of Jude's separation, Jacob continued his studies with the elders of Damascus and the mystics of Emmaus. He had already accomplished his time of separation many months earlier, having braved the heat of the day, the cold of the night, and the days of endless isolation that were meant to bring one closer to HaShem. He felt that it was only proper that while his brother endured these things and sought for HaShem, that he should spend time in deep meditation. For that, Emmaus was an excellent place. Emmaus was the seat of the mystical Hechalot in Judea, and was actually the old mystical city of Bethshemesh, which had been transplanted from On, Egypt at the time of the Exodus. In fact, Jacob and his family and community knew Emmaus as Bethshemesh. It meant the House of the People of Shem, the House of the Sun, or On.

It was there that Jacob began to realize that the idea of two mashiachs as understood by Chananya and the elders of Damascus may not be entirely correct. It appeared to him that the mysteries referred to a single mystical and universal mashiach far and beyond a mere king. It was a small seed that would grow in his mind for many years. To him at this time, it looked as if there may be a difficulty in the interpretation of two pillars, or individuals, meeting the prophecy of messiahship.

Of more immediate concern to him, however, was his own relationship to HaShem. He studied the Torah and the Hechalot, trying to absorb the meanings of the words of the sacred texts. He knew he had to rightly divide the words of HaShem and the Torah to decode the true teachings, prophecies, and designs of HaShem. The methods had two purposes: to cause him to meditate deeply and precisely, and to reveal hidden truths in the words of the Torah. He did this under the direction and supervision of the great seers of Emmaus, as no man could rightly ascend into the chambers of the heavens alone. It was too dangerous, even for one as pure and righteous as Jacob.

So, he had retired to an upper room of a small building in Bethshemesh dedicated to the faithful where he recited his words that enabled him to enter into a deep mediation. He had ascended through many chambers and was approaching a very high level when he suddenly heard a voice of an archangel guarding the path ask him, "What of your bishirtah?" The question stunned him and he lost his concentration.

"Brother, Jacob," a human voice called him, "Return." Jacob slowly aroused from his meditation, realizing that he was shaking and sweating, something not usual in his prayers.

"You went too far, brother. I thought it best that as the elders advise, you must go and then return lest you receive the kiss of God." He was referring to an ecstatic vision where the person goes so far that he has no desire to return and his body dies. The man was much older than Jacob, his eyebrows thick and bushy, but his face sparsely bearded, offsetting his piercing blue eyes. He was dressed similarly to Jacob with a tzitzit, or prayer shawl, over his linen garments and no shoes on his feet.

"The Spirit of the Lord has spoken to me in my meditation, Brother Elazer," Jacob spoke in whispered tones, still unable to catch his breath. Jacob stretched and brought his arms down to his side as he looked up at his companion.

The man was Jacob's senior in the ways of the Hechalot, Rabbi Elazer, a disciple of Menachem the Essene. Menachem, now gathered to his fathers, had been acquainted with King Herod and had been respected by him because Menachem had prophesied that Herod would be king. It was primarily because of Menachem that the Essenes were believed to only be pious ascetics. They also took on some of the aspects of the Pharisees, but differed in all ways having to do with placation of Rome. However, they wisely kept this to themselves with the exception of a few of their number who were becoming more and more active and vocal in their contempt for the empire.

Jacob's older brother, Joses, had also followed the paths of these mystics, but had gone to On in Egypt, as well. Jacob, however, felt that the traditions of the Jews in Judea were most important and therefore followed the commands of Ezekiel the prophet to avoid Egyptian ceremonial representations. Jacob rejected Joses' extended training and had warned him repeatedly of the dangers of ignoring the Oral Tradition as held by the elders and even respected by the regime friendly Pharisees.

"Do you wish to share it, or would you rather pass?" asked Elazer.

Jacob was unsure. He had taken additional vows to HaShem. One of these was that he had agreed never to have the company of a woman unless he had received an assurance that she was his female counterpart from the pre-existent realms. In other words, he believed he had a soul mate. Any other woman was not acceptable as she would be only for comfort in life, not as a spiritual necessity.

"I go so far and then cannot go any further," Jacob said as he breathed in deeply and then exhaled slowly. Still somewhat shaken, he looked at Elazer and reached out for his hand. The two men clasped their hands and Elazer helped Jacob to stand.

"You are yet only a very young man. Most men are not permitted to even begin studying the mysteries until they are forty years old. Do not disparage yourself. Your piety and righteousness are not in question. Remember, HaShem through the elders of the Way have chosen you, you have not chosen us. Besides, you cannot expect to stay in the Presence, but must go and return—go and return."

Jacob listened intently. He was not as concerned about the duration of his meditation as the message he had received. As they stood facing each other, Jacob finally decided to explain his problem.

"My promise to HaShem was that I would be separate from the world all my life. Part of that was that I would not marry, save to a woman HaShem would show me. The sign would work similar to the situation where the servant of Abraham would find Isaac's wife (Genesis 24). Without HaShem's intervention in meeting the signs, I will not take a wife. Yet..." Jacob paused, trying to make sense of his vision.

Elazer, seeing his confusion, held Jacob firmly with his left hand on Jacob's back, pulling him closer. "If it is not clear, it is not your place to assume what it means," he said. "It is obvious this has been hard for you to share with me. But, it is right that you should. Your vow is intact, and while no man can point your path to you, it is obvious that HaShem sees your condition and is responding to your vow."

"I will tell you the words I heard," Jacob responded. He looked down, and then raised his eyes to Elazer, looking directly at him. "The voice asked, "What of your bishirtah?"

"Your feminine counterpart, yes," Elazer ventured. "Interesting: You have vowed to not marry without a sign, and yet HaShem asks you about her. Obviously, it is in your hands. What was the sign you agreed upon in your vow, if it is fit to ask you?"

"It is not lawful for a man to even look upon a maiden that HaShem has not given him," Jacob began. "My father died before he brought one to me, and Joachanin has said nothing to me concerning it." He hesitated, then sighed and lifted his hands in front of him as if ready to receive something, "The sign I agreed upon was that Joachanin would bring me my wife, and she would be holding a water pot."

Elazer creased his brow, looking deeply into Jacob's eyes as he pondered what Jacob had just told him. The air was silent for several moments. Finally, Elazer spoke to his companion, "Joachanin is not much older than you. While the rightful heir of the High Priesthood, and mature beyond his years, he has barely entered marriage himself. However, his contacts are numerous and his influence strong," Elazar nodded as he reasoned with himself, glancing sideways at Jacob. "You have never discussed this with Joachanin?" he asked.

"It is beyond the bounds of my vow and should it be done, the mere action would nullify my promise, breaking that which I hold most sacred," responded Jacob.

"Then, it must remain as you have formed it," responded Elazer. "But, as the High Priest cannot go into the Holy of Holies without his wife near, so you cannot enter into the final chamber without yours. The Lord and His Shekinah (God's female aspect) are one and no man can enter into the Presence unless he is like Him. A word of caution here, young man," Elazer paused as he pointed to an ark or cabinet in the corner of the room that contained a Torah Scroll, "HaShem expects us to do works worthy of His kingdom. Even if your wife is not in this world, perhaps not to be born for one hundred years or having traveled through this life one hundred years ago, you must have her bound to you while in this life or you cannot enter the Holy of Holies nor the upper chambers of the Heavens."

Jacob was puzzled. "I have no idea what that means," he said. "How can I bind a woman to me that is not here?"

Elazer pointed again at the Torah Scroll, "The answer lies in the Word. Search it and divide it, rearrange the letters and study the numbers. You cannot go further, as righteous as you are, until this is resolved. However, you still have much time in your life. While most young men are married by eighteen, you have not yet reached that age. Rest from it and allow it to happen as HaShem sees fit. It may not happen until you are much older. Only HaShem knows."

Jacob nodded affirmatively. There was another issue related to this one. "Can the mashiach not reign without a wife?"

Elazer was shocked. Was Jacob seeking to claim the position of the mashiach? He looked away from Jacob and turned towards the corner of the room, rubbing his chin with his right hand, obviously in deep thought and reflection.

"The direct answer to your question you already know," Elazer said. "A king is no king without fulfilling the Torah and bringing forth posterity to HaShem. I have known you now for many years, and I know of your family history, even better than you do. I trust this question is not concerning you?"

"It is only a question," responded Jacob. "Events are now transpiring that will define the future and my desire is only to ensure my understanding of them."

Elazer looked carefully at Jacob. "All that has come to me says that your brother Jude is progressing well in Torah and the Way. While he is not yet a master of the Hechalot, he has not neglected his duties, either. If it is of him that you concern yourself, there is little doubt that his actions will fulfill all that is required of him. But, there is little which I can say at the present time. There is a mystery here. And it concerns the seed of Joseph who was sold into Egypt, the same who was the son of Jacob who was renamed Israel by HaShem, the son of Isaac, the son of our father, Abraham, blessed be his memory. As proclaimed by Israel, Joseph received the birthright blessing from his father, Jacob, and Joseph passed it down through his son, Ephraim. Does this mean anything to you?"

Jacob partially understood what the wise sage was saying to him. But, this had been a subject of controversy for many generations. The sages had tried to use the Torah words themselves to interpret the hidden secrets by breaking the words down and expanding them. But this had not shed any greater light on the subject. A polite agreement had grown amongst the elders to avoid the issue.

Historically and politically it was one of the major points of the initial breakdown in the Davidic Kingdom many centuries before. The northern kingdoms of Israel had broken away from the Davidic Kingdom and formed their own political entity. This tragedy happened shortly after the death of King David's son, King Solomon. It split Israel into two camps, the Kingdom of Judea which was the old political kingdom of David, and the northern kingdom of Israel. The historical event seemed to defy the prophecies that David's lineage would rule forever over the entire nation of Israel, not just the tribe Judah and the southern kingdom. Yet, even now Herodian descendants, not Davidic, occupied that throne. The underground, of which Jude was a part, claimed to be holding the true Davidic line in waiting for the return of the messianic king, the rightful heir of the Davidic line and the throne of Israel.

"The Psalm plainly states that HaShem took David as His firstborn," Jacob said, although he was primarily just thinking out loud. He then looked up and asked, "Does this not show that Ephraim was superseded by David and the birthright remains with his descendents?"

Elazer did not answer, but just raised his eyebrows and waved his head side to side.

"With the defeat of the Kingdom of Israel by the Assyrians centuries ago, and the northern ten tribes taken into captivity and lost, I thought this was now just more proof of the validity of the Davidic Covenant?" Jacob posed to his senior.

"Well, outside the Torah are many things. In response to your question concerning the captivity of the Ten Tribes, what did the Prophet Jeremiah say?" Elazer put the question to Jacob. "He was certainly well after David. What is it that he said? Oh, yes...'They will come with weeping, and with supplications will I lead them: I will cause them to walk by the rivers of waters in a straight way, wherein they shall not stumble: for I am a father to Israel, and Ephraim is my first born.'[5] Does that not bring much to your remembrance?"

Jacob stared at him with the look of youthful confusion.

"There is more, but I dare not say it now," answered Elazer. "Just keep this in your mind. HaShem keeps His thoughts hidden, and His ways are unknown to us. We go as far as we can, that is all." He paused for a moment and then brought up another point. "In the same light, it is interesting that your parents paid the ransom of five shekels for Joses, as the Torah requires for the redemption of the firstborn[6] to free him from a life of service only to HaShem. Yet, HaShem later said that instead of the Firstborn of all Israelites, He took the Levites to him. So, to be safe, we do as the Torah suggests, 'Therefore, I sacrifice to the Lord all that openeth the matrix, being males.'[7] Yes, it is a narrow path we trod. I suppose Jude has the way opened to sit on the Throne of David. But, let us not take the works of HaShem into our own hands. Prudence dictates that we wait and see what the Creator has in store, and, as I said, do the best we can."

Jacob was not sure what to make of these words. He decided to do as he was counseled and let the issue rest for now. He thanked Elazer and began his return to Damascus to meet Jude who was now approaching the end of his forty days of separation in the Wilderness, and Jacob knew he needed to be there for Jude's return.

***

Jude had faithfully completed his forty days of separation. He had consumed only wild plants and pure water, meditating upon Torah and seeking direction during his ascents to the chambers of heaven. Chananya had met him often during this time to assist him in the deeper meditations that Jude undertook to receive the spirit of prophecy. The king must know the will of HaShem in order to rule righteously and justly, and Jude was submitting, exercising all the necessities and tools at his disposal. Chananya helped him in the mysteries of the Hechalot, the use of spiritual meditation to ascend through the chambers of heaven. And, Jude had kept his vows of separation.

"You are now ready to take your rightful place and prepare yourself for the next step," explained Chananya. "You will immediately go to the Community Council and present yourself to them."

It was just getting dark, the beginning of a new day in Jewish reckoning, as the two men walked together down the rocky dirt hills on the side of the settlement and approached the hall where the governing council, the Twelve Elders or Community Council, met to decide important matters. Jude was deep in his thoughts, but ever attentive to any words from his mentor. They paused at the door and embraced each other, then turned and entered. Just inside the room, Menachem removed his horn of oil that he had at his side and Jude knelt next to him facing the group of men inside. At that moment, Jacob and Joachanin entered the hall. Chananya and the men of the Council acknowledged them as they took their places.

"The Mashiach ben David," announced Chananya as he poured the consecrated oil on Jude's head. After Chananya had anointed Jude, he assisted him to his feet. Every face in the room was aglow with contentment and gratitude. The members of the Council all arose and turned toward the two men as they made their way to the low round table in the center of the room. The flickering of the small flames from the oil lamps illuminating the room caused the men's shadows to dance erratically on the stone and clay walls. Chananya stopped at his point at the table as Jude continued walking around to greet each man and shake their hands. After he had greeted each man in order, he stood by Chananya. The group all sat down in reclining positions around the low table in one almost coordinated motion.

"Jude has completed his forty days of separation and his vows are intact. You have witnessed his anointing as the Mashiach ben David. He is now ready for your inquisitions," Chananya said as he gestured toward Jude and then to the council.

"King David was anointed by the Prophet Samuel as a young boy," began the eldest Councilor, Ivraham. His long flowing white linen robes matched the whiteness of his long beard and locks. "You, too, have been anointed, Mashiach ben David, by our prophet and priest, Chananya, and await the approving vote of this council. You are yet a very young man and needful of more instruction even though you show your understanding and wisdom in so many ways, bringing knowledge and awareness to all of us. How does the future King of Israel make straight the path of justice and mercy and bring about the beauty of Israel and the government of HaShem?"

Jude responded almost without hesitation.

"HaShem guides us toward a reconciliation of Israel through victory against the kittim and the glory of his remembrance to all the twelve tribes of Israel. We will prepare a foundation and build an army of light with the efforts of the brethren to bring the lost back to the fold. With this army of the righteous, we will attain the kingdom and, HaShem willing, secure peace and prosperity for all men."

"Well said," responded Ivraham. "How do you intend to build this army of the righteous?"

"We will preach to the people the Way of the Torah, and find among them those zealous for HaShem, the Holy Temple, and Israel. These we will instruct further and try them with ever increasing responsibilities. After we have proved them, we will place them into the ranks of the army and allow them to continue in their lives, waiting for the command of HaShem and their King." Jude looked over at Jacob and their eyes met. Jacob was smiling with approval.

"That will bring knowledge of HaShem to the people and prepare the people of Judah and Israel for the final battle," Ivraham said. "It is fitting that the King would be able to accomplish such holy goals. It will also mask our true intentions from the kittim. This is brilliant."

Ivraham reclined again and motioned to Chananya who then raised his hands in a gesture of invitation. "Who is next?" he asked, his eyes scanning over the elders seated at the table, whose heads were nodding, signifying agreement to what Ivraham had said.

A middle-aged man arose at the other side of the table. His kipa (the small covering men wear on the crowns of their heads) nearly slipped off as he stood to speak, his right hand instinctively grasping it and placing it back in its proper position.

"Yes, Gideon, speak," instructed Chananya.

"In all honesty, it seems unnecessary to proceed any further as everyone here knows what Jude has accomplished. This plan to increase the ranks of the Army of Light, and his attention to the expulsion of the kittim are in line with all we have sought to undertake. Jude should be accepted as the Mashiach ben David. He will, no doubt, become one of us, a Son of God."[8]

Chananya stood. "Do we all agree? Show by raising your right hands to the square."

All the men arose and raised their right hands to the square. The vote was unanimous.

"Well then, if there is nothing else, go in peace and may HaShem bless you all, all honor to His Name.

"Amen," the men all responded at once.

As each man returned to his own home, the importance of what was discussed and the path upon which they were about to embark became clear, and weighed heavily on the heart of Jude. He knew there was much for him to prepare. Jacob came to his side.

"With the sustaining vote of the Council, there is nothing to stop the salvation of Israel, HaShem willing," Jacob said as he hugged his brother with his right arm.

"We have much work to do," Jude responded as he looked into his brother's eyes and the two men exited the hall out into the warm Judean desert night.

CHAPTER THREE

Miriam was the daughter of Benjamin ben Nikdimon. She was of noble descent, stately in her appearance, slight of build but well-shaped, clear complexion and, some said, had the most beautiful face in Judea. While unable to perform anything in a noble capacity due to the usurpation of the ruling class by the Herodians and their miscreants, she still had the knowledge and sophistication to direct business and official actions that she assumed for her father on many occasions in his absence. She was well educated, knowing how to read and write which was rare among women.

She was slightly younger than Joses by a mere six months. They had met for the first time when the two of them were fifteen at a gathering hosted by Joseph of Arimathea that brought the families of Cleophas and Benjamin together. It was an arrangement understood by all for the purpose of allowing the underground actual heirs of the kingdom to meet each other. Joseph's home was the perfect place for such an event as it was large and spacious with garden walkways and high ceilings. He had his household and the servants attend to every detail to make the guests feel welcome and comfortable.

In fact, the get-together was strained. The Nikdimons were not fanatics. Actually, neither had been Cleophas. But Cleophas' sons, with the exception of Joses, had more passionately followed Chananya ben Menachem and had formally espoused the lifestyle of the Community at Damascus by the Dead Sea, also known as the City of the Nazarenes. Even at their young ages, they were determined Messianic adherents, and they were already demanding that the family obey the strict interpretations of the Torah pronounced by their leader. While all in attendance at Joseph's home desired to follow the Torah as well as evict the kittim, or Romans, the Nikdimons felt that the Damascus group had added to the Torah against the commandment in Devarim (Deuteronomy) not to add to or subtract from the Law. In the view of the Nikdimons, Damascus had done just that with their community discipline, and the result was that the Community had actually alienated otherwise potential allies.

Uncle Joseph did his best to place the differences aside.

"My friends and family, please feel free to find comfort in my home anyplace you like. The food has been carefully prepared according to the Torah. You may wash in the basin, there." After all had washed, Joseph brought them around the table. He then raised his hands as he recited an often-said prayer. "Blessed are you Oh Lord our God, Creator of the universe. We praise your Holy Name, Alleluia. And, we thank you for providing this fruit of the earth, the food, the water, and all that we have for we have so much. Amen."

Everyone repeated, "Amen."

"This is wonderful, Joseph," Cleophas said as he embraced his brother and then turned to Benjamin. "Benjamin, how special to see you and your family," he said with outstretched arms to embrace his old friend and ally. As they did so, Cleophas winced from a sharp pain in his back. Benjamin could see the pain in his friend's face.

"Good to see you, too, my friend," echoed Benjamin, "are you alright?"

"Yes, yes, just fine," answered Cleophas.

"This is a good time. Our young ones needed the time together," said Benjamin. He looked past Cleophas and saw his wife, Miryam.

"The pure mother of the House of David, how are you?" Benjamin asked in a respect that revealed his devotion to her and her family, despite his differences with the younger men. "I trust you are doing well."

"We are, Benjamin," said Miryam. "My husband is a little down, but he seems to be on the mend."

"Yes, Cleophas, what is it that has been making you sick?" asked Benjamin.

"My age," mused Cleophas, "and a strange ache in my back that does not stop. But, my wife eases my torment."

"Not mine," interjected Arimathea with a laugh. "My wife has not taken up the same skills as Miryam even at my request that she teach her."

"Where is she, Joseph?" asked Miryam. "I have not seen her since we arrived."

"Right here," a woman's voice spoke from the other room. "I am right in here. Come on in and help me finish this, would you?" said Tamar, Arimathea's wife. At that invitation, Miryam left the men and went to lend a hand.

The adults continued their visitation as the young men and women went about oddly discordant activities. Benjamin's children, with the exception of Martha the oldest and her next younger sister, Miriam, were anxious to hear of the activities of Joses' brothers, Jude, Jacob, and Kefa. The brothers of Joses, already upset at the prospect of eating and associating with people outside their Damascus Community, did not show a great deal of interest in the other young people, not even Eleazer, the brother just a year younger than Miriam, much less the two other boys and Lata, the youngest daughter and sibling. The Nikdimon children entertained themselves with a game in the large courtyard, hoping Jude, Jacob, and Kefa would eventually join them. However, these sons of Cleophas continued to separate themselves from the other children, discussing their religion and plans directly across the courtyard. Seeing how the boys appeared distant, Salome, their younger sister who was always sensitive to others, went to play with Lata.

Martha and Miriam approached Joses to talk to him. Miriam, in particular, found herself staring at Joses, trying to make sense of what she was seeing...and feeling.

Joses had been sickly as a child, and the infirmities had not altogether dissipated. He was barely as tall as his younger twin brother, Jude, and his hair was just beginning to fill out, a sign that his nutritional deficiencies were abating. His shoulders were slightly slumped with a noticeable curve to the upper part of his back, a bodily characteristic that was considered a blemish by some of the brethren at Damascus. The rules of the Community barred those having perceived bodily deformities and this blemish kept him from full fellowship with the Community as much as his independent position which many considered an unwillingness to submit to the Community authorities. He was not the handsomest of the boys. But, Miriam found herself inexplicably drawn to him.

"Nice to see you, Joses," she said. She stood about two-arm lengths away, unsure of her own intentions. It was then that she looked deeply into his eyes, and his voice seemed to fill her.

"It is wonderful, and an honor, to see you both," responded Joses who commanded a surety in his address, but with a humility and demeanor that immediately exposed his feelings. He wanted to ensure that both girls felt acceptable, but he had been studying Miriam from the safety of the side of his father until Cleophas had gone to talk to Benjamin. He hoped Martha did not notice the attraction. But, she had, and stepped forward a little to try and obtain more attention from him.

"You have decided not to go with your brothers?" Martha asked.

While he had considered moving to the area where the other boys were meeting, he did not feel inclined to expose himself to their ridicule and really wanted to get to know this family they were visiting. So, he had remained in the main room. He was about to answer Martha when he noticed Jude and Jacob watching him from the doorway.

"Are you coming out with us?" asked Jude.

"Not right away," responded Joses. "I have a few things to do for father before I can come."

"Keep your distance, brother," said Jacob, even with Martha and Miriam in earshot who knew that he would be referring to Joses' proximity to the girls.

Joses smiled at the older sisters and responded to his brother.

"The purity of Benjamin's daughters is already known to me, so you need have no concern."

Jacob looked at him disapprovingly. "How can he presume to know such things? He is always pushing the boundaries of proper behavior," his thoughts betrayed by his barely audible whispers.

"How do we know that Martha and Miriam are not experiencing their monthly impurity?" Jude commented quietly in Jacob's ear, who nodded in agreement. "He had better not so much as touch their garments and then come near us."

"Their parents have taught them the Torah so they would be in separation if they were unclean," Jacob responded thoughtfully. The young men looked at each other and shrugged.

To avoid any further confrontation, Joses smiled and turned to exit the home to obtain his father's belongings. Once outside, he walked to the gate where he had left his father's travel bag and placed it over his shoulder. Just then a group of Roman soldiers passed by. He watched for several minutes, thinking about the constant presence of the Empire until the soldiers turned the bend in the road and walked out of sight. "Will the land ever return to HaShem?" he thought. He then strolled slowly to the house and took the bag to Cleophas, who motioned to him to come aside as Joses placed the bag in the corner of the room. Cleophas drew the young man close to him.

"Joses, do you know why your uncle has had us come here?" asked Cleophas. Before Joses could answer, his father continued. "You are already past your bar mitzvah and approaching the age that men should marry. That is what this is really all about. You can take your time, but just be aware of what is truly transpiring here. With your brother, Jude, already having a wife promised him from the Nazarenes at Damascus, you should seriously consider this family as a possible source for a wife. Jude already has his future wife betrothed to him according to the dynastic rules for the king. He will complete his training and studies at Damascus over the next two years. Your mother is very proud of that. But, do not let yourself fall behind. This is an honorable family."

Joses nodded as his father looked him in the eyes and gave him a reassuring smile.

"We will talk more of this later," Cleophas said to his son as they turned to enter the dining area together.

Later never came. Cleophas died within the week. The family held the funeral in the Nazarene Community of Damascus and they took the body in a procession to Hebron for burial in the family sepulcher. After the funeral was completed, Joses' mother, Miryam, asked Cleophas' brother, Joseph of Arimathea, to take Joses with him on his business voyages. Miryam wanted Joses to pursue his interests, and it would keep the family from quarrelling. She also favored Jude to some degree for his commanding appearance and self-assuredness. She believed him to be true kingly stock, and wanted him to solidify his alliances without interference. Young Jude had sacrificed his youth for the kingdom, remaining at Damascus throughout most of his young life. He had shunned the normal activities of young men and was scheduled to take his final vow and separation when he turned seventeen, then marrying in the dynastic tradition near his 18th birthday.

A short time after Cleophas' death, Joseph of Arimathea, recognizing the situation and still holding to the right of Joses to be king, approached Benjamin and asked him about how his daughter Miriam might respond to a proposal of marriage to Joses.

"My friend," Benjamin greeted Joseph who was walking briskly up to the door. The men reached out and embraced each other. "I received word of your arrival and decided to meet my esteemed friend and offer you a bowl of water for your feet."

The customary greeting and presentation of water for the washing of the feet was meant to secure trust and to show respect, as well as to rest the feet from walking and to clean off the dust.

Joseph sat down on a small stool at the entrance to the house and submerged both his feet in the large clay bowl. The coolness of the water gave him immediate relief and the look of pleasure and rest on his face gave Benjamin a sense of satisfaction.

"You come for a visit, but it has a special purpose, does it not?"

queried Benjamin. Joseph could see his anticipation. "But, before we talk, come and eat, drink, and refresh yourself," gestured Benjamin as Joseph dried his feet and put his sandals on. He stood and the two men entered Benjamin's home. Benjamin's wife brought some food and drink to them as they reclined and discussed politics.

"What do you make of the attacks on the Romans in Galilee?" asked Benjamin to obtain the insight of his friend who was also a member of the Sanhedrin. "What will the counselors (members of the Sanhedrin) do? They certainly cannot support the efforts of the resistance, so they must assist to seek out the people responsible."

Joseph trusted Benjamin, and he answered him accordingly.

"You know how I feel about the kittim and those they have placed in power over us," responded Joseph. "The goyim control the affairs of the true blood of Israel and there is little we can do to deflect their power. I am afraid few of us are left, oh..." he rubbed his left arm and then stroked his beard, "Gamaliel, your father, Nikdimon, and myself. Only HaShem has the power anymore, and that man who is His Hand. Otherwise, I fear much can be lost in a very short time." He stopped and looked at Benjamin who had a look of concern in his eyes. "But, enough of that for now. I have come for a more joyous reason. I am acting as Joses' father to ask a question of you."

"Yes, please go ahead," Benjamin answered as he leaned forward slightly to make sure he could hear all of his friend's words as clearly as possible.

Joseph stood and Benjamin followed. The two men looked deeply into each other's eyes.

"I am here to ask Miriam's hand in marriage for Joses."

"I am overjoyed! My dear, come here!" responded Benjamin as tears welled in his eyes and he called for his wife to join them. As she made her way from the next room, Benjamin could not contain his exuberance. "Yes, yes! The wife of the line of kings shall she be!" and he ran to his wife and embraced her. As the reality of the request settled on him, he turned back to Joseph. "What about the eldest? What about Martha?"

Joseph had anticipated this concern. It was customary for the eldest daughter to marry first. But, it was clear to Joseph that Miriam was Joses' bishirtah, soul mate, and chosen vessel of the royal seed. He had seen it in meditation and it had been confirmed to him by his mystical contacts in Emmaus and most notably by Joses himself.

"Martha will not be left behind," Joseph assured the couple. "She will have her husband shortly and that will be presented to you in Emmaus if you would take the journey. I can only talk for Joses right now."

"Emmaus?" asked Benjamin. "Oh, I see! HaShem has prepared for the eldest daughter so the royal line will pass through Miriam without contest!" he realized that the sages had spoken through Joseph and that his oldest daughters would both need their dowries. "We are overjoyed! And, yes, we will speak to the wise ones in Emmaus concerning Martha. Thank you, Joseph. Yes, yes, we consent. Miriam has already made known to us her feelings and what you have requested is in accordance with her desires, as well."

Joseph was pleased that Miriam had already committed to Joses in her heart. It was merely up to Joses to complete the request, and Arimathea would allow some time before he brought that up to him.

"You are dear friends," Joseph grasped Benjamin's hand and smiled at the couple who seemed to hang on his every word. "I will give your message to Joses. The betrothal will not be for some time as he has some other business to attend to. But, upon his return, hopefully in less than a year or two, he will be ready."

"Our home will be ready as well, and so will our daughter," said Benjamin. "In the meantime, we will take Martha to Emmaus."

"Please take Miriam, as well. She should enter a time of separation if she is to accept betrothal. It will be a long wait, but she will understand, won't she"

"Absolutely! Blessed are you Lord our God, King of the universe," said Benjamin, raising his hands and eyes to the heavens to thank HaShem for this opportunity for his daughter. Then, bringing his gaze back to Joseph he asked, "Where will you go for now?"

"To the sea!" Joseph excitedly declared and stepped briskly along as he waved goodbye.

The promises made, Joses accompanied his Uncle Joseph on his voyages for the next couple of years. They traveled to Briton, Egypt, Rome, Gaul, and even to India. The young man grew more wise and experienced. He also took the time, as occasion would permit, to study with the mystics of these other lands. It was his habit to investigate the breadth, height, and depth of HaShem's dealings with all the other nations. A wise ruler must be knowledgeable, and the leader of Israel must understand firsthand why HaShem commanded Israel to pray for the seventy nations of the world. Indeed, Israel was HaShem's chosen people, but the whole Earth was also the work of His Hands.

Others, however, looked upon him as a coward for not standing to fight the Romans over their usurpation of the land and their stealing of the fruit of their labors and the treasures of HaShem. Among those most displeased with him were his own brethren.

While Joses was gone, his brothers became more active in the Community. Each took their place, Jude preparing for kingship, Jacob for priestly duties, and Kefa as a Zealot leader. Jude and Kefa began assisting the Zealots in planning and executing attacks on Roman interests. Jacob, on the other hand, looked to Chananya ben Menachem as his mentor and he refined his asceticism and discipline even more. With Joses out of the way, Jude began in earnest to seek support for his claim to the Throne of David, the right he felt Joses had lost, especially with his seeming flight from Judea with Uncle Joseph.

The schism between the brothers and Joses continued to grow even with Joses' absence. Jude had completed his Nazarite vow and entered full fellowship into the Way of Damascus. As the Mashiach ben David, the anointed son of David soon to be king, he had led many fierce battles against the kittim and had been victorious. The brothers were set to control the events of all Palestine should they succeed in expelling the kittim. How could they fail with HaShem on their side?

But, it was a sad time, as well. As the fighting became more intense, the Romans turned more and more to a scorched earth policy to enforce their will. Resistance to their rule was met with the most horrendous revenge. Whole villages and some towns were completely destroyed. Lack of command emphasis to prevent atrocities was, in fact, more like command approval in allowing the soldiers to have their way in the land.

Roman Legionnaires were not permitted to marry, although many had women and some children who followed them, staying outside the main camps. The soldiers, having kept the requirements of their enlistments and having no sensitivities but to Rome and their own pleasures, unleashed their lust and destruction upon the populace. They were not against raping, pillaging, murdering, and burning beyond the necessity of battle. With no one to hold them back from whatever their hearts desired to take, and the willingness of their commanders to allow them the spoils of war, the devastation to the people was without mercy.

Many staunch members of the Community, and many followers from around Judea and Galilee, had family and friends maimed or killed by the Kittim. Too many had been crucified, left to hang on the stakes by the hundreds, to remind those who survived not to question the power and glory of Rome. Peace with Rome was the only road to peace.

It was about this time that the sons of Herod the Great clamored for control of the government and petitioned Caesar for solidified positions of power. Many uprisings occurred in defiance to the maneuvers by these Idumeans who were supported by Rome. The choice of government lay either with Roman governors or the Idumeans, and neither was satisfactory to the people of Judea and even less so to those allied with the resistance and the movement for independence. It could go on no longer for those who saw resistance as a necessary tool to secure the freedom of Judea and all Israel.

Opposing the resistance was the Roman Procurator, Sabinus.

A man of many desires, foremost was his thirst for riches. Seeing the turmoil of the people in trying to maintain a semblance of unity, then a breakdown in confederation, he saw the opportunity for plunder. He was older than most of Caesar's representatives, having entered the service of the Emperor after the demise of his own estates due to miscalculations of commerce throughout the east. Tall, with a head of distinguished gray hair, he was an imposing figure of power. He wielded it for his own gain.

"In the land are many fortresses built by Herod, and many places of secret storage of treasure, not the least of which is the Temple," Sabinus explained to his friend and confidant, Romulus. They were watching the guard force just leaving Jerusalem that was escorting the Roman Army Commander Varus to Jaffa where he would board a ship for Syria and then proceed on to Antioch. Varus had been modestly successful at his efforts to put down the many rebellions and uprisings that had occurred throughout Judea, and there were many Zealots who might try to assassinate him. Sabinus was to stay in Judea with an entire legion at his disposal in Jerusalem and many cohorts available throughout the area for reinforcement and to keep the peace.

Sabinus continued, "Varus is a man of great talent and ability. He emphasized to me that the Jews need us, that they need good rulers to bring them safety and security. But, he did not fail in his own operations to take booty and send it to Rome for the cost of the wars." He stopped and turned, giving Romulus a sinister grin. "I see going a step further. It is important, moreover, for us to ensure that the Jews do not have the means to wage war upon each other, or us. So, I need you to advise me of the next area of operation after the post at Mar Saba, of the forces necessary to seize the citadels guarding the treasures, then we will consolidate the money for Caesar, keeping a sizeable reward for ourselves."

"Yes, your excellency," replied Romulus, a tall man also, but with a much more cerebral demeanor than exhibited by the warrior, Sabinus. "Where will you maintain your portion of the king's money? It is growing to a sizeable amount and you will relieve the people of more of it. You will need a safe place for many reasons, foremost that if you are discovered by Caesar, he will not only imprison you, or worse, but put the money in his own treasury."

"I can handle Caesar," Sabinus said confidently. "He is not altogether unaware of my ambitions, and my needs. He has said as much." Sabinus poured some wine from a silver pitcher taken from the Temple and placed in the service of the procurator. He offered a cup also to Romulus. They raised the cups and saluted each other. Then, Sabinus continued, "Obviously my storehouse at the port of Caesarea is the most secure location. The problem will be getting it there from the many locations we take it from around the country. That we can handle with sizeable escort forces or disguised caravans that look like local merchants. I really see little difficulty in this."

"The disguised caravans are an excellent idea," responded Romulus. "I have people that would fit this assignment very well, and no one will ever interfere with them even if they suspect something is amiss."

"That is why I keep you as a friend and counselor," Sabinus said to him, smiling with closed lips as he swallowed another sip of wine. "We are ready for our operation in Mar Saba then?"

"As we speak. Varus will set sail tomorrow, and you can attack the local treasury at Mar Saba in the evening just as the Sabbath starts and the evening meal has taken the fight out of them."

"Brilliant! Bring the commanders of the forces to the west of Bethlehem and stage them there tonight. I will arrive in the morning and we will proceed to the hills just west of Mar Saba. We will attack after dusk."

"As you wish," Romulus replied. "Hail Caesar," he said as he turned to depart.

"Hail, Caesar…indeed," Sabinus said under his breath. "Call for the High Priest," he said to his servant who entered the room as Romulus departed. "I need to talk to him."

"Yes, your Excellency," replied the servant who hurried off.

A half-hour passed and a soldier announced the arrival of the High Priest, Joazer ben Boethus. Joazer was the son of Boethus, the High Priest before him who was of a priestly clan brought from Eqypt by Herod the Great. Herod had married Boethus' daughter after disposing of his Maccabean wife, Mariamme. Ironically, Boethus' daughter was also named Mariamme. The Boethusians had bought the High Priesthood and were loyal to the Herodian rulers and to the Romans, certainly not to Israel or the Jewish people. In fact, Joazer, like his father, was a man of intrigue, hungry for power, envious of riches, and a sycophant. He was soft, almost feminine in his appearance and the fine texture of his skin was typical of rich Jews from Alexandria, Egypt where expensive oils were in abundance. He walked not so much with grace, but arrogance, maintaining his chin at a level a little above its natural position.

"Your Excellency," Joazer saluted as he entered the Procurator's chambers. "You have called for me."

"Yes, Joazer, I need your advice," said Sabinus who poured a little more wine in another cup and handed it to Joazer who immediately sipped the sweet and fragrant liquid, running his tongue over his lips after swallowing. Sabinus retrieved his own cup and walked to the porch, Joazer following. "Tomorrow we attack at Mar Saba, the resistance has many members there and we need to route them, taking as many captive as possible so that we can obtain more detailed information concerning their activities. The operation will be another expense upon Caesar and we intend to pay for it by seizing the treasury. It is apparent that is the source of the support for the resistance, anyway. Can we depend on the assistance of your local administrators?"

"As always, your Excellency," responded Joazer. "May the Procurator at his pleasure explain the way in which he desires me to encourage those administrators?"

"As has so often been necessary, I will pay them for their trouble, and for your assistance I will deposit a tenth of that seized into your hands," responded Sabinus.

They smiled and raised their cups. "To a successful campaign," said Sabinus.

"To the health of my friend and ally," toasted Joazer. "And to Caesar, Hail Caesar!" he said with conviction.

"Hail, Caesar!" responded Sabinus.

***

That same afternoon found Jude in contemplation while walking by the Temple in Jerusalem. He was doing all he could, he assured himself, but he knew that the tasks ahead would be crucial. His concerns sometimes drifted from his own necessities while he sacrificed his personal comfort to ensure the hope of the people. When he was not planning or executing a military operation, he was teaching and preaching to the people about the coming of the Kingdom of Heaven to Israel. Even though still of a relatively young age, everyone who knew what he was about recognized him for the king he would become. One of the principle steps was to properly prepare the Israelite virgin chosen by Chananya to become his bride. Chananya had the young woman's parents notified and she was placed in a separation from all but those women chosen to train her and maintain her purity. Jude was ready to assume his destiny. Nothing could prevent him from fulfilling his life's purpose. He sat pondering all of these events. It was approaching evening and the Sabbath when he realized that Joses' plans were still very similar to his own. Joses was back from his voyages, and Jude anticipated friction and antagonism with his brother should they meet. Undoubtedly Joses would challenge him in every way.

But, Joses continued to mind his own business, a feat which seemed intolerable foolishness to Jude as he continued to ponder recent events as he watched the business about the Temple during his walk.

Upon their return from the voyage to India, Arimathea had approached Benjamin and confirmed the plans for Miriam to marry Joses. They were both now eighteen years of age, and Joses had increased in stature. He was still smaller than his brethren, but he was, gratefully, taller than Miriam. The problem was that he did not have the recognition of the people as a revolutionary as his brethren did, especially Jude and Jacob. To him, that merely meant that he would proceed with his life the way he saw fit, for he knew he could not bow to the fanaticism of his brothers. The marriage was scheduled for the month of Tishrei (September), and the bride's father, Benjamin, would preside. The ceremony and feast would take place in Bethany.

When Jacob learned of Joses' plan to marry Miriam, he went to Jude and warned him of the danger to his claim to the throne. Jude responded by having Chananya ben Menachem complete the arrangements for his own marriage that was then planned also for the month of Tishrei just like Joses'. With his mother Miryam's help, Jude was able to proceed quickly. His betrothed, a daughter of Gideon ben Simeon from the Community of Damascus named Rachel, was more than anxious to become the wife of an heir to the throne of David. By following the dynastic requirements of marriage for the King of Israel as proclaimed by the Teacher of Righteousness at Damascus, Jude's marriage would further guarantee his success as the heir apparent to the Davidic Throne.

Chananya deferred to Joachanin and Jude's brother, Jacob, for the final ceremonial rituals. It was a good move; principally because Jacob would perform part of the ceremony, further solidifying Jude's position as the rightful heir. Jacob was highly respected in the Community and in all Judea, even at his young age. He had abided by his vow, was a strict vegetarian, and followed the rules of the Community to the letter. He was quickly becoming popular with the resistance and the people of Judea at large who knew of him because of his piety, righteousness, and dedication to HaShem. His revolutionary side was veiled from ordinary view because he stood in the place of a preacher and teacher at all times, never discussing the resistance outside of a very small circle of confidants.

It was Jude who became the military revolutionary known to the brethren. His identity was also veiled, but not nearly as well as Jacob's due to the manner in which he had to operate, physically and frequently leading military operations. But, as a whole, the cover of the ascetic, disciplined, religious observing community tended to divert Roman attention away from their resistance activities.

While Jude was still lost in thought concerning these events, he only subconsciously noticed the figure approaching him from the Court of the Gentiles of the Temple. It was Kefa, his brother.

"Sabinus' troops were seen moving toward Mar Saba this afternoon," Kefa spoke quietly. "There is a rumor that Sabinus is after the gold and silver there just as he was in Hyrcania."

The news startled Jude. "Not again, not so soon!" He shook his head to clear his thoughts so as to better focus on the dire news from Kefa. He stood slowly, however, to avoid any detection of his alarm. The brothers then walked slowly toward the gate to exit the Temple grounds. "What is the size of the force?" asked Jude.

"The legion has not left Jerusalem. The force is apparently a couple of Cohorts from west of Emmaus, maybe from the border with Egypt."

"Is there time to get word to the Teacher?" asked Jude.

"No way to know. The Romans could attack tonight, or, worse, tomorrow night," responded Kefa.

"Tonight is our Sabbath, and tomorrow night the Sabbath for the people. Not on the Sabbath again," moaned Jude. "They use our religion against us. But, if I were in their shoes, I would likely do the same thing. There is no time to get word to Chananya or Joachanin, we must proceed immediately to Mar Saba and warn them."

They traveled swiftly, making it to Mar Saba in less than three hours. In a valley to the west, they could see the Roman force in an apparent staging area. But, the size of the force was not even nearly a cohort. The information from Kefa did not seem to fit.

"That is a century, maybe two at the most," commented Jude. "And, they don't seem to be all that threatening."

Kefa looked at the Romans, then at Jude and merely shrugged.

They kept walking to avoid looking suspicious. Mar Saba was just ahead. As they entered the town, they could see that there was no sentry from amongst the town's people and they could not locate any of the local leaders, none they could trust, anyway. Finally, they approached Jonathan ben Netanyahu, a faithful man and member of the local council.

"My young friends!" Jonathan hailed them as they came into his shop where he dabbled in carpentry and silver work. "What is the occasion for this surprise visit? Tomorrow night begins the Sabbath, you may have to stay awhile."

"May we talk inside?" Jude cautioned. The three men walked casually to the door, Jonathan noticing concern on Jude's young face. Even though Jude was half his age, Jonathan respected him for his courage and position. They crossed the threshold and closed the door.

Jude turned to Jonathan while Kefa kept watch.

"We believe the Romans are going to attack Mar Saba sometime in the next day or so, probably on the Sabbath," Jude reported.

Jonathan was obviously stunned and he searched Jude's face with a seriousness Jude had not seen in him before.

"On what do you base this alarm?" asked Jonathan.

"Kefa's spies have reported a Roman Cohort moving from the west, and there is rumor that Sabinus intends to do to Mar Saba what he did in Hyrcania."

"You mean despoil the treasury?" asked Jonathan.

"Yes, we think so." Jude looked over to Kefa to ensure that all was still clear and he saw Kefa nod reassuringly to him.

"That explains a few things," responded Jonathan. "I think those in power here have been paid off. We were warned today not to resist Roman patrols and to stay clear of the citadel. Troops loyal to us are there guarding it, but if the Romans seek to attack it, then it will be lost. In Hyrcania we thought the Romans were after the resistance camp on the south of the town, and they did attack it, killing many. But the main thrust was the local treasury. Is this a new pattern of insult?"

"Everything points to this Sabinus wanting all our wealth. I doubt he is really about keeping order. He is here to plunder us and that record is pretty clear. With Varus gone, I would not put the Temple Treasury beyond his greed if he believes he can succeed in taking it," said Jude. "But, can we do anything to defend Mar Saba? Can you help us gather volunteers from the faithful who will help repel this aggression? If you can, I will return to Jerusalem and approach Gamaliel to see if he can use his influence to stop Sabinus."

Kefa could keep silent no longer.

"My brother, you still trust that man?" he asked.

"Sometimes we just have to go with what we have," responded Jude. "Although a Pharisee, and believing that Rome is HaShem's reward for our nation's unfaithfulness, he does not stand for abuse of power. Yes, I believe he can help."

"Then go," encouraged Jonathan. "We will do what we can here."

"Kefa and I will return as soon as possible," said Jude.

They left immediately as Jonathan began to gather men and arms in an attempt to counter any assault. The brothers hurried on the path back to Jerusalem while the darkness of night gathered about them.

"We should turn aside at Beit Lechem for the Sabbath and a rest," said Jude. Kefa agreed. "We will not linger, however, as HaShem understands the urgency of our situation. As holy as our Sabbath is, HaShem would not want us to rest when His people stand ready for the slaughter." As they approached Beit Lechem from the south they noticed a glow that was out of place on the west side of the town.

"What could that be?" Jude asked Kefa. It then dawned on him. "It could be nothing but a Roman camp, and a sizeable one. We had better take a look."

The two men raced to a hillside to try and see what they feared most, but on the crest of the hill they could see what appeared to be a Roman sentry. To avoid detection, they turned south again and approached from off the road. As they got closer, they could hear the sounds of an army. A few more feet, and they proceeded on their stomachs through the sparse brush and scattered rocks. There, in front of them, were at least two Roman Cohorts encamped in a small valley.

"I knew it," said Kefa quietly. "Now what can we do?"

"Mar Saba cannot defend against this," said Jude. "We can only hope to delay them until our friends in Jerusalem change the Procurator's mind. The resistance resources in Mar Saba are not sufficient to warrant such an attack. This must be to seize the money. I am afraid we must split up. I will go to Gamaliel, you return to Mar Saba. Organize what forces you can and delay the cohort. But, do not risk capture. It just isn't worth it. Ask Jonathan if there is any way to encourage a reinforcement of the citadel."

The brothers backed away and stood when it was safe. They looked at each other and embraced. No more words were exchanged. Kefa headed south to Mar Saba and Jude made his way to Jerusalem.

Jude arrived at Gamaliel's home near midnight. The sage was still awake, a flickering light from a lamp coming from a back room where he was known to study Torah and pray. Jude knocked on the door. The sage's wife greeted Jude.

"Son of Cleophas," she exclaimed as she had respect for this young man who showed such promise. "I presume you seek my husband. Come in, I will tell him you are here."

Jude felt somewhat out of his element. While he knew this was the best course of action, he still felt uneasy associating so closely with those not in the Way of the Community.

"Jude ben Cleophas!" Gamaliel called to him. "What a time of night to be wandering the streets of Jerusalem. This is the time you hold as your Sabbath. A mere visit this is not."

"Rabbi, my visit is not for pleasure, but for the saving of life and the offerings to HaShem," Jude said earnestly. "The Romans are staging near Beit Lechem to prepare for attack against Mar Saba. We think it is to plunder the citadel, but many will perish as well."

"Oh, no!" Gamaliel muttered. He looked at Jude with imploring eyes. "Are you sure?"

Jude nodded in the affirmative. "We have seen the Cohort, maybe two, on the west and a century to the south. They are armed for battle."

"Then the Romans are not going to stop this robbery of our

lives and goods. I heard that Joazer gave an assurance to the effect that Sabinus was satisfied that the rebellion had subsided and there would be no more raids. It has put us at a disadvantage."

"Is there anything you can do with the Sanhedrin? Anything?" asked Jude.

"These are still dangerous times, Jude," responded Gamaliel. "I will do what I can. But, my influence is minimal anymore. For now, take a rest until morning. You will need your strength in any event."

Jude accepted the invitation to rest for the night. He would not get anymore of a Sabbath observance than this.

It was all for naught. Sabinus had moved up the attack time.

At daylight, a Roman Cohort attacked Mar Saba from the north, and another from the west. The century Jude and Kefa saw the day before was placed as a holding force to the east, the only possible escape route from the slaughter. Kefa, too, was caught off guard, not having had time to prepare lookout positions or defenses. He looked at the approaching columns and did the only thing he could do—obey his brother's instructions not to be captured. He did not even have time to warn Jonathan. He ran as quickly as he could to a hiding place prepared for resistance fighters on the south side of the town. It was somewhat of higher elevation, but the approach to the rock cavern was well concealed from most angles of view. As he closed the rocks and brush in behind him, he felt overwhelming emotion at his failure. He broke down and sobbed.

The Romans fired volleys of arrows into the town from both cohorts. Any people in the open were cut down, men, women, and children. The resistance fighters were still not organized, although Jonathan had a small group gathered not far from the citadel where they were preparing their equipment. The attack came as a surprise, and Jonathan and his men ran to the only place they felt they could do any good—the citadel.

Now the infantry from the Cohorts was entering the town, breaking down doors and killing the occupants or taking them prisoner as they pleased. Kefa watched as small groups of people tried to escape to the east, right into the hands of the century that was the holding force. Most of them were killed or maimed by volleys of arrows until the soldiers decided that those remaining were not a threat and could be taken prisoner. None of the townspeople were armed, and none offered any resistance. Most who survived engaged only in pleadings and cries for the salvation of their lives.

The Romans were now burning homes and chaining the few remaining women and children, separating the men still alive, or barely alive, into heavily guarded areas for interrogation. Kefa looked over to the citadel and could see that Jonathan and his men had still not gained entrance. There seemed to be some sort of disagreement taking place between those at the gate and the soldiers in the citadel. Then, as Kefa watched, he saw the citadel guards fire volleys of arrows into Jonathan's small force. They were all killed to a man, their blood running in small streams down the earthen embankments of the structure.

It was all over in a matter of half an hour. Only the southern portion of the town remained undamaged and there appeared to be no casualties in that vicinity. It was where the local aristocracy friendly to the Romans lived. Friendship with Rome had spared them.

The citadel doors were opened from the inside and the Romans entered unopposed. They methodically emptied the treasury into carts and wagons that were then escorted west out of town. Kefa watched to see the fate of the guards who had apparently been convinced to repel Jonathan's men but not the Romans. They never left the citadel. The Romans departed and all was quiet except for the moans of a few women and children who had been ignored by the attackers. No one from the south side of town had yet exited their dwellings, not even to assist those who were suffering.

Early that same morning, Gamaliel had tried to approach members of the Sanhedrin to petition Joazer and Sabinus concerning any planned military actions near Beit Lechem or Mar Saba. But, he learned that the attack had already commenced to destroy members of the resistance hiding in the town of Mar Saba. Heartbroken, he returned to his home and reported the information to Jude.

"It was not to happen before the Sabbath of the people!" cried Jude. "That was our information. What happened?"

"The Romans are flexible, Jude. Any information that gets to them that they believe will alter their plans causes them to respond in whatever manner is favorable to them. Obviously, Sabinus kept the exact hour of the attack to himself and his subordinate commander to prevent any interference. I guess he figured the Sanhedrin could not accuse him of anything if he acted before our Sabbath. He is a very sly enemy."

"Kefa!" Jude cried out. "Kefa is still in Mar Saba. I must go to find him!" He gathered his few belongings and began to exit the door when Gamaliel stopped him.

"If Kefa was caught, there is nothing you can do now. Go to your elders, and try to decide on other options," said the sage.

Jude was unsure now of what he had done. Should he have trusted a Pharisee so close to the establishment. Maybe Kefa had been right. But, there had been no time for anything else, and it did not appear that Gamaliel had betrayed him. There were no soldiers here to carry him away in chains.

"Yes, you are correct," sighed Jude, breathing hard while trying to regain his composure. "I will return and report." With that he nodded at Gamaliel and left for Damascus.

Kefa stayed hidden until near nightfall which was also the regularly celebrated Sabbath of the people not wise to the Way and the true order. Before the sun dropped too low in the sky, he left his hiding place and made his way to the east, then north, as far as he could before the Sabbath began. He sat down on a rock just east of Beit Lechem and considered entering the town for the night. He had already violated the Sabbath he recognized, but he had no desire to interfere in the observances of others. However, he was afraid that with the raid on Mar Saba, he may be identified as a member of the resistance. He decided to go ahead and proceed to Damascus under the cover of darkness.

In the meantime, Sabinus was elated over his defeat of Mar Saba and the seizure of the citadel's treasure. According to the Roman commander, the amount of money was substantial, and the treasure was almost all ornate gold, silver, and precious stones. As planned, Sabinus gave ten percent to Joazer, several pieces to the collaborators in Mar Saba, and a more than substantial portion to Romulus to transport to the storage in Caesarea. The bulk, however, still went to Caesar. Rome's coffers, and those of her supporters, swelled again as innocent Jewish blood soaked into the ground.

As Sabinus gloated over his success, Kefa arrived at Jacob's tent where he also found Jude. The men exchanged information in preparation for the briefing to Chananya and the Council later that morning.

"It was cold-blooded murder," Kefa stated with disgust and hatred. "Many, many deaths and it was obvious treachery. The guards in the citadel unleashed their volleys upon Jonathan and the resistance, killing all of them. But, justice was returned to them for their treason. The Romans killed them all, too. Dead men tell no tales, and you don't need to pay them, either."

"I should have stayed," Jude lamented. "Maybe I could have rallied a better defense."

"No, brother," Jacob tried to assure him, "it was lost before it began. Perhaps, the only thing you would have succeeded in doing is having the Romans kill or capture you. It would have complicated too many other concerns. Come, let us go report this to the Teacher."

The brothers left Jacob's tent and walked several yards to where Chananya was discussing matters with several other men. Word had already spread of the action of the kittim in Mar Saba. Joachanin also arrived at about the same time and the group entered the smaller room in the Community Hall. As soon as everyone had assumed a place, Chananya asked Jude to speak.

"Teacher, there is no end to the atrocities of the kittim, and they have the help of these thieves in the Temple," Jude reported to Chananya who sat in his tent with Joachanin and Jacob. "For the sake of gain do Boethus and Sabinus spill the blood of our people and destroy our edifices. It is no longer just to control us. It is to rob us!"

"Yes, it is time to oppose these heathens more directly. It is appropriate for you to go and prepare an army to punish Sabinus. The place to lay siege to him is at Jerusalem. But, be aware that Rome will quickly come to his aid. You must secure your alliances and convince the strays of Israel to band together. It is time to begin a cleansing, HaShem willing." Chananya then turned to Joachanin and Jacob. "You, as the tzaddiks of HaShem, should accompany Jude in this endeavor. You may not shed blood, but you can support Jude and encourage the people to do so as well. So, make your plans and do nothing in haste. Do these things and yet do not leave undone all else that life requires of us."

The brethren arose and did as Chananya instructed. It was the beginning of the Messianic age.

***

As Chananya had advised, the brothers made their plans for the revolt against the kittim and the Herodians. But, they also took the time to engage in other important aspects of their lives, even when they all could not agree, such as the wedding of Joses and Miriam.

The day for Joses' and Miriam's wedding arrived. The marriage feast was prepared by Joses' mother, Miryam, and planned at the Galilean meetinghouse. The house, a large but unpretentious structure, was a cover for the Zealots and a short distance from Damascus. Miryam attended to all the details of the ceremony and celebration with the aid of Joses' uncle, Joseph of Arimathea. The brothers and other members of the family were all invited, and all of them came out of respect for their mother. Several servants were hired by the family to assist in the festivities.

Benjamin ben Nikdimon stood in his capacity as governor of the feast. He began by singing a hymn and calling the bride, his daughter, to him. Her gowns were beautiful, white and flowing, with the veil fully covering her face. The father and the bride walked to the chupa, or marriage canopy, and waited together for the entrance of the bridegroom. Then, all stood for the entrance of Joses. He entered the hall and walked more stately than he ever had before. It thrilled the bride to see him so commanding and dressed so finely, even almost like a king. She nodded at Joses' mother who had done a wonderful job in supervising the manufacture of the dresses of the women in the ceremony, and especially of Joses' gowns.

The brothers shook their heads and shrugged at what they saw next. The symbolism Joses was trying to convey did not escape them.

Joses carried a sword in his left hand and an oil lamp in his right. He wore a blue sash and a blue and white mantle. He was in the regalia of the royal house. Joses arrived at the chupa where Benjamin and the bride stood, and the ceremony began. Each answered the questions of vows, and the bride walked around Joses seven times, as was the custom. Joses then placed a ring on the bride's finger. Joses lifted the bride's veil and kissed her for the first time. They then walked together to a small tent or bridal chamber where they were allowed to embrace each other in marital union. During this time, the wedding feast began and the participants enjoyed food, drink, and general celebrations, awaiting the arrival of the new couple from their first time alone.

The brothers, particularly Jude and Jacob, were disturbed by this break with the customs of Damascus and the pretense of the royal robes, sword, and lamp with which Joses adorned himself. This was somewhat out of the ordinary, and the brothers and several guests scoffed at Joses' continuing alterations of tradition, laughing amongst themselves at the apparent pretensions and yet seriously disturbed by the wedding ceremony. After sometime, the couple exited the bridal chamber. Joses' mother, as was the custom, dutifully entered the bridal chamber to confirm the consummation of the marriage by attesting to the blood on the bedding from the breaking of the bride's hymen. With her declaration of the union, the party renewed again.

Jacob and Jude approached Joses to ask him what caused the oddities of the ritual. The two brothers were confused. But, Joses felt no need to explain the situation to them in any detail, which only brought them to a higher level of interrogation. During the discussion their Uncle Joseph approached them. Quelling the apparent disagreement, Joseph said he understood the plans and asked Jude and Jacob to open their hearts and minds. Joses would perform the proper subsequent rituals for a complete dynastic marriage as needed later. Jude and Jacob merely shook their heads, but wished their brother and his wife happiness. As they walked away, Uncle Joseph again confidently introduced the couple to the guests.

In Jude and Jacob's minds, Joses had not abided the terms of dynastic marriage. Jude and Jacob were appalled at Joses' behavior and this insult to the family. But, Jude also knew that his position as heir to the throne grew stronger even as the event concluded. He realized that with this action by Joses and his own dynastic marriage to Rachel merely days away, he would have more weight in the Community and with the Teacher than Joses could ever hope.

After the marriage, Joseph of Arimathea took Joses and Miriam on a short voyage for their honeymoon and to assist them in settling in their new home. Joses was out of Jude's way, for now.

Jude's marriage was now imminent. Unlike Joses, Jude and Rachel were to have their ceremonies performed in Damascus. Also unlike Joses' marriage, Jude would marry Rachel in the method of the dynastic succession, securing his claim to the Throne of David. All he needed after that was a son born to him the following Tishrei. There was a method to this procedure, and the Community was there to ensure that success to the best of its ability. Jude's mother and brothers were ecstatic.

"Tomorrow is the day you will begin your final preparations for the throne," Miryam said to Jude, keeping her distance from him so as not to defile him prior to the wedding. "You have been the light of this family," she said with an admiration for him that clearly identified her preference for this son. "You make your parents proud, and you honor HaShem."

A maiden entered the room and reported to Miryam that the bride had completed her immersion in the waters of a mikvah and was ready for her. Rachel had been sequestered from all men, including Jude, for the last three months since her betrothal to him. It was now time for her final preparations and the rituals that prepared her for her rightful place. Miryam excused herself.

Jude passed through another door and then outside into the area near the living quarters of Chananya and Joachanin, mere tents just on the outskirts of the town. Joachanin also had a small cave up in the hills where he kept his few personal belongings and some scrolls. Both habitations were the most humble in the settlement. The High Priest in Jerusalem had a palace, furnished with the luxuries of kings. The heir to the Teacher of Righteousness in Damascus was a man committed like the "poor," those senior elders of the Way in Damascus who had donated all their earthly wealth to the Community. As such, Joachanin lived as most others in Damascus, in tents or small caves using the clay buildings primarily for community tasks.

"Jude," Chananya called to him as Jude entered the building, Jacob standing as his brother entered. "Tomorrow you will enter into the most sacred of covenants with HaShem, a likeness of His Shekinah shall be given you. Have you been to the mikvah?"

Jude bowed his head in the affirmative as well as in respect and thoughtfulness as the initiation rites began. Chananya asked Joachanin to officiate in the ritual and Joachanin, using a small basin, symbolically washed Jude while repeating the words of sacredness. At the same time, the women led by Miryam washed Rachel, uttering similar words. The two rituals were being performed simultaneously, but well separated from each other. After the washing, Joachanin then placed oil upon Jude, repeating sacred words of promise to him and admonishing him to follow through on his destiny. Likewise, Miryam placed oil on Rachel, repeating similar words.

As the daylight slipped away and night began to fall, the couple, with their respective chaperones, prepared for the wedding the next day.

In the morning, Rachel's father stood at the center of the ritual canopy surrounded by family members, Jews from various villages and towns, and the members of the Community, as his daughter and her entourage were brought to him. Miryam and the maidens appointed to guarantee Rachel's purity escorted her to the canopy. She took a position just in front of her father.

Chananya and Joachanin then entered the area with Jacob and the rest of the twelve elders of the Community. They took their places as Jude, dressed in the purple robes of the king, came and stood at the entrance of the building. He carried an unsheathed sword in his right hand and a lit oil lamp in his left hand. As he walked between the assembled guests, all stood to honor him. The bridegroom approached the chupa (canopy) and Rachel. She was facing forward with her veil over her face, watching out of the corner of her eye as her King stood next to her. Gideon ben Simeon, Rachel's father, then began the ceremony, offering his daughter to Jude. Jude accepted and the father pronounced his blessing. At its conclusion, Rachel, now unveiled, walked around Jude seven times and was then brought next to Jude. Her father now recited the final words of the ceremony, and had Jude place the ring of promise upon Rachel.

"You are hereby sanctified unto me with this ring according to the laws of Moses and Israel," he said to her. They looked at each other, smiles breaking forth on their faces, Rachel also slightly flushed.

Finally, Rachel's father read the royal ketuba (marriage contract) and recited seven marriage blessings upon the couple. They then kissed for the first time. Before joining the rest of the celebration, the women escorted Jude and Rachel to an adjacent room, where they were to spend some time together alone. With that, the festivities for the guests began. Upon the completion of their time alone, Jude and Rachel exited their private room and the assembled crowd ecstatically greeted them as Jude's mother, Miryam, entered the chamber to verify that the joining had occurred. Rachel was again blushing slightly, burying her head into Jude's shoulder, as Miryam returned to the gathering and nodded her head in approval.

Jude kissed his bride lovingly on her cheek to reassure her and gaze into her eyes.

Jude and Rachel would now remain together until she became pregnant. Once that confirmation was made, a second ceremony would be performed at a later time to declare the dynastic character of their marriage and perform an additional ritual. The twelve elders would then separate the couple again until the child was born. Jude knew that at that time he would then be recognized as the Mashiach ben David without question.

CHAPTER FOUR

A year passed and Joses and Miriam were content and happy. A child had been born to them, a son they named Joseph. The family lived in two places depending upon the time of year and other circumstances. In the warmer parts of the year they stayed in Capernaum while in the cooler parts of the year they lived in Bethany. Joses traveled often, sometimes with his Uncle Joseph, at other times just to accomplish work projects around the country, as he was an architect and builder, like his father, Cleophas. In fact, Herod had used Cleophas on a number of his palaces and even parts of the Temple of Herod. The fact that Cleophas never revealed, nor pushed, his Davidic right to rule over Israel kept him in semi-good graces with the ruling Herodians and Romans, at least as far as his business was concerned.

So it was with Joses. He often felt incensed toward the ruling classes of the Herodians and Romans, and he pretty much kept to himself, devoting his time alone to study and meditation. Often, his meditative periods would last for hours as he applied the techniques he had learned in On and Damascus in his younger years.

But, Joses had something calling to him and he could not refuse its refrain. While he knew that the responsibility he had of taking the throne of David was his Uncle Joseph's greatest desire, Joses had to search to find how he could best attain it. To claim it directly and publicly would not only be dangerous, but would likely cause a greater rift in his extended family than he had already experienced. Well he knew that Jude was claiming the kingly mashiach position. Furthermore, while his physical condition had continued to improve, he was still not of a kingly stature, and certainly not strong enough to become a kingly warrior.

Then there was the problem of the Torah and the Community's interpretation of it. Sadly, they were the only voice in Palestine that even came close to upholding the Law and having a right to do so. The problem for Joses was their brand of asceticism and discipline that went beyond Torah requirements. In fact, Joses felt that these beliefs were their greatest weakness. Yet, to attempt to ascend to the throne without their approval would, again, be met with failure due to the support they demanded, and received, from all Jews.

So, Joses remained patient. He studied the Torah diligently, and prayed often. Having attended the schools at the City of On in Egypt, which were presided over by the priesthood there, he had a massive repertoire of the mystical side of the Torah, the Hebrew language, and its application to kingly acquisitions. He knew he would need to return to On, or commit to some degree at Damascus, at the appropriate time and at the proper age prior to his final ascension to the throne. His travels and studies in foreign lands, especially the east, had polished his understanding of all these things in the light of the descent of the teachings of Abraham to others outside of Israel. Israel had, in fact, lost or misunderstood so much of it since the Babylonian captivity. His ventures around the world had brought many things regarding the secrets to his mind.

His studies were not, however, limited to purely spiritual matters. He worked hard to improve his physical condition. He even requested from his Uncle Joseph that he obtain an instructor for him in the ways of combat and weapons employment. He studied the wars of the Jews from Moses' time to that of the Maccabees, even the guerilla tactics of the Community revolutionaries. He did not allow himself to remain idle, as time was growing ever shorter. He was now approaching his twentieth year of age.

Throughout this time the other brothers continued their resistance activities. Rome was becoming more and more adamant about controlling Judea and Galilee while the people's anger against Rome was reaching a fever pitch. The Romans had responded by increasing troop strength and also considered sending in a new Roman Governor. All the while, any hint of resistance was crushed immediately. The resistance won many skirmishes, but they could not defeat the entire Roman Army. The Romans, on the other hand, realized that they needed to do more than merely occupy the land. They needed to discover the leadership of the resistance. The question was how to accomplish it.

Jude, Joachanin, and Jacob had been working together to determine how best to ensure the addition of new members to the Community. The righteousness of the members of their resistance army was also a great concern, as they knew HaShem would bless them only if their men were pure. The success of all their plans depended on their diligence in managing these two issues, and in honoring and worshipping HaShem. As they discussed these issues, it occurred to them that they needed to accomplish a feat that would endear the population to their cause. A new move was needed to impress the people with the true need for fighting back, and the means to do so. It was time for a bold act, out in the open. But, what should it be?

Several days later, while on his way to Emmaus, Chananya ben Menachem and several of the members of the Community were attacked and killed by a Roman patrol. The Romans believed them to be members of a Zealot raiding party that had attacked a Roman camp not far from Jerusalem. Their bodies lay in the ravine for several days where they were killed before a search party from Damascus found them. The Community was devastated. Not only had these pious men been slaughtered without cause, but also their bodies remained unburied and desecrated.

Joachanin and several of the remaining elders from the council went to the Roman Governor, Sabinus, and demanded an explanation. While the Community had no actual respect for the Romans or their Herodian administrators, the fact was that Herod had looked favorably upon the Essenes as a whole because of Menachem the Essene. They had not been formally implicated in any seditious activity, and they needed to emphasize their case to the Roman and Herodian authorities. The fact was suspicions would be raised if the Community did not offer a protestation before the authorities discovered whom their soldiers had killed.

Sabinus had the affair investigated for the sake of Herod Antipas, Herod's son, and found to his satisfaction that Chananya and his fellow travelers were not the seditious attackers that had killed many of the Roman camp. He issued a formal apology to the Jews, especially the Community at Damascus. But, he refused to punish the renegade Roman soldiers who had attacked the men with no real justification. They were his men whom he had ingratiated with any pleasure they might have as long as they brought the spoils and the booty to him. This was all according to the methods of Sabinus to obtain riches and power. He had now even set his plans in motion to obtain the treasure of the Temple, and there were those who perceived his intentions.

It was then that the Community elders recognized Joachanin ben Zechariah as the Moreh Ha Tzedek, or Teacher of Righteousness. Joachanin and several other men were chosen by lot (vote) by the remaining council members to replace those who had died. Joachanin was specifically voted as the new Teacher of Righteousness and there were no dissents, even with his younger age. His zealousness was tempered by his wisdom, but he still did not hesitate to identify the true issue in his heart. He read the War Scroll to the whole Community, which was the plan for the war of the Sons of Light, the Community, against the Sons of Darkness, the kittim and their followers and supporters. But where would these legions of soldiers for the Army of the Sons of Light come from? The plan was bold and broad.

The Community believed the end times were approaching. The people needed the Kingly Mashiach to lead them into freedom, and Jude was still consolidating his support. At twenty, he now commanded a respectable following that trusted his prowess, judgment, strength, and commitment to the requirements of a Davidic King as dictated by the new Teacher of Righteousness, Joachanin ben Zechariah. He had developed an efficient recruitment campaign for the Community. Speaking in public places as a spiritual leader, he would collect followers and introduce them to Joachanin ben Zechariah who would immerse them in a mikvah (later called baptism by Christians) or in the flowing waters of the Jordan River.

This group Jude would then mine to find those willing and able to join the fighting unit he called HaShem's Army. This was a very effective tool, allowing him to sort through large numbers of individuals and access their true state of mind. Once he ensured that his choices were appropriate, he would introduce them to the Messianic Movement and the Zealot Resistance. But, this was the one area of the Community's activities that was the most susceptible to Roman infiltration and intelligence gathering. While slow to react to this threat, the Romans were going to catch on soon enough.

After recruiting a great number of followers through their ministry, and then identifying potential Zealots, Jude and Jacob found that they had the numbers and the general support to formulate bolder actions than any in their war of resistance to date. The Zealots served as a core upon which they could build larger forces as an action progressed, encouraging locals and others to join in specific resistance efforts as the need developed. In this manner, they could keep an operation secret until just before or immediately after they initiated hostilities. One such event was the planned assault upon the Royal Armory at the palace in Sepphoris of Galilee where Herod and the Romans kept a store of weapons and supplies. The attack, if successful, would allow Jude to seize weapons so badly needed by the resistance. It would also send a message to friend and foe alike that the resistance was strong and capable.

Jude and Jacob met their closest followers south of Jotapata, a city approximately four miles north of Sepphoris and well situated for planning an attack against the Royal Armory. Sepphoris was the pride of the Galilee, located nearly in the middle of the land between the Mediterranean Sea and the Sea of Galilee, surrounded by mountains, hills, and valleys. The fact that Herod and the kittim constantly occupied it was a source of severe irritation to the people, and especially Jude who understood its military significance. In general, the terrain made the Galilee a favorable location for resistance activities against the kittim. The resistance could engage in small and large scale attacks and then disappear into the hills. On this occasion, Jude staged his forces in the hidden valleys and prepared them for the attack. During nighttime, in a large tent surrounded by nearly a hundred men, and more arriving, Jude finalized his plans with his leaders.

"Here is the palace," Jude pointed to a map of Sepphoris he had constructed out of rocks and sand. "Here is the armory. The Roman Garrison is here on the east side of the palace, and here are the quarters for the Herodian Guard. Our objective is the armory, here, inside the palace walls. The Romans and Herod's troops heavily guard it. A century is in reserve at all times, located here at the southern gate. At any particular time, there are ten Romans and twenty to thirty of the King's guards manning the entrance, watching from the tower walls, or standing about the armory. These forces are a mixture of infantry and archers. There is no cavalry." Jude motioned to his right-hand man, Laban. Laban was young, physically powerful, and extremely strong willed. Only a leader like Jude could command him. While intelligent, he was often given to a slight impetuousness-a risk taker. But, this made him a flexible and capable field commander who could take advantage of enemy weaknesses.

"We have watched the changing of the guard," explained Laban, "and we have found that it occurs twice a day, once in the morning immediately after sunrise, and again immediately before sunset. In other words, the forces are at their strongest at all times but these because at all other times the armory is secured very well. While the number of men is doubled around the armory during the guard change, the gates are opened and there is some confusion in the command and control. We plan to attack during the morning guard change on the third day of the week, which is tomorrow. Although the reserve century is moments away, they are typically involved at the time we have planned in replenishing their supplies and are not usually capable of immediate deployment. They are unaware of this weakness, or just plain stupid," he smiled and looked over at another leader, Jude's brother, Kefa.

"So, where will our forces concentrate?" asked Kefa. "To guarantee surprise and gain the initiative this will need close coordination and access. I have seen the area and can't say that there is a convenient spot."

"Here, on the north," Jude pointed to the map. "This is the best approach. We will attack in the lingering darkness before the sun rises above the hills to the east. We will converge from three directions, Kefa on the left, Laban on the right, and my forces in the middle. We will make our way through the city and enter the palace at the moment the main gate is opened for the supply wagon. Laban will act as a rear guard and reserve, protecting us from any surprise from the Roman Century. He will also supply the spies and messengers to help us coordinate the attack. You, Kefa, and those with me will enter the gate and proceed directly to the armory. I have six men who will use a small battering ram to break down the door. As your men continue to battle what forces the kittim have in and around the armory, mine will remove the weapons. Laban will ensure the east gate is opened and we will make our escape to the east. The kittim will never expect such a daring act. It will take them completely by surprise."

Another voice spoke in the darkness.

"Barabbas," Jude's brother, Jacob, called to Jude using a name of affection meaning more than just a brother, but a more sure 'son of our father.' It had a two-fold meaning, one referring to their blood relation, and the other Jacob's recognition that Jude was the Davidic King. "Several in the city have informed me they have enough men that once the battle begins, they will join it to keep the Romans from reaching the armory. They intend to do this not only by force of their swords, but also by placing a herd of sheep and some oxen in their path. It should delay the reinforcements long enough to grant your retreat as long as you do not take too long to gain entrance. Laban's men have but to signal the battle by blowing the horns we have given them."

"Then we are ready," said Jude with satisfaction. "Inspect your men," he instructed Laban and Kefa. "We move tonight."

Laban and Kefa along with the many men who had been standing around stepped away into the darkness. Jacob and Jude were alone.

"This is the big one," Jacob said.

"We have done many things, blessed be HaShem," responded Jude. "But, this will be the most important so far. If they had not murdered Chananya, we would not have had to proceed so quickly and so mercilessly. Is Joachanin in agreement?"

"He knows the danger," Jacob said as he lowered his head and nodded. It was a somber occasion for him. Many could die. The Romans could, and likely would, retaliate. He didn't like the spilling of blood. He had always wanted it to be a last resort. But, Chananya's murder proved that the people could never trust the kittim and the Herodians. "However, he also knows that HaShem expects us to do all we can to free ourselves and to honor His Torah. So, that is enough of that for now. Let us eat to renew our strength and prepare for what is to come."

Jacob and Jude raised their hands and looked up as if to see into heaven. Jacob thanked HaShem for all they had and for providing them with their food and sustenance. The two men then sat and ate.

Two hours later the forces were moving to Sepphoris. In all, Jude estimated the immediate forces at his command at over one thousand men. Added to that the men Jacob was promised in Sepphoris itself, Jude was reasonably certain of success.

As Jude rounded the crest of the last hill before the city, he could see the light of the torches of the palace. Clearly silhouetted against the light were the guards on the walls. He moved his men closer to the city until he could see Kefa's forces on his left and Laban's on his right. Jacob would remain in the rear in the hills to ensure that, should anything go wrong, he could get a message to Damascus. The sun's light was just piercing the eastern sky. There were no clouds, but there was a subtle red hue to the morning light.

Exactly as he predicted, the supply wagon approached the gate and Jude waved his men to move forward. The gate opened to allow the wagon to enter, and Jude's forces rushed the guards. Laban's men began blowing their horns to cause more confusion and to signal the movement of the sheep and oxen into the likely path of any enemy reinforcements. The changing guards were, in fact, caught by surprise and the two guard commanders began giving conflicting orders.

The confusion of the Romans and Herodians was to Jude's advantage. While Laban held the gate and moved a contingent of men to the east to secure the escape route, Jude and Kefa with their forces fell upon the defenders. Swords and sicars slashed and stabbed, men on both sides were yelling and screaming, falling, dying, or running. The Romans and Herodians were taking the greatest losses due, no doubt, to the surprise and confusion. But, it was also obvious that the virulent attacks by the Jews against the kittim were accomplishing their destructive intentions. Pools of Roman and Herodian blood formed around their dead and dying.

Roman and Herodian archers began to release their arrows, several striking the Jews who were rushing their positions on the corners of the armory building. With no armor to protect them, the arrows penetrated deep into their bodies, immediately killing six and wounding four more. But, Kefa and his men tuned on the archers before they could draw another arrow. As one Roman archer looked into Kefa's eyes, Kefa cut off his arm with his sword and then slashed his throat with his sicar even before the man fell to the ground. Kefa's men dealt the same to the others, and in only two minutes, Jude and his men had used the ram to break down the door and were in the armory.

They took the swords and archery equipment stored in racks and in stacks around the walls of the main room and loaded them into large sackcloth bags or carried them in their arms. Men armed with sicars and swords protected the flanks of those who carried off the weapons and supplies. These all moved quickly to the east gate and escape.

Jude looked around to try and take an accounting of the

situation and perceive any dangers. No enemy reinforcements had arrived. Jacob's men from the town must have succeeded. Laban held the gate and looked at Jude who then waved him to move to the east. Kefa was already on his way to the east gate as well, his men carrying their dead and wounded. Jude then realized that there were no enemy soldiers actively fighting them. It appeared that Jude and his forces had killed or severely wounded all of the guards. If his forces could now escape in their entirety, a greater success he could not have imagined.

As Jude and his men fled to the east, the Roman Century finally arrived at the armory. There was not much they could do but secure the palace and ensure that none of the Zealots remained. Their commander knew better than to pursue a superior Zealot force into the hills. Such adventurism would mean utter annihilation of his command.

The Zealots were successful, thanks to Jude. They formed an efficient distribution system to arm all the men they could in the resistance. A price was put on the head of Jude, although the Romans were not able to accurately identify him, thinking him the son of one Hezekias instead of his real father, Cleophas. His fame, as Barabbas and the Mashiach ben David, was the talk of the people in all of Galilee and even Judea.

After Sepphoris, Jude and Jacob returned to Damascus while Kefa remained in Galilee. The Roman retaliations that so concerned Jacob began almost immediately. It was now a war of tit for tat. Over the next several years, the Community and its attached Zealots carried out a widespread campaign against the Romans and the Herodians. The brethren kept silent, even on threat of torture and death, if they were captured. Their tenacity even amazed the Romans who were, by far, better equipped and experienced in the art of interrogation and torture. The tactics by the resistance were, by and large, a series of guerilla type hit and run missions to disrupt communications, seize equipment or weapons, and to inflict maximum casualties. They were certainly not strong enough to confront the Roman Army in open battle although they had been successful in several minor campaigns.

While the common Jews were supportive of the efforts, they could not see any real advantage to providing other than food, supplies, and shelter to revolutionaries. At times, that was even difficult, because, as after Sepphoris, the Romans would often answer an attack upon them by raiding the closest town or settlement and killing groups of people or taking them away into slavery. It was a brutal and difficult time.

With all this, Jude had other things troubling his mind. He and Rachel had not yet conceived a child. For a man who desired to be a king, especially the promised Mashiach ben David, he could not afford the absence of posterity. While not truly jealous of Joses and Miriam who had already had their first child, it did disturb Jude that HaShem seemed to deny him the needful fruits of his marriage. He never made Rachel feel inadequate as he realized that he was very likely at fault for his constant movements and obligations away from home. They both talked about it frequently, comparing themselves to other ancient families who had a difficult time bringing children into the world. They tried to view it as a test of their trust in HaShem. Rachel's dedication, and Jude's confidence in dealing with this developing crisis, actually brought them closer together and their love for each other grew.

Jude continued his efforts to increase his alliances and gain more soldiers for the resistance. His success in these endeavors was due in part to his abilities, but also because the people were tired of Sabinus and his excesses. Thousands, many not even Jews but others such as Idumeans, were now angry at Romans and Sabinus over his abuses of their lands and riches.

Several other resistance groups now began asserting themselves against the Romans in an attempt to claim leadership over the Jews and to dislodge the kittim. One of these was the rebel leader, Simon, who had been a servant of Herod Archelaus. Simon had himself declared King and attacked the Herodian Palace at Jericho. His forces burned the palace and destroyed the images it contained. They also removed what gold, silver and other valuables they could find. After killing the attendants and servants, they departed. This

Simon made several such attacks, killing Romans, other foreigners, and collaborating Jews. His fame reached Jude, who decided that he needed to attempt to consolidate these revolutionaries with his own forces.

After meeting with the leaders at Damascus to secure their approval, Jude sent several dispatches to Simon that went unanswered. Jude finally decided to try to meet him and negotiate a mutual agreement. With only a small band of fighters to avoid Roman detection of their purpose, Jude set out for Galilee from Damascus. They dressed themselves as pious Essenes, which they were, but whose reputation was not, as yet, associated with the resistance of the Zealots. So, at this point, the dress allowed them to travel undetected. Through a contact in Galilee, Jude managed to acquire a meeting with Simon.

It was late at night on the shores of the Sea of Galilee near some fishing boats that were anchored close to shore and rocked slowly back and forth with the gentle waves. Jude and his band made a fire and cooked some food while they waited for Simon to arrive. He did so within the hour. The designated contact approached Jude's party. The appropriate exchanges were made and the contact disappeared into the darkness. A few moments later, Simon and his men arrived.

"The legendary descendant of David," snickered Simon.

Jude avoided any comment of a negative tone. He did, however, stand up, as did the few of his band that were beside him. For safety and security, Jude had placed the majority of his Zealots in a hidden location near the boats to facilitate any unforeseen emergency.

Simon then took a seat by the fire and helped himself to a few morsels of food.

"Why do I have the idea that you want me to join your pious brethren and leave my own success to offer it to you?" asked Simon.

"What makes you think I am desirous of that?" remarked Jude. "The fact is that you have been very successful in our war on the kittim. My desire is to ensure that we all conduct ourselves for the benefit of our people and the will of HaShem."

"HaShem has smiled on me," responded Simon. "Besides, all I have heard you do is preach niceties to the country. Where is your scepter of power?"

Jude's public preaching as his alias, Yeshua, had been successful in gaining pious converts, but Simon was not apparently aware that from that group Jude had fashioned a formidable army. He did not feel inclined to let Simon know the true extent of his power.

"The people need hope, and I can give that to them without the necessity of too much bloodshed," said Jude. "I think that, as you have already observed, I have the right to the Throne of David. All I am asking is that you council with me before you act so that we can increase the odds of our success as a people."

"What you really are saying, Jude, is that you want me to be subject to you," Simon said as he tossed a pebble into the water. "What is in it for me?"

"The approval of the heir to the throne," responded Jude.

Simon laughed. "That and a little minnow may buy me a matzo." Simon's followers laughed along with him. "Look, Jude," Simon continued, "I know you are no pushover, but I think we are doing just fine on our own. You do your thing in Judea, and we will do ours here in Galilee."

"Divided efforts and separated forces will not win against the kittim, Simon," Jude cautioned. "Not in the long run. We need a wide-ranging and coordinated plan of action. Working together we can conduct effective, timed, and mutually supporting actions."

"And who do you want me to answer to in this organization you propose?" asked Jude.

"Kefa ben Cleophas, my brother, is the contact leader in Galilee," answered Jude. "All coordination would come through him."

"Kefa!" exclaimed Simon. "A man of strength he is, a man of planning he is not."

"No, Simon," Jude interjected, "Kefa will merely be the communications coordinator. I will be directing the actions."

"Ah, I see," said Simon. "Well, I don't think so. We will do our own fighting."

"Simon, you need the efforts of more than just the few you have here. You must know that some of our own from Damascus have been aiding you in your campaigns. That is really no more than an extension of what you have already managed."

"If I will not answer to Herod, why would I answer to a dreamer of the Throne of David?" quipped Simon.

Jude did not answer, but looked at Simon's followers and walked past each of them, looking them in the eye. He wanted them to see the determination in his countenance, and let them ponder the wonder of a descendant of David actually before them. He then returned to Simon who was still tossing pebbles into the water. Jude gazed at the men of Simon and could see that their minds were at work.

"I tell you what, Simon," said Jude. "Take a few days and consider what I am saying. We have an effective plan for increasing our numbers and re-establishing the Kingdom of Heaven of HaShem. You would do well to become fishers of those recruits with me."

Simon scoffed. He turned to Jude and looked above him to the stars now shining brightly above them, as the moon had not yet risen.

"I will ponder what you have said, Jude, but I am the King here in Galilee. Any agreement I make will be as an equal to you. So, for our mutual interest, I will consider your offer, but it will need to be in terms of an alliance, nothing less."

Jude was not hasty. He recognized that the kingdom had been fractured for sometime. It was not easy for those from the area of the former northern kingdom of Israel to fashion themselves a part of the Davidic dynasty. Jude tried to see several moves in advance, and he was not greedy. His true interest was the restoration of Israel as a sovereign kingdom under HaShem with the kittim gone.

"OK, Simon, why don't you think about it? We should meet again before the beginning of Av (the time of the year around July and August)."

"Fine, I will agree to meet then," said Simon.

He didn't. And in a botched operation where Simon tried to

attack a Roman column, he was roundly defeated and beheaded by Gratus, a Commander of King Herod's troops. Jude had lost one potential ally. He would lose more. Several of Simon's followers broke away and fought battles throughout Galilee. But, even though moderately successful, they were not coordinated with any major overall operation. So, while they burned the royal palaces near Jordan at Betharamptha, only a few of Jude's forces could assist because of the short notices and Jude's ongoing plans to attack Sabinus at Jerusalem.

During this time of Roman weakness and general rebellion, another man, named Athronges, set himself up as king. The word of his actions reached Jude who also learned that Athronges directly challenged Jude's right to the throne of David. Athronges, a poor shepherd who had no legitimate genealogy to prove his claim, still had the support of the people because they were anxious to throw off Roman rule and would listen to just about anyone who had the right words and an army to back it up.

Athronges gathered a superior force for the time and proceeded to war against the kittim, the Herodians, and anyone who opposed him. He was also willing to fight Jude. After Athronges attacked a Roman Cohort at Emmaus, killing their Centurion Arius and forty of his troops and stole their corn and weapons that the cohort was transporting to their legion, the people began to believe that he might be their mashiach.

This concerned and even angered Damascus. On more than one occasion, Jude had tried to make a pact with Athronges, but Athronges had no interest in placating him. Athronges' claim to the throne made cooperation impossible, and he had four brothers who were as adamant in their support for him as Jude was against him. As a result, Jude and Athronges began to fight each other at the same time they fought the Romans.

The bloodshed became so pervasive, that the Romans worried they would lose control of the entire province. Jews killing Jews was not so much a concern as the side effects. But, the Romans learned to use the internal strife and violence between the Jews, and the tumult in Jerusalem, as a way to justify their continued occupation of Palestine, and even increase their control. The occupation, so they stated, was to protect the people from the unscrupulous and destructive actions of the different factions in the country. This whole problem would continue for many years. But, the suffering of the people only increased as Rome responded to the unrest.

All that was apparent to Jude was that he needed to consolidate these efforts and point them in a concentration of forces to one objective-Jerusalem. The liberation of Jerusalem would be the catalyst for his ascension to the throne and the freedom of Israel. He tried once more with Athronges. Surprisingly, Athronges agreed to a truce and a meeting to discuss a confederation.

They met just before Passover at Tarichaeae on the south side of the Sea of Galilee. This area was a famous rebel stronghold that the Romans had not yet perceived. It was noon as the two men approached each other with their bodyguards close by. They sat down together and tried to act like old friends. The air, however, was thick with distrust, recollections of recent battles between them fresh on their minds.

"Jude, I trust HaShem blesses you and your family," Athronges said with reasonable tones unlike his usually boisterous manner. Jude's caution did not abate.

"And likewise to you," Jude responded. He looked around quickly to check the area and noted it was clear. "I think we are sufficiently alone to talk seriously. Let me begin. I know that we have a disagreement over the right to the throne, but something else is in danger right now that overrules our differences. Sabinus, according to my sources, is likely to take Jerusalem and the Temple treasury sometime between Passover and Shavuot (Pentecost-See glossary). This will be the death of any hope for our independence."

"Don't you think you are a little young for this sort of thing?" laughed Athronges. "What are you, all of nineteen or twenty? I know you have been very successful and have quite a reputation under many other names, but you are still too young. Who will take you seriously?"

"Jerusalem, the Temple treasury!" Jude emphasized. "We must talk about these issues. Time is quickly getting away from us. I tell you that in this thing we must consolidate our forces. You can keep yours, but we must join now and bring as many others as will join us. If we act as if we are only going up to Jerusalem for the Passover and subsequent celebrations, we will not be noticed. There will be nothing more to the Roman's eyes than a larger number than usual devoted faithful. We can encompass the city and take it. We have so little time."

"The Temple treasury, huh?" asked Athronges. "My concern, of course, has always been Mount Ephraim and the promises to them. What concern have I for the Temple?"

"Again, despite our differences, our peoples have placed their riches there, have offered them to HaShem. Even if Herod and the Romans pollute the Temple, the heart, the sweat, and even the blood of the people are still there. More importantly for you, though is the chance to break the will of the Romans and the collaborators. It is a chance to give them a wound which shall not heal," Jude was passionate.

Athronges looked at him for several seconds before he answered. The answer was a surprise. "Yes, Jude, I see your point. We have a confederation. Let us begin our planning together."

***

Sabinus had finally concentrated his efforts at Jerusalem. With the legion Varus left him and the assistance of Joazer, he was now prepared to use any ruse to accomplish his designs of greed. But, the fates were stacking up in a way he had not considered. As was the custom, this was the time of year that many in the land traveled to Jerusalem for the Holy Days between Passover and Shavuot, anyway. This time the pilgrimage was also a cover for the resistance whose leaders believed that Sabinus had designs on the very Temple Treasury, itself. They were, of course, not incorrect.

After the Passover and just before Shavuot, Sabinus ordered the legion in Jerusalem to seal the gates of the Temple. At the same time, several cohorts of soldiers surrounded Jerusalem. No one was allowed to enter or leave under pain of death.

"Romulus, I am now going to be the richest man in the world, second only to Caesar himself," Sabinus stated boldly. "We have led Varus and even the Emperor into a concern that Judea is on the verge of total collapse because of the uprisings and commotions we have been able to engineer for our benefit. As a result, I have been given a free hand in ruling this country, allowing me to plunder it for Caesar's glory..." he paused and laughed, "...and mine. With our report to Varus of a revolt in Judea and even Jerusalem itself, no one will question my subjugation of the Temple to destroy the last remnants of this wicked religion and its people."

"Indeed, Procurator, you have been brilliant," Romulus praised Sabinus. "Who else could have even obtained the assistance of the High Priest in bringing about such a momentous and total defeat of these ungrateful people?"

"Your Excellency," a voice came from the main entrance. The men turned to look. "We have relieved the Temple of a great portion of the offerings that were kept in it and are now preparing the great wealth we have found there for transport to wherever you command."

It was just then that Joazer entered the Procurator's palace.

"Ah, Joazer," Sabinus welcomed the High Priest. "We have succeeded and you will receive a great reward."

But, the High Priest did not seem so confident or happy.

"Your Excellency, I am the bearer of grave tidings. There is, even now, a force of tens of thousands of armed revolutionaries approaching the city. Somehow, your plot was perceived and this counter set in motion long before this day. See for yourself from any high vantage point."

Sabinus and his companions nearly ran to the top of the King's Palace where Sabinus kept himself. They viewed the areas surrounding the City on all sides. The Cohorts placed around the walls of the city were under heavy attack from the armies that had surprised them.

"What have I done?" cried Sabinus. He realized it almost immediately. "By consolidating my forces too soon and with no security in the countryside, I signaled my intentions. And without that security, these forces were able to quickly join. Who is their commander?" he asked Joazer.

"How should I know, your Excellency? There are many leaders of these people. Who could be their one mashiach, I know not," replied Joazer. "But, I had better leave you and return to the Temple lest I be detected and we lose what influence I may have."

"Agreed, go now," ordered Sabinus. Joazer took his leave without a moment's delay.

"Send a courier immediately to Varus and request his help with haste. Send it now before the siege makes any escape impossible," he ordered Romulus who ran to the Commander of the legion who had his post at the entrance to the Antonia Fortress, but was now also on the top of the palace watching the battle unfold. After receiving Romulus' directive, he immediately left for the Fortress.

"Your Excellency," a senior Roman Officer saluted as he entered the tower of the Palace. "We have received word by courier that there are several attacks occurring simultaneously throughout the countryside. This uprising may be a general action across all of Palestine. We have not the strength to counter them. I suggest we consolidate our forces now inside the walls and defend the city. We must send word to Caesarea and to Antioch. We have allies in the field, but the situation has turned grave quite quickly and unexpectedly."

Sabinus had to stop and think. There was too much coming too fast for him to adequately process. He was silent for several minutes. Romulus spoke up.

"Your Excellency, I would advise that we concentrate our forces at our immediate disposal into the city at several critical points. Those would be the Hippodrome, the east wall of the city, and the western wall of the city here at the palace. These are the likely points of the enemy's main effort. What other forces we have after that commitment we should have at various points around the perimeter of the city and keep a reserve at the Antonia Fortress to counter any major breach of the defenses."

Sabinus wanted to respond in a rage and defend his honor, reminding Romulus that it was he, Sabinus, who was the great military commander, the Great Procurator. But, he realized that his lack of planning and attention had now created in him a form of stupor due to the gravity of the events building upon him in such a short time.

"It is a disaster that our forces have not gathered the evidences of these developments over the last while. What happened to those responsible for gaining information about the enemy and about these revolutionaries? Why were we caught off guard?" He looked directly at Romulus.

Romulus knew the answer, but dared not state it. He thought to himself that the objective of taking the riches of the country as plunder had become the object of Sabinus' concentration at the total expense of sound military and political activities. They had not considered all aspects of the information that was available, only that having to do with the plunder, forgetting that the people might indeed revolt at last.

"Your Excellency, our focus was not on a general rebellion of such magnitude probably because we did not see it as an option for the revolutionary leaders. I have failed you," Romulus said, bowing his head in shame.

"Yes, you have," and Sabinus drew his sword and beheaded Romulus on the spot. The body stood for a second and then crumpled to the floor, the head rolling several feet away and finally stopping next to a golden vase.

Sabinus yelled at the Roman officer, "Do as Romulus directed. Place forces at the east wall, the Hippodrome, and the west at the Palace. Keep a reserve at the Fortress and intermittent security forces around the wall of the city as we are able!"

"As you command, Hail Caesar!" responded the officer.

"Yes...Hail Caesar," Sabinus coughed, a lump in his throat making it difficult for him to breathe.

The officer immediately left and commanded his subordinates to deploy their forces. "Do what you can to bring the remnants of the cohorts outside the city into the walls. But, do not risk further casualties, as we need every soldier! I will deliver these orders from the Procurator to the Legion Commander. Go!"

The subordinates saluted and separated to their areas of responsibility. The Roman Officer then proceeded directly to the Legion Commander at the Fortress of Antonia.

Confusion reigned in Jerusalem and outside its walls for several hours. The defending Romans and Herodians made every effort to return those who had been caught outside in the surprise attack. Most had been salvaged and were now available for the internal defenses and lines of communication that would prove invaluable in countering the siege. Roman archers selectively fired on the attackers as the occasion permitted, and this allowed them to keep the enemy forces from approaching the walls for several hours. But, the reverse was true, as well. No one could now leave Jerusalem without suffering death or capture. The siege had begun.

Jude stood on the Mount of Olives viewing the forces he commanded. While he was only one of several leaders of factions involved in the siege, his negotiations and alliances were working quite well. His responsibility was the eastern wall of the city. The result of his political and military skills was now before him as he stood ready to defeat the Romans and recover Israel's liberty.

Jude's forces assisted in an attack on the city from three sides just as Romulus had predicted. The resistance army attacked at the Hippodrome, the east wall, and the area of the King's Palace. The idea was to close the Romans in and press the fight. Jude had been primarily responsible for the spies in the city and he used the spies to inform him of dispositions of troops and the general condition of the inhabitants who were unable to flee before the assault began. He then gave this information to the other revolutionaries, principally Athronges and another named Yitzak. Yitzak, however, had left the siege to attack Romans and collaborators throughout the countryside to create diversions and prevent possible Roman reinforcements to the area of Jerusalem. Jude's intentions were clear; all his future plans, the survival of Israel, and the purity of the Temple all depended on regaining liberty, starting here at Jerusalem.

"I will command from the highest tower of the Phasaelus Fortress," Sabinus instructed his aide, "Ensure that you inform the legion commander so he can establish lines of communication with me." In reality, Sabinus desired that location not only to observe the battle, but also for his own safety, and the aide realized it.

Yes, Your Excellency," responded the aide and he hastened to the Legion Commander to report as Sabinus had instructed him.

Sabinus rushed to the Phasaelus Fortress and climbed to the very top to watch as the siege progressed. He could immediately see that the Jewish fighters had not yet consolidated their positions and Sabinus gave the Roman Commander the order to fall upon the Jews outside the west wall. The counter attack force was nearly a cohort in size and it rushed in mass outside the gate nearest Herod's Palace falling upon the Jews and inflicting a terrible slaughter. The Romans discovered that this group of revolutionaries was poorly equipped and trained. Many of the fighters were armed only with rocks, some having slings with which to hurl them. They were no match for the Roman soldiers who pierced their line and drove them back and to the north of the city. The Romans slew hundreds of Jewish fighters while suffering only a few casualties themselves.

Sabinus, watching from the tower, felt a rush of hope for his deliverance. But, then, just as quickly, he could see that the some of the rebels ran around the north wall and began ascending the wall to reach the cloisters[9] above the outer court of the Temple, where they again continued to hurl stones and arrows at the defenders of the city. The rebel archers shot their arrows with deadly accuracy from the top of the cloisters down upon the defenders. The height of the cloisters was such that the Roman archers on the ground could not gain sufficient elevation to engage the enemy. As a result, the stones and arrows from the Jews on the cloisters were causing numerous casualties among the defenders down below.

At the same time, the rebel forces on the west managed to

break through the defenses and enter the city. But, they could not reach beyond the citadel near to Herod's Palace due to the ferocity of the defense by the Romans and King Herod's soldiers under the command of Gratus. While Gratus had checked the breach, the fighting now settled into several days of attrition, neither side gaining much over the other.

During this time, Sabinus stayed in the tower of the Phasaelus Fortress, not even interested in descending for the sake of his friends. He paced the floor and constantly ran his fingers over his face and through his hair. He would sit down and then stand again, finding no comfort. His dispatch to Varus should have reached him, but he had no certainty of it.

On the morning of the fifth day of the siege, Jude could see by his observation from the Mount of Olives that the Romans had commenced some activity below the cloisters of the Temple. He realized too late that their intention was to set fire to the cloisters, thereby consuming the rebel attackers on top of them. The fire was roaring nearly out of control before Jude's runner could reach the wall of the city. Jude could now only watch.

The flames spread quickly and murderously due to the coverings on the wood used for their decoration and preservation. Without any direct route off the cloisters, the Jewish fighters were trapped save those who could begin the descent, and that only a few. Those still struggling to inflict casualties upon the Romans found themselves engulfed in the fast moving inferno, their clothes, and then their bodies, catching fire. These fell from the heights and perished in large numbers. Jude and Sabinus both watched with equally disparate emotions as many of these hopeless ones chose their own blades to the punishment of the fire, hurling themselves onto their own swords when they perceived that there was no chance of escape. Most however, became walking torches and then disappeared from sight.

Among those who successfully managed to obtain to the ladders met nearly as immediate an end as those who died from the fire. Jude could now see the Romans systematically killing those

Zealots who had begun the descent; Roman arrows unleashing a merciless fusillade against those on the ladders as their swords also cut down the desperate and disorganized Zealots who reached the bottom. Not one of those brave souls who had ascended to the cloisters escaped. All were killed.

Sabinus was gleeful, as much for the defeat of the brave rebels on the heights of the cloisters as the scene, which next greeted his eyes. The Roman soldiers now rushed through the areas where the fire had subsided and relieved that portion of the Temple of its treasure, that which was the sacred money of the Temple. The soldiers took much for themselves, but Sabinus sent word that 400 talents were his and his alone.

As Jude stood watching, his legs weakened, and he sat down heavily on the ground, unable to control his anguish. He did manage to send word to Athronges of the catastrophe. He soon received a message from his compatriot that they should encompass the palace and concentrate their forces there. Jude saw the wisdom in the suggestion and immediately ordered many of his forces to join at Herod's Palace. There, they gathered torches and began threatening to burn the palace and all inside. The Romans, cut off by their retreat beyond the Palace of Agrippa at the surge of the rebels through the gates and over the walls near Herod's Palace, dared not attempt an attack through the narrow streets. Such a maneuver with nearly no frontal power due to the narrow passages would prevent them from safely overwhelming the enemy to any satisfaction that would make the attack worthwhile. They decided to defend the areas they controlled and that offered the best means of repulsing any attacks.

It was at this point that Jude and Athronges learned that Varus was now approaching through the Galilee. Athronges agreed to take a portion of his forces and try to engage Varus, slowing his progress. Yitzak could only do so much. Jude, on the other hand, would stay with the forces at Jerusalem. Athronges left and traveled north with the forces he selected for the delaying actions.

At the city, the threat by Jude to burn the palace convinced many inside to surrender, especially the majority of King Herod's troops. However, Gratus, and another of Herod's commanders, Rufus, refused to join the rebels, even though Jude promised that they would not be harmed if they left. Knowing that those remaining would fight to the death, and unable to inflict the suffering by fire he saw upon the cloisters, Jude continued with the siege of the Palace, digging mines and passages under it to weaken its structure and seek other ways to enter it.

Sabinus watched it all from the Tower, still safe from the weapons of the rebels. He now understood that the entire area of Palestine continued in upheaval. Varus was his only hope of survival. But, once Varus arrived, he would have a great deal of explaining to do. He now began to weigh his options, even considering the possibility of escape from Varus once Varus had broken the siege.

Varus, having received the request from Sabinus, as well as dispatches from the commanders at Caesarea and even Herod, had immediately formed his forces, several legions from Syria, and attacked the Galilee in an unrelenting drive south to Jerusalem. He burned Sepphoris and, because the people there seemed to back the resistance, he enslaved most of them sending them back to Rome and elsewhere. Small groups of Jude's forces joined in the effort to conduct a number of delaying actions to keep the Romans at bay while his main forces surrounded the Roman Legion at Jerusalem. At the same time, elements of Athronges forces were now engaging the Romans in an effort to slow Varus' advance. But, it was too little and too late. Nothing could stop the Roman juggernaut, and many of the Jews began to realize that their hopes were slipping away. Varus then marched to Samaria to destroy any evidence of the resistance there. But, he found that they had not joined the sedition against Rome or involved themselves in the civil war amongst the Jews, so he ignored them. He turned south and took Sampho, Emmaus, and finally Jerusalem where the resistance had besieged the Roman Legion commanded by Sabinus.

Having found themselves at odds with the Romans at the same time, the various factions of the resistance had no choice but to consolidate their forces against this concentration of Romans attacking from the north. The siege had been quite successful, but the actions to delay Varus were paramount to victory. That, Jude realized, was untenable. The resistance could not continue to fight on two fronts, especially against the superior forces of Varus. Jude and Athronges' forces began to withdraw from Jerusalem. Jude returned to Damascus to again take up the life of an apparently devoted Essene, a cover that had worked for a very long time and would continue to do so. But the withdrawal was not quick enough for all of the resistance forces to escape. Varus caught up with several of the larger forces and fought them, capturing about 2000 men belonging to Jude and Athronges. Archelaus, a son of Herod the Great, captured one of Athronges' brothers as he made his way back north. Two of Athronges' other brothers were killed in battles with the forces of Ptolemy and Gratus. The final brother surrendered to Archelaus after his force was decimated and he had no choice but to ask terms. Archelaus agreed to accept his surrender and not kill him. Jude and most of his forces escaped.

The siege broken, many of the Romans sought out and welcomed Varus. But, Sabinus hid from him. Knowing full well that his actions had brought these catastrophes upon the country and upon the legions of Caesar, he left Jerusalem under cover of disguise and fled to the seaside. He was never heard from again and Caesar would eventually obtain the stolen treasures at Sabinus' storehouse in Caesarea.

Varus assembled those captured to interrogate them as to the purpose of their cause and the leaders. Among the captured was Athronges who was trying to secret himself within the mass of prisoners Varus had placed in a temporary stockade. While interrogating the prisoners, Varus' officers found that the vast majority of the captured had fought merely to rid foreigners from the land. He collected these from out of the number and addressed them all at once while under guard several furlongs from the camp. He found that these had no messianic interests. He spoke to them about the benefits of Roman rule to keep the peace and prevent such insurrections for the good of the people. At that, he forgave them and sent them away. He also sent a number of the lesser leaders back to Caesar for questioning. Caesar eventually forgave many of these, but those related in any way to Herod he executed for treason against their family.

Varus decided to crucify about 2000 of the prisoners because of their activities that he concluded were to seat a new Davidic King. During this procedure, he noted that one of them was commanding some attention. His officers told him that the man was Athronges, and that he claimed to be the Yehoshua ben Joseph of the Jews, a less often used appellation for a messianic leader, but not the Davidic King of the Judeans. It was not a familiar title to Varus, but he assumed it meant the same thing as a king. Varus brought him to his seat and pronounced the execution order directly upon him. He immediately delivered Athronges to a scourging in preparation for his execution by crucifixion.

They removed his garments and left him wearing only his loincloth. Then the beatings began. Time and time again they spat on Athronges and struck him across the face and body with their hands and with sticks. They mocked him and begged him to resist in sarcastic tones as they had a personal hatred for him as one who had caused the deaths of some of their own comrades.

Athronges was already near unconsciousness, bleeding from the nose, ears, and mouth when they tied him to the upright stake upon which they would soon hang him in crucifixion. They took a pot of cold water and threw it on him to ensure he was conscious. Then, they took turns beating him with the whip which had pieces of sharp bone attached to the ends. Each strike tore more flesh from Athronges' body, wracking him with indescribable pain. He gasped for breath and screamed at every lash.

The continuing thought in his mind was that he would never again see his loved ones. This was the dread that left him even more weakened and destitute of hope. Maybe he should have cooperated more with Jude. But, he would never tell the Romans about him, even if Jude were his rival. The fact as it made its impression on his mind was that, until the Romans could be defeated, he should have more fully allied himself with Jude. It was a mistake.

Athronges could no longer see them clearly, his eyes swollen from the beatings. Furthermore, he had long since lost the concentration to pray and call upon HaShem for strength. Pain and desolation were all he perceived, and those were hardly real, either.

They then stood him up. He could detect that they were bringing the crossbeam for his crucifixion and saw them put it on the ground. But, he was delirious, merely moving as the guards commanded him, not sure of what it all meant. He seemed to be unable to formulate any independent thought, but he realized that recognizing that state of mind in himself was reason enough to believe that he still had his senses to some degree. He no longer feared death or solitude; he simply accepted both.

The soldiers pushed Athronges down onto the crossbeam while removing his loincloth, and then placed the crossbeam beneath his head and tied his arms to it. What he could only partially see filled his heart with terror. Two soldiers, each carrying a hammer and an iron spike were approaching his sides. Despite his understanding of the futility of resistance, he involuntarily attempted to avoid the fastening to the crossbeam. Familiar with the efforts of their victims in times past, several soldiers held Athronges' massive but weak arms to the beam as one of them drove the rusted, dark brown spikes through his wrists below the joint, crushing the nerves and causing a new pain that swept Athronges into a bitter agony that made death seem paltry. His arms and chest convulsed, the contractions searing his sanity and yet not sufficient to bring on unconsciousness or death. His fingers and hands burned and ached with uncontrollable distortions. He kicked his legs and tore at his arm sockets in his attempts to flee the pain. Again, his actions were dictated not by reason or hope, but involuntary efforts of his body to escape the pain. The executioners then used a set of ropes and pulleys to lift the beam to which they had fastened Athronges and placed it on the upright stake.

Now another form of intense pain enveloped his body as his own weight caused the wounds in his wrists to feel as if they were tearing apart the very joints and muscles. Every breath was a labor of vanity. He faintly noticed a soldier with another spike approaching him as unseen hands held down his right leg hard against the upright. An unbearable pain filled his right foot and leg as he felt bones and sinews separate and shatter as a piercing blow thrust the spike through his foot at the instep. Then, the same pain came again as the right foot was placed over the left and the spike hammered through the instep of his left foot and into the upright. The tendons in his feet and calves contracted violently, sending new waves of excruciating pain throughout his beaten and abused body. Gathering himself as best he could, he looked down at his bare body exposed to the world, broken, bleeding, humiliated and suffering. Why had he allowed this to happen? What good was it? He had failed in his attempt to defend the land against the invaders from Rome, the usurpers of Herod and the false religions of the heathen gentiles.

Athronges hung on the crossbeam for nearly two days. The birds had begun to peck at his open wounds and even his eyes. He could no longer see, and breathing was nearly impossible. He had long ago lost all sense of time and the environment surrounding him. Then, he felt his legs shattered by an unseen object. A soldier had received orders to break the legs of all those who had not yet died from their wounds. The legion needed to move on.

Immediately his lungs failed to expand and he felt his shoulders separate from their sockets. His subconscious effort to push himself up to breath was now no longer possible. His chest felt as if it was being ripped open and the spasms of the muscles tore them from their sinews.

How long he was there he could not tell. Then he felt his arms and body being wrapped in cloth. Unseen hands were touching him and voices were consoling him, encouraging him to stay alive. Several of his followers had waited until the Romans left and then they came to rescue him. They pried the nails from his flesh and bone and out of the wooden planks. His limbs limply fell to the side and his head he could not control. They placed him upon a litter and dragged him several miles to a shelter on the side of a hill. There, they tried to nurse him to health. But, the loss of blood and the injuries were too extensive. He was swept with fever as an infection raged within him.

He died before morning.

***

Jude was very angry that Joses had not taken part in the attempt to return liberty to Israel. As Jude saw it, Joses had kept himself from the dangers and had devoted his time to questionable meditations and domestic concerns of family. He certainly had not conducted himself in any kingly manner. Jude approached his brother in Capernaum and they agreed to meet on the shore near the fishing vessels. They met alone. Both brothers walked silently side by side for a short distance without saying a word. The breeze off the Sea of Galilee mingled strands of their hair, but their thoughts had no common ground. Finally, Jude spoke.

"Joses, it is time we have a serious discussion. It seems to me that we no longer have any reason to question the heirship. I'll just cut to the quick of it. You have made no attempt to act in the interests of the people or HaShem. The war we have fought over the last several months was our greatest chance to free ourselves. We did not fail because we were without you, but you have failed because you were not with us."

Joses did not remove his gaze from the sand, nor raise his voice to the ears of his brother. He continued walking, as if all alone in thought. Jude looked at him and saw that his back was still slightly humped, and his frame still not as strong as that of Jude's. The realization brought Jude to empathy for his brother's frailty. He continued, but from a more gentle position.

"In all our disagreements, we have never resorted to violence or hatred one for another. Admittedly, I cannot tolerate your insistence that you have any right to the Throne of David, but you have also done nothing to trouble me concerning the matter. Not really, at least not that I have seen. So, I will trust that it will remain so. Is that correct?"

Joses finally answered him.

"My place is as all that has transpired says of me. The crimson thread was placed upon my wrist, and I have not sold it."

Jude was bewildered.

"Then why don't you act more as if you claim it?" queried Jude.

Joses did not answer at first. The brothers walked some distance in silence, and then Joses finally answered.

"My time has not yet come," he said, turning to look into Jude's eyes.

"So, when you think that time has come, you will more actively oppose me?" asked Jude.

"We are not on the same path," responded Joses.

"But you claim the Kingdom?" asked Jude.

"It is my burden," responded Joses.

Jude could not make sense of Joses' answers. He seemed totally without emotion or aggression towards what Jude was saying. And, there was no avarice in Joses' eyes. Jude felt he needed to press the issue no longer.

"I must return to Damascus," Jude said. "Let me know of any issues that come into your mind."

Joses smiled and then said, "You will be one of the first to know when my place and time has arrived. Take your journey safely."

The brothers embraced and Jude left to meet his escort for the return to Damascus as Joses made his way back to his home. The brothers shared the same thought that they may never meet again.

Unsure of the circumstances around him and still not fully capable of responding to the tyranny and destruction, Joses continued in his efforts to strengthen himself in body and spirit. He and Miriam had many talks about his future and his responsibilities. As often as occasion would permit, he consulted with his Uncle Joseph of Arimathea and even Nikdimon ben Gurion who was also a member of the Sanhedrin, the Jewish governing council. Joses was convinced that the resistance against Rome and the Herodians was justified, but he could not, in good conscience, back Jude or the extremisms of the Nazarenes of Damascus. Like his father, Cleophas, he felt the Community had gone beyond the requirements of Torah in many ways. While it was proper for those who desired to take the additional restraints voluntarily, especially those of the priestly lineage, it concerned Joses that they would often enforce requirements upon Jews and foreigners when there was no requirement for them to obey.

While protection of the purity of HaShem's Temple was tantamount, the Temple built by Herod with his depravity and defilements, in Joses view, probably had no legitimacy whatsoever. Joses looked to Shiloh, a small area northwest of Jerusalem, as the proper place for the Temple. The Temple's main purpose had been to serve as a house for the Ark of the Covenant, which held the stone tablets upon which HaShem had written the Ten Commandments for Israel.[10] But, the Ark, the true purpose for the Temple, was no longer there. It had been missing for hundreds of years.

Yet, he was not sure where he could find the answer to his dilemma. He felt confidant he was the Mashiach ben David, the king to be for all Israel. But what was his responsibility as far as priestly duties? Should he return to the priest-kings of his forefathers? Could he slay the kittim and the backsliders of the Jews? Should he?

Joses decided he needed to return to On for instruction, and he made the proper preparations. He decided to take his family with him. This was the defining moment of his life, for he felt that only the priests at On would guide him through the Jewish Mystical secrets that he needed to finally master in order to make the proper decisions about himself and the future of Israel. Also, he needed to ensure the he and Miriam completed a required ritual for him to fulfill the terms of Davidic Kingship. He would remain there for several years refining his understandings, building his family, and strengthening his alliances. He was still at a young age for a man to study the secrets of Jewish mysticism, but he felt it necessary to complete this training as soon as possible so he could take on his leadership role in earnest. He and his mother Miryam discussed it at length.

"Joses, of course I recognize why you see On as so important. So do I. But, doesn't the Community have these same methods? They have safeguarded these things since Zerrubabel." She loved Joses and his family and just really did not want them off to Egypt and so far away. Joses had been gone so much as a child and very young man.

"Mother, you know I am not eligible for Damascus. Growing up there from time to time I was accepted, but never actually a part of it. My feelings about the extreme interpretations of Torah and especially my back where the bend is make me ineligible in my own mind, and certainly by the rules of the Community. Besides, all they talk about is the priesthood of Aaron, the Cohanim. While they accept and encourage righteousness to the point of the priesthood of Malchi Tzedek, they set a path to get there I cannot follow. You know my interest in On..."

"Oh, son," Miryam interrupted, "I know what you are going to say. Remember, my father, Heli, was named after On. They mean the same thing. We both know why. And I know the family and friends there will treat you so well, as will those in northern Egypt. I can even understand their reticence to come here with all the difficulties and dangers. But, this is the home of our fathers. This is where we should be. When we left Egypt with Moses many generations ago, we brought On with us and established it at Irshemesh[11]. Part of it is there, and part of it is here in Damascus. Maybe those in Irshemesh can accomplish what you search for."

"As I said, Mother," answered Joses, "Damascus is not going to accept me, even if Joachanin were to invite me. Besides, while On went to Irshemesh, the greater part of the mysteries were taken back to On when the captivity occurred, you know that. And, mother," Joses looked deep into her eyes, "the prophecy is that HaShem will call his sons out of Egypt. In many ways a metaphor, but as pertaining to me, I must return and obtain the full initiation of the secrets of Moses."

"Yes, Joses, you received the crimson thread, I know," sighed Miryam. "Your works have been wonderful, Joses, but, honestly, look at what Jude has accomplished for Israel. Look at what Jacob has done. I love you, son, but this is not for you."

Joses smiled lovingly at his mother. He understood her and her difficult situation.

""Mother, I will be in On very soon. I will send you word as often as occasion permits."

Miryam smiled and hugged her son. "Yes, I know. You cannot blame a grandmother for trying."

Joses and his family departed for On within the next few days. At about the same time, as if designed to give credence to Joses' concerns for his people, Augustus Caesar decreed a census and a tax. Caesar assigned Coponius as Governor of the land and appointed the Roman Senator, Cyrenius, to preside over the census. Joses wanted nothing to do with this Roman villainy and desired to protect his children from the methods the Romans would use to gather and use the information. According to Torah, Israel was not to be numbered, and taxation of HaShem's people by the Romans was, in his sight, an abomination. His brothers, however, considered his departure merely another manifestation of his cowardice. But, Joses was concerned only with his preparations for his destiny, and he could let nothing deter him from that quest and a sure knowledge of HaShem and His principles. Jacob met him in Bethshemesh to try and dissuade him from his journey. They met at Rabbi Elazer's home along the Dismis River.

"My brother," Jacob saluted him, "it is a gift from HaShem that you and your family are well. But, what are your concerns for Israel? Jude, your brother, risks all he has, indeed his very life, to defend the people and the land against the kittim. Do you not feel strongly that you should do the same?"

Jacob was never one to hold back the words he felt may be necessary to effect resolution of an issue. To Joses this seemed to be not only an insult, but also another claim that he was abrogating his birthright.

"Jacob," Joses began, "how is it that you, one of those closest to the mysteries, cannot see that my path is defined by HaShem, not by men? If I follow man because of what he expects of me and ignore HaShem's call, what does it profit?"

"Jude is following the dictates of HaShem, and so should you by doing all in your power to help us overcome the kittim," Jacob painfully explained. "There is a time and season for everything, and it is now the season to fight the kittim for the honor of HaShem and the establishment of a free Israel."

"And how is it to be accomplished?" asked Joses. "The war has gone on for many years and Jude, even with his alliances, cannot break the grip of the Emperor of Rome. The eagle's talons are locked, and it will hover about the carcass and feed off of it until there is nothing left. Anyone who looks and perceives can see it. Why not you and Jude? No, I go to seek the will of HaShem and my relationship to Him. That, above all else, is my task."

Jacob could not really contradict Joses' words. He knew, as did Joses, that above all, HaShem had commanded them to seek for Him. "Yes, Joses, what you say is true." He paused and looked out over the hills. He could see Joses' family quietly waiting for him. The air was calm and no sound penetrated to his ears, no sign presented to his eyes, and no words formed in his heart. He sighed, "Your search for HaShem is admirable, my older brother. To have HaShem's word and will revealed to you, and thereby aiding Israel, may be as important, even more so, than combating the kittim and spilling their blood and your own. Our mother, also, has seen your departure as needful for you, and possibly to merely allow Jude his space. Hopefully, you understand that he deserves my loyalty and his courage is like that of the lion."

Joses smiled and looked at his younger brother who, despite his strong feelings, was obviously maturing into a much wiser man. While Joses recognized that Jacob still held to the extremes of his Nazaritism and the dictates of the severity of the law beyond the mark, he could not fault his brother for his dedication and loyalty. That was an indication of his spiritual strength and fortitude that Joses could easily mold later if HaShem so desired.

"Jacob, my brother," Joses spoke and placed his right hand

on Jacob's shoulder, "the dangers of fighting the Romans do not frighten me. HaShem says to us that He is to be our fear and our dread. Do you not recall your meditations? We will return when I have a greater understanding of HaShem and the Hechalot."

The brothers could formulate no more words between them. It was obvious both were set on their individual paths. They looked at each other for a long moment, and then embraced. Joses then departed and returned to his family to continue the journey west to On.

A thought came into Jacob's mind as he watched his brother leave. The words of his thoughts came to his mouth and he uttered them quietly, "Yes, Joses must be considered a warrior," he pondered as he nodded his head, a breeze now catching the locks of his hair and blowing them toward the back of his head. He recalled the dangers of the higher meditations and the angels who guarded the paths and the gates with drawn swords ready to destroy the unworthy who attempted to approach the higher realms. "Whose wrath would I rather face; that of a Roman Centurion or one of the armed angels of the heavens like Kaptziel or Metatron?[12]"

Joses would be gone for ten years.

***

The tax of the people of Judea and Galilee unsettled the entire nation, and even neighboring Diaspora Jews. While the relations between the establishment High Priest, Joazer, and the Torah-dedicated Sadducees had been strained for sometime, Joazer's support of the Romans in collecting the tax was the catalyst for Jude to divide the faithful from the Herodians. As with Joses, this was a straw that broke the camel's back as the Torah faithful Jews had no intention of honoring Caesar by giving him their strength that should go to HaShem. Despite the efforts of the Herodian Jewish rulers to try and keep the people in line, things were quickly spinning out of control. Jude and Jacob again seized the opportunity presented them by the Census of Cyrenius. Using his oratory skills to the maximum, Jude pushed for an all out revolt against Rome, telling his countrymen that they would be cowards to pay the tax. He convinced the people to whom he spoke of the necessity of liberty from foreign oppressors so that the people could worship HaShem as their laws required.

A split occurred between the Sadducees along the lines of supporting the Romans and their tax, or resisting the same. Joazer, the High Priest, led the group supporting the Romans and the establishment. Jude and Jacob led those who were against the census and the tax, and the faithful who were trying to follow the Torah. There was widespread support for Jude and Jacob, and this support grew stronger as each year passed. As for Jude, Joachanin, and Jacob, they believed that the collaborators with the Romans and the Herodians, those who were foreigners and not Jews, but pretended to be Jews, had polluted the Temple. More and more of the people realized the same thing as time progressed. The Messianic Movement was gaining momentum.

Simon, Jude's brother, remained the greatest of the fighters. They continued to call him Kefa, or rock, for that is what he was. He had remained reliable, steadfast, violent, and faithful to the Community. He looked to his older brothers, Jude and Jacob, as the heirs of the messianic titles and he supported them without question. He had led a lion's share of the raids, producing stores of supplies for the Zealots while filling the Romans with dread when they traveled through isolated areas of the country. He had also recruited some stalwart Jews to the movement. But, the Romans were never positive of the identities of these Damascus Essenes. Their cover as ascetic, pious, other-worldly worshippers put the Romans and, some of the Herodians, off guard.

As these events were unfolding, the Roman Governor Coponius and the Roman Senator Cyrenius removed Joazer from the position of High Priest. They replaced him with Ananus. Along with this, they appointed the Herodian rulers merely as tetrarchs over much smaller areas. Over the next several years, the succeeding Roman Governors continued to remove and appoint new High Priests from the Herodian establishment who had no legitimate claim to the office. The office went from Ananus to Ismael, then to Eleazer the son of Ananus, then to Simon son of Camithus, and then to Joseph Caiaphas. This entire administrative activity had nothing to do with the Israelite law of succession of the lineal descendants of the High Priest. These men either bought the High Priesthood with bribes to the Romans or were all Herodians, Roman puppets. This action further incited the flames of revolt against Rome and was proof to the Jews that Rome had no intention of honoring their laws and customs. Bloodshed increased in Palestine. The Romans and Herodians tried to maintain control while the Zealots of the Jews attempted to disrupt their administrations and attack their interests.

This Roman effort to control the situation continued with some success for the next few years. But, as a result of the uprising, Rome continued to tighten its grip on all of Palestine. In approximately 18 CE, Caesar sent a new Governor to Judea. The man, Pontius Pilate, had earned Caesar's respect because of his administrative skills that had enabled him to accumulate a great deal of wealth. But, Pilate was also an ambitious and ruthless demagogue who would employ any stratagem to obtain the desired results. Caesar needed such a man to bring order to Palestine. However, it was a gamble, as well, for Pilate proved to be more brutal in dealing with the attacks and activities of the resistance, torturing and crucifying hundreds, maybe thousands, of Jews. The scales could go either way; forcing the Jews to capitulate and willingly submit to Roman authority, or catapulting them into a more widespread and deadly revolt.

The Herodians were also attempting to gain a more firm control over the land. But, despite all their efforts, they could not effectively convince the lineal Jews to cease their revolutionary acts, even with widespread bribes, torture, and threats of denial of access to the Temple. The Herodian Priesthood, with Roman encouragement, began instituting requirements of an oath of loyalty from the people before allowing individuals into the inner courts of the Temple of Herod. Without this certification, the Jews could not find a place to worship. Losing their temple access was something most of them could not bear, and this act alone prevented some of the Jews from otherwise actively assisting the resistance because they held their access to the Temple in higher esteem than overthrowing the Roman powers.

To pay for these additional actions, the Herodian priests and leaders brought merchants and money changers into the Temple where they would collect what amounted to a tax for the oath and the right to enter the Temple to offer prayers or sacrifices. The normal duties of these changers had been to ensure that only coins without forbidden images produced by Jews were used in the Temple. But, even that appeared to be changing as Caesar's image appeared more and more often on coins offered for the Temple Treasury.

All of this only further angered the Community and the Zealots. Against the wishes of some of his followers, Joachanin ben Zechariah decided to more openly accuse the establishment priests and leaders of the Herodians as sinners and usurpers not fit for the Kingdom of HaShem. Whenever he left Damascus, he removed his white linen robes and donned sackcloth to emphasize his message. He openly began preaching of the coming of the end of times and the retribution HaShem would take upon the liars and deceivers of the covenant who everyone knew were the Herodian priests. He openly accused them of incest and sleeping with women during their periods then entering the Temple as unclean, taking multiple wives and committing the same actions with each of them, marrying and divorcing at a whim, and also of sacrificing to idols in the Temple. Most of these, to one degree or another, were prohibited by Torah and further restricted by Joachanin.

Furthermore, he proclaimed that HaShem, through his mashiach, would overthrow the Romans. Since he was in ragged clothes of sackcloth and of a generally unkempt appearance, railing against the Herodian leadership and actually making a comic spectacle of their lives, the Romans did not consider him a necessarily immediate threat. He was playing with fire, but at this point the Romans merely considered him mad. That allowed him to continue for a much longer time than otherwise possible.

But, the Herodians were sure they knew differently. Their spies had seen him throughout Judea obviously commanding a large number of followers, from all walks of life, even the Essenes from Damascus. While he did not seem to have a close association with Essenes, as the Immerser (as Joachanin was also called) did not dress like them when he was outside of Damascus, he did have those around him who had been seen conducting Sicarii operations. Their activities were getting out of hand, and Joachanin seemed to fire their passions of liberty and nationalism. Zealots had again begun seizing anyone not of Jewish descent who talked about the Torah and demanded that they be circumcised. If they refused, the Zealots killed them saying it was a requirement of their law.

One such tragedy took place just outside of Jerusalem where a Roman soldier and young Herodian were discussing Torah and Jewish customs. Jude's lieutenant, Laban, and a group of eleven Zealots, dressed not in their white linens but as simple peasants, approached the Damascus Gate near nightfall. They had prepared themselves for a strike against the kittim and the Herodians, one that would send a message to the invaders and, they hoped, please HaShem. Many of the independent Zealot groups were beginning to do the same thing, and Laban wanted to ensure Jude's honor amongst them so as to strengthen Jude's position for the throne. The opportunity came easily as Laban spotted the two men and overheard their discussion when he and his men passed close to the Damascus Gate where the two men stood talking. Once beyond the earshot of the Roman, Laban stopped his men and gathered them close around him next to a turn in the wall where the Roman could not see them.

"My brethren, what you have just witnessed is an attempt by a usurper to disrespect HaShem's law by informing the kittim soldier," explained Laban. "The Torah is to us, the rightful heirs, not to goyim. As the Teacher has instructed, this angers HaShem and defiles all of us. It is right for us to act to avenge this encroachment upon us." As Laban talked, he removed an object wrapped in linen from the bag he kept attached to his waist. Unfolding the linen revealed a small, flat, smooth stone designed for circumcision, sharpened on the end to an edge capable of shaving a man's beard from his face. "As required by Torah, I will use this on the Roman. You," he nodded towards a Zealot named Taddai ben Netanyahu, "will check the Herodian." Taddai immediately withdrew his circumcision stone from his own bag and began to unwrap it from its linen. "If he is not circumcised, do so. The rest of you will take them to the ground and hold them until Taddai and I have done the duty."

The men all began to prepare themselves for the confrontation, checking their sicars beneath their clothes and preparing cords of linen to bind the victims. This would be no easy task. No man, including the weakest of men, would resist any violation of the integrity of his manhood, even to the point of inflicting death on those so seeking to do such a deed.

As the Zealots made their final preparations, Laban peered around the protrusion in the stone wall, a gust of wind blowing particles of dust into his eyes. He shielded his face and blinked to wash away the stinging grit. Once he had cleared his vision, he looked again. He could see that the two men were so involved in the discussion, that they were nearly oblivious to everything around them. "So it is for all men who study Torah," Laban whispered to himself, "even these who are unworthy. But, it will work to our advantage." He then motioned for the Zealots to follow him. As they turned toward the gate and began to pass the Roman and the Herodian, they all pulled their shawls up over their heads to help conceal their identities, and Laban's followers seized the two prey.

The Roman attempted to fight and call for help, desperately trying to maneuver his lance for a strike. But the Zealots succeeded in taking the lance from him and laying hold of his armored torso to try and force him to the ground, their drawn sicars waving threateningly near the Roman's face. He managed to draw his short sword, but Laban struck it from his grip with a sharp blow from his own sicar. The force of Laban's blow and the weight of the other Zealots finally took the Roman to the dirt.

Taddai's group had no trouble. When they seized the Herodian and placed their sicars to his throat, he whimpered and fell to the ground almost voluntarily. It made Taddai think that the little usurper probably had no idea what was about to befall him if he was found not to have already obeyed the Torah. If he did, he would likely not have succumbed so easily.

The Zealots with Laban now secured the Roman's silence with a linen rag pulled tightly around his throat, and pinned him to the ground with their hands while they fastened more linen cords about his limbs. The linen about his throat cut off his air like a garrote and an initial panic seized him. He struggled all the more ferociously, trying to kick and strike his assailants. But, with little oxygen to fuel his efforts, his struggles were obviously losing their effectiveness and he seemed to realize the uselessness of his resistance. With thoughts of impending death and no way to alert his fellow soldiers or cry for help, he said his prayers to Jupiter and prepared to enter the afterlife.

It was then that he felt the tug on his clothing that obviously exposed his genitals. He made the effort to look down and he saw a man holding a sharpened stone and moving it toward his groin. He again began to struggle, this time with all the might every fiber of his body could gather. He managed to free his right leg and kicked the unseen man who held it so hard that the man fell backwards, allowing the Roman to now use the free leg to kick at those about him. But, almost when he thought he might free himself, his leg was again immovable and pinned to the ground. All he could do was arch his back and rock slightly from side to side. The man holding the linen rope about his throat now tightened it, and the lack of air brought on a stupor upon the Roman's mind, almost to unconsciousness.

A small number of men and women who were traversing the area of the gate stopped for but moments to watch the scene before them. Most of Jerusalem was now at supper, few traveling the paths about the outside of the city. Those who did witness the disturbance were not numerable enough to be of any real concern to the Zealots, and few remained long enough to see the details. Most knew that it was better for them to put distance between them and the skirmish as more soldiers could arrive and exact revenge.

The Herodian was also now bound and gagged to prevent him from making audible screams, and he could see what was about to befall his Roman friend. The terror of the moment seized him, for he knew he had not obeyed the Torah, and was, as the Roman, about to lose a part of his anatomy. He felt a tightening of the linen rag about his throat and a tug about his hips. He then saw a man with a shawl over his face holding an object in his right hand. The dim light of the torches reflected a small glint off the object, and the Herodian realized it also to be a circumcising stone. Realizing their intent, he struggled as he had never done before in his life, but was overpowered by the strength and number of his captors. He gnashed his teeth and tried to scream, but only a muffled groan proceeded from his chest as he felt someone grab his member, stretching the foreskin with no intent of gentleness. He writhed in agony as the sharp edges of the stone cut through his taut flesh. The pain was such that no other sensation, no sound, no glowing light from the torches above the gate, nor even the efforts of his captors to immobilize his limbs made any impression upon his mind.

"I almost have it!" exclaimed Taddai to the men holding the Herodian to the ground. "There! It is done! Glory to HaShem; the Torah is honored!" he called out to all as he held the excised foreskin in his hand. The Herodian, now merely allowed by the Zealots to curl up to try to hide himself and alleviate the pain, could see the blood about his legs and the mutilation of his organ. Between the pain and the exertion of the struggle, he lost consciousness and rolled further over onto his side.

Finally, Laban was able to seize the foreskin of the Roman and stretch it to a length that allowed him to begin the removal. His method was well practiced and the cuts were quick and precise. But, even in his near unconsciousness, the pain to his member awoke the Roman to a new level of combativeness. As if receiving strength from the pain, he again heaved his body and limbs at his attackers, forcing not only the man at his throat, but also the men holding his arms, to lose their balance and fall backwards. He saw his shorts word in the dirt only four cubits from him, and despite the pain, leaped toward it and grasped it with his right hand.

Laban was caught off guard. Even though the Roman's foreskin was in his hand, it was obvious the situation had now turned to one of life and death. He stood and took a step backward, dropping the foreskin to the ground and drawing his sicar from beneath his clothing. As the Roman stood, blood trickling down his legs from the mutilation, staggering from the loss of blood and the exhaustion of the struggle, he waved his sword toward Laban. Laban backed away slowly.

"Get going," Laban calmly ordered the Zealots. There was no reason to encourage the taking of this Roman's life. The circumcision would be a meaningful message to the Romans and the Herodians. That was the important issue.

As the Zealots heeded Laban's command and made their escape back to the north and into the darkness, Laban lowered his sicar and followed them. The Roman tried to pursue them, but tripped over a stone and fell. Gathering what strength he had left, he kneeled on the ground holding his groin.

"You are cowards!" he yelled as loud as he could, the emotion evident in his failing voice. "You have defiled me and stolen my manhood, you filthy Jewish vermin! I will hunt you down and see you all crucified!" he shouted as he slowly collapsed to the ground.

Just then, a maniple of roving Roman soldiers arrived and found the two victims lying in blood. Several of the soldiers tended to the Roman and Herodian while others entered the city to call for reinforcements. The leader of the soldiers was horrified more by the mutilation of the men's organs than the attack itself. As he checked his injured soldier and the Herodian, he grimaced at the sight of their loss. He turned from the mayhem and peered out into the darkness, searching for any sign of the perpetrators.

"We will do the same to you!" he screamed into the night. "We will make you all women and then crucify you!"

The Romans' anger and hatred toward the Zealots, and all Jews, grew from that day onward.

Many Romans, Herodians, and foreigners were killed as a result of these fanatic interpretations of Torah. The more conservative of the Jews also thought these actions were beyond reason, prudence, and Torah. The extreme dictates of Joachanin were beginning to leak out as coming from him. So, the Romans and Herodians needed to begin a plan that would take Joachanin out of the picture. The Herodian leadership became more afraid that the Romans might remove them from their seats if they did not remove the leaders of the resistance.

As all of this was coming to pass, Jude and Rachel, now well into their dynastic marriage, were still without a child. The extended separations required by Jude's work and the rules of the dynastic wedlock were taking their toll on Rachel, making her feel like the Patriarch Abraham's wife, Sarah, who did not conceive until she was in her old age. Her concerns for Jude's royal line made her the more desperate, as she realized that without an heir, the throne may be lost for him. But, there was little they could do about it other than pray to HaShem that her womb might be opened.

They came together again in Kislev and Tivet (basically the month of December), and separated as required to await the possibility of pregnancy. They had followed this program for so long, that even Jude was concerned about some other possible answers to the problem. Finally, in the month of Adar (February-March) Rachel could make the announcement that she was pregnant. Accompanied by Community midwives, she calculated the time of the birth to be exactly as it should be, Tishrei, the month of Yom Kippur. If the child was born and survived, Jude would have his heir. To recognize the official nature of the pregnancy and receive HaShem's blessing that indeed Rachel represented the Shekinah through her becoming one flesh with Jude, the final ceremony of the dynastic marriage forging their bond forever was completed in Iyyar (April-May).

As expected, the baby arrived during the month of Tishrei amidst an outpouring of joy from Jude, Rachel, and their friends.

The infant was a boy Jude named Jacob, and he would be the heir of his father. Following the commands of the Torah, Jude had Joachanin circumcise the baby, and the dynastic succession was well underway.

Best of all, Joses and his family were still in On and far from any influence over Palestine, the Community, or the throne. Jude hoped Joses would find On so much to his liking that he would never desire to return and interfere with Jude's plans. It had been nearly ten years since his brother departed the land of his birth, and Jude looked upon the apparent self-imposed exile as a just reward for a wavering faith and a destructive, but fortunate, delusion of grandeur.

As the Community brethren and Jude's compatriots began to earnestly celebrate his apparent victory concerning the claim to the throne, Joseph of Arimathea sent a communication to Joses regarding the attitudes in Judea, Galilee, and especially the Community at Damascus. He emphasized that Jude was gaining more and more support and that Joses may indeed lose his birthright unless he returned quickly. Even then, Uncle Joseph cautioned in his letter, it may take an action by HaShem to correct the situation.

Several days later as night was approaching in On, the beginning of the new day, Joses was preparing for another night of meditation at the Temple in On, just a half a furlong from his home. Joses was enjoying his family and friends, some of whom were the selected allies who had accompanied him to Egypt years before, and some who were new supporters he had gained while discussing Torah and the politics in Palestine. Many of these people had taken part in some of the rituals and instructions Joses took upon himself, and all were edified as a result of their determination. Of course, none dedicated themselves to the levels Joses had, but his evaluation of his studies and meditations suggested it was approaching the time where he could no longer be the student, but must take his position as the master, the example. It was time to claim his position and he could only do that on the soil of his own country.

As this issue became a point of discussion with those who

surrounded him, a knock came to the door. Miriam looked at Martha who immediately nodded and excused herself from the group. She opened the door and greeted a man she did not recognize, but she could see he had a scroll with what appeared to be Joseph of Arimathea's seal. She allowed him to enter and he announced he had a message for Joses from his Uncle Joseph. As the courier delivered the scroll into Joses' hands, Joses knew the time had come to return home even before he unfolded the document.

CHAPTER FIVE

The Egyptian city of On, Heliopolis as it was called in Greek, or Irshemesh as it was called in Hebrew, was a place of contrasts and dichotomies. Less than thirty miles east of the Great Pyramids, it was located on the east bank of the Nile River adjacent to the fertile Nile Delta in the area called Goshen. It was a paradise, green and lush, with palm trees and natural fruit growing in abundance. It was also a desert; the hot wind scorching the nostrils while the sun's brightness removed the sight from one's eyes.

The buildings were a mixture of fallen down clay shacks, humble but well kept structures, and a plethora of exquisite mansions. Dispersed throughout the city were various temples and holy structures representing nearly every possible view of gods and goddesses. Markets offering fresh foods and merchandise literally littered the city, and one could find anything the heart desired.

And, yes, there were the prostitutes, the sacred Temple sirens of the Pagan religions who encouraged men to honor the female deities, and the street women who offered their services for the lonely, the lecherous, or adventurous. Yet, On had been a mystical center for thousands of years before Joses' birth and continued so even as he spent the last ten years walking its streets and considering its shortcomings. Good and evil are always best discerned in the presence of the opposite, and On was just such a place.

While many mystical disciplines had always thrived in the area, the Hebrews, prior to the exodus, had looked to On as the seat of their religion. It was a disciplined and sacred place in those days, with no room for the dross or profane. Before Moses, Goshen and the city of On had been the home of the Patriarch Jacob and his twelve sons after Pharaoh gave it to the Hebrews out of respect for the notable services of Jacob's first son by his second wife, Rachel. This son, Joseph, had saved Egypt and the entire known world from famine by interpreting the Pharaoh's dreams using the mystical techniques of the Hebrew prophets. Pharaoh's respect for Joseph compelled him to make the young Hebrew the second most powerful man in all of Egypt, second only to the Pharaoh. Thus, an Israelite had ruled Egypt for a period of time. Indeed, it was a strange world.

Moreover, Joseph had received the birthright of his father's family, and that then fell on to his own son, Ephraim. This family passed on the mystical secrets to their descendents, and Moses helped them take these secrets out of Egypt and to the Promised Land after the polytheist rulers of the Upper Kingdom again obtained control of all Egypt around 1400 BCE. The Pharaohs of the Upper Kingdom from Thebes routed any and all relatives of the Hyksos, including the Hebrews, from their land. Once the Israelites reached the land they would call Israel, the center of this mystical knowledge was kept at Irshemesh, also known as Bethshemesh, the city of the sun or the light of the people of Shem, and also the house of the people of Shem. While the secrets were passed by mouth to ear only to those deemed worthy of them, the actual training was confined to Bethshemesh.

However, after many years, the secrets were again returned to On, partly as a result of the efforts of the High Priest Onias who the Greek Seleucid King Antiochus deposed nearly two centuries before Joses' birth. Onias had escaped Judea and built a fortress and a Temple at On. The Temple took the shape of a tower, unlike the Temple in Jerusalem. It was made of large stones and rose to a height of sixty cubits. Onias enclosed the Temple in a brick wall and controlled access by the use of several stone gates. Wisely, he accepted the assistance of many followers and well-schooled mystics who helped him reinstitute the rituals and requirements of the Torah, as well as the secrets of the Hechalot. Over the course of the decades, and despite the political shufflings and pollutions in Jerusalem, the

On Temple remained. It was a sanctuary for the devoted. The Ark had long ago been lost, the Jerusalem Temple defiled, the secrets compromised, and the dangers to the mystics in Bethshemesh or Emmaus too great for them to remain there. As a result, many of the greatest mystics returned to Egypt as they had so many times in their long and tumultuous history. They returned to On. It was for this reason that Joses now found himself in this same place.

Diversity of culture, elegance and poverty, refinement and dross, solemnity and apostasy, even elements of depravity all coexisted in On while Joses visited there. Rome's influence had spread more quickly than the influence of the Greek family of Ptolemy who had ruled Egypt for several centuries before Rome defeated them. Yet, it was this very environment that concealed the great mystics and allowed them to go undetected in their Torah study and meditations. Here, Rome was not threatened as all went about their business. Leisure for the rich and privileged, education, business ventures, philosophical debate, and access to any and all of it kept the people, and the government of Rome, from any concern of the messianic hope in Palestine. In the depths of darkness, behind the blackest smoke, that is where one finds HaShem in His hiding place.

Joses had chosen to be here, for he knew this was the school where he could go forward without fear of reprisal or revenge. Reassuringly, his family was safe while they were here with him. Hidden in the belly of the beast, as Jonah had been imprisoned in the belly of the whale, Joses could contemplate his destiny and ascend through the heavens in search of HaShem. His earlier training from the priests at On and the most exquisite school under their tutelage when he was a young boy concentrated primarily on Torah study and the methods of ascertaining different levels of meaning from the texts. In those years, he and his brothers were still too young to develop the mastery of the Chambers in meditative disciplines. That training began after they returned to Damascus as teenagers. Even then, these techniques were unusual for such young men. The sages required that most men not enter the meditative states until they were much older, even in their forty's. But, these young sons of Cleophas and Miriam were of a special lineage and took to the training as few others could.

Now he had spent nearly an additional ten years refining his understandings and developing his meditative techniques with the help of the priests and mystics in the On Temple. He had braved the unknown and approached the guardians of the gates to the Seven Chambers or heavens. However, even though he had studied diligently and was gaining more knowledge and experience every day, he had not overcome his fear of the darkness at the Seventh gate and the ferocity of the angels who guarded it. Indeed, even his brother Jacob had shuddered at Joses' willingness to confront the drawn swords of the angels of the gates. Yet, Joses' teachers, as they had when he was a young boy, marveled at his grasp and command of the disciplines. Joses' contacts also increased, and he became closely allied with like-minded and well-connected people in Alexandria and in other parts of the world. Ever insistent on the requirements of Torah, he did not forsake the commandments of HaShem or accept the manners of any of the Jews who wanted to become more like the Hellenized world. He fulfilled Torah, and provided that example to all he knew.

"Joses," called Elazer, the same man who had often helped Joses, Jude, and Jacob in Emmaus. He had also returned to On a few years earlier as the unrest in Judea began to interfere with his life and studies. "The Priest has told me that you may return home." Elazer was concerned, but more for himself. Joses had been a good friend and he was not certain that he wanted to see him leave. Now much older and feebler, Elazer wanted to remain closely associated with this young contender for the throne of Israel.

They were both in the preparatory area of the Temple prior to entry into the upper room for meditation. The preparatory room housed a mikvah and some ashes of a red heifer so they could ritually purify themselves before uttering the sacred words and Names. Joses, who was just drying himself, looked up as Elazer again spoke to him.

"Is it true?" asked Elazer.

"Yes, my friend, we are leaving for home in a few days. My Uncle Joseph sent me word, just tonight, that I should return. He is right, of course," Joses continued to prepare for his meditation, donning his white linen robes and reciting words of Torah. He then stopped his recitation and renewed his conversation with Elazer. "The last ten years have been fruitful, but it is time for me to put my training to its rightful purpose. Plus, the family is ready to go back. My son, Joseph, has reached young manhood and needs to see his homeland, and it is there he should find his wife. So it is for Martha's son, Jochanan. My Miriam, and her sister Martha, also long to again walk the paths of their native land. They have supported me here, and encouraged my efforts with untiring devotion," Joses informed Elazer. Even with his decision clearly made, Joses showed a furrow in his brow. "I have yet to enter the Seventh Chamber, the Kingdom of Aravot, but I know what I must do to accomplish it. I must return to my homeland and complete the meditation in the presence of my bishirtah, my sweet Miriam."

"Yes, I understand," Elazer sighed, holding back his emotions. "We will miss you here. Your wisdom and understanding are most appreciated and informative. But, when you find yourself in Emmaus, feel free to use our facilities. They are always yours."

"May HaShem bless you," responded Joses. "As for today, this will tell me if my decision is proper. I still cannot penetrate the darkness, the veil that hides the Throne of Glory. Apparently, while individual worthiness is adequate for most visions, home seems the only place where this mystery can be revealed."

"HaShem's ways are certainly not ours, "responded Elazer. "Who will be with you in the upper room?"

"The High Priest of On again," answered Joses.

"You are in good hands, then. But, I doubt that HaShem would kiss you and take you from us before your mission is done," said Elazer.

"And what mission is that?" asked Joses in a way that caught Elazer off guard. Certainly Joses knew the answer. "You have known all along, my friend," Joses said with a little amusement.

Elazer smiled, but did not say a word.

"My destiny at present has nothing to do with the Davidic Throne," Joses continued. "It will be up to Jude to seize that, if he can make the demonstration."

"Yes, I know," Elazer said almost with sadness in his voice. "I suspected as much all along, but just did not know if, or when, the truth would illuminate your mind. So, it comes to pass?"

"Yes, the father of Israel," responded Joses.

"Alleleluia and Amen," responded Elazer. "You are the Mashiach ben Joseph."

"Only if I demonstrate it," Joses said with determination. "I need to receive the confirmation of HaShem."

"You will," responded Elazer. "See me if you can before you leave."

Joses smiled and waved at his friend as he climbed the stairs to the upper room. His thoughts rushed back to his first meditation after he arrived in On many years before tonight. He was in this very building and had completed his purification in the mikvah, then climbed the stairs and sat down in the upper room with the priest after he said his prayers of thankfulness. What came was more than he was prepared for.

As he repeated the Divine Names to enter the vision and ascend to the First Chamber, darkness gathered all around him. He refused to turn from his purpose and concentrated more and more until the darkness dissipated and he saw a green field. The grass of the field was waving gently in a mild breeze, the subtle changes of hue from the turning of the blades of grass catching his eye. Far in the distance was a cave nestled in a crevice of a hillside. He approached the cave, but stopped just before entering it.

Suddenly, out of the cave came a huge and hideous beast with one eye and the body of a man. The creature must have been twenty cubits tall and was dressed only in a loincloth and a belt from which hung a chain connected to a large stone. The creature roared like a lion and the sound of it was deafening. Joses looked for a way to escape. On his right was a high cliff and he realized that he had no retreat but across a system of nets to his left. Was it the Three Nets of Belial?[13] Was he to cross the very sinful field that was forbidden to the members of the Community and all the righteous? How could he use this very evil to escape the certain death that awaited him as the creature approached? The temptations of riches, fornication, and pollution of the temple were what the nets symbolized, and he could not justify traversing them to save his life.

He turned again to the beast. Yet, here again, there was no purpose served other than his death. Was this all HaShem required of him?

He heard a voice call to him from across the nets and he looked to see two men standing on a small hill far on the opposite side. The men were dressed in white linen robes that glowed with a light he had never seen before. The hair on their heads was white and their skin as alabaster. Each had a glistening bow of the most exquisite crystal and a flaming arrow prepared for flight.

They motioned for Joses to come to them even if it meant to cross the nets. He obeyed, as his judgment discerned that temptations must be overcome, but to die wantonly was of little purpose. He hurled himself into the net as the beast grasped for his leg. Joses stepped lightly through the netting and was making his way toward the men in white when his right foot became entangled. The creature was still too close and again reached for Joses' leg. Just as the creature was about to seize him, the men in white shot their flaming arrows at the beast, striking him in his only eye. As the beast retreated to an uncertain fate back into his cave, the men in white reached down to Joses and pulled him out of the net.

"Remember the Orchard," said the man on the right. "Each level has a meaning, yet all are unified and support each other. Remember the Orchard, PRDS[14]: Peshat, the literal; Remez, the allegory; Darosh, the meaning drawn out for comparison; and Sod, the mystical aspect of Torah. This is the Garden of Eden, a place in Aravot, the highest heaven, where the souls of the righteous are stored. These you can enter upon your diligence and worthiness even in life. Now continue your journey."

His uncertainty of coming to On was answered. He had to risk temptation in a foreign land to avoid the dangers at home from Rome and the Herodians. He needed time to mature. He could still live a life of separation amongst the wicked. In fact, to do so was the only test of his true nature and his commitment to HaShem.

Now free to continue his search, and still in meditation, Joses continued to repeat the combination of Divine Names and he suddenly arrived at the gate to the first chamber. The gate was made of what appeared to be a solid piece of the finest cedar from Lebanon. On both sides of the gate were four angels: Dahaviel, Kashriel, Gahuriel, and Buthiel on the left and Tofhiel, Dahariel, Mathiel, and Shaviel on the right. These angels were of a fierce countenance, clad in white robes with swords at their sides and listening intently as Joses pronounced the Names. Satisfied that he knew the correct Names, the angels allowed him to approach the gate. Suddenly the gate opened and Joses felt a wind from the west, and he could see a very bright star in the sky. The clouds rushed past him and a thunder sounded near the horizon. Or was it thunder? The wind became stronger and not a breath passed before he heard the thunderous sound again. This time it was closer.

"I know that sound," he said to himself. "That is not thunder! That is the voice of HaShem!"

Now the thunder surrounded him and closed in on him. There was no place to go or escape and he hurled himself to the ground, covering his head with his hands and drawing his feet and knees up underneath his body. The sound powerfully reverberated around him and through him, penetrating every fiber of his being. He was terrified and relegated himself to destruction. He could not breath; he could not move; he could not speak; and he knew that all he had left was his will; his will to surrender to the will of this powerful voice, the voice of HaShem. He gave himself over to the Voice and said so in his heart. Then, he heard the voice of a man speak to him.

"Son of Joseph, you have forsaken the blasphemers and the evil ones and sought only for Me," said the voice which was now still and gentle. "These, My servants," Joses could feel the presence gesture toward two other beings just off to the left, "will guide and protect you. Go forward and seek Truth."

Joses then felt the vision drawing away. As the earthly light and sounds of the meditation room returned to his senses and the meditation ended, he could hear the voice of the Priest of On.

"Yes, my brother, it is time to return, return, come back" said the Priest.

He still could not move or speak. He lay helplessly for a time he could not measure. Then, finally, he was able to move the large toe on his left foot. Then he moved the large toe on his right foot. Slowly, and ever so carefully, he tested other parts of his body as he continued to return from the vision. With the help of the Priest from On, he finally came back to the world.

That was nearly ten years ago. While he had meditated many times before, that event was the most dramatic he had experienced in his entire life up to that time. Since then, he had progressed through the chambers and received more and more instruction. Yet, he had still not overcome the fear and trembling he felt when he neared the Seventh Chamber and the guardians there with drawn swords, the Throne of Glory behind the Gate in total blackness. Now, he was here in his last days in On. What could he finally accomplish?

As he entered the close confines of the upper meditation room, he greeted the Priest of On who was already sitting in the center of the room facing to the west. The Priest arose and greeted Joses with a bow of his head and they then stood together and put their tallits over their heads and attached the tefillin to their heads and arms. Then Joses opened the meditation with his prayer of thankfulness.

"We thank HaShem for all that we have, for we have so much," Joses began. "We praise your Holy Name, ALLELUIA."

"Alleleluia," repeated the Priest.

"Shema Israel, The Lord Our God is One Lord," Joses recited the words from Torah.

Joses then sat down and started to breath rhythmically. The Priest sat down next to him and just to his right. But, instead of repeating the Divine Names in various combinations, Joses did something new that the Priest had never heard before.

"Yichud Jacob ha Adonai Elohim,"[15] Joses said as he continued to breathe in a rhythm. "Unite with Jacob, the father of Israel, the prince of God, of the Lord God," Joses repeated over and over. "Yichud Israel, Yichud Israel, be one with Israel..." and Joses ceased speaking.

Then after a time had elapsed, Joses spoke again.

"Yichud Yitzak ha Adonai Elohim," Joses said as he continued to breathe in a rhythm. "Unite with Yitzak, the son of Abraham, of the Lord God," Joses repeated. "HaShem, make me one with Yitzak, whose experiences made him strong and full of valor, nothing wavering," Joses said as his words expanded beyond what the Priest expected. "Yichud Yitzak, Yichud Yitzak, be one with Yitzak..." and the words drifted into the night.

It was the same Yitzak from the story in the Torah, Beresheit (Genesis), whose father, the great Patriarch Abraham, placed him on an altar to sacrifice to HaShem after HaShem commanded him to do so. The Angel of HaShem spared Yitzak's life by staying Abraham's hand. Joses wanted the strength exhibited by such a man as Yitzak who would submit wholly to HaShem's will.

***

His tasks and schooling in On now completed, Joses was just returning to Palestine as he had planned when he became aware of the increasing troubles between the kittim and people. He had sequestered himself and his family while he studied and meditated, and he had been somewhat out of touch with some of the particulars of the difficulties at home, receiving only limited information. While this lack of detailed information concerned him, he felt that the time spent upon his training was extremely important. Even though still of a relatively young age, he was now a master of the mystical Hechalot of the Jews, as well as several other mystical systems, some which he had developed on his own.

Returning with him were his family and several new friends he had acquired who recognized him as the heir to the title Mashiach ben Joseph, or Yehoshua ben Joseph. This realization had occurred to him during his training in On, and he received the affirmations of the priests as well as the assurances of his meditations. It was a revelation to him that still maintained his right to rule Israel, but not under the Davidic Dynasty as he had once thought. That position was Jude's, if he could accomplish it, or do what the Hebrews described as the demonstration. Joses believed he now held the position of the Mashiach ben Joseph as the heir to all Israel, the patriarch of the entire nation just as the patriarch of old, Jacob the son of Isaac, also known as Israel, had held and had so been proclaimed by HaShem with the change of his name to Israel. "Israel" meant, "he is the Prince of God." Joses would never again lay claim to be the Mashiach ben David.

Information concerning the extremism of the Zealots, not just their efforts to expel the Romans and Herodians, but their treatment of foreigners generally, concerned him, as well. He fully supported the resistance and the actions to expel the Romans, but he also knew that by obeying Torah there was no reason for the Zealots to go beyond the mark, regardless of any other vows they might have taken. He felt, as he had all along, that they and those of the Community had gone too far. It threatened to bring the cause, a righteous and noble cause against the kittim, to a danger point of failure.

He pondered one of the most absurd and heinous activities of the Zealots, that of forcibly circumcising anyone who was not a circumcised Jew but who was found to be discussing the Torah. He knew this to be an action totally at odds with the freedom espoused to all by the Torah. Besides, without proper discussion, how could those of the gentiles learn of HaShem and his laws so that they could make an intelligent decision as to the possibility of conversion? Joses was, in fact, angry with his brethren who were obviously ignoring the problem, or worse, sanctioning it. This issue would become a further wedge between Joses and his brethren.

Joses was greeted by his mother, Miryam, on his return to

Capernaum in Galilee. He discussed with her his intentions to claim the right of the crimson thread, but now explained it was pertaining not to the Davidic line, but to that of Joseph of Egypt of old. Miryam was confused. Had not they determined that their family line was through the tribe of Judah, which her husband Cleophas had claimed? Joses explained what he had found in On. The friction between the brothers would not be abated by this new development, and it could even cause a greater rift. But, she knew this was inevitable, anyway.

Joses began speaking more openly to those who would listen to his explanations, even in the synagogues. But, he never explained his new understanding of his lineage; he left that out of his discussions. Those loyal to Jude and Jacob were incensed that he would return and cause this difficulty for his brethren who had born the brunt of the resistance for so many years.

And, there were other details that troubled Miryam. Her wayward son was going even further. He was instituting secrets from On that she had not forgotten. But, although she was not certain it was correct, she could not find fault in her oldest son. After Joses' discussion with her, she rushed to Joseph of Arimathea to discuss what was happening and to get his wise counsel.

Jacob was also hearing this disturbing news concerning Joses. His sources were informing him that Joses was now telling close associates that he was preparing to move ahead with his plans to lead Israel. Jacob went to Jude and informed him of the development. Jude was concerned, but was calm as usual. The crimson thread was his by default, and all of his actions through the years had properly prepared him to assume reign. What needed to be done? Jacob told him that the Kingly Mashiach must have the approval of the administrator of the succession, and that Joachanin ben Zechariah was not going to agree to Joses' claims. He had not performed the duties required by Joachanin in the Community. Indeed, Joses had forsaken the requirements as dictated by Joachanin. All of this reassured Jude. He would continue his plans and try to allow Joachanin and Jacob to handle the problem. But, so as not to ignore his responsibilities, he would meet with his errant brother just once more.

Joses met with Jacob and Jude even though he knew they considered him an outsider, almost a foreigner. But, as the oldest brother, Joses always attempted to accommodate his brothers' desire to see him. They met in Beit Lechem in the middle of the market so as not to bring attention to themselves. They blended in well as they shopped, then chose a place to sit as many of those attending the market would. It was amid the people, but near a wall that was offset enough from prying ears to ensure their privacy.

"Joses, I love you because you are my brother," said Jacob, "But you cannot think that you have the right to assume the throne. You are not qualified. Please try to understand. Jude has been obedient and respectful of the Law, and he has the backing of the Community," Jacob reasoned with Joses.

"My brother, HaShem has delivered me to the instruction of those you know in On and has given me wisdom not comprehended, but lost to most of our people," Joses began. "I am the rightful heir, and my training is no less than Jude's. It is actually more than his."

"On is a den of priest craft," Jude said as patiently as he could. He had been in On, too, as were all the family during their younger years. In fact, a short distance from On was Alexandria, Egypt, which had been the dwelling place of one of the largest populations of Jews in the Diaspora (Jews outside their homeland of Palestine). "The Teacher, Joachanin, is the rightful priest and his son is his successor. They administer the secrets lawfully, but you refuse to accept their authority! How can you give credence to anyone else, especially those who have not the courage to answer HaShem's calling to gather here and claim our land?"

"I do recognize the authority of the Teacher," answered Joses calmly. "And I will obtain the blessing of Joachanin."

"Ha!" laughed Jude. "Nothing you have done proves your worthiness, brother. You must repent of this nonsense. The true lineage descended to Damascus, as you know because you are part of that. What good is On?"

"What good is the Galilean Movement (another name for the resistance) if we are no better than those we seek to overthrow?" responded Joses, ignoring his brother's denunciation of On.

"Let's be practical, Joses," interrupted Jacob who did not want secrets discussed in the possible earshot of others. "You have no alliances, no subjects, no weapons, and no recognition from Joachanin or me. You are not the mashiach."

"I am consolidating my alliances," Joses informed Jacob, "and I will succeed. It is clear to me the path I must follow to free Israel and hold the ensign of the Torah to the people. The Torah is not to be subtracted from, or added to, and you have assisted in doing just those things. I believe my demonstration will prove my point to the people."

Jacob, also now incensed, could not have any of this.

"How can you solidify alliances, Joses? Where are they going to come from? Who will recognize you? You have not even been in our land for many years," Jacob rebutted.

"I know what to do," Joses said. "I do not yet ask for your assistance or agreement, but I will show my worthiness by what I do. One thing for certain I must do, and that is to restore the Torah to our people as it is, not going too far and by not failing to go far enough. It must be done exactly, no more and no less. Israel is to be the hand of HaShem in bringing salvation to the nations and to all people, not unjust coercion. What is this that has come to my ears that our brethren are mutilating the kittim found discussing Torah?" Joses' eyes betrayed his anger.

Jude and Jacob were steadfast. "You have no jurisdiction to counsel us!" they exclaimed, nearly in unison.

"The kittim are here unlawfully, and we will insist upon their removal from the land or their obedience to Ha Shem," Jude stated emphatically. "Now, no more talk. I can see that we will not agree. You are either with us, or against us."

"Brethren," Joses spoke slowly and deliberately, "for us, circumcision is the door to HaShem. Do you wish it so to be for the kittim? Do you wish to give them entrance to the kingdom, even when it is against their will, and yours?"

The question stunned Jude and Jacob. Joses had just told them that the action of supporting these forced circumcisions and helping the kittim into HaShem's Kingdom was actually contrary to their plans. They stood in silence as Joses continued.

"My intention is to overthrow the kittim and restore Israel. I will not demand allegiance to any but HaShem in that task. In all things, but of my understanding of Torah, my intention is the same as yours."

Despite Joses' logic, Jacob had enough and stood to depart. He did not feel that his arguments were getting to Joses. "I will speak of all this to those of the Way, and to our mother."

Joses nodded his head in the affirmative. What Jacob was about to do would only strengthen Joses' position. He was now going to go and seize his rightful destiny by using the secrets of Moses kept by the Priesthood at On that had protected the secrets even better than had the Way of Damascus.

Jacob's first order of business was to meet with his mother, Miryam. The two met in Caesarea so as not to raise any questions. While the seat of Roman rule, no one would believe that they would be discussing messianic subjects so close to those so opposed to it. Miryam confided in Jacob that Joses was indeed now discussing his rightful heirship with small groups of supporters. The most shocking news, however, was that he was denouncing the Oral Torah as proclaimed by the Teacher and even the mainstream Jews as going beyond Torah in many of its determinations.

"What do you mean, mother? He has never understood this part of our law. Do you think that he is ever going to subject himself to Joachanin and follow the dictates of the requirements of the Community?" asked Jacob.

"No, I do not believe he will do that," responded Miryam. "In fact, his intention is to follow the example of Joseph of Egypt. He claims the heirship of Yehoshua ben Joseph and has received an anointing by the priests at On."

Jacob had to stop for a moment and consider what his mother had just revealed to him. The thought horrified him.

"A claim to the Patriarchy of all Israel?" asked Jacob, his eyes widened and his breathing turned to gasps. "He is conducting the secrets outside of the Way."

"Yes," replied his mother.

"This cannot be! This is one of our charges against the Herodians. They defile the sacred and honor idiocy. This is an outrage!" Jacob, normally composed, now stood and paced. "Mother, I have remained a Nazarite and celibate my whole life to devote myself to HaShem. My vow is intact. It is proper. Should HaShem give me a wife, she will be my bishirtah and no other. I do not violate Torah by waiting upon HaShem. Jude has a dynastic wife and submits himself to Joachanin. He follows the rules of dynastic wedlock. We, as brothers, have performed the law. Joses has forfeited these things, and now he enters into a spurious claim to dishonor our family!"

Miryam sat silent, allowing the anger and frustration in Jacob to run its course. She knew he would not allow it to overtake him. He was holy from the womb and anger would not remain in him. He finally composed himself and sat down.

"When does he plan to do this thing?" he asked.

"His plans are ongoing," she was brief and to the point.

"A man outside the Way, no less," he said in further disgust. The Herodians had made a habit of also subverting the Torah, and this was a constant charge against them by Joachanin. Jacob saw no other recourse. "Mother, we must reject him and inform all others to do the same. His excuse for this action certainly involves correct interpretations, but we are of the Davidic line."

"Jacob, he is my son, too. He was born first and received the crimson thread. I am not sure this can be changed, despite all you have said."

Jacob looked into his mother's eyes, incredulous that she seemed to be wavering from her commitment to Jude.

"Mother, what of Jude? He has performed and is the rightful

king!" stated Jacob with no hesitation. "Are we to lose a brother to the sword to defend the honor of HaShem and our family"

Miryam's eyes flashed. "He has children, and he has not broken the Law! I must tell you something." She tried to calm down, but she was speaking in hushed tones with some distress. "Your father did not follow Chananya simply because he felt his attitude toward Torah was too far beyond the mark. Your father also, while not preventing you boys from following your consciences, did not approve of the stakes Chananya, and now Joachanin, placed around the Torah. I do not think he would approve of Joses' course, but I don't believe he would find fault with his interpretation of Torah, or its applicability to him in this matter. Jacob...(she paused long) I cannot find fault in him."

While the two sat staring at each other, a figure in the shadows moved toward them. It was Joseph of Arimathea, Jacob's uncle and long-standing supporter of Joses. Jacob was startled to see him as he thought his mother had come alone. But, he should have known that his mother would never travel unescorted seeing that she was, in fact royalty herself, even if she was effectively in exile.

"Jacob, I did not tell you he was here because I wanted you to have free vent of your feelings. But, now, I feel that your Uncle must further address your concerns," said Miryam. She moved aside as Arimathea came close to Jacob.

"Uncle," Jacob spoke in respect for this elderly and respectable man who had done so much for the family. "I mean no disrespect, but do you still support Joses, even in this?"

Arimathea did not immediately answer. He stood for the longest moment looking Jacob in the eyes. Then, he grasped Jacob's right hand.

"You, my boy, have been pious all your life, freely giving your life to the service of HaShem. I want you to know that I recognize this." Arimathea waited for a sign of acquiescence from Jacob, and it came with a firmer grip. "I also know that Joachanin ben Zechariah is the legitimate Tzedeq. He, too, has dedicated his life to the service of HaShem. He has pronounced the law to Israel, and Israel must listen. Even Joses says there is no greater prophet than Joachanin."

Jacob was puzzled. If Arimathea supported Joachanin, how could he also support Joses? "Then, Uncle, Joses is not beyond the dictates of the High Priest. He must consent to the decrees of the Teacher. He cannot go outside of the Way, further defiling our lineage from David. Is this also your position?"

"No," Arimathea was not one to mince words. "I will tell you why. You may not accept this, but I must also yield to the Torah. The Torah is not to be added to nor subtracted from. You know this. But, you take the position that the Lawgiver speaks through the current High Priest and that his word defines the Torah. Jacob, there are other factors here even we were not aware of. These have been revealed to Joses, and he is empowered to do what will ensure the survival of Israel. That is his calling. And as long as he does it in the confines of the Torah, no one, not even the High Priest, can find fault in him. It was through the kingly and priestly families by order from mouth to ear that the secrets have been passed on.

Joseph paused and looked his nephew over. He could tell the young man was not comfortable, leaning slightly away from him.

"Have you not understood that the enmity of Judah and Ephraim will depart?" Joseph continued. "I have carried this secret all of my life, and it is the true meaning of my name, which is from Ramathaim of Mount Ephraim, or HaRamayahu. The Hebrew-Greek rendition I call myself, Arimathea, is nothing more than a smokescreen to protect this secret from the Herodians and the kittim. We are of the tribe of Ephraim, the birthright of Joseph lies with us. There is a responsibility here you have yet to grasp. If it had not been your father, or your older brother, it would have been me. But, I took another path when I could see what was developing in the family and in our land. I needed to remain outside the turmoil, so that I could be of the greatest value at the proper time."

"Those issues were decided long ago when the northern tribes were taken into captivity by the Assyrians," responded Jacob. "Judah stood fast, and HaShem has shown His favor to Judah." Jacob thought he had effectively negated his uncle's position.

"Then why does the Torah say that the scepter will not depart from Judah until Shiloh comes?" asked Arimathea.

Jacob realized that there was something to what his uncle had just told him. He recalled the teachings of Elazer, but he would consider that in depth later. There was another concern.

"You are sounding like there was something more to what Joses has done in On," Jacob pointed out. "Jude told me that Joses had good things to say about those pagans. I say they are nothing but pagans."

"Jacob, be wise," Joseph tried to be reassuring but not altogether conciliatory. Jacob was usually calm and thought deeply, but Joseph was finding him impetuous at the moment. "Think about what I am going to say. The term "pagan" has become something of a joke in Judea and amongst our people. Is a Pagan just someone other than yourself, like Goyim?"

Jacob was incredulous and not so easily persuaded. "No, Uncle, that is not the whole of it. I cannot discuss it with you further, at least not now. But, I do want to know if Joses will do anything more for his marriage to Miriam. Will he ever attempt the dynastic requirements outside the Community?" To Jacob, it was unthinkable for anyone to perform the secret rites of the mystics outside the control of the Community Council and the Teacher of Righteousness of Damascus.

"It will be at the end of Tishrei in Cana of Galilee," answered Arimathea. "It will follow the tradition and Benjamin ben Nikdimon will perform as governor of the feast. You and all the family are invited."

"I, for one, cannot partake in this," Jacob said. "I will not attend. I rather suspect Jude will not attend, either."

Arimathea watched as Jacob departed towards Jerusalem. After some short span of silence, he turned to Miryam. "This is going to be a serious test for Joses. How are you handling this reaction by Jacob?"

"I do not know what to think," Miryam responded. "It seems my sons will forever be in disagreement. I feel like Rebecca, wife of

Isaac, who had to contend with the feud for the birthright between her sons Jacob and Esau. She, according to Torah, stood by HaShem for her younger son who obeyed Torah. Am I wrong in supporting Joses in this thing? Jude has met all the requirements, not Joses."

"The Davidic profile would appear to support Jude, I agree," Arimathea said as he thoughtfully placed his hand on his chin. "But, I maintain the lineage to be different than you and the family have thought and that Joses has done nothing to abrogate his heirship. This explanation of the Mashiach ben Joseph has great merit in the Torah and our traditions."

"At this point, I am just following the only path I can see," Miryam stated with exhaustion and a hint of grief. "I will support all my children as long as they seek HaShem. I believe, despite his nature, that Joses has not forsaken that quest. I will prepare the feast for the marriage."

The new marriage was still several months away and Joses was now prepared to make a decision and approach Joachanin ben Zechariah. Before his second marriage to Miriam signifying his recognition of her as the one who would have the right to anoint him, he would enter into a Nazarite vow for forty days. He had decided to approach Joachanin ben Zechariah while Joachanin was washing initiates into the order in the Jordan River near his usual spot at Bethabara. The washing in a living or moving water was as acceptable as the ritual baths called mikvahs which actually were constructed to allow moving water to go through them. The Jordan River was merely a tool to allow the work to proceed faster for larger groups of initiates. As Joses approached the banks, Joachanin was not sure what to think.

"Joses ben Cleophas, what are you doing here?"

"I recognize the priestly position of your calling, and I call you the father of our community," responded Joses. "I submit to the washing to fulfill my responsibilities and to fully show my commitment to Israel."

"You have been observant, Joses, just not valiant." Joachanin did not see any flinch in Joses concerning this accusation. "You must also see to it that you take up the cause of the kingdom and more actively seek the defeat of the kittim. Can you not do this?"

"I see that this is part of the way, and I am prepared to do what is required of me," responded Joses.

"What of On?" asked Joachanin. "What have you done there? Have you partaken of their ordinances?"

Joses knew that Joachanin understood On, but was not sure he would recognize what Joses had accomplished there outside of Joachanin's oversight. He answered boldly, nonetheless.

"Your student has committed himself to the Torah, having lived it all my days," Joses began. " As such, all the ordinances of my fathers have been accomplished to me but this washing by you and the final ritual of kodesh keetoonoah (holy matrimony). Furthermore, I do not claim the throne of King David, but the rights of the patriarchy of all Israel, the birthright of Joseph and Ephraim."

Joachanin raised his eyebrows, slightly stunned, and nodded his head.

"So, you know?" was all Joachanin asked.

"Can we proceed to fulfill the Torah and all righteousness?" asked Joses.

Joachanin looked about the area of the Jordan River where others seeking the washing and his own initiates stood watching the proceedings. The witnesses, all of those here, would mean there was no turning back should he accomplish the administration of this ordinance, effectively publicly recognizing Joses as a keeper of the Way and, by the nature of the circumstances, the legitimate head of Israel because of Joachanin's acceptance of him. The Teacher had acted his part as the Tet or instructor to this young man for many years, possibly without Joses even knowing it. He had delivered to Joses the most contradictory positions to test him, even seemingly recognizing Joses' own brothers and encouraging them to their tasks. Despite all that he had done to test Joses, here he was, standing before him and HaShem, having completed nearly all the requirements. And, he had sought it all on his own, a testament to Joses' fortitude and conviction. Joachanin was amazed.

"And what of the crimson thread?" asked Joachanin.

"It is still the sign of my birthright, my leadership of the family and all Israel. That is the right of the firstborn," Joses said with authority.

"The burden you take I am not worthy to even comment upon," Joachanin looked away, tears welling in his eyes. He took Joses' hand and led him into the waters of the Jordan. Once they reached an area of the water that was nearly chest high, they stopped and faced west, toward Bethel, Shiloh, and Bethshemesh. The crowd immediately noticed the change in the ordinance, as Joachanin normally had those he washed face east toward the rising of the sun. A hushed silence fell on all present.

Joachanin placed his hands upon Joses and immersed him in the waters of the Jordan River. As he brought him forth from the water, Joachanin spoke loudly so that all could hear him. "Behold the ben Adam, Yehoshua ben Joseph," which meant the son of Adam, the Mashiach son of Joseph, the rightful patriarchal head over all Israel. He had effectively, as Samuel of old who anointed David the son of Jesse, King of Israel, proclaimed Joses the Mashiach ben Joseph, or legal heir of the birthright of Israel. Joachanin then reached in his bag and poured anointing oil over Joses' head, again pronouncing his earlier words. "Behold ben Adam, Yehoshua Ha Mashiach, Yehoshua Mashiach ben Joseph ben Adam.

The followers of Joachanin, including Andrew, a close friend of Joses' brother, Kefa, who witnessed this ceremony were astonished. They were unsure of what Joses' purpose may be, and they were puzzled that Joachanin would agree to perform the ordinance upon Joses. They moved closer to try and hear the conversation.

"I will separate myself for forty days in a Nazarite vow," said Joses, "and prepare myself for what is to come so that I may lead the people."

Joachanin understood. "The Spirit of HaShem has descended upon you, Joses, as I believed it would. You have kept the Law, no more nor less, and have shown your right to this anointing by your discernment. I have washed you in the living waters to prepare you for your sojourn. May HaShem bless you with all you require. In this time you will show the people and later you will rule."

At that, Joachanin and Joses came out from the water, and began a short walk to the shore, looking quietly at each other. At the bank, they sat down together. None of the assembly took upon themselves to approach the two men, but allowed them to continue their discussion. After all, not only was Joachanin the final word, he was Joses' first cousin.

"Joses," Joachanin began, "How have you come to understand that my requirements were a test for you?"

"I did not recognize them, as such" responded Joses. "I merely could not reconcile the Torah with the fences you constructed around it in all cases. I think I came to understand that those fences were designed to teach the people how to obey Torah, as the Torah is to teach us how to deal with HaShem and each other."

"Ah, yes, Joses," Joachanin stated. "And, I was inspired to see how you would respond to the difficulty. You know, your brothers are at odds with you, and you will not easily deal with it. But, as Joseph the son of Jacob saved the known world from famine and as King David defeated the hosts of the enemies of Israel, you must be willing to reconcile all contradictions. As David never raised his hand against HaShem's anointed, King Saul, and proved his faithfulness, so have you respected my calling and station. It seems the wisdom of Solomon is in you."

Joses felt somewhat uncomfortable, changing his position slightly as he formulated his next few words.

"Jacob, my brother, is a man bound to Torah, but he has taken a stand that I must submit myself to your fences. That, as you know, I cannot do."

"As you should not," replied Joachanin. Joses showed no surprise. But, he had one more issue to resolve.

"I will claim the Mishpat (kingly role) and Tsedeq (priestly role) based upon my birthright. I realize this will be a process," he said. "But, something else superseded Aaron." He looked into Joachanin's eyes, which betrayed no surprise at hearing his words.

I will be the Malchi-Tzedeq, the Priest-King of Israel in due time," said Joses.

"You have learned well in On," said Joachanin with a slight grin. "What I do see is the secret HaShem has given to you of the true line of succession for the Mashiach of Israel. Can you recite it to me?"

Joses and Joachanin again stared quietly into each other's eyes. It was Joses who broke the silence.

"If I am to lead Israel, I must protect the Torah from additions and subtractions that could cause errors. Individual efforts through Nazaritism cannot bind the nation to the very same requirements. That alone, if taken to the extreme, could result in the destruction of Israel. So, it cannot follow that these rules are or should be, universal. For selected priests or individuals, for a time, yes, perhaps. And, that was what Damascus was meant to be, the hidden priesthood, the Zadokites. But, their order was not to be to Israel as a whole, and certainly not upon the heir of all Israel, or the King, who must perform their functions."

Joachanin could not find fault in the reasoning. "As I said to you, Joses, I have watched this rift with uneasiness. But, I felt it necessary to push the Community of Damascus into a direction where the efforts to purify our people would perfect us in the Torah. I will concede your point, and surrender to you on that. I am not worthy to step beyond Torah, or to unlatch your shoes in this regard. Jacob will come to understand. Jude, on the other hand, may be more of a problem. While not tacitly claiming the throne of David, you supersede him. You are reclaiming what he felt you abandoned. I cannot say what this will cause, but I see it as a potential for danger. So, will you repeat to me what I have asked?"

Joses closed his eyes and began, quoting from the Torah at Beresheit (Genesis), "The scepter shall not depart from Judah, nor a lawgiver from between his feet, until Shiloh come..."

And what does that mean, Joses?" asked Joachanin.

"HaShem has seen fit to bring all things together, a restoration of Israel and a return of His Holy Covenant. This will bring tranquility and peace to Israel and the nations of the earth in their turn. So I will return the Law to Shiloh, and will unite the two sticks of Israel, Judah and Joseph, beginning the process of the reconciliation of Ephraim and Judah. I have the proper genealogy to be the heir to the promise to Joseph, son of Jacob our patriarch, that his seed would receive the birthright to rule the House of Judah and the House of Joseph, in other words, all Israel. I will be Mishpat (pillar of judgment also known as the pillar of Boaz) the Mashiach ben Joseph as well as the Tzedeq (pillar of righteousness also known as the pillar of Jachin) to function for Israel."

Joachanin was satisfied and shook his head. "Yes, Joses, that is correct and I can see that the breath of the Creator has whispered to you. But, there is still more. When will you solemnize your kodesh keetoonoah?"

"During Iyyar (mid-April to mid-May). She will be three months pregnant with our second child," responded Joses.

"Very good," Joachanin said with a smile. "If it is a son, he will be born in Tishrei (September to October)." He paused and looked into the sky, pondering his next words. "Despite your detachment from the Community Way at Damascus, you have fulfilled the requirements of Torah and, I believe, will continue to do so. You are righteous, Joses, and you are, indeed, a son of God, as much so as any of the righteous brethren of the Way. There, see it? The testimony of my words and the spirit of prophecy," Joachanin pointed to the sky where a white dove hovered on the breeze. "The sign that these words are true."

Joses had his victory. Joachanin was a man of intelligence, reason, and spirituality. But, how would Joachanin's followers react? Joachanin answered Joses as if he had heard his thoughts.

"I will go this much further, Joses," said Joachanin. "I will tell them that I must diminish and you must increase, and that it is for the good of Israel. It is the time of the King. But, the secret of that kingdom I will not reveal, for that is your calling. You will release men from the evil of the kingdoms of this world, and return to give them the Kingdom of HaShem. Will you go also to Samaria?"

"I welcome all you have said, and I will go there to find more of the lost House of Israel," said Joses. "But, I think what I do will not resolve it in the minds of those even here today. That will take a great deal of patience and instruction, if it works at all. Israel is always difficult to gather." He could already see the danger of his position even if he did not fail. The thought of it was very much like an epiphany.

Joachanin arose first, in deference to the one he recognized now as the next King of Israel. He turned to his followers waiting nearby and told them what he now expected.

"Behold Yehoshua ben Joseph, HaMashiach, Barabbas, Mashiach ben Joseph ben Adam," which was Joachanin's priestly way of declaring Joses the promised leader of Israel at the times of the reconciliation, and an adopted son of God according to the standards of the Way.

Andrew could not believe his ears. Here was the Teacher of Righteousness, the leader of the Damascus Community, declaring Kefa's first brother, Joses, the Mashiach ben Joseph and a high-ranking initiate of the order of the Way! This was a turn of events that Andrew recognized would likely result in a serious confrontation between Joses and his brothers Jude and Jacob. But, he could not deny what he had witnessed. He approached Joachanin and Joses.

"What of Jude?" asked Andrew.

"Joses is the rightful heir, the Davidic line has always been in question. But, Jude may still claim it if he can hold onto it," is all Joachanin would say.

"And Jacob?" asked Andrew.

"That is for him and HaShem to decide," Joachanin stated with a stern voice.

"I seek to begin my mission," said Joses as he approached the men and looked directly at Andrew. "I am separating myself for a period in the Wilderness (Damascus) and charge you, Andrew, to notify my brother Kefa to begin gathering those who have the ears to hear and not deny what has transpired here. But, for the sake of the kingdom, do so carefully, and I will take charge upon my return."

"Yes, Joses," responded Andrew, though still somewhat stunned. He looked at Joachanin again who merely shook his head in agreement with what Joses had just instructed.

Then Joachanin made it definitive. "Andrew, the time of the King is at hand. Shiloh has come. Follow the King and do as he instructs."

Andrew turned and began to assess how he would accomplish his task as he watched Joses begin his walk toward Damascus to begin his Nazarite vigil of forty days in preparation for his mission.

***

Jacob and Jude were at the Community when Joses, in white linen robes that were the characteristic dress of a Nazarite, entered Damascus. His arrival was unknown to them until a brother informed them that Joses had taken up residence in a spot on the south end of the camp closest to Jerusalem. It was also the spot of the symbolic Jerusalem for the Community. Startled at the development, Jacob and Jude approached Joses.

"What are you doing here?" Jacob asked.

"I have entered into a vow for forty days," replied Joseph.

"So, you have entered the Wilderness unclean, Joses?" Jacob thought Joses had not arrived washed and purified. Furthermore, Joses' physical appearance of his back and shoulders made him unfit for membership in the Community where every man admitted to it must have no physical blemish.

"The living waters of the Jordan Joachanin used to wash me, and he instructed me to sojourn here for my vow."

Joachanin's instructions? What was going on here? Jude and Jacob were puzzled and could not bring themselves to sort out the right thing to do. At that moment, Joachanin arrived as well.

"Brethren," Joachanin saluted them. "You can allow Joses his time here. He has much to meditate upon. He is acceptable to us and can eat at our tables if he so wishes. He is a ben Elohim (son of God)."

Jacob had no intention of questioning the Teacher at this

point, although questions of a married man and one outside the Law being present in the Community without having fulfilled all the prerequisites troubled him. The Twelve Community Elders had not even interviewed him. He drew Jude's arm close to him and returned to the center of Damascus. Jacob told Jude that he would discuss this development with Joachanin after the Sabbath the following week. Jude, somewhat puzzled and near to anger, agreed to leave that issue to Jacob, as he needed to return to his preaching and recruiting campaign.

Jacob waited for the Sabbath to end, and then consulted with Joachanin. It was nearly as troubling to him as his discussion with his mother prior to Joses' marriage.

"Teacher, I am confused as to the truth here and need further light and knowledge. This decision reflects on us, and affects the ability of our people to wage the war against the kittim. Joses is not worthy, is he? And, what is the purpose, what calling will he fulfill?" asked Jacob.

Joachanin was firm, and to the point. "The rift in your family is symbolic of the rift in Israel, and it is HaShem whose right it is to effect a reconciliation in the manner HaShem sees fit. I have taught you well, and you have learned well. You have excelled. But, you lack the discernment of the truth, in this instance, and Joses has shown the ability to rightly divide truth from error. He is the rightful King."

Jacob was startled. The King? Joachanin referred to Joses as the King.

"Yes, I have washed him in the living waters of the Jordan," explained Joachanin, "and he will be anointed as the King of Israel, Yehoshua ben Joseph, Mashiach ben Joseph, Yehoshua HaMashiach, savior of his people and the Torah. He is the father of all Israel by birthright and the voice of HaShem. All he has left to do is to fulfill the Law with his holy matrimony as taught to us by Moses."

Jacob was unable to respond. His thoughts were mixed, even confused. Then he thought of Jude. His marriage had already been according to the holy matrimonial contract and was abiding the terms of separation. Where was this all to lead? He vaguely remembered the words of Elazar that there was a mystery to all this and the division of Israel. He quietly obeyed Joachanin's intimation that he not argue. He decided to depart into the wilderness also and enter into a meditative period. Joachanin left the Community with a group of his followers and resumed preaching on the Jordan.

Joses spent forty days in separation, meditating, and studying Torah. He bathed several times a day in the mikvahs of the Community, seeking a closer relationship to HaShem so that he would know what his course of action should be as he began his mission to consolidate Israel and expel the kittim. After his forty days, he performed his final mikvah and donned his regular garments. He thought he was alone as he began his journey back to Galilee where he would begin consolidating his power in earnest. He was met by Jacob, who had taken a short reprieve from his meditations. The significance of Elazar's statements and the events of the last month had opened his mind to other possibilities. But, he was unsure.

"Joses," Jacob was going to find out himself what this brother's metal was. "What are you trying to accomplish? Do you think you are Bar Abbas, able to turn the stones into bread?" which meant in the Community symbology that he could now bring in new members to the Community on his own.

"We cannot survive on mere converts," Joses replied. "Further, we must trust in the Torah as it is given us, not fencing on all sides and adding to it, but living by the Word of HaShem. That also means that I must act according to the rights of my heirship, and I do not need approval from anyone."

Jacob was taken back by Joses' direct and adamant answer.

Jacob asked another question, pointing his finger at Joses. "Are you the Mashiach ben David?" He did not give Joses any time to answer but continued quickly, "Or are you Bar Abbas, Yehoshua HaMashiach ben Joseph ben Adam? If you are you will succeed. If not you will fail. So, go ahead and we will see if HaShem will help you."

Joses, before responding, raised his right hand. "I place my faith in HaShem and can only expect that I must do what is right, hoping that HaShem will bless my efforts. As we enter the Community in faith, so must we go about our destiny in faith, trusting in HaShem. To this calling, ben Joseph, was I born. I have the crimson thread."

Jacob was not prepared to let it go so easy. He parried his final question. "What you need is for me to give you my support, and you and Israel will rule the world after the War of the Sons of Light against the Sons of Darkness if you will but submit to the rules of the Community and acknowledge us."

"Again, Jacob, I say to you that Torah requires me to obey HaShem. Adonai[16] I must worship and serve only Him. You can help me, or you can stand against me, that is your choice. Consider, that before Aaron was brought forth from Abraham, was he to whom Abraham paid tithes, the priest of the Most High, Malchi-Tzedeq."

"You have defiled yourself by failing to remain separate from the world. How can Moreh ha Tzedeq allow you in the Way? What has he not told me? HaShem could not permit this," Jacob was pointed.

"If we are to pray for all nations, then truly Israel is HaShem's hand in the world, and if his hand is in the world, it must work in the world. That can be done while maintaining our separation from what the world does, and what it can do to us. Otherwise, how is the Torah of any worth if its righteousness is not seen? It is like a light, which cannot be hid under a basket if it is to be of worth. It is possible to be in the world and guide it by example without being of the world. Is that not true, brother?"

At that, Joses turned and walked away leaving Jacob to ponder what his test of Joses' metal told him. Was it rebellion, or was it the proof of the character and strength of a king?

***

During this time, Andrew had talked seriously with Kefa and several other men, some of whom had already shown an interest in Joses' position. Kefa talked at length with Andrew and had decided to break from the tradition he had believed in and support Joses in his claims. Considering that Joses now had the support of Joachanin, how could he do otherwise?

The new followers of Joses attended the marriage at Cana. Miryam, Joses' mother, was the hostess. The father of the bride, Benjamin ben Nikdimon, was the governor of the feast as he was the first time. Most of the attendees were new to the concept of Joses actually declaring his messiahship. When the question was brought up to Joses' mother, Miryam, she instructed them to do all that Joses asked them to do. Joses was not sure that his mother should have given so much away, especially since he had not had time to fully explain the matters to his brothers, and it seemed a little premature. But, he went ahead and presented his intentions to the crowd, fully explaining his intent to assume the role as the head of Israel.

Some of them accepted his message, and he brought them into his order that he began while he was in On. Anyone who wanted to be a part of the new Israel, with Joses as king, received membership. It was turning water into wine, a euphemism and code for the ordinary people becoming enlightened. This action upset those who were part of Damascus and saw Joses instituting the secrets outside of the confines set forth by the Community Council and the Teacher, Joachanin. Yet, Joachanin now seemed unconcerned and distant from the matter. So, some of them began to talk amongst each other, wondering what action, if any, they should take. But, the ceremony began, anyway.

The marriage proceeded in secret, with the attendees outside the covenant chamber. They had not yet seen the bride. The only ones allowed to enter and actually witness the ceremony were those directed to do so by the priest from On who came to officiate the marriage. After the ritual was completed, the wedding party entered the area designated for the festivities.

Everyone noticed that Miriam had now taken her hair down from her head and allowed it to flow naturally about her. It was quite obvious she was pregnant. Some in attendance were aghast that a married woman would commit this infraction of customs, for women were not permitted to have their hair down except in the private company of their husband. They did not understand the significance of the kodesh keetoonoah, holy matrimony or sacred marriage of the royal line or the method of the birthright. That was not for their understanding, but only for those initiated in the knowledge of the king-making rituals secretly handed down from Moses through the mystics of the royal line of the tribe of Judah and the patriarchal line of the tribe of Ephraim. Due to this ignorance, many who saw her believed Miriam to be acting like a prostitute, and they gave her the name "Miriam Mgadla Mshaya, or Miriam Magdalene (meaning a hair dresser) In fact, she was now Joses' most holy wife, the mother of the royal line. She would now be the key to his final ascent to the throne.

To emphasize the importance of all this, Benjamin ben Nikdimon made a proclamation, for he was also of the Israelite nobility and had an understanding of the requirements.

"HaShem has accomplished what he said he would do. He has called his son out of Egypt." Coming from the father of the dynastic bride, no one, not even those most opposed to the arrangements, dared to make an issue over Joses' right as the Mashiach ben Joseph. That would come in time.

The wedding party, including a number of men and women not known to the guests, left for the town of Bethshemesh, formally called Irshemesh, meaning the light of the people of Shem. Its sister city, indeed its original location, was On in Egypt. Joses would need just one more ordinance at that location after which he would also leave Miriam there until their next child was born.

Joses' acceptance by Joachanin and his subsequent use of a Nazarite vow and period of separation were but minor irritations for Jude. But now, this completion of the Kodesh Keetoonoah outside of the jurisdiction of Damascus was just too much! What was this Mashiach ben Joseph nonsense? He knew he could not let it stand in the way of his plans. So, Jude continued in his recruiting work near Jerusalem. While Jude was preaching under his alias of "Yeshua," he was approached by the Herodian, Amelaus and his servant, Reu, whom he had encountered on many occasions. Amelaus was known as a loyal subject of Herod and a close ally to the Romans, but he had always treated Yeshua with respect. Reu, on the other hand, was a true Jew because of his mother even though his father had been Herodian. Most importantly, he had showed an increasing interest in the Torah. As before, Reu was very interested in the message Yeshua was speaking about.

Yeshua finished his oration and instructed his assistants to help anyone in the crowd who may need further information. He then turned to Amelaus and Reu who were waiting on him.

"I see you have returned," Yeshua addressed them with some apprehension evident in his voice. He felt a need to remain cautious.

"Yes, Yeshua, we see you often on our walks about," responded Amelaus. "Reu constantly tells me how impressed he is with your message, and I just continue to tell him that the truth lies with the leaders of our faith, as they are presently constituted under Caiaphas. I know it is a point of disagreement, but I think your preaching concerning our love for one another is evidence of the validity of my position. If HaShem wanted it different, would it not be so?" Amelaus elaborated as on prior occasions. Yeshua smiled and nodded in the affirmative. "Well, I must be going, and Reu has some other places to go on his own, so we will see you again sometime." Amelaus then left and headed up a stairway leading to another roadway. Reu, however, after he had walked a few steps in the opposite direction, turned around and again approached Yeshua.

"I am interested to see what more I can learn about. I do not want to be seen talking to you, however, as the authorities are suspicious of me. Can we talk somewhere out of the public sight?"

Jude was uneasy. While Reu was obviously sincere, he was terribly close to the Herodian power elite. But, Jude could not totally put aside the possibility of converting such a person. Reu had, actually, come to him on good recommendations. Furthermore, such a conversion may, at least in Jude's mind, be helpful to his plans once he decided to complete his move to seize the throne.

"Yes, Reu, we can. Follow Laban here and he'll take you to a place near the center of town where we can talk a little easier. I'll join you shortly."

Reu nodded in agreement and followed Laban on a winding course through the city to the place of the meeting. It was a typical brick building that housed a number of living quarters within another group of structures. Laban and Reu went to what seemed to be the innermost portion of the building several doorways from the main street. It was dimly lit with candlelight and had only one narrow hole into the ceiling where fresh air could enter from the roof. Jude was already there waiting. He greeted Reu as he entered.

"Welcome," he said to Reu while motioning for him to take a place at a table on the floor. There were no chairs; the parties basically reclined around the table, as was customary practice. Jude then asked Reu what he could do to answer his questions.

"Yeshua, I am in some danger," Reu began, "because I have not been very good at showing my wholehearted support to Joseph Caiaphas, the High Priest of the Temple."

Caiaphas was not a recognized High Priest by the majority of Israelites because he was not of the proper Israelite lineage, and worse, he was a supporter and collaborator of the Herodian usurpers. He had received his priesthood on the order of Herod and agreed to by Rome.

Reu continued, "I have studied the Torah now and can answer any question you might have for me. I want to be received into full fellowship. I know this is startling, but I will do anything to prove my sincerity. The salvation of my family is more important to me than the position with the Herodian nobility. What can I do?"

This was not unlike some of the other conversions Jude had seen before. More importantly, as he had already realized, a conversion this close to the Herodian ruling family was a definite asset to his final thrust for regaining the Throne of David back to the Israelites.

"You are really serious about this?" asked Yeshua.

"Absolutely," responded Reu with a sincerity in his voice and eyes that almost moved Yeshua to agree right then. Reu continued,

"My family has searched for the truth for so long," said Reu handing over a small scroll. "If the Teacher can accept my records and me, I will do whatever is necessary to prove my convictions."

Jude examined the scrolls showing Reu's family history and assets. He now had to determine how best to test Reu.

"Well, my friend," Yeshua began, "the first step is an offering and then a period of repentance followed by a ritual bathing. HaShem expects us to follow the Torah in these regards and to renounce our past. We will begin there."

"Yes, but I want to do more. What more can I do to prove to you that I am sincere?" The men looked at each other for a long moment. Then, Reu spoke again. "May I offer this suggestion?" he asked, and Yeshua gave a slight nod and a shrug to encourage him to continue, which he did. "The requirement of the Community is that the convert offer all he has and I have the documents here to prove my personal wealth. I will give it all to the brethren…all of it."

Jude remained calm but realized what this transfer of wealth entailed. It could provide a needed boost to the battle preparations for the resistance. It was, in and of itself, enough to make him agree. Then Reu produced another resource.

"I will also provide the brethren with goats and sheep," and he handed Yeshua a scroll privately transferring ownership to him of a substantial set of flocks, without any strings attached that was effective at that moment whether Reu was accepted as a convert or not. Reu's generosity and sincerity won Jude's decision to accept Reu's request.

"You are such a fine example of the true believers that HaShem has placed in our midst," Yeshua told him. "But, you must understand that we will not permit you to give any of your substance to us until well after your admittance. In fact, you cannot part with any of your substance to the "Many" until such time as you take upon yourself the higher life. But, I will arrange for your initiation with the Teacher. He will want to meet you. When can we proceed?"

"I am at your disposal, but we must be as secretive as possible," replied Reu.

"What of your family, especially the Herodian side?" asked Yeshua. "You will need to forsake them and..." he stopped short. He needed to keep this convert on the inside to acquire information he needed.

"Actually," Yeshua reconsidered, "your greatest contribution may be in being a quiet example to your extended family, remaining amongst them but quietly providing a new hope for them in subtle ways. That may also be a good reason for you to hold on to the bulk of your assets rather than give them all to the Community right away." Jude wanted the new convert to be an effective insider.

"Whatever you require, Rabbi Yeshua" responded Reu.

"I will arrange your meeting with the Teacher on the day after tomorrow," Yeshua informed him. The men stood and embraced each other.

As they left the small house, they could see the High Priest's guards clearing the way for the High Priest, Joseph Caiaphas. Adorned in his priestly vestments and making an appearance of nobility and piousness, he loved to show himself to the people. But, more and more often, as now, the guards did not have to make much effort to clear his path. Most of the people, rather than walk near him, would cross the street of their own accord. Such was the disgust for the man held by the people. This aversion did not go unnoticed by Caiaphas, and his hatred for Joachanin multiplied in his heart. But, he was gloating, because he knew his rival's days were numbered.

Jude watched Caiaphas as he passed, Reu taking his leave and running far ahead of the entourage to avoid the shifting of the crowd from slowing his departure. Jude's eyes met Caiaphas' as the men neared each other, Caiaphas giving a smile of arrogance. Jude turned his back to him and wiped the dust from his feet.

At that moment, members of Herod Antipas' Guard arrested Joachanin ben Zechariah as he was administering to followers by the Jordan River. The charge, as he and members of the Community were to learn, was sedition against Herod for accusing him of marrying unlawful wives and of polluting the Temple. He was transported to a cell to await his call to Herod who wanted to see his accuser himself. Furthermore, the pre-emptive arrest would take any suspicion away from Herod's and Caiaphas' new spy who was now well on his way to a deep infiltration of the suspected movement's leadership.

Reu turned through several streets and stopped at a local market to take time to shop. He wanted to ensure that no one was following him. After an hour, he began his journey back to the area of Jerusalem near the Temple. His home was there and he was in quite a hurry to return lest a prolonged absence raise more questions than necessary. Entering the gate by his home, he turned now to the right and proceeded into the shadows next to the Fortress of Antonia and stopped. Another figure moved slowly toward him out of the corner. It was Amelaus. The two men conversed for several moments, and then they separated.

Amelaus walked into the Fortress of Antonia where the Roman Army kept watch over Jerusalem, especially the area of Herod's Temple. He passed the guards without any delay, whisking his cloak to the side so as to ensure their recognition of him. He entered a large hall that then gained him entrance to a secluded room, quite large and spacious. In the room, among others, were Caiaphas, Herod's vizier, and the commander of the Roman Legion. They were obviously anxious to discuss a matter of grave importance.

"Hail, Caesar!" saluted Amelaus as he approached the group. They all returned the salutation, almost in unison.

"We have awaited your return and report with great anticipation, Amelaus," stated Herod's vizier. "Are you in?"

"Your Excellencies," responded Amelaus, "Our man has again met with the Essene known as Yeshua and he has all but accepted his conversion and offerings. Yeshua has scheduled him to meet with the Leader of Damascus in the next few days. I trust we have already taken care of that difficulty?"

"Joachanin ben Zechariah was arrested again at the Jordan earlier this evening. He is in confinement," answered Caiaphas. "I rather suspect that if we keep him too long, the people will use that alone as a reason to cause riots as they did before. We must remove him to Herod as quickly as possible. Herod will remove him to his fortress at Machaeros where he will spend what days we give him. At least the people will then not rest in the hope of his release but will believe him dead. If that provokes an uprising, we will be prepared for it and finally identify the root of these insurrections."

"I detect a jealousy of this man in your tone, Caiaphas," commented the Roman. "Is there more to your hatred of this man than his mere babblings?"

"He is an enemy of Caesar, Herod, and the people," answered Caiaphas in a deep, foreboding tone. "Regardless of my personal feelings for the man, we need to silence him for the common good."

"All of this is as per the instructions of Pilate," interjected the Roman commander. "His excellency is more than ready to get rough with these revolutionaries and their collaborators if they kick up too much of a fuss. Pilate has no problem spilling blood-the more the better. Enough is enough with this rabble. They have no appreciation for the new order we have brought to them," said the Roman commander.

"Are we going to be able to obtain the names of the collaborators and especially the leaders of the revolution?" Caiaphas asked Amelaus. "Are our suspicions going to be verified, that Damascus is behind all this, or at least involved in supporting the resistance?"

Amelaus spoke without hesitation, "Yeshua is presented to me as nothing more than a spiritual leader. But, there are some others, core men of the descendents of the Davidic line. I cannot be sure, yet, but I think you are correct that we have unmasked the ringleader of the movement in this Immerser, Joachanin. I need to give the man Yeshua more time to trust Reu, and we need to interrogate Joachanin as soon as possible. As with so many of these people, I imagine he will not tell us much on direct examination, so we must trick him into giving us related information that we can corroborate and make our deductions from there."

"You are too good at this sort of thing, Amelaus," remarked the Roman commander. "No wonder Caesar made you a citizen of the Empire."

"It is my greatest reward," Amelaus responded with a wide smile.

"A word of caution, gentlemen," the Roman commander moved to the center as he spoke. "This is going to be an extended, long-term operation to learn everything we can about this revolutionary movement. We cannot be hasty. This cult of David has been waxing and waning for a thousand years. We must ensure that it and all of its sympathizers are universally and forever wiped out. So, let us proceed with intent to be thorough. As such, I will be the focal point for the information gathered by our sources. Amelaus, from now on I expect you to report directly to me or to Herod's advisor. I will then determine what we need to distribute to the rest of those here assembled. The final action we take, if any, will be ordered by Pilate, and Pilate alone. Is this understood?"

All agreed to his terms.

"I really have no intention of forfeiting my personal belongings and wealth to make this gesture to this Yeshua by Reu more desirable," said Amelaus, "even though I am willing to put them in jeopardy for the sake of Caesar and Herod. So, may I have some assurance that what I put up is replaced once we have accomplished our goals?"

"Caesar is appreciative of all who serve him as you do, Amelaus," answered the Roman commander. "But, this is Herod's responsibility, and Caesar is not subject to any requirements. Herod will ensure the offer is repaid in the event it is lost. It is his rule we are really protecting here. Is that not true Caiaphas?"

"It will be done according to Caesar's desires," answered Caiaphas.

"Then we are done for the night?" asked the Roman.

"Yes," answered Caiaphas.

"Hail, Caesar!" the Commander saluted as he stood and left with his aides.

"Hail, Caesar!" responded Caiaphas and Herod's vizier, and Amelaus.

The men stood side by side until they were alone in the room.

Then Caiaphas spoke. "The Romans do not understand the culture of these people as we do. Caesar would not give them any quarter and move more quickly to silence these suspects, if his representatives here fully understood the danger."

"Yes, Holiness," the vizier responded. "May I inform the High Priest that Herod is fearful of this madman, not merely cognizant of his motivations as you are? What is your desire in the matter?"

"The Immerser needs to disappear. Whatever Herod wants to do, he must never allow Joachanin ben Zechariah to be seen by the people again."

"What of uprisings in his defense?" asked the vizier.

"A most unfortunate side effect that we must smash with the might of Rome." Caiaphas muttered through clenched teeth. "I want no more interference from this madman and deceiver. I am the High Priest! He is not even permitted in the Temple!"

The vizier backed away. This was no man to cross or question. "Your words will be delivered to Herod," the vizier said as calmly as he could.

Amelaus looked at Caiaphas, nodding approvingly.

Caiaphas turned away and looked over at the Temple. "Very well," was all he said.

***

Jude received word of Joachanin's arrest and transport to Tiberias in Galilee. He met with Jacob and they assembled a large group of the brethren of the Way and traveled to outside of Herod's palace in Tiberias. Along the path, they stopped and gathered other Jews who respected Joachanin and the pious ones of Damascus. The people, led by Jacob and Jude, became incensed and surrounded Herod's palace day and night demanding the release of their true High Priest. Herod called Joachanin into his chambers.

"Why do you foment this sedition against us, Joachanin?" asked Herod.

"You are not a Jew, not until you and your house truly fulfill the law of the third generation for an Idumean Edomite."

Joachanin was referring to a law in the Torah that stated Edomites could fully convert after three generations of loyal followers of the Torah. Joachanin was pointing out that none of the Herodians had accomplished the requirements. "HaShem has given to me, by the lineage of my birth, the right and duty to interpret Torah. The niece marriage is but part of a bigger problem. Torah says a man should take his dead brother's wife to raise up seed to his brother. But, you married your brother's wife who already had children. My problem is your insistence on taking wives of your relatives and sleeping with them in their periods, then allowing them and yourself access to the Holy Temple in this defiled state, not even taking the time for immersion in a mikvah. You also offer sacrifices to idols, and to Caesar. You cannot do this. Caesar is not HaShem, and you must stay out of the Temple!"

"I am the third generation, Joachanin!" Herod stated emphatically. "In fact, it was the Maccabean Jews who forced my family's conversion. You know this. By our own law I am able to claim Israel as mine. Furthermore, my father built the Temple, and you owe it to us to recognize that fact."

"Your fathers never truly converted, and I cannot be responsible for others forcing you to take on the appearances. And that is the point; you took upon yourselves the outer appearances and immediately began to pollute all you touched, all the while calling yourselves Jews. Jews you are not. And as far as the Temple, in all reality, an unclean man with other unclean men built the Temple. If HaShem would not permit King David to build His Temple, a man who had shed other men's blood even for HaShem's glory, why would HaShem honor that which Herod built? Yet, I still find you foul and your intentions pollute what is otherwise holy, for the first rituals conducted there were done by a legitimate priesthood until your father destroyed them and brought Boethus from Egypt to replace them, he not even a Jew or of the priestly lineage. Herod pawned him to the people as a Jewish priest. That, he certainly was not! Over the last few years, the Romans have constantly changed the priests as if it is their right to dictate to HaShem. This is wickedness, and it pollutes the holy place as assuredly as your foul acts. If you truly seek to set all this right, then allow me to enter the Temple and perform my rightful duties as High Priest, and insist that the Romans depose Caiaphas."

Antipas could see that Joachanin would not back down. He wanted to kill him, but was afraid that the people would riot and overcome his guards. Rome was not privy to these wranglings and had not sent sufficient troops to guard him. Besides, he wanted to appear conciliatory to the people to try and gain their respect. Herod, partially out of fear of the people, released him before he consulted the Romans or Caiaphas.

Jacob and Jude and other members of Joachanin's community were joyous when the Rabbi Tsedeq came out to greet them. They could not believe their eyes.

"By the will of HaShem I will live another day to the glory of His Name!" praised Joachanin as the crowd cheered.

Jacob and Jude along with the brethren from Damascus took positions around their master to protect him from the people pressing to get near him. They could hear the crowd calling him "Yeshua," meaning savior of the people. While this seemed appropriate to the men of Damascus, Joachanin stopped and begged the people to listen to him.

"People of Israel listen to me," he began. "HaShem has blessed me that my words have filled your hearts to His glory. But, there is another who has come that you must look to for your liberty and salvation. My time is coming to an end, even now, and while these here with me are the salt of the earth, you must prepare yourselves for the chosen one of HaShem who will lead you to the Kingdom. You have heard this good news! And, the one who will replace me is here before you, and I say unto you that Jacob is my heir when I am taken by HaShem."

Jacob was stunned. Jude was angered. The crowd was bewildered. While word of Joachanin's recognition of Joses had spread through the brethren of the Damascus Community, which had caused enough confusion, this announcement went beyond the realms of reason in the eyes of Jacob and Jude. Jacob was not of the line of the High Priest Aaron, and could not hold such a position. Had the Moreh Ha Tsedeq's imprisonment caused some unseen damage to him that impeded his normal wisdom? As the brethren encouraged the Teacher along his way, he leaned over to Jacob and whispered in his ear.

"You shall go to your brother, Joses, and ask him for a gift, which he shall reveal to you. From that moment, you become my heir."

Jacob stared at Joachanin's eyes that were as clear and self-assured as he had ever seen them. Jacob's own emotions became unsettled, and his mind raced from one part of Torah to another, from one code of the Community to another. Joachanin could see his discomfort.

"I am not of the priestly line, Teacher," Jacob responded so that Joachanin would know he had heard him. "How is it lawful, seeing as we disagreed with the Hasmonaeans over this issue? What have I missed?"

"Fear not, ben Abbas," Joachanin said as he slowed his pace. "HaShem will confirm it to you in His own time, and you and your brother, Joses, shall be the manifestation of HaShem's will for us."

"Your son? What of your son? He is your heir. It is his right!" exclaimed Jacob.

"Of the line of Aaron, yes, but until he is grown and ready, it remains with you," said Joachanin.

At that moment, Miriam and Joses were participating in the ceremony at Bethshemesh that would assure his right before HaShem to assume the heirship of all Israel. He had met all the requirements but this one, and it was his wife Miriam who needed to complete the ceremony. Gathered about the couple were a number of close associates and priestly leaders from On and Israel's own Bethshemesh, as well as Kefa, Andrew, Eleazer and Martha.

Miriam held a small bottle that contained tears she had collected from herself over many years. While a type of pagan custom that was condemned by pious Jews, the tear bottle still had an important and required significance in this ceremony. She took the stopper out of the small bottle and poured them over Joses' feet. She then used her long hair to wipe the tears away. All of this was symbolic of Israel giving up its connections to other gods and the return of a repentant Israel to HaShem as well as the recognition that Joses was her King. She was representing the position of the goddess giving life to the king, an ancient ritual practiced by the royal Egyptians. But, they had learned it from Abraham, the patriarch of the Israelites.

Then, using water carried from the Jordan, Miriam washed Joses from head to foot repeating sacred words taught to her by Joses and the priests of On. Miriam then anointed him with oil of spikenard on his head after the manner of the Davidic Dynasty, but then moved on and further covered him from head to foot with the sacred oil repeating sacred words of the ritual as was part of a secret handed down from the hidden law of Moses, a secret ritual from the descendants of Shem from ancient Egypt and delivered to the more righteous heirs of the Israelites.

All were silent as Joses spoke.

"I tell you all the truth. The father of Israel is in me, and I in him. All who have ears to hear, let them hear. The Kingdom of Heaven is at hand. All that is the father's will be mine. I hold the birthright of Israel as I stand in the place of Joseph and his father Israel. But, see that you tell no man, for this calling is completed only at the time of the reconciliation and remembrance."

Joses was now ready for his destiny.

CHAPTER SIX

Herod confided to Caiaphas what he had done in releasing Joachanin ben Zechariah. Caiaphas was outraged, and would have killed Herod himself for his stupidity if he could have gotten away with it. Yet, while not at all supportive of Herod's decision to allow Joachanin to go free, he recognized that Herod was Tetrarch of Galilee with full power over the Jews of that region as decreed by Caesar. Reluctantly, Caiaphas finally accepted the fact and tried to again coordinate with Herod. The men agreed that they needed a new plan. It was time for another meeting with Pilate's officers, or maybe even Pilate himself.

After a few days, the meeting took place.

"No more mistakes!" Caiaphas still could not calm himself. He had been angry for days. "I tell you that Joachanin is the leader of the Sicarii. I am certain of it! His words fire the passions of the people and he accuses us of all manner of iniquities. These people have been uncivilized, warring nomads most of their history, and when a civilized society tries to show them the way to peace and prosperity, they kill them!"

"Calm down Joseph, I know you are not one of their kind," Pilate said to Caiaphas in a meager Greek, as he did not know Aramaic. "I can assure you that I will obtain absolute control over all of Palestine. How many of these impudent rascals have I already dispatched? We will find their weakness and exploit it. Now, this Joachanin?"

The meeting between Pilate, Herod, and Caiaphas was taking place at the Palace of the High Priest in Jerusalem. Here was the most appropriate place to discuss the issues and survey the breadth of Judea. Galilee, about seventy miles to the north, had ample and lush facilities, but the rulers wanted to feel the heartbeat of the people. There was no better place than Jerusalem and the Temple.

"I tried to explain to Caiaphas that it was better to let Joachanin go than to risk another rebellion over gnats and vomit," explained Herod, referring to Joachanin's and the people's anger over small issues that he felt did not concern them. He also reviled against the filth of the words the people had pronounced against himself, Caesar, and Caiaphas. "While he may indeed incite small groups to violence, I find his words console most of the populace and they await their deliverance from their god. That," he chuckled, "will never happen. He dulls their sense of reality and they wait like lambs for the slaughter."

"Enough of your ridiculous estimates of their abilities and intentions! We have tortured endless numbers of these Sicarii and they refuse, by what power I cannot fathom, to answer any question put to them. That is not the mindset of one who is waiting like a lamb to the slaughter. This shows their resolve!" Caiaphas shook his fist at Herod as he spoke, barely able to contain his fury. "Joachanin travels far and wide, seemingly calling no place an abode. He dresses like no other man and yet he is held in high respect by all of Palestine! He has followers throughout the land and he is the Teacher in Damascus where he preaches to the Essenes. Fortunately, most of them seem wholly unwilling to follow his notions against us. All they do is meditate and tend to their duties. If it were not for his appearance, so unlike theirs, I think he would even lay claim to their consciences. And you," he pointed to Herod, "do nothing. I have commissioned spies to find these things out when you should have done so!"

"Sit down!" commanded Pilate, directing Caiaphas to take his seat. He could not afford the High Priest to show such disdain for Herod. It could be bad for Pilate in the long run if word ever got back to Caesar. "We must approach this problem with a methodology and ruthlessness, yes, but we also must take advantage of time. That, I believe, we have plenty of. To do something in too much haste could return us a disadvantage. We need to lay a foundation."

As Caiaphas took his seat, Pilate stood and moved to the center of the room. "You have the key to it, Joseph," he said to Caiaphas. "These people need civilization, a way of life that only Rome can offer them. We need to take the time to convince them that we are their saviors, saving them from endless toils, the invasions of other nations, filth and blood, and the civil wars constantly being brought upon them by their own kind. Rome is their friend, not their enemy. I think we can all agree that Caesar is the key to stability. But, I realize that even their years in the Babylonian Captivity did not impress these facts upon their minds as a people. So, how should we proceed?" He looked at both Herod and Caiaphas, each choosing not to respond, or not knowing how.

Pilate continued, "Varus destroyed so much of this land years ago, even attacking and destroying the armies of the Judean resistance that had besieged Sabinus' legion here in Jerusalem. Do you remember what happened when he approached the Jews in Jerusalem after he defeated the resistance? The people of the city said that the sedition began because of the numbers of people who came here for the feast, and they placed the blame on their own people from outside the city, and that they, the people of Jerusalem, were as besieged by the revolutionaries as Sabinus' legion. Look at the people's disdain for the Samaritans who in every way but blood are like themselves. Here is their weakness. They are too independent and cannot forge any lasting alliance for their own good. Varus forgave many, even some of the leaders. He also crucified many, principally those who showed no remorse or were in any way associated with messianic sympathies. My point is, gentlemen, that we can use their own political and military ineptness to our advantage. When Varus forgave so many, he infected their passions with doubt for their cause. But, he also ruthlessly destroyed the instigators, putting the blame for the unrest and destruction squarely on them. It is a divide and conquer, gentlemen, a famous maxim of Julius Caesar. Let's create more division and mistrust of their own kind, all the while pointing out the benefits of Rome."

Herod and Caiaphas looked at each other, nodding in somewhat of an agreement.

"What of your spies, Antipas?" asked Pilate. "Are we getting good information from them?"

Caiaphas interrupted, "Actually, your excellency, I have a man in a particularly admirable position who is, even at this moment, inside the very core of the suspects. Antipas and I both agree that he is our best resource."

"Very well," Pilate commented. "Now we need more of that information, all he can provide us. It is possible that there is a weakness that we can exploit, create a problem, and then proceed to provide its resolution. Do you see what I am getting to?"

"I believe so," said Herod Antipas. "If our man can get into a position where we can feed disinformation to the resistance, we can manipulate them to our advantage, even making ourselves look like the champions of the people."

"Now you are thinking," Pilate praised Herod. "Let us use the Immerser, uh, I believe that is what they call him, isn't that right, Caiaphas?" Caiaphas shook his head in the affirmative. "Yes, well, let's use him not only to embarrass the resistance, but to be the bait for its demise. If not him, then one of the other leaders we uncover. Agreed?"

Herod and Caiaphas again nodded their heads in agreement and Caiaphas then spoke. "The Immerser will have appointed a successor, it is one of the things these men do as a habit. But, it also tends to cause divisions. That may be the best seam for us to exploit. I will instruct Reu to find that seam."

"My friends," Pilate raised his arms wide and high, "I see that we have come to a significant milestone. This will be the beginning of a long and prosperous relationship. Hail, Caesar!" he saluted as he left the hall, his right hand raised high and then striking his left breast.

"Hail, Caesar!" responded Herod and Caiaphas in unison.

"I think I am going to like this Roman," said Caiaphas. "He is vicious and thorough. We may keep our positions yet."

***

Jacob had returned to Damascus after leaving Joachanin and those with him once they reached Jericho. Joachanin never let much time go by without teaching by the Jordan River, and he anxiously hurried to his traditional spot again. However, Jacob knew he needed time to meditate and study, so he continued on to Damascus. The information from Joachanin was startling to him on a number of points. He would remain in separation and meditation for many, many days.

As Jacob returned to his spiritual affairs, Jude and Joses both realized that time was growing short. On Jude's part, his concern for the ever-growing rift in Damascus over the Teacher's acceptance of Joses had to take a second seat in his priorities. The Romans were gaining in strength and power everyday. The survival of Israel was obviously at stake, and there were too many independent and uncoordinated efforts by various resistance groups throughout Palestine. Jude's earlier efforts at consolidation had been remotely successful, but he could not forge any lasting alliances, especially once the leaders of those groups were caught and executed. Even the Zealots were becoming splintered. Joses' separation from Jude made coordination and any concentration of forces nearly impossible, especially since the Roman Varus' success against the resistance years earlier. The two men decided to meet once again and try to resolve their differences. They would meet in Pella, east of the Jordan River.

"My brother," Jude spoke first as the men approached each other. It was daylight, the preferred method of meeting at this time as it appeared less suspicious. Although Jude would not normally travel with women, it helped to cover his real purposes. Two women and several men accompanied him, all of them armed with the notorious sicar Arabian dagger, from which the Romans gave them the name "Sicarii," hidden under their clothing. Jude embraced his brother and spoke again, "It is good that we can come together for the good of Israel and the glory of HaShem. It has been too long."

"Yes, I agree," Joses said as he returned the embrace of his brother. The two men held each other at arm's length studying one another's eyes. "How is your family?"

"Rachel and Jacob are very well. And we expect another child soon," answered Jude. "And what about your family?" Jude did not like his brother's familial arrangements, but he would not violate custom and etiquette by failing to inquire of their welfare.

"All are well, Miriam is expecting in Tishrei as is your Rachel, so we should have an eventful month," Joses laughed, again hugging his brother with his right arm as they turned and walked to a sitting area under some fig trees. "Let us sit here," Joses pointed to a cleared area that would work well for them. Joses had not brought any women, but his four guards were armed with the same familiar weapons. The two men and their companions sat down in the shade. Jude and Joses looked at each other for a long moment. Joses broke the silence.

"My brother, we have been at odds over many things for most of our lives. What is important, however, is that we share the same goals for Israel. It is doubtful that we will agree on the terms of the Throne, but we can agree on everything else until that issue is unavoidable."

Jude was impressed that Joses wasted no time and cut to the important issues at hand. It was not like him. Jude had remembered Joses always dealing in circumventions and excuses. "Agreed with this exception," Jude was adamant, "that my leadership in the resistance is secured and we have the resources in place to give the kittim a wound which will not heal. I cannot abrogate that position of leadership. The command of the resistance, for now, must remain with me."

Joses knew it would come to this. If Jude remained in command of all available forces, it would be unlikely that Joses could gather the support of enough of the people to assume overall rule. He looked into Jude's eyes for a long period, thinking back to his earlier years, his schooling at On, and the paths he had chosen. If HaShem determined that he would take his rightful place as the bearer of the crimson thread, then nothing Jude could do would supplant him.

Besides, the success of the resistance and the salvation of Israel was the important issue here. But, he had a caveat.

"My brother, I cannot in good conscience abdicate my claims or I may forfeit all that HaShem has promised me." Jude squirmed on his seat, preparing to defend his argument. But, Joses quickly continued, "My agreement is that we allow you to continue in command, and you will get the majority of the new members for the Community. Only allow me to keep those already under my command, and give us a tenth of those recruited so that we may give them a chance to choose whether they be with me, or with you. But allow all to be in the Way, so that none are left out. The command of the tenth of the new members for my use is all that is asked of you. You get all the rest. The Teacher has accepted me, but I will not deprive you, my brother. You are able and willing. May HaShem decide that issue."

"Let me understand, Joses," Jude said. "You will gather the people as I am doing and keep only ten percent of all who enter the Community? My right to the throne is not in danger, and you will lead your forces under my overall command? All you ask is that we let HaShem determine who will be King?" Jude tilted his head slightly sideways, looking at Joses from the corners of his eyes, conveying a slight disbelief. Jude did not understand Joses' ease of alliance. "This sounds like devilish talk to me," Jude explained. "It opens the door to severe strife unless we resolve it now."

"This is a treaty, if you will, until all Israel is secure. A house divided against itself cannot stand. If I fight the kittim and defeat them, it is a victory for you as well. And the same goes for the other; if you defeat them it is good for me. If they depart, whose power has achieved it?" Joses waited for an answer.

"HaShem," replied Jude.

"We must unite for now and put aside the issue of the throne," Joses explained. "If you do not accept these terms, my campaign will still continue, and all care will be taken not to interfere with you. I only look at the chance to better concentrate our efforts."

Jude's suspicions could not allow him to agree to any future debate over the throne. But, he could see the wisdom in this alliance for the defeat of the kittim. Joachanin, the Teacher, had recognized Joses, but also said HaShem would be the one to ultimately decide based upon the works of the brethren. Jude felt he still had an edge. His thoughts raced as he looked for a compromise that would keep him in the best position of power. Joses would take a tenth of all the new followers? Not a chance.

"How about you keeping a tenth of only those you and your followers personally bring into the Community?" asked Jude.

Joses thought a moment. This was designed to keep Jude's number superior by such a large margin that Joses may never attain the support needed to gain him the rule of all Israel. Still, it was reasonable under the circumstances, and Joses knew he had little time anyway. The kittim could smash all Palestine before much longer. That would make the ultimate question of who obtains the throne over Israel totally meaningless.

"That is agreeable to me," Joses answered. He realized that he had not gained all that he had wanted. But, he had not revealed his entire plan. "I will remain primarily in Galilee and do the work there, keeping a tenth of all the new members. That leaves you with Judea and Perea. All that is left is the question of Jerusalem itself. In that regard, I only ask that you agree that we have access to the Temple."

Jude realized that the best conversions to the resistance came from Galilee. But, he would get the majority of them, plus all from Judea and Perea. And, as far as the Temple, that seemed only right to share it. Besides, Joses never thought much of the Temple in Jerusalem, anyway. "Yes, we can share the Temple in Jerusalem, and, I will take Perea also," he stated. Perea was the area east of the Jordan and included the town of Pella they were now in.

Joses looked somber for a moment, and then responded to Jude's demand. "Yes, that is agreeable. So be it."

Jude was more than confidant. He arose first and assisted Joses to his feet. All of the members of the party arose with them. "This is a momentous occasion," Jude was feeling more excited by the moment. "We need to set into place a method of communication as soon as possible so that we do not have to meet again personally, or at least not so often. I think our similarities are close enough that most anyone would think us the same person. So, why not use that to our advantage?"

Joses recognized that Jude was right. It was a brilliant idea. "Yes, brother, that is a most effective weapon for us. Why not use a similar name for both of us. That may better serve our purposes."

Jude knew exactly what that should be. "Yeshua," Jude said. "In the hands of HaShem we are the saviors of our people. There is no other name given for such a glorious purpose."

"Yeshua it will be," replied Joses.

The method for communication was then decided upon and the names of the carriers identified. With these last issues of administration and coordination, the men shook hands and began their return to their respective homes.

As he walked out of the town with his guards, Joses spoke to his most able man and confidant, Eleazer. "Jude has agreed to take only Judea and Pella," Joses said, smiling at Eleazer as they walked north toward Galilee. "He is not interested in the fate of Samaria nor the dispersed Israelites living outside of Judea and Perea. We have won a great victory today, Eleazer." Both men began laughing in disbelief at their good fortune, and the other guards joined in. "Jude will have nothing to do with Samaria as he considers them unclean, even though there is Israelite blood to be found there and multitudes of those who serve HaShem and the Torah. We also have great support in the Diaspora, especially in Egypt, India, and the gentile lands of the north."

As he spoke, Joses walked more briskly, hardly able to control his excitement. He had spent his younger years traveling with his Uncle Joseph, gaining a huge following throughout the known world where he had been. "Jude will have the tenth of the converts from Galilee, and all those of Judea and Perea, but we will have all the rest from Samaria and the world!" He felt his ascent to the throne was assured. "HaShem has blessed us," Joses told his men."

"Alleluia, Alleluia, Alleluia," responded Eleazer and the guards. "HaShem has blessed us with your presence and wisdom. You are Yehoshua ben Joseph, Yehoshua Ha Mashiach ben Joseph," they all said in hushed tones that they wanted to shout from the housetops.

"Ben Adam is my name," Joses said to them. The appellation meant the Son of Man.

They looked at him with an even deeper respect. He was telling them he had reached the highest initiations in On. But, they knew they needed to keep the secret quiet, and that they could tell no one.

While Jude more earnestly sought for followers in Judea and Perea, Joses concentrated in Galilee and Samaria. Joses would keep his recruiting efforts in Samaria from Jude as long as he could, and would concentrate on Jews outside Egypt in the Diaspora after he solidified his following in Samaria and Galilee. With his reputation in On, he could easily count on the Jews in Egypt. Joses knew he would need to get as many of these people as possible into Palestine for the final decision on the throne, but that would come in time.

Both men sent representatives out identifying their master as Yeshua, just as Jude and Joses had agreed. The method of conversion was quite simple. As in the past when Jude would preach, he would interview the new members and identify potential Zealots for the resistance. These would then be worked through the system of the Community Way of Damascus and given the secret tokens for their missions against the kittim and Herodians. Joses was doing the same in Galilee and Samaria, keeping all the converts from Samaria and only a tenth from Galilee. The rest from Galilee were referred to Kefa who remained "neutral" in the disagreements over the throne. He would accomplish the necessities for Jude without parting from Joses. It was somewhat uncomfortable, but the system seemed to work for now.

This procedure was in place for many months, and the bitterness in the country seemed to quiet down. It appeared to the Sanhedrin in Jerusalem, the Herodians, and the Romans, that there was a massive religious revival underway. What dangers would such a revitalized Jewish population present? And, who was this 'Yeshua' they were hearing about? With what information they had, they suspected it was Jude alone, as all the descriptions they had gathered sounded like him. But, no bother; The Essenes were always fervent in their spiritual ways. As long as he didn't attack the establishment like Joachanin ben Zechariah had, who would care? Stability was more important than a few religious fanatics.

Caiaphas, on the other hand, remained skeptical. He pushed his informants harder and demanded more information. His suspicious nature and his craving to eliminate Joachanin and the resistance drove him to emphasize his belief that more violence would soon descend upon the nation from these robbers and innovators. His arguments to Pilate finally won over the Procurator's concerns.

As Pilate and the Herodians suspected, the relative calm again gave way to sporadic and increasing violence. The days and months passed as more unrest claimed the land. Pilate lost his patience and bore down harder on the people, setting up images in the land to honor Caesar and insult the populace. In retaliation, groups of people would revolt, only to have Pilate crush them, killing most and selling the survivors into slavery. The actions by Pilate and the Herodians were actually the best reason for the continuing success of Jude and Joses. Caiaphas, on the other hand, could not understand Pilate's wavering from shrewd manipulation and covert operations to overt violence. Caiaphas sensed instability in Pilate as he came to better understand him. As he had in the past, Caiaphas relied more and more upon his inside man, Reu.

Like his brothers, Jude and Jacob, Joses was quietly building a following, preaching to the "multitudes" (a code word to describe the people from whom he would take those committed to him as Jude was doing from Damascus) in areas from Capernaum in the north of Galilee and on into Samaria. His message was not unlike that of his brothers. As he agreed, from Galilee he sent all but a tenth of those he converted to Kefa for Jude who would attach them to the Community in Damascus. But, of the tenth Joses kept, he did not introduce to Damascus. He instructed them all on his own and built an organization similar to that of Damascus, save the governing council of twelve elders, which he respected. His intent was to show his ability to obtain followers and then to demonstrate leverage that would convince Damascus of his abilities. While risky, this method could be well disguised from the kittim and the Herodians, and a great asset to the Way when, and if, he obtained the throne.

One afternoon, in the heat of the day, Joses was walking through a section of Capernaum talking with his disciples. The topic of the conversation was the coming of the "kingdom of heaven," a codeword for those who had been initiated into the resistance. To the uninitiated, it seemed that Joses was only talking about something more along the lines of a spiritual awakening, a rising of consciousness or awareness of HaShem and his ways. But, for those initiated, the phrase meant the coming of the Israelite Kingdom in Palestine. So, Joses could speak to both groups, and have them each understand him in a different way, yet edify all who heard him.

A Herodian tax collector named Mattathias was sitting at his post of collection where the people were required to pay various taxes. Normally, he worked only in Judea collecting the Roman tax there, but he was now expanding his services to Herod in Galilee. He looked up just as Joses was passing by. He had seen Jude, Joses' brother, preaching when he was in Judea and thought this must be the same man.

"Brethren, come over here, please," he requested of Joses and his disciples. The formality of "brethren" was his way of trying to ease the burden of the communication. He knew that these men would never consider him a true brother, even if he were a Jew. Joses stopped to listen to him so as not to appear obviously disgusted with his profession, which kept the Jews subservient to the Herodians and the Romans. Mattathias continued, "I have seen you before, Yeshua, in Judea. I have always been fascinated by your teachings about how we should obey HaShem. What should I do about the tax from you? Are you Judean or Galilean? Have you paid the tax yet?"

This was a difficult situation. Roman soldiers were standing a short distance away and any hint of his unwillingness to subscribe to the tax and the occupation would be dangerous.

"You are from Galilee, are you not?" asked Mattathias again, hoping for more money. He could not require Joses to pay if he were from Judea and paid the tax there.

"Did you not see me in Judea?" asked Joses, trying to avoid giving Mattathias any money.

"Yes, Yeshua, I did, when I went to the Temple," answered Mattathias.

"Then you should know that I do not have to pay the tax here in Galilee," responded Joses. His response was overheard by one of the Roman soldiers in the group just a few cubits (i.e. a cubit is about eighteen inches) from Joses. The answer Joses gave seemed reasonable, so the soldier turned back to his companions.

"Ah, yes," answered Mattathias, "But I never received a tax from you there."

"There are many tax collectors in Judea," answered Joses. The Roman then looked back towards the small gathering around Joses, staring intently at him.

The hearers of the "Way" who were not yet members but were disciples or followers were called fish. This simply meant that they were not yet part of the community. One of these disciples, not yet fully understanding Joses' teachings, brought out a Roman coin from his pocket. "Here, Mattathias, take this for payment."

Joses reached for the coin and looked at it. It was a Roman coin. While he would not have ordinarily paid this collector, it seemed only appropriate to do so now. The coin was Roman, not Judean, and it was not really from Joses, nor a member of the Way.

"See the image on the coin?" Joses showed his followers and Mattathias. "Whose image is it?"

They all answered, "Caesar's." Judean coins did not have graven images on them.

"Then return to Caesar what is Caesar's, and to HaShem, what belongs to HaShem," Joses said in a veiled language. It seemed appropriate to the Roman, who understood little Aramaic and could tell this was no unruly group. To Mattathias, a schooled man, the answer seemed strange.

"HaShem says that if we obey his laws, we have no reason to disobey man's. So, what are you saying, Yeshua? Does not Caesar rule the world? Has not HaShem delivered it all into his hands?"

"Caesar's money is Caesar's," replied Joses as he turned to walk away, "But, Caesar never gave man life, nor heart, nor mind, nor body, nor spirit. And, HaShem never gave him the earth as his own, only as his administration, and that not over men who do not seek it. Men's hearts and minds are HaShem's as well as all that is in the earth. No man is HaShem. The Lord Our God is one Lord, and we have no other, certainly no man.

The veiled language was not entirely lost on the tax collector. He realized that Joses was really saying that Israel is not to pay a tax to anyone, but only to offer their sacrifices to HaShem. As he watched Joses walk away, he went to the Roman who had watched part of the exchange.

"Do you speak our language?" asked Mattathias.

The Roman answered in Greek, "I speak Greek much better."

Mattathias also spoke Greek and he responded, "Did you witness that incident?"

"Yes," said the Roman. "It seemed as if it was of no consequence."

"On the contrary," said Mattathias, "that man has gathered Judeans around him in Jerusalem, and he always says very strange things that I think border on sedition. I think he would deny the tax if it were not for his disciple who had a coin. Maybe you should keep an eye on him."

The Roman could really care less. There had been no unruliness and a tax was paid. Who cared? "I am satisfied as is Caesar," the Roman said. "Should I see him again I will watch him closely."

Mattathias shrugged and walked away, returning to his post to collect more tax.

***

The month of Tishrei was approaching and Miriam was about to give birth once again. Joses returned to Bethshemesh for the arrival, and to take part in the rituals for the mother and child. The household and the attendants, as well as the Priest from On, then traveled to Beit Lechem for the birth itself. The child was born almost on Yom Kippur, the Day of Atonement, just as the traditions of the Dynastic Code outlined. Joses named his son Joshua, and he was the second heir to his father's throne. The name was a commemoration and sign that all his preparation and effort would soon free his beloved Israel. It was also to mark his passage into the Workings of the Merkava, the ultimate goal of the Hechalot. This was the culmination of the teachings and secrets of the prophets, the means by which they attained knowledge of HaShem and His will. The name of Joses' second son was a symbol of Joses' determination to become an adopted son of HaShem.

Likewise, Jude's wife Rachel gave birth to their second son in Damascus. Jude named his son Simon, and he was second in line to his father's throne.

Surprisingly, there was no enmity between the brothers during this time. The agreements they had made seemed to be successful, and much was being accomplished. However, the undercurrent whispered that they were merely postponing the inevitable clash that could come in the future.

After the births, Jude returned to his preaching in Jerusalem and Joses' family went to Bethshemesh while he returned to Galilee. They were not sure when they may see each other again. But, Miriam and the family would stay only for a few more days.

At about that same time, Joachanin ben Zechariah again became the obsession of Caiaphas. Through information received from his spy, Reu, Caiaphas was certain that the man was not only inciting the populace to revolt, but was insulting Herod, Caesar, and those in power. It was sedition, not just preaching. Furthermore, Reu had learned that there were other members of Joachanin's sect that were dispersed throughout the land who initiated actions independent of him. But, Reu could not ascertain the mechanism of their communication and coordination.

Caiaphas decided that Herod needed to act again. Sending a

message to Herod, Caiaphas reminded him that the people must see Joachanin as the source of their sufferings, and they must see Herod as the answer to free them from those same sufferings. The plan called for an influx of Idumeans, cousins of Herod from the south, who would pose as Judeans destroying, looting, pillaging and raping at Joachanin's insistence. These men would attack throughout the southern border of Judea and the area of Perea on the east. That way they could better disguise their actual movements and origins. The people would believe that the warring Jewish factions of the past were returning.

The plan went very well, at first. For weeks the raids produced the desired effects. Roman soldiers and Herodian representatives would respond to an area that had been "cleansed" by these "avengers of the Immerser" who claimed they were rooting out the evil in Israel. The people believed themselves the victims of madmen. They complained that they were not guilty of the accusations made against them by the religious fanatics, whoever they really were. When questioned by the Herodians, the common sentiment was that they believed Joachanin had been talking about the Herodian family and rulers, not the people as a whole. Yet, they believed these henchmen were certainly his followers. As they "cleansed" a village or settlement, one of their numbers would read the Torah aloud, pronouncing the judgment of the Immerser upon them. The Herodians assured the people that they would bring Joachanin to justice.

During this time, Joachanin had heard of these accusations and vehemently denied them. His followers and allies, among them Jacob, Jude, and Joses, also tried to dispel the accusations. But, they were not privy to the expert manipulations put upon them by the Herodian and Roman apparatus. They could only react at this point, not proactively counter the negative propaganda concerning them. It all happened so fast.

Taken in chains from the northern part of the Jordan River where he had again been preaching against the Herodians, Joachanin was transported north towards Herod's palace in Tiberias. He would never again see freedom, and Herod and Caiaphas hoped that the wheels were set in motion for the dissolution of the resistance.

Word of Joachanin's arrest raced through Galilee and Judea, even before the Teacher left for Herod's Palace. While the settlements that had been raided by the Idumeans acting as followers of Joachanin welcomed the arrest, others were not convinced and several small uprisings started here and there. These uprisings were anticipated, even welcomed by Pilate, and he had the leaders accused of collaborating with Joachanin and his butchers. Upon arrest, the Romans immediately executed them. In the space of a few hours, Pilate had given orders to crucify anyone who was involved in any way. Confusion reigned throughout Palestine. Keeping the people unsure of their true enemies and offering them the hope of stability and security was an excellent way to gain their confidence and loyalty.

Joses heard of the news of Joachanin's arrest and brought his principle disciples together. No one at that time had made any concerted effort to mount a unified attack to free Joachanin. Furthermore, with all the confusion over the events surrounding the reason for his capture, those loyal to him had found it necessary to proclaim his innocence. But, the rescue was the important thing. If they could not do so before the Teacher reached the Palace at Tiberias, there would be small hope of freeing him. Joses sent scouts to keep an eye on the location of the detail, which, as it turned out, was an entire Roman cohort with several units of the High Priest's guards attached as reinforcements. The situation seemed hopeless as Joses realized he could not mount a force large enough to attack the column. In fact, the Romans would probably just kill Joachanin on the spot should such an eventuality take place. Joses sent word to his brother, Jude. But, the distance would delay any return word for a day or more. Kefa was south, conducting business not far from Pella. Joses sent word to Kefa, as well.

While busy preaching near Jerusalem as 'Yeshua,' Jude received word from Reu of Joachanin's arrest. It was deliberate information from Pilate and Caiaphas to set a trap. Jude was not aware he was being manipulated. Reu told him that he was not sure how large the escort detail was, but that he thought it was small and heading to Tiberias. Reu asked him who he could find that would be able to take some action. Jude, wisely, told him that it was all in HaShem's hands, that they could do nothing. Reu was not at the level where he could be privy to any of the military plans of the Zealots. However, Jude excused himself and asked Reu to send a message to Jacob who was in Damascus. Reu reluctantly agreed, as he did not want to depart Jerusalem without notifying Amelaus that the news of Joachanin disturbed this man called 'Yeshua' and that he seemed to be preparing some response. Before leaving for Damascus, he hurriedly went to Amelaus and left the information.

Realizing the danger of the situation, Jude still made arrangements for a possible counter to what the Herodians had done. He organized a small band and sent runners north to locate Kefa. He also wanted to try and join some of Joses' men or other Zealots placed in the area of Galilee. Believing the size of the Roman force securing Joachanin to be small, he had only fifteen Zealots meet him at Jericho. His hope was that Joses and Kefa could secure more fighters for him before he reached the area of Tiberias. He followed the Jordan River north to Pella. There he learned that his runners had found Kefa before Joses' had. The runners told Jude that Kefa would meet him at the Jordan River southwest of Pella with approximately fifteen more Zealots. He hoped his swift movement with a small force would be rewarded with more Zealots once he arrived.

The movement of his small band went undetected, and they were swift, traveling the near 80 miles in little less than two days. He met Kefa at the designated spot, just outside of the town. They then moved north.

"I doubt we can have any hope of freeing the Teacher," Jude said to Kefa, "But we must at least try." He kept moving but redefined the situation again. "Actually, even if we were to free him, he would need to go into complete hiding. They would never let him be free again."

"What is the plan, then?" asked Kefa.

"Where is Joses? Has word reached him so he can bring us reinforcements?" asked Jude.

"I don't know. I have not seen him for days. I doubt he even knows I was in Pella," answered Kefa. "He may have taken Miriam to Bethshemesh for sacred ordinances or instruction. No one knows for sure at the moment."

"No matter," Jude said with a slight disappointment in his voice. Here was a grand opportunity for a combined allied operation and they did not have time to respond adequately. New plans were probably in order. He slowed his pace and called for a stop while the group rested. "I suppose this was in haste, brother. I should not panic. Jacob is in Damascus and can handle all the affairs of the Community. I doubt we can reach Tiberias in time, so maybe we should conduct some reconnaissance and formulate a plan."

He was up and moving again before Kefa could respond. But, it sounded like a good idea for them not to rush into an unknown situation. The Romans likely had a vastly superior force than they could assemble on such short notice.

As they entered a small valley, Jude realized that his haste to obtain his objective beyond the Jordan was possibly an error, but he proceeded anyway. He needed to observe the areas and get as much information as fast as possible. As they approached a depression in the road, several Roman soldiers appeared out of nowhere and attacked them from the west out of a small ravine. A quick assessment by Jude led him to believe it was a maniple, a small unit of infantry useful for mountain fighting and special missions normally amounting to only a dozen soldiers. The Zealots counterattacked to try and overwhelm the small Roman patrol. Jude and Kefa, leading the charge, hurled themselves forward, blades slicing and thrusting as they moved into the Roman line. Jude had felled two Roman soldiers when he turned to check the disposition of his fighters.

It was then that he saw the second line of Romans with archers aimed at his unprotected guerillas. He yelled as loud as he could, but it was too late. The Roman officer ordered the archers to release, and the arrows found their marks. Jude saw the majority of his men fall, and he himself felt the pain and pressure of an arrow's penetration into his right chest just underneath his arm.

Kefa saw Jude get hit with the arrow and slump to the ground, but could not defend him. He had worked his way down the Roman line and was now not far from the archers who were again preparing to release on the Roman Officer's command. He could see that the Roman force was not only superior, but that they had gained the surprise and may totally annihilate his men. Those of the Zealots who had not been felled by arrows or otherwise wounded were running to the hill on the west and hiding behind rocks. It appeared that the Romans had not covered that flank. In the split second he had time to react, he yelled to his men to escape and ran for the same cover. It would be easier to handle the Romans with the rocks to act as obstacles.

The Roman Officer again gave his command to release the arrows. Kefa heard a whizzing sound about his head as he hurled himself to the ground to escape them. He looked up at his men in the rocks and saw two of them fall who had not made it to the cover. The others then started to run up the hill keeping the rocks between them and the archers. Kefa, fleet of foot, was quickly behind them urging them upward and out of harm's way. Closely behind him came several Roman soldiers.

"Too close to allow them to stay on their feet," thought Kefa out loud as he turned and struck the first soldier across the neck with his blade in a surprise and violent attack that was totally unexpected, slicing through the flesh and sinew to the spinal cord. The second received the same fate as he tried to put his sword through Kefa's stomach. The blade glanced off Kefa's sheath and gave him the instant he needed to dispatch the man, and then Kefa was running again up the hill, urging his men forward. He heard the Roman Officer again order his archers to release.

"Down, now!" Kefa yelled and the Zealots dropped behind any available rock. The arrows ricocheted harmlessly about them, most breaking from impact on the rocks and gravel. The men were up and running again, sweating profusely, gasping for breath, some bleeding from wounds or abrasions, some with Roman blood on them.

But the Romans had their prize. It was Jude they really wanted. While the Zealots who had escaped were now near the top of the hill with several Romans trying to reach them, the Roman Commander felt confident that further pursuit was not in their best interests. He recalled his troops and turned to his next in command.

"Leave them. The second Cohort is pushing to the south and will cut them off," he said. "If there are more, they will be destroyed, too." He then walked over to Jude. Looking down at him on the ground, he could see that Jude was severely wounded, a pool of his blood staining the sand.

***

"We must keep moving," Kefa gasped as he pushed one man ahead of him who was particularly slow. "The ambush was only a small part of the Roman force here. See," Kefa allowed the men who dared to look over the adjacent hilltop, "Over there is the main body of the Romans, and they are trying to maneuver around us to stop our retreat." He was pointing to the west where a visible cloud of dust was already rising above the hills, an unmistakable sign of a sizeable Roman force on the move, possibly a century or even a cohort.

"We have only the hope that HaShem will conceal us from their eyes. We must keep moving and make it across the Jordan before they encircles us to the south." Kefa continued to push them, some stumbling as they headed down the opposite side of the hill and on toward the Jordan River some three furlongs to the east. None dared stop until they reached the river.

"There, see? Cross at the widest point so that the water can cover our footprints," Kefa commanded. Two of them men hesitated. "What are you waiting for?" Kefa demanded.

"We are afraid we will drown!" one of the exhausted men replied.

"Go, now!" Kefa yelled, making the men fear him more than the uncertainty of their abilities. As it turned out, the water was also relatively shallow at this point as none of the men's heads went below the surface during the crossing. The water cleansed their flesh and their clothing, most of the blood and dirt washing off, while it cooled their hot and stressed bodies. Once all were on the other side, the party split up, doing their best to cover their footprints with weeds and other vegetation until they reached a traveled path.

Kefa separated from the last of the band and headed north to the Sea of Galilee, the area where he had taken up residence. Most of the rest of the men had to travel much further south near the Dead Sea to the Community at Damascus. But, they were now far from the action of the past day and the likelihood of discovery by Roman soldiers and scouts who would recognize them was remote. Kefa knew that he had to get word to Joses or his men who should be in Tarichaeae at the south tip of the Sea of Galilee. That was almost a day's journey for him, and that only if he took advantage of all the available time with little rest.

He reached Tarichaeae the next night. He found Joses was indeed there, still gathering his forces and preparing to move north to Tiberias once Jude reached them.

"Kefa!" a startled Joses called his brother's name as he saw him approach their position just west of Tarichaeae. Joses could see that he was exhausted and nearly to the point of collapse. "What has happened?" He took Kefa by the arms and assisted him in the short distance to the encampment. Kefa had not slept in three days, and it showed on his face. He was approaching delirium, but he could still tell his story.

"Joses, my brother, oh, oh, our brother Jude is captured, maybe dead!" he sighed, no strength now left in him. "We were heading north and were ambushed just west of Pella and the Jordan by a Roman century. Jude was wounded and taken prisoner. I don't know if he is alive."

Joses tried to calm him and called for water from one of his men. He brought a large vessel with fresh water and gave it to Joses who then assisted Kefa. As Kefa drank until he was satisfied, Joses looked him over carefully. He noticed that there appeared to be remnants of blood on his hands and clothing, his clothing was torn, and there was a noticeable slash on the sheath for his sword. Joses pulled the sword from its sheath and found dried blood and fresh impact marks on the blade. A fight had certainly happened.

Joses held his brother and then offered him some food. Kefa, hardly able to maintain his composure, slipped in and out of consciousness. Joses put him into the care of two of his men.

Jude must be rescued. There was no other alternative. Failure may mean the identification of Damascus as the seat of the resistance and the most certain death of a valiant, faithful brother. He turned to his men.

"We need to leave immediately. As we head west we will request that the Samaritans give us additional support. Our allies there will give us any aid we need. Eleazer!" he called to his brother in law, his best scout and friend.

"Yes, Joses," Eleazer answered as he ran to his side.

"Run ahead with your men and keep me informed of all that transpires. Also, send word to gather any allies the Samaritans can afford us. Here is my seal." He handed Eleazer the seal. Even though his friends and supporters in Samaria knew Eleazer, Joses did not want to take any chance that his messenger may not have the proper recognition of authority. Eleazer called his men and they ran off to the west. Joses turned to the remainder of his force.

"Only HaShem knows what is ahead of us. Who will go with me?"

All of the men, approximately 100, raised their hands and said, "I will!"

"So be it! May HaShem bless us and our loved ones!" He raised his sword and waited until all with him did the same. Then with a commanding resolve he prayed, "For HaShem, our wives, our children, our brethren and our nation!"

"Amen," came the reply.

At that they began their journey to the west.

CHAPTER SEVEN

With the events now brought to the present, the story continues from the battle Jude and Kefa had with the Romans in the small valley where Jude was captured after being wounded, losing nearly all his band of Zealots. Kefa had escaped with a few survivors, and watched from a distance as the Romans bound and interrogated Jude. All of the other wounded Zealots appeared to have died during the torture the Romans inflicted upon them, their bodies left for the birds and animals. As Kefa and the survivors continued on from the scene of the battle, the Romans prepared Jude for transport to Caesarea and further interrogation. In his mind, Jude was recalling a scripture from the Torah.

"And it came to pass in the time of her travail, that, behold, twins were in her womb. And it came to pass, when she travailed, that the one put out his hand: and the midwife took and bound upon his hand a crimson thread, saying, This came out first. And it came to pass, as he drew back his hand, that, behold, his brother came out: and she said, How hast thou broken forth? This breach be upon thee: therefore his name was called Pharez. And afterward came out his brother, that had the crimson thread upon his hand: and his name was called Zarah." Genesis 38:27-30

The firstborn always had the birthright in Israel. For a man to be born of a woman who had never before given birth entitled him to the heirship, whatever that may be. However, on occasion, circumstances rearranged themselves. Such was the case of Pharez and Zarah, born of Tamar and the patriarch Judah, son of Jacob who was the son of Isaac, who was the son of Abraham. In the case of twins, the recognition went to whichever twin was born first. But, in their history, the descendants of Abraham had confronted some very technical questions relating to the birthright.

For instance, in the case of Jacob and Esau, Esau was the firstborn to Isaac through Rebekah. However, Jacob, according to Rebekah, was supposed to be the firstborn son. She contrived a ruse to fool Isaac into conferring his heirship blessing upon Jacob. The ruse was approved by Isaac's own words even above the protests of the first born son, Esau. In his later life, Jacob then witnessed a similar division in his own family. His son, Judah, had twins born to him through Tamar, Judah's former daughter-in-law whom he married because of a foul indiscretion on his own part. While the breaker of the matrix was technically Zarah, who received the crimson thread on his wrist that came forth for only an instant, it was Pharez who actually was born completely before Zarah. In other words, while possessing the thread claiming heirship, the pronouncement at Pharez's birth should have changed the mistake. As the midwife proclaimed when Pharez was unexpectedly born first, "This breach be upon thee."

All of this was weighing heavily upon the mind of Jude during his detention in the Roman camp. His wounds were healing thanks to the physician provided him by the Romans whose only real concern was keeping him conscious and well for interrogations. His mind now clearing from the fever of the wounds, he again resumed the thoughts that often occupied his mind. Had his heirship been a mistake? Was there now a circumstance being thrust into the forefront that would alter his right, indeed cause him to lose it? Would the right of the kingship now revert to his sloppy and irresponsible brother, Joses, who found it better to travel the world than to commit himself to the Torah and the resistance, and who was contrary to the order of the Community? No, that could not be allowed to happen. Certainly HaShem had the welfare of Israel closer to His heart than that!

The sound of a harsh voice of a soldier commanding him to stand brought him out of his contemplations.

"On your feet, you vile piece of camel shit," growled the soldier as he pulled up on Jude's hair to force him to stand. Jude's hands and feet were still bound and he could not stand well on his own. Two other soldiers took him by the arms and dragged him out of the temporary stockade. As they pulled him across the sand, he could make out the canopy of an officer's headquarters just ahead. Under the canopy was the Roman Officer who took him prisoner and another soldier who stared at Jude whose face and appearance was still dirty and disheveled from the battle. The second Roman's eyes widened as he believed he recognized him. In fact, he mistook him for Joses.

"This is the man I saw in Galilee that was pointed out by one of the tax collectors there as instructing the people not to pay the tax to Caesar!"

The Roman Officer then studied Jude more closely as the guards brought him to the front of the canopy.

"Are you certain?" asked the officer.

"I remember his face quite well, and his is a match," replied the soldier. "He seems taller and more robust, but that could be from different clothes." The soldier walked over and turned Jude so that he could more easily see his face. Satisfied, the Roman pushed him away and to the ground. "Yes, he is the man."

Jude and Joses were certainly not identical, and Joses' shorter stature, an obvious distinction with his slight back deformity, would have been hard to judge from a distance. The only positive way to tell them apart was when they stood side by side.

"So, not only are you a killer of Romans, but an insurrectionist against Caesar's tax," the officer said with a vile disdain. "This man, alone, killed two of my soldiers," he said to the other soldier, forming a spitball in his mouth that he spat on Jude's face. "Put him on his feet before me," the officer commanded two soldiers who grabbed Jude's arms and forced him to his feet.

"Our information is correct. You are the leader of the Sicarii, just as I accused you," he said to Jude. "You have been very active in Galilee for many years, even when but a boy," the Roman deduced. Jude did not respond, but looked at the stones on the hill beyond the canopy. The Roman continued, "No, I know you will not answer me. But, I have a proposal for you. If you agree to talk to me, I will go much easier on you than the professionals that wait for you in Caesarea. I am a practical man. My only concern is money, and I will receive that as soon as we deliver you to Pilate. I have already sent word of your capture and we are awaiting a unit from Caesarea to assist in your transport. I will not free you, but I can reduce your suffering. Talk to me," his words were like a harlot's caress.

Jude remained silent. The Roman had no other words, but he slowly drank from an ornately adorned cup as the soldiers dragged Jude off to a waiting wagon. Once the detail was prepared, the Roman Officer mounted a horse and ordered the group forward to Caesarea, about a day's journey away. All Jude could think of was to pray to HaShem for deliverance. It would come, and he would not be sure how to receive it.

The trip to Caesarea would take Jude through the despised land of Samaria. For the Judeans and Galileans, it was not a friendly or likeable place. Part of the old northern kingdom of Israel before its destruction many centuries before, Samaria was still anathema to those who saw the inhabitants as either interlopers, remnants of the northern tribes now defunct, or just goyim gentiles. In Jude's mind, it seemed only proper that if the Romans were to have their center for administration in the land, it may as well be in Samaria.

As the guard company with their prisoner entered a narrowing of a small valley, a volley of rocks and boulders struck several of the guards causing them grievous injuries. Hurled by men expert in the use of slings, these projectiles were as deadly as arrows. The arrows came next, striking many of the remaining soldiers in the exposed portions of their bodies as they attempted to organize themselves. Two arrows had found their mark on the Roman Officer who fell from his horse, breaking his neck in the fall.

The sudden attack confused the remainder who tried to rally to the origin of the missiles, only to be attacked from their rear they had failed to protect. In a short five minutes it was all over. A group of Zealots had effected Jude's rescue. All of the Romans were dead or wounded and unarmed. The Zealot's surprise and violent attack had caused them only a few minor injuries. As Jude's bonds were cut, a familiar, yet strangely out of place voice spoke from the rocks to the south. It was his brother, Joses.

"We may not have much time, Eleazer has spotted another group of kittim approaching," Joses stated in a tone more commanding than informative. "Collect the weapons of the dead and take what necessities you can carry and follow me." The Zealots collected all the military hardware they could carry and headed into the rocks with Jude in tow. He was still too weak to accomplish a flight from the area solely under his own strength. Two of the Zealots placed his arms over their shoulders and allowed him to sit on their crossed hands, a form of a speedy litter effective for short distances. Joses had not yet taken the time to formally address his brother. The approaching Romans, while not yet aware of the battle, would soon be upon the carnage of the prisoner escort detail. Joses climbed the rocks to the vantage point of the scout who was watching the Roman movement.

"They are right there," Eleazer pointed to the west toward the city of Caesarea. The Roman unit was about ten furlongs away (well over a mile) and was in a march formation moving in a modified column of threes up the grade. By Joses' estimation, it was likely a century. While the prison detail was relatively small and manageable for the Zealot team, this Roman force was much too large to even consider a quick hit and run tactic. The other factor was the remnant of the century that Jude and Kefa had battled earlier. Joses was not sure where the bulk of that century might be. Joses made his decision.

"Too much for us right now. We had better depart the area and ensure that we can put enough distance between the Romans and us until we can get to safety. Besides, Jude needs care. He doesn't appear up to another battle," Joses smiled at Eleazer who grinned back at him as they moved off the vantage point of the rocks.

The raiding party moved swiftly and silently through the terrain, hardly noticing the burden of the injured Jude. Once they reached the crest of the hill, they put Jude in a litter they had brought along to make his transport easier. They were now able to travel quite quickly. At different points along the route, small groups of the party would break off and head in alternate directions to conceal the size and ability of their forces from Roman patrols or the eyes of spies and informants. Joses' group traveled for several hours until they arrived at their destination, the town of Sychar in Samaria. Jude and Joses had still not spoken to each other. It was now well after dark and the remainder of the band split up just outside of the town so as not to attract attention. Even though it was dangerous for Joses and Jude to be together, Jude still needed medical care. With three other companions, Joses and Jude approached a well-manicured and relatively expansive home on the south side of the town. There they were greeted at the door by a group of friends who were special to Joses.

"The poor have arrived and need a place to rest," a man standing at the door stated to a woman and several men who Jude could partially see through the door. It was obvious the woman was preparing a room for the expected guests.

The use of the word "poor" by the host did not go unnoticed by Jude. It was one of the code names for the upper members and leaders of the Community at Damascus. However, Jude did not recognize the people, and while he understood Joses' position with Joachanin, Joses had not attained to any formal rank in the Community. The only person around who met the requirements of such a salutation was Jude. However Jude considered this strange situation, the only real important thing was that he heal as quickly as possible. He would figure the rest as time and opportunity occasioned. So, for the moment, he was thankful for the hospitality of the people. As the group entered the home, Joses spoke first.

"Simon, thank you for inviting us. How is the family?" Joses was trying to behave innocuously until all were inside and the door was closed.

"Fine, fine," the man identified as Simon responded, playing along. "We have been anxiously awaiting your arrival for the beginning of the festivities."

These were Samaritans. Jude could tell by their accents and their mannerisms. What is Joses doing with Samaritan associates? He could not make immediate sense of it. As the door closed and the men assisting him helped him take a seat in the corner, he also noticed a young woman assisting the older woman he had seen as the door first opened. His wound was again bleeding from the effort of the travel and he felt more and more tired as the moments passed. Joses came to his side for the first time as the men again dressed his wounds and covered him to keep him warm. Leaning down beside him, Joses placed his mouth to Jude's ear.

"My brother, thankful to HaShem are we that your life has been spared. Fear for your welfare and the salvation of our father's house brought me word of your predicament. Kefa has maintained the lines of communication well. Word went to Damascus, and of course, to me. Praise to HaShem that we found you. Now sleep and let your spirit be strengthened." Joses embraced him as best he could in the confines of the corner with the men attending to him.

Jude did not know what to say. This was all not according to what his understanding brought to him. But, he was exhausted and his mind was no longer able to distinguish and process the events. He drifted now into a dream state, the warmth of the fire and the comfort of the bedding lulling him into unconsciousness.

***

It was Simon Magus! Jude had awakened abruptly at an hour of the day that allowed rays of sunshine to enter the home through every opening. He was in the home of pretenders and sorcerers! What was the meaning of Joses having fellowship with these unclean and...

"You are awake," he heard the familiar voice of Kefa, his younger brother.

Still groggy, but wanting answers, he raised himself up on his elbows and looked around to see Kefa standing near him. He was eating a piece of fruit and knelt down to offer a piece to Jude.

"I prepared this myself, brother, so it is clean to you. Eat," Kefa held a piece close to Jude's lips. Jude wanted answers, but he needed nourishment as well. He whispered a prayer to HaShem and then took several bites of the fruit that provided much needed moisture and sustenance. He immediately hungered for more. Kefa obliged him and assisted him in consuming several pieces. After a drink of water to further quench his thirst and cleanse his mouth, Jude laid back onto his bed.

"I did not want to leave you, my brother," Kefa began as tears welled in his eyes. "I had no choice. The Romans outnumbered us and I knew that it was a trap. I could not let the possibility of word concerning our fate failing to get to Damascus. I could see that you were wounded, but..."

"Its fine, Kefa, I understand. You did the right thing," Jude said slowly and with a hoarseness yet in his voice. "I erred in not planning more appropriately for the mission. If you had not escaped, where would we all be now? You showed the ability of a fine field commander."

Jude was sincere. He realized that with Kefa's tactics he was now alive and free from the Romans who would have possibly tortured him for information. The resistance did not need to lose the heir to the Throne of David. That reminded him of another brother.

"Kefa, where is Joses?" asked Jude.

"He has gone to talk to several men concerning his plans. He asked me to stay here and look after you with the help of Joanna, the daughter of one of his associates.

A woman was in this house alone with him and Kefa? In Samaria? This was not appropriate and he again rose up on his elbows to try and depart.

"Are there no other men here besides us?" he asked Kefa.

"None at the moment," responded Kefa. "All of them have important tasks to accomplish. A man well schooled in the arts of healing has administered to you, and you already look the better for it. He will arrive again toward the end of the day to check on you."

"It isn't the Magus, is it?" asked Jude.

"What if it is?" Kefa retorted with a laugh. "You are alive and healing. Thank HaShem for His deliverance. Better by the Magus than the kittim."

What was this attitude in Kefa? While Jude knew he had agreed with Joses' claim to the throne, that did not do away with the law of the Way. What was going on?

"Kefa," he said as he rolled to his side to better see his brother and the surroundings, "Where is Joses?" As he asked the question he could make out the form of a woman passing by the door to the adjoining room. "Who is that?"

"That is Joanna, daughter of one of the Samaritan leaders, and she is actually a purebred Israelite," replied Kefa. He looked around to see Joanna again walk past the door. "The Samarians are with us, but will not tip their hand to the kittim or the Herodians as to their true loyalties," he explained.

Jude did not want to go there.

"What is that to me?" Jude spat. "I have no mission to the dogs, only to the House of Israel. What is Joses up to?"

"Joses is looking for more allies to our cause," Kefa said carefully, expecting Jude to react immediately. But, Jude wanted to hear this, so he remained calm. Kefa continued, "Not all Samaritans are goyim or gentile. Many converted to HaShem, as you know and keep the Torah even though only converts. Some, though, have proven their lineage and are of the blood of Israel. Joses has entered into an alliance with them. It will all remain beyond the power of the kittim and Herod until the time is right."

Jude was incensed, and wondered who Joses thought he was? He needed to take this to the Teacher...

"Where is Rabbi Tzedeq?" Jude asked concerning Joachanin as he recalled the original purpose of his mission. "What has become of him?"

"He is still in Herod's custody," replied Kefa. "The word is that Herod is going to execute him."

"For what? We surmised it might come to this!" Jude could not contain himself. Herod was as fickle as ever. He had arrested and released the Teacher once already. Nothing had changed, but now Herod seemed bent on ridding himself of Joachanin.

"The same charges," responded Kefa. "But, we do not know

all the details. Jacob is handling things and may try to work with Caiaphas on the matter. Last I heard, he had not done so, but was still considering the possibility."

"He should not even try. That evil snake is not going to assist Jacob, and he is the likely source of this plan of murder," snorted Jude. "Jacob may only endanger himself and the resistance."

"No, he has removed himself from any activity other than teaching," replied Kefa. "He will only represent himself as a pious one, that he is anyway, and remain in Damascus or teach. He will not reprove the establishment and endanger his position. But, the people support him as they did Joachanin, and his demeanor is not seen as a threat. So, the kittim and Herod will want to appease the people to prevent an uprising over Rabbi Tsedeq.

Jude felt a betrayal amiss.

"How does Jacob relate to Joses' claim to the throne? Has that changed? For that matter, where do you stand?"

Kefa winced. These were his brothers. But, he knew the Teacher recognized Joses' position as the Mashiach ben Joseph. On the other hand, he did not want to excite Jude or appear disloyal to the Community, the Way, and this, his brother, who had done so much for the Kingdom.

"I must support Rabbi Tsedeq," answered Kefa, for once choosing his words carefully. "I love you, and respect all you have done. You are an heir, but Joses is the first-born. He received the crimson thread."

Jude felt anger and resentment swelling in him, but he held his emotions. Kefa continued. "There is nothing wanting in you, my brother. The Teacher has not abandoned you, either. But, Joses has claimed his position, and is fulfilling the requirements. He has made new allies and is bringing more and more faithful into the resistance everyday. We are not strong enough in Damascus to do it alone."

Jude had to stop him. "No, Kefa! That is not the answer. HaShem expects a pure and obedient people that only the Way can produce. The siege of Jerusalem was merely a confederation, a first effort, and it proves the point. HaShem did not bless us because we had the unclean amongst us. We failed! It is not numbers that HaShem needs; it is cleanliness and pureness of heart with the works of righteousness. Remember Gideon? HaShem had him dismiss almost all his soldiers until he had but a small remnant. With obedience and righteousness, Gideon defeated the Midianites. Recall King David, how he slew Goliath and that with a mere sling for he had trust in HaShem. Don't you see? Joses is wrong. He will cause HaShem to turn away from us."

Kefa was not sure what to say. Had not the Teacher declared Joses the Mashiach ben Joseph? He had heard it with his own ears. And yet, Jacob still supported Jude. Not in opposition to Joachanin, but because in Joachanin's own statements he intimated that Joses would have to prove his position by his works, just as with Jude. Maybe it was not such a cut and dried decision after all. Joachanin had been testing his followers all along. Maybe all this was a test, too. Blessings and prophecies are pronouncements based upon works and worthiness, not mere gifts of birth! Of course, that would be how to approach this. Maybe he should agree to wait and see.

"You are wise, my brother," Kefa said. "I have thought it over, and I will do as you ask. I love you both, and all I want is for us to be together, a righteous arm of HaShem. It really matters little to me, as it is all in HaShem's hands. Wherever this goes, I will follow."

Jude was not sure this was what he wanted to hear. But, for now, he needed to get moving. He did not want any chance of defilement or any chance of being recognized in Samaria. "I need to leave, now," he said to Kefa.

"You are not strong enough," Kefa shrugged and reached for Jude. "You have more mending to accomplish. And, it is daylight, maybe that is not the best time."

"No, I can manage if you will help me. In fact, daytime is the best time as we will not look as suspicious. Help me up," Jude was adamant.

Kefa, not wanting to argue, assisted him. Joanna, a vibrant and attractive young woman, entered the room to see why there was so much going on. But, she would not speak, for she knew who these men were and did not want to be presumed disrespectful. She watched quietly, but received no word from Jude. Only Kefa spoke.

"I must assist Jude in an important task," Kefa said to her. "Tell Joses that we will make our way back to Judea."

Joanna looked at Jude who seemed much stronger, but she doubted his strength would remain over the long journey. However, she obediently assisted the men in their preparations. Soon, they were walking slowly out the door. As Jude passed over the thresh hold of the home, he immediately felt relief that he was no longer in the company of the unclean. His return to Judea, and Damascus, would take many days.

Joses returned later that afternoon from the conferences he had with selected men of the area. He was satisfied that the day's work had gone well. His concerns again returned to his brother, Jude. He hastened his walk, accompanied by two other followers who were his bodyguards. They approached the home where Jude was and knocked upon the door. Joanna answered.

"They are gone," is all she said. Joses, walking past her, looked around and saw that the bedding was folded neatly and that Jude had left. He thought the worst.

"Was he discovered?" No, that could not be it or the house would be under guard and all inside seized. "He encouraged Kefa to help him leave, didn't he?" Joses asked Joanna. She nodded in the affirmative.

Resolved to the development, Joses stated his feelings. "May HaShem deliver them to safety."

At that moment, Simon appeared as well, cloak about his head to shield him from the sun and any eyes that may be watching. With him was the father of Joanna, the owner of the home.

"Joses," Nicolaus said quietly as he entered the home with Simon, "How is Jude?" A quick look about and he already knew the answer.

"He has returned to Damascus," Joses answered as Nicolaus looked to his daughter, Joanna. "He is a man of conviction and strength," said Joses, "This is no real surprise. He has the common disdain of Samaria that infects most of Judea. May this not disturb your house," Joses said respectfully to Nicolaus.

"No, may it not disturb you," Nicolaus responded. He motioned to Joanna to come closer to him, as she did so he placed his arm around her. "My daughter has informed me that her intention is to become the wife of your brother-in-law, Eleazer. If that is agreeable to him we wish to arrange the betrothal. Perhaps this will demonstrate all of Samaria's allegiance to you."

Simon Magus nodded in agreement. Joses was surprised, yet with the death of Benjamin ben Nikdimon, it was proper for Joses to act as his father. Joses recovered from his reflections and addressed them.

"Yes, Joanna is a pure and noble woman, and she would be worthy of the station. Perhaps we could speak one to another for a short moment?" asked Joses.

Joanna nodded again, smiling with a mild anticipation.

Nicolaus and Joses shook hands. "Would you care to discuss these matters between you?" Nicolaus asked as he gazed at his daughter.

Joses looked at Joanna, who again nodded in the affirmative.

"Then, if it pleases you, go sit by the Jacob's Well and let your discourse bring peace to your minds and spirits," Nicolaus motioned to the area about fifty cubits from the house. Joses moved first toward the door, and Joanna followed. Once outside, Joanna drew water from the well as Joses sat upon it on one side, waiting for her to ask him anything of concern to her.

"Will you give me a drink?" Joses asked her.

"This is all so strange," she replied, "As the Jews have had so little to do with us. Why are you so friendly?"

Joses smiled and answered her, "You know my claim is to the crimson thread of Israel. The one who speaks to you is the Mashiach ben Joseph. While this has been a difficult road, my commitment is steadfast. Through this method, HaShem will free us from the kittim."

Joanna could see the truth in Joses face. "Yes, I want to be a part of this, so is marriage to Eleazer possible?"

"Let me speak to him," Joses tenderly replied. "It is likely that he has feelings similar to yours."

They then returned to the house and Joanna told her father of Joses' wisdom in dealing with her.

The next morning, Joses and his bodyguards began their journey back to Galilee. After several days of a leisurely travel, they parted company and each went to his own home. Joses entered his large well-furnished abode and found Martha preparing a meal and taking care of other household duties while her sister Miriam was instructing the boys who had just returned from their schooling in Emmaus. Martha was a little out of sorts as the hired help she was accustomed to in doing house work was unavailable because of some family difficulties. Yet, Joses' safe arrival excited her.

"Joses!" she exclaimed. "Miriam, boys, Joses is home!" She hurried to his side, but did not touch him, the dishware in her arms almost falling from her grasp.

"Shalom," Joses greeted Martha as he saw her approach him. "We were successful and it will be wonderful to experience your culinary arts again," he praised her abilities as only he could. Martha, however, felt a pang of discomfort. She just didn't feel like her efforts were properly rewarded. She had given so much of herself to Joses and Miriam to try and make their burdens lighter.

Miriam then came to him and the two embraced.

"You're safe, praise HaShem!" Miriam said excitedly as she gently rubbed his back, trying to ease the certain discomfort he must feel around his spine. The deformity was less pronounced, but still visible.

Joses kissed Miriam and then placed one arm around her waist as they played with Jochanan, Martha's son, and Joseph for a few moments. Martha watched as her son, Jochanan, who was somewhat older than Miriam's boy, moved closer to Joses.

"Jochanan, come let me look at you," Joses affectionately took him in his arms and embraced him. Jochanan snuggled up to Joses even though he was now in his teens and past his Bar Mitzvah. "You grow everyday, and when I do not see you for awhile and return, I really notice how quickly you are becoming a man," Joses praised him. Jochanan's face beamed and he looked over at his mother to see her approval. She smiled and nodded gracefully.

"And you, Joseph!" Joses also drew him closer and kissed him on his head, squeezing him at the same time. The boy looked into Joses' eyes, then wrapped his arms around his father's neck. "You are getting stronger and growing taller. Soon, I will have to look up to you when we stand together. Remember to grow in wisdom, too," he said to the boy, now also a young man who had completed his Bar Mitzvah. He then turned his attention to the smallest boy, Joshua, taking him in his arms and hugging him tightly.

Martha hurried off to the dining area to place the dishes on a table. Then, as was customary, Miriam asked about the activities of the brethren, especially the dangerous mission Joses had just undertaken.

"All went well, then?" she asked. Being his dynastic wife, Joses knew it was important for her to understand all the particulars, something he shared with few others. While these discussions normally took place away from other ears, Joses did not take that precaution this time and Martha over heard. She was upset that Miriam was privy to this information all the time, but she had to ignore it, concerning herself with the order of the home. But, the disparity got the better of her and she came back into the main room.

"We were entirely successful, and only a few were slightly injured during the movement of the goods to the warehouse," Joses said in veiled language which Miriam and Martha understood.

"Blessed is HaShem that He protects you and our loved ones," Miriam responded.

"Yes, we are so grateful," echoed Martha. "But, Joses, when I am so close to all that transpires, and give myself to you and your house, why is my sister the only one with whom you desire to discuss the issues? While you do this, there are so many other duties about the home that need someone to address them. Could not Miriam assist a little more?"

Miriam was slightly annoyed at Martha's assumptions, especially given the fact that Miriam was Joses' dynastic wife. Why would he not talk to her, and not to Martha? Joses, ever understanding, did not disrespect Martha's concerns. He allowed the boys to run off after giving Joshua over to Joseph so he could watch him as the adults talked.

"Indeed, what could we do without all the attention you pay to the careful preparations of the home? That is your gift, and what better thing to do than that which brings you joy and fulfillment?" Joses said to her in the kindest voice Martha had ever heard. It immediately diffused her agitation, and Joses finished his explanation. "It is Miriam's duty as the mother of the heir to do the things needed for that. This brings her joy and fulfillment. It is her station and no one can take that responsibility of her's lightly nor take it away from her."

Martha acknowledged the situation and recognized the weakness of her complaint. She was here of her own volition and could not righteously complain. She regained her composure and pardoned herself.

"There is nothing in life I would rather do than be here with those I love, assisting them in so great a work," she said with tears welling in her eyes. She loved Joses, too.

Joses arose and smiled at her like only he could do. Refreshed and comforted, she returned to her work that pleased her heart. She did not like dealing with the difficulties of the Kingdom, anyway.

The home was then quiet and serene until supper time when Joses informed Miriam and Martha of the proposal by Nicolaus that Eleazer marry Joanna.

"Yes, she is a wonderful young woman and Eleazer has been fond of her for a long time," said Joses. The two women squealed with delight. They were all reclining around the dining table, the young boys experimenting with their food, tearing the grapes apart and picking out the seeds, listening to the conversation of the adults but trying not to appear too interested.

"When do you plan to inform Eleazer?" asked Martha.

"At sunrise," responded Joses. "We must meet on other business, but this will invigorate his day," and Joses laughed softly as Miriam and Martha clapped their hands with joy.

Joses met with Eleazer the next morning concerning Joanna. Eleazer told Joses that his feelings for Joanna were strong and that he desired to marry her. As a result, the marriage took place and Joses presided over the wedding. His brother-in—law now had the beginning of his own family and the couple was obviously a perfect match, each complementing the other. Furthermore, the marriage provided another strong alliance with Joses' movement that could turn the tide in his attempts to claim the right to rule all Israel.

***

Pilate walked briskly through the Antonia Fortress, his lush white robes flowing freely in the slight breeze of the afternoon, his thoughts upon what rewards he hoped Caesar may bestow on him for his willingness to govern Judea in such troubled times. Abject ruthlessness with controlled information to Rome; Yes, that should protect his future. He would just have to ensure that these Jews did not go around him. What mechanism could prove so valuable?

"Hail, Caesar!" a guard saluted as Pilate entered the portico of his offices.

"Hail, Caesar!" responded Pilate, enjoying the prestige of the salutation from his subordinates. He had always reveled in the privileges of rank.

"Your Excellency," a voice called from the hall. It was Julianus, the Centurion who was the watch commander. "There is word from Caesarea concerning the escape of a prisoner and the destruction of the detail that was transporting him."

Pilate almost froze in his tracks. No, that would not be possible, not the man they had just captured days before. The intelligence indicated he was the leader of the Sicarii, or that he was at least very important to the resistance. Pilate caught himself, not wanting the soldier to perceive him as easily frustrated. He continued again into his chambers motioning Julianus to accompany him. Once he had arrived at his chair, he sat down and reached for the scroll in the hands of the Centurion. Julianus handed it to him and took a step backward as Pilate read the report.

"All dead, but one? The prisoner and all the Sicarii escaped?" he asked rhetorically as he read through the report. The Centurion watched as Pilate's eyes grew intense with concentration and, apparently, anger. "I cannot believe it! A sensitive mission and a prisoner of such importance mismanaged by a soldier because of his own greed!" Pilate was inconsolable. "This is inconceivable! It's a good thing that Centurion died in the battle or I would have killed him myself!"

"Your Excellency," Julianus said hesitatingly, "What do you desire?"

"Send word for Caiaphas. I need him here immediately."

The centurion left and had Caiaphas notified. It was only a matter of about one half an hour before Caiaphas arrived with Amelaus in tow. Pilate was sipping on some wine and trying to look controlled and poised, but Caiaphas sensed a pretension about him, and could see in Pilate's eyes that he was seething just below the surface.

"Yes, you called for me," said Caiaphas.

"I see you have brought Amelaus along. That was wise." Pilate placed his cup on the table and crossed his legs. "As you know, your man gave us information that if we informed him of the direction of the detail, he could notify his contact who may have an association with the resistance. As it turns out, the Sicarii attacked the detail and all but one of my men were killed. The prisoner escaped without a trace."

"Your Excellency," Caiaphas was livid about this error on the part of the Romans, but he dared not put that at Pilate's feet. "What would you have had us do?"

"What does our source tell us about the possibility that the man he informed performed this rescue?" asked Pilate.

Amelaus spoke up. "Reu has informed us that he did not see Yeshua for several days. But, he has apparently been near Jericho and Damascus, the city of the Nazarenes and Essenes."

"It is possible he could have gone to Galilee and returned in that time," Pilate reflected. "What about the rescuer of the man who was taken prisoner? Is there any word on whom that may be?" asked Pilate.

"None, your Excellency" answered Amelaus, his hands shaking as his gaze dropped to the floor.

"Well, then, I suppose we have underestimated our enemies," sighed Pilate. "All we can do is try again. I want your man back on this and to gather specific information on what anyone says, especially the identities of those involved. I need your resources on this day and night, without fail. If you cannot flush them out, I may have to do something much more drastic. You are dismissed."

Caiaphas and Amelaus drew a deep sigh of relief as they immediately and silently took their leave of Pilate.

***

Joses had decided to go to Jerusalem and use the time while Jude was recovering to do some preaching there himself. He went to the Temple with some of his followers as he and Jude agreed he could, and he began to expound the Torah to the people assembled there. Immediately, the Herodian Priests and Pharisees reacted to him and sent out representatives to question him. Reu was also told to go and watch and listen by positioning himself in the crowd as a supporter. The Romans, on the other hand, watched from the Antonia Fortress.

Joses remained low key for most of the afternoon. He sat on the steps and talked with small groups of men and women. He could see the Herodians watching him, and he did not want to attract more of their attention. But, Caiaphas did not want anyone in Jerusalem that he did not have as much information on as possible. So, he sent his representatives, Pharisees and Sadducees, to question him.

After trying to patronize and flatter him by saying he was

a great teacher, the Herodians asked him if it was lawful to give tribute money to Caesar. Joses had heard this trap before. But, the crowd had grown much larger with the anticipation of a debate, and Joses could not let the opportunity pass.

"You are hypocrites," Joses said to them. He laughed quietly and moved higher on the steps. "Since you are the servants of Caesar, where is some tribute money?"

One of the Pharisees handed him a coin that was minted by the Romans and had Caesar's image. Joses held it up and asked those assembled near him, "Whose image is this?"

They all answered, "It is Caesar's."

Joses explained, "Then if it is Caesar's property, render it to Caesar, but render yourselves to HaShem if you are His. The bounty of Israel belongs to no foreign ruler, but to HaShem, as do the lives of the people."

Reu thought to himself that this teacher sounded just like the teacher in Galilee that had been reported to the Romans and to Caiaphas. It was interesting to Reu that this man looked so similar to Jude. Yet, having been so close to Jude, he knew it was not Jude. He got closer to listen more carefully and to study the man.

"If a man has a wife, and he dies without having children by her," one of the Herodian Sadducees began, "Torah says his brother shall marry her and raise up seed to his dead brother. Now, there were with us seven brethren, and the first died having no seed, so the wife married his brother. But he died also, not having children by her. This continued through all seven brothers until the last one died, and then the woman also. In the resurrection, whose wife will she be, for they all had her?"

Joses shook his head. These Sadducees did not even believe in a resurrection, yet here they were trying to alter a well-known story about seven brothers who had given their lives for the freedom of Israel and for HaShem. They were belittling the sacrifice of those brothers and the honor of their mother. It was an insult to the war of liberation fought by the Maccabees almost two hundred years before, and an insult to those seeking the present liberation of Israel from the Herodians and the Romans.

"You are greatly mistaken in your supposition," answered Joses. "How can you, who do not believe in a resurrection, ask a question concerning its disposition? These brethren of whom you speak gave their lives for the liberation of Israel and the glory of HaShem.[17] To insult them is to insult all Israel and HaShem. You do not understand the scriptures, and you mock the power of HaShem. For in truth, HaShem is for the living, not the dead." He had answered them in a code, telling them that they were dead to the law and outside the covenant. He, effectively, had called them "goyim."

"They who are unto HaShem, cannot die, for they are equal to the angels, and are the Sons of HaShem, the sons of light and life. You are not so, even denying the power of HaShem."

Joses was angry over the attempts by these usurpers to challenge him on the Torah. He had long desired to say publicly what he felt, and his temper flared while his voice rose so that the people around him could hear what he had to say.

"People of Judea, fellow Israelites, listen to me. We know our people, we know our lineage, and we are commanded to govern ourselves. Moses instructed us to have no other form of government but a monarchy, and to always cherish that form of government. But, the Torah also commands that we have none over us but those of our lineage, never permitting usurpers or imposters, or even the adopted. Think about what I am saying. I tell you the truth." He stopped and looked around. The Herodians were all ears as well as the people standing about him. This could be dangerous, but he could not fail to speak the truth. He motioned for the crowd to sit down. They did so almost in unison.

"The family of Herod is not our nation, but of Edom and at the most, adopted to us after the third generation of conversion. As such, they are not permitted to rule over us. But, due to the alliances they have made with Rome, we are obliged, under pain of death, to accept their administrations, as unlawful to us as they are."

The Herodians sent a few of their number toward the Antonia

Fortress where the Roman Garrison housed its troops and monitored the Temple and all Jerusalem. Joses knew he had only a short time to deliver his message.

"The Herodians sit in Moses' seat, whether we like it or not, and we must observe what they command or suffer retribution. But, do not do the same works they do, for they say and do not. For they are the administrators of the invaders, placing heavy burdens, grievous burdens upon our people while they themselves will not move them with one of their fingers. All their works they do to be seen of men, making broad their phylacteries and enlarging the borders of their garments. They take the uppermost rooms at all the feasts, and the chief seats, and they love the greetings they receive in the markets and to be called, Rabbi, Rabbi. These men should serve HaShem and His people, not insist that they are our masters, our mashiach, or an idol for worship. The greatest of us, should be our servant, not a taskmaster. Whosoever shall exalt himself, shall be abased, and he who humbles himself shall be exalted in HaShem's eyes."

One of the Herodian Pharisees who was a lawyer asked him, "Which is the greatest commandment of the Torah?"

"Hear, Oh Israel," Joses began quoting from the Torah, "The Lord Our God is One Lord. We must always remember this and the day HaShem delivered our fathers from the Egyptians at the Red Sea. From these we see that the first commandment is to love the Lord your God with all your heart, soul, and mind. This is the first and greatest commandment. The second follows because of it, that you shall love your neighbor as yourself. Upon these two sayings are based the Torah and the prophets. All wisdom emanates from these sayings if we take them to heart and not the dogmas and instructions of men."

All the people's eyes were upon him, even the younger children. Every ear was turned to catch every word he spoke. Joses then turned to the Herodians, the pretenders to Israel and the Jews, the supporters of the establishment of the Romans and all their cruelty, and he spoke directly to them, not sparing his words.

"Woe unto you, hypocrites! For you shut up the kingdom

of heaven against those seeking to find it, and you will not go in yourselves. You go so far as to lay bonds upon those who seek to enter, passing laws punishing them for seeking and doing the truth that is their right from HaShem and injures no man. Woe unto you Herodians, for you devour widow's houses, and for a pretense make long prayers. HaShem commands no rote and lengthy words, but a sincere heart and good works. For your pretenses you shall receive a greater condemnation. Woe to you, Pharisees, Herodians, for you look all across the world for proselytes, and when they are made you make them twice the children of hell than yourselves, pretending to adopt them into Israel when all you do is give them a name and take their tithes for the goyim. Woe unto you, you blind guides who say that to swear by HaShem and the Temple are of no concern, but them who swear by the gold of the Temple is a debtor, and you do this to enslave our people and steal their property. In your world, a man's children are slaves before they are born. You are fools and blind, for HaShem and His Temple are greater than gold. But, what and where is the true Temple of HaShem, for this building here is but a defilement, a pretense to all that HaShem has set. Nothing here is of any efficacy, but within these borders a new Temple and altar shall HaShem erect." Joses, unlike his brethren or most of the Jews, had little use for Herod's attempt at this temple. Joses recognized that all things in it were invalid, and he looked to another, but did not reveal it.

"Woe to you, for you pay tithes on the little things such as mint, anise, and cumin for a show, but you omit the more important matters of the Torah such as righteous judgment, mercy, and trust in HaShem. Without forgetting the smaller things, you should not have forgotten the more important ones. You are blind guides that strain at a gnat and swallow a camel. Woe unto you, for you make the outside of a cup and platter clean, but on the inside you are full of extortion and excess. In like manner, you are whited sepulchers, which indeed look beautiful from the outside, but you are nothing on the inside but dead men's bones, and of all uncleanliness. You appear outwardly righteous, but are actually full of hypocrisy and iniquity. Woe unto you, for you build the tombs of the prophets and garnish the sepulchers of the righteous, but you would kill them if they were here today. You are the children of them who killed the prophets, you and the backsliders of Israel whom you have bribed through many generations. All Israel, pray that HaShem will leave unto them houses of desolation, and these men not see me again until they say 'Blessed is he that cometh by HaShem and shall do his works'."

Joses then departed, as he knew the guards would be hurrying to the scene. As he left, several of those listening wanted to know more about the temple Herod had built. He responded tersely as he hurried from Jerusalem, "This is not the House of HaShem, and it will come to destruction."

Reu decided he had better leave. He had seen all he needed to for now. He was sure that the Romans would arrive soon to break up this gathering and he did not want to be caught in the melee.

The messengers sent from the Herodian Priests to report about Joses arrived at Caiaphas' location and reported to him the commotion at the Temple. Caiaphas then sent word to the Roman Garrison at the Antonia Fortress that a riotous disturbance was breaking out. But, the Roman Commander, who had been watching the oratory, only laughed.

"Tell Caiaphas that we have monitored all that has happened and that the people did not arise in rebellion. We will keep an eye on the situation, but the madman has left."

In fact, the oratory by Joses, while inflaming the Herodians and those who supported the establishment of the Romans, had only caused the ordinary people who heard it to contemplate all that Joses had said. They slowly walked away from the Temple, dispersing into the streets and gates as they went, wondering whom this new preacher was. But, everyone pondered the words of the man they found upon the steps of the Temple.

Caiaphas, having heard that the Romans did not intend to react, immediately called for Amelaus who was in another part of the city. Once he arrived, he and Caiaphas decided that they needed to send Reu into the crowd to ascertain whom this man was and what his alliances may be. From all they knew at this point, the description of the individual sounded like the man Reu was meeting with, Yeshua, who had been preaching simple spiritual doctrines in the past and not attacking the establishment, at least not directly. They wondered if it could be the same man or someone like him who was trying to step into the place of Joachanin? Amelaus did not think so, but Reu could probably provide the answers.

"He appears very similar to Yeshua, but it is not him," Reu explained to Amelaus and Caiaphas. "I was some distance from him, but this man looks shorter with a slight bend to his back that seems to keep him from standing up straight."

"Every time we get rid of one of these deceivers, another pops up to replace him," Caiaphas grumbled as he adjusted his robe before he stood up. "There seems to be no end to these mashiachs. The Immerser agitated the crowds against us, and this man does the same. It must be one of his followers from Galilee. Was there anything that gave away his place of abode?"

"Or maybe you heard someone in the crowd say something that could help us?" questioned Amelaus.

"He had several men that seemed to be with him, but they said nothing and I did not recognize any of them. I heard some in the crowd call him 'Yeshua.' But, these people call every new hero that name," said Reu. "The Rabbi you are having me see is also 'Yeshua.' It is a popular name."

"Yes, well we know," said Caiaphas. "I suggest we go back to your known contacts and see what you can learn there. We need to know who this man is and where he is from. If you spot him again, follow him for as long as it takes to get the information we need. I want to know about his family, his friends, his work, everything," Caiaphas turned to Amelaus, "You need to release Reu from all his duties but this one. I want him to have some help so get him some others and cover more area."

"Good idea," responded Amelaus. "We may have several." He motioned to Reu and the two men began to leave.

"One more thing," Caiaphas stopped them. "I am inclined to believe this new hero is a very dangerous man. He has dared to treat us like dogs, demeaning us to the people. The Romans don't seem to care much about religious disputations as long as the people stay orderly. The next time we see this man, I want you and your men to start a fight. I want blood on the ground. We will ensure that you are not held responsible. Do you understand?"

Amelaus and Reu both nodded affirmatively.

"No more allowing any speech about us that is derogatory. We need an aggressive posture to defeat their propaganda," Caiaphas said as he thoughtfully stroked his beard. "This may take time, but as Pilate said, time is something we have, as long as we use it to bury these rabble."

Amelaus and Reu departed.

***

Joses and his companions were well outside Jerusalem and making their way north. As they reached Bethany, they saw a man in white linen walking towards them from the direction of Damascus. It was Joses' brother, Jacob. Jacob was alone, and he seemed to be deep in thought.

"Jacob!" called Joses.

"Joses!"

To one another's surprise, they embraced almost involuntarily. Jacob was weeping.

"What is wrong, Jacob?" asked Joses. "Is there something that must be done? Is anything amiss?"

"Everything is fine," Jacob responded. "I have spent much time searching and meditating. Joachanin told me the reasons for his support of you, and instructed me to study it out." Jacob paused, as he habitually made the choice of his words a task of importance, believing language a gift from HaShem deserving sanctity and respect. "The Holy One of Israel has whispered to me, showing me the path now to travel. The gate is through the gift you have so righteously deserved, and claimed. Truly HaShem cultivates our spirits as individuals, not just the destiny of Israel."

Joses listened carefully. He knew that Jacob was holy, truly a seeker of the will of HaShem. His intensity and strict interpretation of Torah were simply a result of his devotion. He needed to see a bigger picture, and Joachanin had directed him along to see it. Joses turned to his companions and directed them to continue on, giving him a moment alone with Jacob.

"My brother, joy fills my heart!" Joses told him. "I see you understand that my path was to search out the entire truth of the matter, looking for the goal spoken of in Torah that Abraham knew HaShem who declared him His friend. Israel is HaShem's hand in bringing forth his purposes. But, he has another hand that was before Jacob, before Moses, indeed before Abraham. It was that aspect of HaShem that I needed to search for and confront. There was no intention in my heart to abandon the ways of our fathers. Both can be done without any contradiction."

Jacob nodded his head in agreement."When you study it out and search the chambers of your soul, you will find it, for you have no guile and seek only the will of HaShem," Joses said to him.

"This truth will open my heart and mind?" asked Jacob.

"You will understand the mysteries of HaShem, and receive Ruach HaKodesh, and see that it was before Abraham," Joses explained. "As we know, before Abraham, was Shem. And Shem was the father of all those who are to receive these gifts, an expanded family of those who have the genealogical right to the consciousness of HaShem, administered to each according to the separate covenants of their fathers. And he made covenants with the fathers of Abraham, who fathered other children and gave to them gifts, as Abraham also received the gift and passed it to his children who would receive it. HaShem guided them to the knowledge of Him. Then came Moses, and through Moses HaShem gave Israel the Torah, and our mysteries are bound to it. It is the straight and narrow way. In our condition, the Way of Damascus has provided us with the gifts, passed down from mouth to ear and in the code of the Torah. We just need to see them. In On, the Chambers were further revealed to me, showing me the paths and refining my trust in HaShem until He bestowed upon me the surety of His will in all things. As was Malchi-Tzedeq, so are we if we abide the mind of HaShem. It is our birthright. It is true freedom. I do not have a contest with Jude, for my claim is as the father of Israel, the Mashiach ben Joseph, not ben David."

Jacob felt a surge of renewal in his being, an inexplicable magnification of the hope he had long nurtured. However, he remained silent and followed Joses as they walked on towards Joses' home where Martha was preparing for their arrival. Joses' companions ensured that the group was not followed and reported the reconnaissance to Joses who then knew it was safe for him to proceed to his home. Martha was surprised to see Jacob and numerous questions arose in her mind. But, she was most happy to see Joses.

"Miriam sends word that she is well and misses you," she said to Joses who nodded affirmatively. Miriam had gone to Emmaus with the youngest son, Joshua, for some special duties.

Martha then turned and nodded graciously at Jacob, knowing that he would prefer her not to touch him so as to preserve his holiness. Jacob responded to her kindness and understanding.

"Martha, may HaShem bless you and your house," Jacob said as he smiled with loving kindness. Jacob realized that this association is something he had missed. Wiping his eyes, Jacob recovered his emotions and smiled in gratitude at Joses.

"Are you willing to go forward?" asked Joses.

"Yes," answered Jacob.

"You will learn quickly. If you desire, you can go to On and see more for yourself," Joses said.

"My brother can teach me and I will find no need to leave my duties here," Jacob responded.

"Excellent," said Joses. "We can retire to the hills this evening. There is a cave there that we can use for these purposes."

"How do I know I am worthy?" Jacob asked.

Joses smiled and shook his head in amusement. "You, not worthy?"

After the sun went down signifying a new day, Joses and Jacob along with several of Joses' companions who were already initiated, arrived at a large cave east of Bethany. The instructions and rituals took several hours. Jacob learned more in those few hours than he had almost the entire rest of his life. Then, the group entered hitbodedut (meditation).

***

Dawn approached and the men walked slowly and thoughtfully back to Bethany. Jacob, even though having had no rest for the night, could hardly contain his excitement. Joses saw a new light in Jacob's eyes.

"Jacob," Joses said, "You will receive more in the near future with Kefa. The time in between enlightenments allows more time for the questions in your mind that will arise. We wait so that you can organize these thoughts and questions, so that you will appreciate the fullness of the knowledge conveyed to you when that time comes."

Jacob again chose his words carefully.

"My brother," he began, "You are indeed the Mashiach ben Joseph, and the Malchi-Tsedeq of HaShem in Israel."

"The secrets from Moses have guided us," said Joses.

Jacob's life long devotion planted a vision before his eyes. He would truly enter into the Holy of Holies. The sun was now shining brightly.

CHAPTER EIGHT

Joachanin had been in the palace prison at Tiberias for sometime, he knew not how long. However, to his surprise, Herod Antipas was actually treating him quite well. He received three meals every day, several walks while under guard, and he could study and meditate as he desired, particularly on the Sabbaths. He could hear the crowds at the gate demanding his release, but the palace was now well fortified with a number of Herod's guards and a Roman Century. Zealots had made several attempts to gain entry to the palace, but all had been discovered by the guards and killed. Joachanin heard of these brave patriots and was overcome with grief that they were sacrificing themselves trying to free him. He feared that Joses or Jude might attempt a grand assault. He knew it would be fruitless. Even if the resistance gained entry to the palace, the guards would kill him before any rescue was accomplished. He decided on another strategy.

Herod permitted Joachanin to have two visitors twice a week. These could be anyone of his naming and they were permitted to stay with him for one hour. Joachanin had not seen Jude, Jacob, or Joses. That was as it should be. They were too important to have their identities clearly made to the enemy. Instead, the visitors Joachanin received would always deliver his messages via code that the guards attending him could not understand. Herod was aware of this possibility, but felt secure in the plan to allow the people to know Joachanin was alive and well. He was sure they understood that any attempt to free the Immerser would mean death for them and certain death for Joachanin.

Over the course of time, Joachanin learned of Jude's capture and the wound he received. He also learned that Joses had rescued him and that Jude had returned to Damascus to fully recover. It also came to his attention that Joses had used Samaritans as allies, which was rather bizarre given the animosity most Jews, but especially those of Damascus, held for them. But, it was a perfectly understandable strategic move. It was obvious from the news that Jude was not happy about this step of Joses to increase his support. More importantly for Joachanin, however, were Joses' efforts to initiate his own followers outside the Way of Damascus. Apparently, Joses was preparing a group under an organization independent of Damascus, yet still recognizing the High Priestly role of Joachanin and using the same or similar ordinances and rituals. Joachanin knew where Joses had learned to do this: On in Egypt.

For Jude, these activities by Joses above and beyond the resistance efforts had been the final straw to break his relationship with him. The proof of his insolence, in Jude's view, was Joses' presumption to act as a kind of priest and king. Jude believed that Joses' conduct was not according to Torah. He considered On as merely a repository for the pagan and materialistic indulgences of the goyim and the refuge for Jews who had no interest in Jerusalem's true destiny. Had not Ezekiel warned the aristocracy not to use Egyptian mystical symbols, but to create ones appropriate for Israel? Had not the Community, Emmaus, and Joachanin accomplished this, having received them from the fathers on back to Yeshua ben Jehozedech at the time of the return from captivity? Of course, they had! Other than recognizing Joses as an ally and coordinating operations with him, Jude considered him and his disciples "dead" to him and the Community. This was simply a euphemism for them not being a part of the true Way of Damascus.

But, Joachanin understood just what Joses had received in On. Yes, Joachanin was the High Priest, from Aaron the brother of Moses. That priesthood was about 1300 years old and had passed down through the generations from father to son and now resided in Joachanin. But, Joses received an initiation into the mysteries, a priesthood or order beyond the scope of Aaron and Levi. It was an order that existed even prior to Abraham. In fact, that priesthood and its rituals had existed at least 1000 years before Abraham. Abraham had received them from the Patriarchs of mankind. Joses knew these mysteries could, with practice, dedication and study, bring him, his followers, Israel, and, he hoped, all of mankind to the presence of the Throne of Glory and complete the reconciliation of the individual's relationship with the Creator. But, that would have to remain a mystery. For none of this would change the Torah. Indeed, Torah contained the secret code for the attainment of this order. Hidden behind the story and imbedded in its very alephbet (alphabet) was the mystery of mankind's true origin and the method to obtain that knowledge. On had shared that knowledge with Joses. And now, as Joachanin understood it, Jacob had accepted Joses' teachings. It was well for him to have done so, and Joachanin was sure his own earthly mission was now nearly complete.

However, the further rift Joachanin had feared when he talked with Joses on the bank of the Jordan was a reality that troubled him. Yet, Joses was doing what appeared right to Joachanin. He was doing as he had been trained and inspired. He was certainly acting like a king, and a righteous one at that. But, Joachanin wanted to be sure. During one of his weekly visits where he had requested the presence of members of Joses' organization, Joachanin asked them to deliver a message. The message was a question. Was Joses going to fully claim the throne and deliver Israel, or was he going to allow his brother Jude, or someone else altogether, to lay their own claim?

Once he received Joachanin's request, Joses had the return message delivered, from his alias of Yeshua, sending the same two visitors only a week later. Joachanin listened to their words.

"The Rabbi Yeshua says to tell you that the blind receive their sight, the lame walk, the lepers are cleansed, the deaf hear, the dead are raised, and the poor receive the message. He has ascended to Ezekiel's vision. The Tzedeq is with him. Also, our rabbi sends word that of all them born of woman, there is none greater then you. You have fulfilled your station."

Joses had replied in the common code of the Way. The blind receiving their sight represented his teachings to his order about the converts to his organization. The lame walking meant that the followers were given the codes so they could understand for themselves and carry out their duties. The leper being cleansed was a code to describe those who had fallen from their vows but returned to the cause. The deaf hearing meant that they who had ignored the call were now responding. The dead being raised was a code that those outside of the Way or removed by Damascus for their loyalty to Joses were now being brought into Joses' organization and their rights restored. The poor being taught the message simply was code for the top leaders of Joses' organization receiving the sacred tokens of the royal court. The words pertaining to Ezekiel's vision meant that he was approaching the ultimate enlightenment of the Hechalot and was seeking to become an adopted son of HaShem. In short, Joses' organization to restore the Kingdom of Israel to its rightful place was serving its purpose. And, most importantly, Jacob supported Joses.

Joachanin was satisfied that his mission to find the rightful king and prepare a people for him was accomplished. The extremes of Damascus were not for the King of Israel, nor those who had gained knowledge of the Tree of Life through righteousness and Hechalot. Joses had arrived where Torah was to take him. That was all that mattered.

***

Caiaphas was walking about the Temple grounds after performing his daily duties. His thoughts were not upon HaShem, however. His mind was contemplating the state of affairs in Judea, indeed all Palestine, and the difficulties he may face if Herod and Pilate could not get a handle on defeating the resistance. His obsession with Joachanin continued to seethe inside of him, causing a state of perpetual anxiety from which he could not extricate himself.

As he struggled with this mental and emotional turmoil, he looked south past the Court of the Gentiles and thought he saw a man similar to Joachanin teaching just outside the Temple. But, this man was wearing white linen, something Caiaphas had never seen

Joachanin do, even though he had heard of the possibility. Having only seen him from a distance, Caiaphas thought it was Joachanin somehow again released from Herod, as no other reliable information seemed available to explain what was happening. He wanted to go check for himself, but the crowds around Joachanin were always antagonistic to him, even dangerous. His anger rose so fast that an inexplicable pressure brought pain to his head and behind his eyes. He immediately called for his guards to arrest the man.

"All can approach HaShem," Jacob said to the people who were gathering about him. "In HaShem's house are many chambers that are not in the walls of the Temple. We must approach HaShem in these chambers and not leave the works of the Temple undone."

"What do you mean, Rabbi?" one of the men in the crowd asked. "How can we worship HaShem without the Temple?"

"Every man is a temple of HaShem, my friend," Jacob leaned toward him and then toward the crowd. "We, as Abraham's seed and the inheritors of deliverance from Egypt are required to perform the ordinances of the Temple, individually and as a people. But, what HaShem desires most is for each one of us to approach Him through the chambers of our hearts and minds, reaching to Him with our spirits. Pray always in the Name of mine, in the name of HaShem, and whatever you ask He shall give to you."

"You mean we do not need to bring sacrifices to the Temple anymore?" asked another.

"What about circumcision?" asked a man who had a little boy in his arms. "It is a law to us," he said.

"By all means we must continue to honor the ordinances of the Temple and the Torah," Jacob explained. "Do that as required, but do not leave it merely to the priests to accomplish a change in your hearts. Seek HaShem in the secret chambers of your mind and heart, calling upon His name with every breath. In HaShem are many mansions, chambers where we may dwell and where HaShem will come near to us. But, we must climb the ladders to the chambers as we increase in understanding and piety."

Jacob paused to look around him. He looked into the eyes of

almost every person there, men, women, and children. He could see that they were perplexed. They did not understand he was talking about more than a mere prayer. He was trying to uplift their consciousness of themselves, each other, and HaShem. Indeed, Jacob now understood that the purpose of HaShem through Torah was to raise the souls and consciousness of the people. But, they were not all prepared for his message. It was still a time of growth, even for those who had been exposed to the mysteries. He realized why Joses had been careful with these things and how he approached the people at large with much simpler words before he brought them into his circle. While Jacob had decided to go to Jerusalem and teach the way he had seen Joachanin do, he realized he had gone too far too fast. He decided to return to Damascus and discuss these things more in depth with those who already had some initiation into his meaning.

"To them who have eyes to see, and ears to hear I give this message with my lips," he said. "If any want more, let him ask me."

"What about the Chief Priests? Why must we do as they tell us?" asked another.

"And even Caesar and Herod?" a voice cried from the back of the group, and yet Jacob could not see the face of the man that asked the question.

A trap?

"The Chief Priests sit in Moses' seat. Therefore, do all they tell you to do, but do not do as they do. Be more righteous than they are, and more righteous than Herod," Jacob carefully said.

He then turned to leave and noticed the High Priest's guards quickly approaching from the porticoes of the Temple. He tried to depart through the crowd, but there were too many people and he could not get past them. The guards caught up to him and seized him. For the guards who had not seen Jacob often themselves, he appeared to them to be similar to Joachanin, but they were not sure.

The people stood almost silent as the guards bound Jacob and began to lead him away.

"Disperse now!" the guard commander bellowed to the crowd. "Anyone who does not depart will face incarceration." He then motioned to the detail holding Jacob to return up the steps to Caiaphas. As Jacob was led away, the people began descending the steps and returning to their other affairs. Many could be seen looking back as they talked in hushed tones to each other over the events that had just transpired.

"What did he do?" one man said to another who simply shrugged his shoulders, not knowing himself.

"He spoke nothing unlawful, all he did is speak of HaShem and our hearts," said another who was walking with his wife.

"Is it now unlawful to discuss our religion in public?" asked another, who then turned around and shook his fist at the guards. "Have the Romans and Herodians decided that we no longer may listen to any other than themselves?"

As the people continued on their way, the guards took Jacob to Caiaphas.

"Your Holiness," the guard commander said as he entered the High Priest's chambers. Caiaphas motioned for him to enter.

"We have the man in custody. He nearly escaped and we had a minor disturbance with the crowd."

"Yes, no doubt," Caiaphas responded, placing his clenched fist on the table. "I will never again permit this conduct in Jerusalem. I will punish anyone who tries, including the Immerser. Bring him to me."

The guard commander motioned to his assistant in the doorway and the detail entered with Jacob in bonds, somewhat disheveled from the treatment he had received. Caiaphas had still not looked at him.

"Joachanin, so we see each other again," he said as he looked around to the rear of his seat to adjust a vase, taking time to control his visible distaste for Joachanin. "How is it that Herod allowed you to leave?"

"Joachanin is not here," Jacob answered. "My name is Jacob."

Caiaphas spun around, knocking to the floor the vase he had

been handling. The shattering of the vessel echoed through the room.

"Jacob?" he raised his voice in volume as he said Jacob's name. He looked at Jacob and motioned for the guards to bring him closer. "An Essene for real and not Joachanin?" Caiaphas paused to think the situation through. "What was your business on the Temple steps?"

"Preaching," Jacob responded.

"Preaching what?" Caiaphas demanded.

"That the people need to approach HaShem with their hearts, not just in the outward ordinances of the Torah." Jacob was almost preaching to Caiaphas.

"Were there any witnesses?" the High Priest questioned his guard commander.

"None that we detained, Your Holiness," the commander said.

Caiaphas was feeling somewhat foolish. Seizing an Essene preacher, an unarmed man and one dressed in white linen was not going to look good to the people or to the Romans. Should he, he thought, accuse him of some crime even without a witness? No, that may not be a good idea in this case. It was probably better just to give him a warning and let him go.

"Jacob, you say?" Caiaphas began, and Jacob nodded affirmatively. "Not this Yeshua we have heard so much about?" Jacob shook his head side to side. Caiaphas continued, "I warn you not to gather the people into such crowds. These are dangerous days and such gatherings are cause for concern. If you follow my instructions, there is no difficulty and I can let you go."

Jacob had kept his head and did not rail against Caiaphas, even though he wanted to do so. "There was no intention on my part to cause any grief to the High Priest or the orderliness of the House of the Lord," responded Jacob.

"Very well, you are free to go," Caiaphas motioned to the guards to remove the bonds and escort him out.

As he departed the High Priest's chambers and the Temple,

Jacob was silently praying to HaShem, thanking Him for deliverance. He had never actually suffered such an event. The closest he had ever come to being captured was when he and Jude had incited crowds to riot against the tax of Caesar many years before. He had spent most of his time in Damascus. Maybe he was not cut out for the type of exposure Joachanin was capable of managing.

Caiaphas was shaken. The mere thought of Joachanin unsettled him. This Essene had showed no disrespect, but something just did not seem right. Maybe he had erred in releasing him without more questioning. No, what was done was done. But he was sure that the movement of the resistance was again gaining momentum. Pilate was in Jerusalem and Caiaphas decided that he needed to meet with him and Herod's Vizier.

The men met the next morning. They agreed on a plot where Pilate would announce a new plan of bringing Caesar's effigies to place around the city and the Temple to incite the resistance. Once a disturbance started, Pilate would then obliterate the demonstrators and the members of the resistance with them. During the discussion, a Roman soldier delivered a message to them concerning a suspected messianist seen preaching in Galilee who was causing a problem over the tax. Pilate had had enough and sent word to prepare for a crackdown. He wanted Joachanin secretly moved to Machaeros in preparation for his plan to totally abolish Jewish Laws and have a stranglehold on Jerusalem. Caiaphas cautioned him against any action that could not be justified to the people and to Caesar. Pilate scoffed at him, realizing that the High Priest was really only concerned about his own position and feared to endanger his lifestyle or position of prestige. Pilate rejected his arguments and returned to Caesarea where he ordered reinforcements from Caesarea to the Antonia Fortress in Jerusalem in preparation for the bloodbath.

The Army reinforcements arrived in Jerusalem at night with Caesar's effigy on their ensigns and they began to erect images and statues at prominent places, including the Temple. The next day the people saw this deliberate violation of their sacred laws and started to join in small clusters of demonstrations against this desecration of their religion and holy sites. Caiaphas watched all this with some trepidation and, fearing a major confrontation, reneged somewhat on his idea to be so forceful once the reality and danger of the situation dawned on him. He again concerned himself about Caesar's reaction and sent word to Pilate that there may be a better way. Pilate was too far on the path to retract his position. The setting was ripe for the flaming of a general rebellion that would allow him to reap glory.

Joses' followers and many people in Galilee including those watching for Joachanin in Tiberias heard the news of the images in Jerusalem and went to Caesarea to protest their arrival in Jerusalem. Joses, however, decided to stay in Galilee to ensure that he could respond if needed. The crowd's numbers surged as they arrived in Jerusalem and Caesarea to protest against Pilate. In Caesarea, Pilate refused to grant the people their ancient laws against the statues and ensigns, so many fell to the ground and refused to move. The crowd continued to lay prostrate for the next five days to protest Pilate's actions in Jerusalem.

During this time Joachanin heard from Herod that he was moving him to another location. To conceal their intentions, Caiaphas and Pilate had demanded of Herod that Joachanin have no more contact with any of his followers. Herod had to accomplish the move in secrecy and would use the events in Jerusalem to his advantage. He arranged for the movement a day after the last visit Joachanin would ever receive. The actual transfer would begin at the time Joachanin usually took his walk and his view from the wall. As more of the people heard about the events concerning the images in Jerusalem, many left the area to go to Jerusalem to protest, or to Caesarea.

At that point, Herod had a man similar in appearance to Joachanin dress in his clothes and walk the usual areas and then appear for a short time on the wall. During this diversion, Herod had Joachanin bound and gagged and placed in a box that concealed him from view and prevented his escape. With a small group of Herodian Guards and Romans dressed as mere merchants, they took

Joachanin from Tiberias. Once they were several furlongs from the palace and out of the view of possible spies, they were joined by a Century of Romans for security and they took Joachanin to Herod's Palace Fortress of Machaeros on the east side of the Dead Sea. Herod planned to depart for Machaeros as well after the operations were completed.

The subterfuge of the man who appeared to be Joachanin walking in the palace area at Tiberias continued for many days. Although he was deeply resentful of the accusations Joachanin made publicly against him and his establishment, Herod was more afraid of what would happen when the people did not see the Immerser any longer. Herod knew the people respected the Essene and, in his own mind and heart, Herod did as well. It was not hard for him to envision a general uprising once Joachanin disappeared altogether.

So, Herod requested further assistance from the Roman Commander and Pilate to ensure his own safety after Joachanin's transfer. They saw the opportunity, as well as the dangers, and agreed to fortify Herod's guards and the Roman Century at Tiberias with a Roman Cohort for the express purpose of putting down any uprising over the affair. The agreement was that the Cohort would camp several miles to the northwest to best use an element of surprise. More support could come from Caesarea as needed.

If Pilate had his way, he would now be able to justify a massive bloodshed under the guise of a civil disorder in at least three places, possibly even forcing the resistance to fight him in the open. Things were falling into place, the people in Jerusalem already upset about the effigies and statues of Caesar, the protests to him in Caesarea also regarding the effigies in Jerusalem, and now the disappearance of Joachanin that would fan the flames in Galilee.

In Jerusalem, the whole city was now in a riot over the statues and effigies. The crowds, many led by followers of Jude and accompanied by people from the countryside, protested the actions of the Procurator, and the Herodians and Jews who collaborated with him. Jude himself went to Caesarea to lead the protests there.

In Caesarea, the crowds continued to gather and Pilate felt

the moment had come. He called them to the open market place telling them he would there give them an answer to their protests and demands. His plan was to kill them all using soldiers in civilian clothing with concealed weapons and regular soldiers who would encircle the crowds and fall upon them. Pilate believed the people were where he wanted them and that his soldiers could easily dispatch many of the resisters. His soldiers in disguise and large reserves of troops were ready to attack and kill all who protested his desires. The plan should unfold equally well in Caesarea and in Jerusalem.

But, as Jude watched the developments, he realized it was a trap. He saw Pilate move toward one of his officers, and he could tell that Pilate was coordinating some kind of plan. Jude watched closely as Pilate gave an order to his soldiers to surround the Jews with their weapons. The soldiers rushed to comply and encircled the crowd in three ranks. Once the soldiers were in place, Pilate told the crowd that he was going to have the soldiers cut them in pieces and ordered the soldiers to draw their weapons. If the people did not immediately disperse, he would put them all to immediate death. Jude, now as his alias Yeshua, was certain of the planned slaughter and entered the fray to tell all the rioters to lie down and say they would rather suffer death than permit the violation of the Torah.

"He who obeys Torah need not fear the law of Caesar this day!" he yelled as loud as he could. "Obey Torah and sacrifice your lives for HaShem, and let HaShem take care of Caesar," Yeshua pleaded.

The people scolded him, but as his warnings became more desperate, the people started to respond to him. They began to lie down, baring their necks while asking for death rather than a desecration of their religion. Yeshua saw it as the only way to prevent a slaughter as the signs of military activity were now plainly taking place with soldiers also moving down several of the side streets.

Pilate could not believe what he saw. The entire crowd was prostrate on the ground demanding death rather than desecration.

"What is this?" Pilate seethed, pacing back and forth, growling under his breath, "I cannot believe what I am seeing! These are the great warriors of Judea? They will not even stand up and die as men! They are pathetic creatures, these Jews." He looked over at his commanders and shook his head again, clenching his fists and gritting his teeth. He then looked away and back at the crowd. "Caesar will have my head if he hears I massacred unarmed civilians lying on the ground. Certainly word of this would reach him and nothing I can do will stop it. He will see this action by the people as an act of submission and a pleading for their religion," he could not help but talk to himself and he shook his head in disappointment.

"Your Excellency," the Roman Commander said, "I did not hear what you directed."

"Nothing," said Pilate, "I suppose if they feel this strongly about it, even Caesar would give it to them. He would consider killing them a travesty of justice."

With a violent wave of his arm Pilate had the soldiers withdraw.

"People of Galilee and Judea," he could barely force the words from his mouth, "I will respect your wishes and will remove these images so offensive to you." Secretly, he hoped that the other portions of his plan, unfolding in Galilee, and Jerusalem, would have better results.

As Pilate gave his new directions and informed the crowds that he would carry the effigies and ensigns out of Jerusalem, Yeshua and the people were ecstatic, believing that HaShem was fighting for them. A battle had been won, and without the loss of blood of a single Jew. But, Jude was concerned about what the situation may be in Jerusalem. Fortunately, once he arrived back in Jerusalem, he found that cool heads had prevailed there as well.

But, Pilate was not done. There was still Tiberias. His only problem, he realized, was that he had spread his forces thinly. Hopefully, Tiberias would be an easy operation and catch the resistance totally by surprise since the disturbance in Jerusalem acted as a diversion.

In the meantime, Joses was having his followers watch for Joachanin at the Herodian Palace in Tiberias when one day they did not see him. The Teacher was not walking at the appointed time, and he made no appearances at any other. Simultaneously, Joses also received word that Pilate had backed down and removed the statues and effigies. The timing of the events caused Joses to fear the worst and instructed two of his men to visit Joachanin. As Joses had anticipated, the guards refused the visit. Joses was now sure that something was wrong and he sent messages to his allies and to Damascus that he thought Joachanin was dead or that Herod had moved him.

Word spread quickly that Joachanin was missing and the people began to protest all across the country in larger and larger groups. As a result, Herod became concerned that the forces he had available to him were not sufficient, and he sent runners to Caesarea that he needed assistance. With the news of the dispatch of the additional Romans from Caesarea, the people's anger brought them to large demonstrations outside of the palace.

"Where is Joachanin?" cried the crowd as they saw Herod walking along the wall of his palace so he could view the disturbance. "Down with Herod and Caesar!" the crowd began to chant. "You take our bread, take the fruit of our labors, and then take our spiritual leaders!" cried men from various locations in the crowd. "What is this that you do?"

Joses' agents were amongst the crowd trying to determine if and when Herod may strike. They kept Joses informed of the developments through a system of messenger runners, while Joses set up an alternate headquarters closer to Tiberias. He knew he would need to interdict any reinforcements coming from Caesarea, at least cutting off the supply lines so that his forces could protect the people from a wholesale slaughter. There was no time to gather a large force to repel the Romans, and it was unlikely to succeed, anyway. It would merely cause a Roman response to indiscriminately attack across the Galilee, a possibility that may happen even as a result of a small uprising.

But, there was little that anyone could do to stop the gathering storm. He was certain it was a plan of Pilate's from the beginning to try and force the resistance to respond in a large-scale open battle so that the superior forces of the Romans could destroy them. But, he also could not stop the people from their anger. While he was well respected, the disappearance of Joachanin was not something he could placate, nor accept. He also sent runners to other resistance leaders including those in Jerusalem and Damascus so that they could prepare for any eventuality. He then began directing his fighters to the most important locations and tasks.

"We have no choice but to attack the Romans as they enter Tiberias, which they surely will do. But we also need to attack the reinforcements and supply lines that proceed from Caesarea," he told Eleazer and his other leaders. "Eleazer, you take the first and second company and set up in the hills to the west. Attack the columns of the Romans from the rear and engage them in delaying tactics to slow their advance. The third and forth companies will remain with me. We will need to engage any attack."

Eleazer gathered his forces and planned to move quickly the rest of the day and during the night to the hills west of Tiberias on the way to Caesarea. He moved with haste because he was afraid he was already too late to slow the Roman advance.

Joses looked at the terrain north of Tiberias and knew he could not meet a large Roman Army Unit on open ground. He decided that he needed to conduct a delaying action at the town's borders to inflict the most casualties against the Romans and allow the people to flee to their homes. It was the best he could hope for. He also continued to try and communicate the dangers of the demonstration to those so engaged. But, it was fruitless.

On the afternoon of the second day of the demonstrations, the gates of the palace suddenly opened and a hoard of soldiers attacked the crowd with swords, arrows, spears, and slings. Many of the people close to the gates were killed outright. The crowd began to disperse, but a small group of armed men confronted the soldiers and began to engage them in battle. Joses received word of the fighting and proceeded to a small hill where he could watch the action and prepare his fighters should it be necessary. As he watched from the hill, he looked to his left and saw a Roman Cohort attacking from the north of the valley, traversing the distance to the palace quickly even though they remained in formation. It was obvious that the attack from the palace and the advance of the Cohort was a coordinated maneuver. He knew he had only a short time to act.

As the soldiers from the palace slew many who tried to flee from them or fight them, more armed men from Galilee entered into the battle. But, they were not in a position to know that they were being trapped. There was nothing Joses could do but to try and stay the slaughter. He had placed his men in their positions on the north side of the town during the night, and they waited for his commands. They took additional precautions to evacuate the people of the area just before dawn to prevent them from being injured or killed.

As the Romans closed the distance between themselves and the outskirts of the town, Joses used a cloth to signal to his commander there that the attack by the Romans from the north had begun. As the Romans approached the edge of the town, the resistance unleashed a barrage of arrows, felling a number of the Roman soldiers on the front line. The Romans would have formed a phalanx at such an event in other circumstances, but the Roman Commander, surprised by the attack, had the soldiers rush the city. As the first Romans ran through the area of small homes at the outskirts of town, the Zealots met them with a fury.

Outnumbered, but having the element of surprise, the Zealots were able to inflict heavy casualties on the Romans. The fight was one of lightening quick attacks, followed by retreats to a staging point, and then new attacks in a different location. The movement of the action confused the Romans who did not know the next direction of an assault. In the meantime, archers on housetops and in concealed positions picked off various individual Romans further disorienting them and preventing their advance.

Joses with his smaller force hurried to the area of the palace where his fighters attacked the Herodian Guards and the members of the Roman Century who were now in a pitched battle with armed

Galileans. With Joses and his force joined against the Romans, the unarmed demonstrators were now able to flee the area. The increase in the force against the Herodians and Romans was sufficient to force them to retreat back to the palace. Joses considered storming the edifice, but was not sure what he may find inside. He held back his men far enough to avoid the archers on the palace walls and allowed the palace gates to close. He then ordered his men, and any of the Galileans with him who were willing, to assist in the attack on the Roman Cohort north of the palace. He left a few spies and a runner to ensure that Herod sent no new troops from the palace into his rear.

To the west, Eleazer was watching as a Roman column moved through the hills. He had already found and silenced many of the Roman force's flank scouts and was preparing to attack the supply line at the end of the column. He estimated that the force was at least a cohort, maybe more. The Roman advanced guard, now about two furlongs ahead and to the east of the main column, was under attack by Eleazer's men. As the main column moved quickly forward to engage the battle, the supply line was left mostly unprotected. At the opportune moment, Eleazer ordered the attack to destroy the stocks and supplies. His men leaped out of their places of concealment and fell upon the few Roman soldiers who were left to guard the equipment and stores. Eleazer's men easily dispatched them, and then proceeded to burn the supplies that they could not take with them. They were mostly concerned about obtaining weapons and battle supplies that could assist in smaller guerilla operations.

With the supply train quickly sacked, their attention turned to attacking the rear of the Roman column that was now in a choke point in the hills because of the ambush of the advanced guard. The Romans had lost many of their men and were trying to array in battle formations suitable for the terrain, but they were surrounded and unable to maneuver effectively. It was then that Eleazer and his men arrived to attack the west of the column and engage them in a major battle. Losses were now heavy on both sides, but the Romans were obviously working to return to Caesarea. As Eleazer doubted he would gain any great deal even if he could annihilate the Roman force, he was more concerned about additional Roman units that could arrive in the area. He moved his line to allow the Romans to retreat west and disengage his forces. The surviving Romans took the opportunity and fled back towards Caesarea.

As Joses now joined the fight on the north side of Tiberias, men of the town and other locals who had been watching the fighting took up weapons and also attacked the Romans. It was obvious the Romans had no idea that they would be involved in fighting prior to their arrival near the palace. While their skill and equipment far surpassed the Zealots and their allies, the Romans could not regain the initiative in the battle they sought. They began a piecemeal retreat out of Tiberias and north to their encampment.

However, several Roman soldiers saw Joses as he disengaged from the fighting and took a position near some brick buildings to evaluate the overall condition of his forces and the actions of the Romans and Herodians. Two of the Romans who saw him thought him to be the same man who may be the leader of the Sicarii, but were certain he was at least the commander of the present action because of his manner of controlling the revolutionaries. They saw that Joses was separated from his main group and decided that they had an opportunity to seize him, or kill him.

"Is not he the man we suspect as the leader of the Sicarii?" said the leader, almost too surprised to know what to do. "Yes, I am certain of it." He looked around and assessed his situation and resources. "Yes, we must capture this one. Think of the honor and the rewards! Come on, let's do this."

Gathering several more Romans to assist them in their design, they went after Joses and the men who were with him. Since he was separated from the main fighting as he was examining a portion of the battlefield, the Romans overwhelmed his small team. The Zealots, realizing their predicament and the danger to Joses, fought all the more fiercely. Joses, himself, was forced to engage several Romans with his sword, easily slaying two of them and wounding a third. However, the Romans killed two of Joses' men and wounded another. Finally, Joses was able to clear an avenue of escape, and he and those remaining with him ran deeper into the town with the Romans in pursuit. As usual, the Zealots split up as they ran away, causing some confusion for the pursuing Legionnaires.

The Romans managed to identify Joses, however, and the main group continued to pursue him. But, he slipped away from them due to his familiarity with the town and its terrain. Concerned for their own lives as they were now separated from the main body of Roman troops, and disappointed at their failure, the Romans fled to the palace for safety and the Herodian Guards allowed them entrance.

Upon reaching the safety of the palace, they reported their sighting to Herod Antipas who became incensed. Here they had a perfect opportunity to confront the Zealots and destroy them and Pilate and the Garrison at Caesarea had botched it. While Antipas had feared angering the populace with the disappearance of Joachanin, Pilate and the Roman commanders had assured him that the troublemakers would be destroyed. He now realized that the Romans had not taken the situation seriously enough to provide the proper strength of forces. Instead, their weak triple-pronged approach had been a disaster, a separation of forces easily defeated by the resistance. He now feared that without additional help, his palace might be besieged and destroyed. But, the word from the walls of the palace was that the crowds had dissipated and the fighting had apparently left the city. Things were calming down. Herod decided to hold his defenses and wait. He was confident that the Romans from Caesarea would arrive soon. But, he did not yet know that Eleazer had stopped them as well. His disappointments were about to increase.

Joses' forces began to reassemble near the edge of town. He knew he had to speak to them and allow them to begin their departure from the area and return to their homes. Despite the victory, Roman retribution could come at any moment and Joses knew he did not have the forces necessary to defeat a Legion or more. He also realized he may never again see Joachanin. He sent word to

Jude and Jacob concerning his efforts, his successes, and his failure to free Joachanin.

Pilate was still not done. He ordered that the leaders of the rebellion in Tiberias must be found and crucified. A legion was sent, as Joses feared, to Tiberias and many hundreds of men accused of being members of the resistance were arrested and crucified. Most of them were innocent, or were never proven to be revolutionaries by the Romans or the Herodian administrators. If anyone looked suspicious, or if they had been recognized as part of the disturbance, they were bound, beaten, and hung on a stake. Tiberias itself was mostly spared, but whole villages in the surrounding parts of Galilee were burned, their inhabitants killed, crucified, or sold into slavery. The soldiers who had seen Joses and mistaken him for Jude reported what they saw to their superiors who then had them looking once again for Joses in particular, although they did not know exactly who he was.

While sorrow, grief, and anger engulfed the Galilee, Joses pondered the results of his attempt to save the demonstrators from their own actions. As he watched the stakes and crosses mount on the land and those hanging from them suffering agonizing deaths, families being burned from their homes, and the general persecution of the populace, he could not help but feel alone and despondent. His mastery of the mysteries and his well developed stoicism still could not prevent him from feeling the magnitude of the devastation. He retired with his family to Emmaus to meditate and come to grips with what he needed to do.

Aggravated over his losses and the embarrassment in Tiberias, Pilate decided on another ruse to get the resistance to take up arms on a more massive scale that he could confront militarily and with superior forces. He schemed with Caiaphas to take the sacred money from the Temple treasury and use it to begin building an aqueduct with images on it from the hills to the city of Jerusalem. This plan went out publicly so as to stir up every citizen, down to the most tame and docile of the people. The matter was on everyone's lips, and all, even those normally supportive of the Romans, began to murmur against Pilate.

"First this Roman placed idols of Caesar in our land and upon our Temple, desecrating our holy places and defying our laws!" one orator cried in Jerusalem, his speech gathering many of the people who shouted in agreement. "He then removed them, thanks to HaShem, blessed be He, but has returned to do a greater profanity. He now takes the treasury of the Temple, the offerings to HaShem, and uses them to build an idolatrous water duct for his own pleasure and to please Caesar, not HaShem!"

"Yes, yes!" those of the crowd yelled. "Down with Pilate, down with Caesar!" they all shouted.

This was repeated throughout Judea and the Galilee. As construction of the aqueduct proceeded, and the money from the sacred Temple treasury was taken, the hue and cry elevated throughout the land.

Jude, as 'Yeshua', and Jacob preached publicly against the actions of Pilate and the unwillingness of Caiaphas to refuse the Roman Governor the sacred treasure. Even after long orations and written demands, Pilate refused to recant his position. It was obvious to Jude, Jacob, and even Joses who was in Emmaus, that Pilate wanted another excuse to justify a flow of blood. However, the people remembered the retributions in Galilee for the actions against the Romans and Herod over the disappearance of Joachanin. While they wanted to fight Pilate, they could not bear another bloodbath of their people. Redress to Caesar, perhaps, should work, they reasoned. But, even with these actions they saw Pilate was not going to back down. As a result, Jude decided that planned military and other drastic actions against the builders of the aqueduct and against the rich in the city who agreed to it, were the only tools the people had left to them. Before launching his offensive, he went to Emmaus to discuss it with Joses.

The two brothers met in Elazer's small house in Emmaus near the River Dismas. It was late in the evening, almost dark, with a slight but noticeable breeze from the west. Joses had just completed a meditation, an instruction to a new initiate in the use of one of the seventy-two names of HaShem for obtaining an answer to a question of merit. Joses did these instructions often, as he was now a master, having ascended the chambers through the workings of the Merkava (mystical chariots), a special type of Hechalot meditation. He introduced his disciple to his brother.

"Nehunia, this is my twin brother, Jude," Joses arose, as did his disciple, greeting Jude as he entered the modest home. Jude extended his hand to Nehunia, but not to Joses. Nehunia, a particularly sensitive young man, could sense a distinct friction between the two brothers. It was not so evident from Joses, but Jude's presence seemed disturbing. He thought he recognized him from somewhere, but Jude looked enough like Joses that Nehunia dismissed the recollection as nothing more than his familiarity with Joses.

"The blessings of HaShem be upon you, Nehunia," Jude said as they completed their handshake and Jude moved to a corner of the room as Joses motioned for him to relax. "Joses has become a great mystic here, I am sure he can teach you many things," said Jude, trying to take any notion from the conversation of his true purposes. He did not know the young man, and merely figured that he was of no consequence.

"Nehunia is a star pupil," Joses told Jude. "He has completed much of his training from me. I suspect he will be a great master in his own right if he continues with his studies and devotion to HaShem. Israel needs the influence and guidance of those who seek the lights."

Jude was slightly offended. "Judah is what matters now," he said, trying to play down the concept of all Israel. Unlike Joses, Jude was not interested in any but the people of Judah and her appendages. "With the insights given down through our Father David the King, we have kept many of the traditions alive despite those who have forsaken them. Have you received this?" he asked Nehunia, obviously in an attempt to see where Joses had taken him.

Joses did not interrupt, but let Nehunia answer for himself.

"I receive whatever HaShem sees fit to bestow upon me," Nehunia responded. "May my teacher allow me to depart?" he asked Joses.

"By all means," answered Joses.

As Nehunia left, Joses turned to Jude. "He is attentive to the plight of Judah and all Israel," Joses began. "It is likely he will become a great mystical master, and he understands the goals and purposes of the movement," Joses continued. "He is well-known to Rabbi Zakkai, but has kept his distance from any actual collaboration with the kittim or the goyim. At the present time, he is my strongest disciple in the Hechalot," Joses concluded.

"You know your situation best," Jude shrugged, "Will he take a position in your new order?"

Joses shook his head, "My intention is not to totally separate from Damascus, you should know that. Our brother Jacob is coming to understand my point of view, and concedes on these points. The issue is not allowing the men of Israel to fall into ignorance. We must raise all those who show a capability, not just those who desire to have their daily routine mapped out for them from morning to night. HaShem wants us to meet the mark, not fall short of it, or go beyond it," Joses was trying his best not to inflame the conversation, but he knew he needed to show his resolve.

Jude grew impatient. "My purpose here is to discuss with you the fact that Pilate is going ahead with his plan of robbing the Corban (i.e. sacred money) of the Temple and using it for his water duct and its idols. There is nothing that can be done to stop him short of attacks to halt the progress of the work, as he habitually meets the demonstrations with violence. Again in two days 10,000 of our people will descend on Jerusalem to partake in another protest. We have reason to believe it may turn bloody."

"Jude, every time we take an action, even a defensive one, the Romans seize, kill, crucify, or sell into slavery hundreds, sometimes thousands of our people. What brought me here was the revenge they exacted against the people of Galilee after our defense of the demonstrators in Tiberias. Even if the Romans planned the whole thing as a slaughter, fewer would have died if the resistance had not become involved. Pilate is baiting us. He is nothing more than a butcher. These piecemeal actions are not providing us with victory, nor even maintaining our position. Without a concerted, diplomatic and military plan, our efforts are doomed." Joses was not afraid of a fight, he had come to realize that if things were to be done right, a new strategy was necessary.

"See, it is obvious," retorted Jude. "You have no desire to put your trust wholly in HaShem and do the works which will free our people. You are no different today than you were as a young boy. Always running off to find something else."

Joses reached over and held his brother's right arm, looking straight into his eyes, "HaShem has revealed to me during my meditative ascensions that the Temple in Jerusalem is of little consequence, defiled and unsalvageable. We do the outward ordinances, but it is a shell. HaShem is no longer there. When HaShem's house is desecrated, HaShem destroys it. Likewise, our people are polluted; their worship has not brought them, as a people, to the requisite consciousness. Have you not read that HaShem is sick of the blood of the sacrifice? Why? Because they have used it as an idol, worshipping the house and its ordinances and not HaShem. Without leaving the works undone, they should also seek to elevate their wisdom and understanding so that they come to a knowledge of HaShem, to beautify their souls with righteousness and mercy. Their works do not bring about a change in their hearts because they refuse to search the soul of the Torah."

"Do not lecture me on the mysticism of our fathers," Jude interrupted. "Your reference to the Tree of Life is not the issue here. Surely the outward commandments and ordinances are to bring our people to a point where they can obtain a higher level, but what I am discussing here is the theft by this Roman of our strength and our sacrifices to HaShem. Surely that is as much an issue as the resurrection of the ancient understandings. If not, how can we survive as a distinct people?"

"The Herodians were forced to convert to our religion by our former leaders, the Hasmonaeans. Do you not remember that HaShem visits the iniquity of the fathers to the third and fourth generation? Our people, as a whole, approved and supported Jonathan the King in this wicked endeavor, and now our people suffer because of it. We brought it upon ourselves, and only a rectification will turn it around," Joses reasoned with his brother. "The Temple is a Herodian edifice, it is not HaShem's. His will needs to be written upon the hearts of the people, and in Shiloh."

Jude stood and shook his garments. "Are you willing to lend your forces to our cause or not?" asked Jude.

Joses shook his head saying, "My path HaShem has shown to me. The righteous must show the way, and bring all creation along with him, or die trying. Shedding the blood of more men will not bring peace. It will bring more destruction. Battle is justified against the kittim and the collaborators, but that is not the wisest path and it is not for me right now. HaShem will show me what we should do if you can remain patient and meditate on the chambers."

"Then we are through," Jude said conclusively. "The Council will be informed, and we will honor HaShem and defend Judah, the people, and the Temple."

"HaShem has shown me the end of the path you now take, Jude," responded Joses as he stood. "What you have proposed shall end in the destruction of many of our people, the end of Judah, and the destruction of the Temple."

Jude looked at Joses in disgust and left the house. Joses immediately sat down and began a meditation.

As he walked quickly to resume the companionship of his followers, Jude saw Miriam, the wife of Joses, standing amongst some men and women not far from the home where Jude had left Joses moments before. It appeared to Jude that Miriam was engaged in some type of instruction to the small group. His curiosity overcame him and he moved closer to listen.

"HaShem desires that all of us, men and women, seek Him out. Search for HaShem in your hearts and minds, for He is in you, and you are in Him. Become Temples of His Spirit, meditate upon the Name, the Ruach HaKodesh[18] will be your reward, and then you can go further into His Kingdom," she was saying to the group as they sat beneath a fig tree.

Just then she noticed Jude. She excused herself and approached her brother-in law.

"No disturbance was intended to you, Miriam," Jude remarked as she came closer to him, standing the obligatory arms length away. "It is not common to have a woman addressing a group like this. And, you seem to be expounding upon the mysteries."

"My husband is my teacher, and he instructs me to instruct others as the Ruach HaKodesh moves me. Principally, however, my children are my responsibility. As I teach my children sometimes the local people hear the instruction and wish to take part. Such was the case this evening. These remained after Martha helped the children to settle for the night," Miriam explained. "How was your visit with my husband?" she asked.

"It is not really my place to complain to a man's wife concerning him," Jude was matter-of-fact. "You know our predicament, and you know that Joses' claims are of no concern to me. However, he has strong alliances and these could be important for the good of Judea."

Miriam had no intention of second-guessing her husband. "Joses is my king," she responded, "even if others do not accept him." As she spoke to Jude, she noticed two men go through the front door of the home where Jose and Jude had just met. She looked back at Jude who nodded his head affirmatively to her answer and excused himself. He walked slowly at first, and then gained speed in his stride as he returned to his companions and headed back east towards Jerusalem.

Miriam quietly walked to the door of the house where Joses and Jude had met and looked cautiously into the main room to see if she could recognize the visitors. She saw no one but Joses who was still in meditation, his head moving in rhythm to some particular words he was uttering. She knew not to disturb him. But as she turned and walked away, she heard him call to her.

"Miriam," he uttered softly, "Return for a moment."

Her heart lightened at the mere thought of remaining in his presence. She entered the room and followed his gesture to sit down and join him. They sat quietly for a few moments, not speaking, but looking at each other. Then, he spoke again to her.

"Of all who are with me," he began, "you are not only my wife, but the most gifted and important of all my disciples. Indeed, we are one, bishirt and bishirtah. To you will HaShem place the burden of our children, Martha assisting you, and the carrying away of the kingdom into another land. However, Martha is the other half of the Life, and we will need her here for my ascension to the next chamber."

Miriam was stunned, unsure of the words she was hearing from Joses. But, she remained silent, allowing him to continue.

"My ascensions have brought me to a place where you both must join me so that we may proceed further. Go and return with Martha."

Miriam arose and hurried several homes away to where Martha was sitting quietly weaving a small blanket.

"Joses calls for both of us," Miriam said in quiet tones. The younger children were fast asleep, but the oldest were sitting close by.

"Jochanan, watch for me," was all Martha had to say to her son. She then placed her weaving materials on the floor and followed her sister Miriam to the other house.

Come, follow me to the upper room," Joses said to them as they entered the house. He stood and helped the women to the stairwell. They climbed the stairs together on the east side of the house. As they entered the upper room where Joses kept his most sacred items, Miriam saw Nehunia and another man in the corner of the room in the shadows. The man, she finally recognized, was one of the priests from On. Joses motioned for them and they all descended the stairs to a small room on the first floor where the mikvah, constructed so that fresh water constantly supplied by the Dismas River passed through it, had been prepared for Joses. The priest from On spread ashes from a Red Heifer in the water as he recited a prayer. Joses then entered the water and immersed himself in it while he said several more prayers. Thus purified, he came out of the water and dressed in white linen robes. The group then ascended the stairs back to the upper room.

Joses closed the door and separated them from the outside world.

"Over the past several weeks HaShem has helped me through the chambers and now I await entrance to the Seventh. Tonight HaShem will bring me near to His Presence, for you are my bishirtah," he said, gesturing to Miriam, "a likeness of HaShem's Shekinah. And you, my dear Martha," he said gesturing to her, "complete the mirror of His image which we are, and the guardians await my arrival in the upper chambers. Stand one step to my right side, Miriam, and Martha, to her right. Both of you hold each other's right hand. Soon, I will descend into the Merkava[19] and then ascend to the angels guarding the supernal chambers, going through the chambers until I finally reach the Seventh and highest."

Miriam's body trembled at the sound of his words, and she could feel the immensity of the event unfolding before her, even in these humble surroundings. Joses nodded at Nehunia who then placed his prayer shawl or tallit[20] over his head. She watched as Joses stood and placed his tallit over his head to create a tent similar to a portable tabernacle. She moved close to his right side as he had instructed, and Martha then moved next to her right side. The women covered their heads with tallits and held each other's right hands. Joses began with a short prayer of thanks to their Creator. The priest of On said nothing, he was there merely to ensure that Joses entered the Merkava vision and that his spirit was still able to remain with his body after entering near to the Divine Presence.

Then, Joses began repeating the Divine Names.

CHAPTER NINE

Jude and his band were still proceeding east toward Jerusalem when he felt what seemed to be an impression so strong that he could not continue his gait. He slowed to an old man's pace and then stopped altogether. His companions, seeing his bewilderment, checked him closely.

"Rabbi, are you well?" asked one.

"Do you need anything?" asked another.

"No, everything is quite alright. It seems though, that some vision seeks to come upon me. I heard a voice and felt a weakness in my heart such as I have never felt before. HaShem's angel may be with me, seeking me to enter meditation. Let us stop here for now," he explained as he sought a place on the ground to rest and ponder. Having placed himself on the ground, he faced east and placed his tallit over his head.

"Stay by me and watch, but only disturb me if you see that I no longer breathe. Then, and only then, wake me, bring me back that HaShem's kiss may not take my soul," he said to his men who were not sure what to make of this sudden development. But, Jude knew from the feeling he had that this vision was not self-induced, but had come upon him when he was unaware. He had no master there to guide him; he had to rely on his companions. The strength of the spiritual call was something he could not ignore, even though he could have chosen to do so.

Almost by instinct he started repeating several phrases in Hebrew to bring himself into a concentration that would lead to a meditative state. It was after the pattern taught by the prophets of old and passed down to select individuals who showed their worthiness. As a student in Damascus, and having been in On, Jude had been received in these traditions and learned a good deal about them, just as had his brothers, Joses and Jacob, even though he had not reached the same levels. His companions merely kept watch as Jude began his rhythmic breathing control and head movements that went along with the phrases he recited with his voice.

Then, he was silent and did not move. Those with him knew that he was now deep in the meditative state, seeing, hearing, feeling, understanding, with spiritual senses, nearly completely tuned out from the real world. They could see his hands held out before him with his palms up, and his head nearly between his knees. None of them dared speak a word or make a sound.

The men waited for nearly an hour before Jude began to stir. He returned to them reciting the phrases a little louder upon each repetition. Finally, he moved his head and said, "Alleluia, Alleluia, Alleluia, Amen." He then brought his hands back to his sides and slowly lifted himself up into a sitting position while removing his tallit from his head. He motioned for his companions to come near to him. They all knelt in the sand just a few feet from him and waited for him to speak.

"My brothers," he began, "HaShem has shown me things that I was not aware of. I must proceed immediately to Damascus and see Jacob, my brother. We cannot stop in Jerusalem, as we must obtain Damascus by nightfall tomorrow. Help me up, please."

They did so and the group again proceeded toward the east.

Nearly this same time, Jacob was meditating in Damascus. His assistant, Gideon, watched over him as he rose higher and higher through the chambers, the places of heaven inhabited by angels and the Elohim. Jacob had done this many times before, but now he stood before the chamber at which he had long been denied entry by the angels that guarded its gate. As before, a voice said to him, "You cannot proceed from here without your bishirtah."

"Amen," said Jacob aloud, so much so that Gideon heard him. But, Jacob did not return from his meditation, and after ensuring his life was still intact, Gideon allowed the vision to continue without forcing Jacob back to the world of matter.

A figure appeared before Jacob's eyes, and it was that of a man, the angel, Metatron. His appearance was as a youth, no blemish in him, wearing long flowing white robes with gold and blue fringes, a golden sash about his waist. His hair was white, adding to the radiance of his face and the majesty of his personage. Although youthful in his appearance, Jacob knew Metatron was one of the elders of the angels. He stood before Jacob and beckoned him to look and see what stood beyond the smoke and mist that surrounded him. Jacob moved closer and looked beyond at the gate of the chamber that was denied him. The gate was like clear, flowing water, yet a solid mass so beautiful, it surpassed anything he had ever seen. Then, he felt the awesome vibration of its power.

For but an instant, if it could be called that, Jacob saw through to the other side of the gate. There, in the smoke and the mist through which he could see nothing more, he saw his brother Joses standing in a brilliant white light with two other beings beside him to his right, one of whom was most certainly Miriam, the other he was not sure. The vision was of such beauty that Jacob now cried aloud with his voice, tears streaming down his face. Gideon knew he was still in his vision, and it seemed to him that what he was seeing was of such splendor that Gideon feared the Teacher might receive the kiss of HaShem and not return to the world. He reached forward and touched Jacob on the right hand, saying to him, "Return, return my brother. Come home,"

Jacob came out of the vision sobbing, but they were tears of joy and that was quite apparent to Gideon. Despite his desire to learn what Jacob may be willing to tell him, Gideon did not speak anything further out of respect for his master. He stood silently until Jacob spoke to him.

"This night my brother, Joses, has entered near to the Divine Presence and he passed through the Seventh Gate. He has sealed the secrets of Abraham and Moses to himself with the will of HaShem. Elazer was right. Joachanin was right. Joses is the Mashiach ben Joseph, the rightful heir of the House of Israel, the true son of Joseph and Jacob in an unbroken line back to Adam. He has arrived because of his faithfulness to Torah and his unwavering devotion to HaShem, blessed be He, who has accepted Joses and brought him into His presence as a son!" Jacob sobbed again, the emotion of the revelation more than he could contain.

"Who would have guessed? Who would have guessed? Joses has obtained the blessings of his religion for himself," Jacob sobbed in happiness and amazement.

Gideon was not sure what to make of it all. He merely stood by as Jacob composed himself and then stood.

"My brother, Jude, will be arriving soon. Let us prepare ourselves for the King of the Jews."

The day went by in Damascus without much change. The brethren did the Torah studies and prepared the needful things of the Community. Nightfall brought Jude and his companions to the city and Jacob's tent. The brothers approached each other and embraced, looking into each other's eyes.

"Did you see?" asked Jacob.

"I saw you looking at Joses, and Joses was above you in the vision," replied Jude. "How is it that he could be above you in a vision of mine?"

"HaShem has spoken to us all at the same time. Our blood is the same, our spirits connected. We are striving to do the will of HaShem despite our separate conditions. The body has different parts with different functions. Yet, the arm cannot say to the leg, 'I have no need of you,' or the head say 'The stomach is not necessary,' but all parts, working according to the will of HaShem will perform their functions."

"But, Joses cannot be above you. What is the meaning of this?" asked Jude.

"It is not so much above," explained Jacob, "as it is that he has attained a greater portion because of his efforts. HaShem let's us each progress according to our strength and desire, or else of what use is our experience? All Salvation belongs to HaShem as a gift, but the glory of it all is our efforts to attain to the heights, as parents rejoice as a child begins to walk."

"Must I submit to Joses?" asked Jude. The question surprised Jacob because he had never seen this type of humility in Jude before, not where the birthright was concerned. But, Jacob knew that a pronouncement from him would not allow Jude his own course, so he answered carefully.

"Do as HaShem and your heart lead you to do. It is not Joses' path to dictate to anyone, but to show by example."

"He has not submitted to the Teacher, to the Oral Torah, or our sages. Yet, you had a vision, and I had a vision, and we both knew it at the same time," Jude was still puzzled.

"Joses has strictly followed the Torah, not adding to it or subtracting from it, keeping himself wholly subject to HaShem, and no man. In what way can we fault him, if HaShem has accepted his path?" explained Jacob. "HaShem may be more concerned with individual progression than we have thought. Maybe the progress of nations and kingdoms is dependent not only on themselves, but upon the individuals that comprise them. Have we not sought to build the righteousness of the people, to present them to HaShem as a Holy Nation that HaShem may support us? Indeed, was not the union of Adam and Eve a political union of two kingdoms, the kingdoms of their bodies and spirits? There is something marvelous in this situation, and as we speak of inviolable liberty, it must be for the people as well as Israel as a nation."

Jude was spellbound. These words coming from Jacob almost sounded Hellenistic, Greek, in character. Yet, he felt there was truth in the words. The problem was Joses' position on the throne. Still, he allowed Jacob to go on.

"It has been said that the secrets were given to the children of Shem, to Abraham, to Moses and passed along by mouth to ear across the generations," continued Jacob. "Moses was first an Egyptian, but the promises reached out across the nationalities, across the abyss and called to him from a burning bush, calling him by his Egyptian name. HaShem never changed Moses' name in the Torah. He was lost from his birthright, but HaShem called him back to it, and he retained his identity. So, we too will be called and raised to a recollection of our true identity. This, it seems, has happened to Joses. Let's see what he brings to us. In the meantime, we have work to do to secure liberty for the people of HaShem and the nation of Israel."

"I will defer to you, for now, brother, as your purity allows you to see and understand more than all the rest of the family, even all of Israel. But, Joses cannot have the throne. That is not negotiable, nor allowable. Do you agree?" Jude emphasized the point with a gesture of opened hands in front of him.

Jacob scratched his brow, trying to choose his words. He realized that, like Joachanin, he had arrived at a point of difficulty with Jude over this whole issue. It could not be something easy to resolve. No, it was at the very core of their beliefs.

"For now, brother, let us meditate together and discuss Torah. It is the best method for resolving our questions."

The brothers walked on into Damascus, new ideas challenging their minds. But the reality of the world they lived in would not let them reflect too deeply for too long.

***

Pilate's 200-furlong aqueduct was proceeding on schedule and the use of the Temple Treasury funds to complete the project was not only an insult to HaShem and Israel, but, as was part of Pilate's design, against the Torah as well. Pilate designed it to incite the people; its decorative statues ensuring their rage, for Pilate also used the funds to pay for graven images of Caesar to adorn the columns. It was a double insult that Jude and his warriors could not let stand without resistance. Even Jacob could not go without preaching against the abomination, accusing Pilate of having no respect for the laws and traditions of the people. Much of what the Romans did the Community could overlook, but not this, and not the collusion of Caiaphas.

Jude made plans he hoped would destroy the kittim while restoring the dignity of the Temple Treasury. He began carrying out more resistance operations, attacking Roman Troops and having

Zealots assassinate rich establishment Herodians and Jews who were collaborating with the Romans. His actions struck terror into the politically connected throughout Judea and even into Galilee, which should have been Joses' area of responsibility. Jude could not wait for his brother to take the necessary military actions to support a general revolt. Not hearing any protests from Joses further assured Jude that his course of action was proper.

Pilate and Caiaphas had still not been able to uncover the identity of the leaders of the resistance, even after torturing many of the rebels they had captured in various operations throughout the country. The only name they consistently pried out of the mouths of their victims was 'Yeshua.' It had not helped them. There were many with that name. Those Pilate found who seemed to be of a revolutionary orientation were arrested and crucified, just like Athronges years earlier. The preaching of one particular man named Yeshua whom their spies witnessed in Galilee and Judea did not rise to the level of political insurrection, and all leads seemed to come to a dead end. They had no idea this particular Yeshua was the code name for the twin brothers, Joses and Jude, acting in different sectors of the country. It was obvious that their spy apparatus, in spite of the on-going efforts of Reu, had not yet penetrated the core of the rebel movement. However, Pilate hoped that the need for further intelligence efforts would be eliminated with the slaughter they had planned in Jerusalem. Certainly this operation would strip the resistance of their leaders by bringing them out in the open where they could be cut down for all the people to see. It would show the might of Rome and the senselessness of resistance to Caesar. The plans were set, and the people continued to gather publicly in larger and larger groups to condemn what Pilate had done and Caiaphas had allowed.

Finally, on one particular day, Jude's planning and efforts managed to gather 10,000 people to protest the unlawful usurpation of the sacred money of the Temple. Dispersed among the people were resistance fighters and Zealots who planned to attack the Romans and any of the establishment priests who were in public. Jude particularly wanted Caiaphas. His leaders ensured that the crowd continued moving closer and closer to the city and the Temple.

This was the moment Pilate had been waiting for. His new plan to incite the people had succeeded. The Romans were waiting for the demonstrators, those soldiers in the crowd hiding their weapons under peasant clothing that made them hard to recognize. The cohorts at the Antonia Fortress were in battle order ready to fall upon the Jews and assist in the killing.

The crowds entered Jerusalem and gathered more to their number as they made their way to the steps of the Temple. All the while the people demanded that Pilate cease his use of the funds, and that if he wanted an aqueduct, to place some other method of payment upon them. Men took turns reviling Pilate and Caesar, demanding that they respect the laws of the country in this regard.

Jude knew there could be a battle, and he had prepared his Zealots for a fight. He did not realize this was no oversight on the part of Pilate, but a deliberate attempt to bait him. Jude realized the danger too late.

At Pilate's signal, the disguised soldiers in the crowd attacked the demonstrators, killing or maiming all in their sight, as Pilate unleashed the soldiers from the Antonia Fortress. The blades of the soldiers did not distinguish between men, women, or children, slaying all that were in their reach. The Romans never knew who would produce a sicar and slash them; hence their eyes in such circumstances spared no one. Jude, his tallit over his head to also help conceal his identity, entered the fight with several of his Zealots to try to turn the tide, but he was overwhelmed. All he could do was fight his way back out of the city, taking as many of the demonstrators with him as he could protect. Thousands were killed in the battle, but Jude and those with him managed to escape as the slaughter continued in and around the city.

As he made his way out of the city, Jude found his planned escape routes were blocked either by enemy soldiers or crowds of people. He had no choice but to go through the Valley of Gihinom, a filthy and unclean place, nothing more than a garbage dump.

Realizing the pollution he was exposing himself to, Jude raised his sleeve to cover his mouth and nose, trying to avoid contact with the very air. But, it was useless. The stench and the filth penetrated every attempted barrier, and Jude heard in his mind the words of Joses, "Shedding the blood of more men will not bring peace. It will bring more destruction." Forced into this valley of hell where the mere dust in the air was unclean with dung and filth, polluting his very skin and nostrils, he felt destruction in himself. Not only did Gihinom pollute him, as had the blood of the men he had slain, but his thoughts, as well.

"Joses has cursed me and those who seek to free us from the kittim!" he exclaimed, frightening his men with an intensity of emotion beyond his normal zealousness. Several who followed him stared at his angry face as they hurried along which caused them to lose their footing and stumble over garbage strewn on the ground, some piles still smoldering from a recent burning.

"No man can curse us," said one. "Certainly HaShem does not do as your brother says."

Jude stopped and turned abruptly, staring in the man's eyes.

"He cursed us in that he did not use his forces to assist us! What else did you think?" yelled Jude.

The man froze, fearful of Jude's wrath. But, Jude composed himself, realizing that his words were not fitting for the moment.

"Take no worry, brother," Jude said to him. "My anger is not against you." He paused for a brief moment, looking over the small number of men who had escaped with him. He then motioned to them to hurry along. "We must make all haste out of this place."

As Caiaphas watched the slaughter from the Antonia Fortress, he realized that Pilate had good ideas, but was really only capable of bloodshed. "We must secure our place," he whispered to himself as he smiled wryly. As with Pilate, he decided that such action was appropriate as long as it was done to appear as an act of defense, that they were protecting the people against criminals and rebels.

His eye caught sight of a large number of dead Jews lying in a grotesque pile, left where the Romans had killed them. He stood watching, emotionless as an executioner, as a river of Jewish blood flowed down from the dead bodies to the east gate.

***

Joses and his family had returned to Galilee prior to the battle in Jerusalem. Despite his earlier military activity, he was now trying to devote himself to the principles of detachment, merely observing what was happening in the world, but not reacting to it. The goal was to arrive at a state where he would remain in constant awareness of HaShem and the Divine Presence, not wavering from its vision. While he had engaged in these mystical routines throughout his life, it seemed to him that now was the time for the greatest dedication to them.

However, he did not ignore the realities facing the people. While he felt the need to concentrate his own energies toward the sure knowledge that only the Torah and the Hechalot could provide, he continued to seek for those who would help stay the increasing power of the kittim until he was sure his time had come.

The day after the Sabbath, Joses decided to meet with some of his followers near Tarichaeae to try and divide out those ready for the mysteries of the Hechalot and those ready to join the forces of the resistance. With Eleazer and two other men, he made his way from Capernaum to Tiberias where they stopped to rest. Spotting a shade tree, Joses made his way to it and found a place to sit. He motioned to the others to rest.

"HaShem has been with us," he stated to the men as they gathered about him, Eleazer pointing where he desired the other two men to position themselves to protect Joses. The men took their positions to the right and left of their leaders.

Joses continued, "My brother, Jude, has done the very best he could under the circumstances presented to him. Unfortunately, Pilate and the dog, Caiaphas, have been one step ahead of him. As you know, many of the people were slaughtered in Jerusalem during and following the protest against the aqueduct."

The men all nodded in agreement. They did not notice, at first, a contingent of Roman soldiers watching them from across the courtyard.

"There he is!" exclaimed the Roman who had seen Jude at his capture and again in Jerusalem not long before. "I know that is him, the leader of the Sicarii! Go, and alert the Centurion," he commanded a subordinate. "We will watch from here until we receive word." The man turned and ran as fast as he could to deliver his message. The other Romans continued to watch the four men under the tree.

"It is necessary that we open our ranks to more of those we can trust to reinforce our numbers and to search for the will of HaShem," said Joses who then noticed the Romans watching from the shadows. He did not alarm his men, yet. "While Jude is against me, he is still doing the very best he can in this effort to expel the kittim and return Israel to its rightful heirs. So, our efforts will likewise support his, and we will hold those closest to us who are ready for the chambers. Now, do not noticeably alarm yourselves, but it appears we are the objects of some curiosity from several kittim in the shadows of the far building across the courtyard.

The other men casually looked, carefully concealing their eyes from the soldiers.

"There are at least four of them," said Eleazer. "It is likely there are more and they definitely have an interest in us. Do you recognize any of them, Joses?"

"No, not really," Joses replied. "But, we had better leave now," he said as he rose and headed directly east toward the Sea of Galilee, his men following and then moving ahead of him in an effort to mask who was the leader.

"They are leaving!" said the lead Roman. Where is the Centurion?" he angrily commented, clenching his teeth and hands. "We should go after them now and not wait for them. Let's go, before they get away from us," and he sprinted from the shadows drawing his sword. The others quickly followed.

"They are coming for us!" said Eleazer. "We may need to fight them..."

"Through the door," Joses said to Eleazer and the men as he gently pushed them through an open door as they rounded a corner. "Go on through to the rear, there is another path there and we can double back. Eleazer, you go with him, and you come with me," he said as he divided the small party up to better escape detection.

"Master, it may be dangerous to split our strength right now!" Eleazer feared for Joses' safety.

"They will not see us if we do as I say, now," Joses responded calmly and walked quickly away. "Meet us where the people are gathering to hear us," was all he said as he reversed his robe to place the light side out, and he was gone. Eleazer hurried away with his companion in the opposite direction.

"Where did they go?" the lead Roman asked as the soldiers entered the alley and could not see the four suspects. "They must have ran ahead, or maybe entered the homes. Quick, split up and search the houses!"

"What?" the other soldiers answered with astonishment and almost in unison. One spoke up.

"There are but few of us and we know of the methods of these assassins. It could be a trap. Don't split us up now in this maze. It could be our end!"

"But, this is the leader of the Sicarii!" the lead Roman pleaded. "This will be a glory to us if we capture him. Think of the reward!"

"Not this time," one of them said. "A reward is no good if you're dead. We need more soldiers and a more systematic search. Besides, you are not our commander but for the watch. The centurion alone can authorize this action."

With that the Romans reluctantly turned aside from their pursuit and returned to the courtyard.

Joses and his men made their separate ways through the town and the hills until they met on the hillside where the meeting had been pre-arranged, not far from the water of the Sea of Galilee. Joses and his companion were the first to arrive. Kefa and Andrew greeted them.

"My brother," Kefa said to Joses, "Blessed be HaShem as He has brought you to us in safety. Where is Eleazer?"

"Romans spotted us in the town, so we split up. He should be along, shortly. Have you divided the group?" Joses looked around and saw many different men, and he knew Kefa had done a good job of gathering possible recruits and disciples.

"Yes, brother, praise to HaShem. These are those who have studied Torah from us, and they are ready to hear your words. Some of your disciples are already in the group, carefully listening to their comments. They will report back to us those they feel are the best choices for the cause. Our brother, Jacob, sends you his blessings and Jochanan, Martha's son, is here to assist us. But one, a Jorah ben Netanyahu, is most certainly a hearer for our brother, Jude."

Joses looked around and noticed this Jorah and his companions mingling in the closest group. He slightly shrugged to himself and moved along.

"Do not concern yourself, brother. Jude will never harm us, or what we seek to accomplish. Eventually, he will see the wisdom in our course. Now, we are ready to proceed?" asked Joses.

"Your place is there," Kefa pointed to a small rock in the midst of the gathering where Joses could sit and instruct those closest to him. Once they received the message, they would then split up and carry the words to other small groups sitting short distances from each other. The design was a good way to spread the message and yet look innocuous to anyone who may be suspicious and watching. If there were spies in the group, the words would still escape their complete understanding, as everything would be in code. Only those needing to hear the message of the resistance would hear it. All others would hear nothing but words of peace and hope. Those who responded to the first layer of meaning would be encouraged on to the second, according to their abilities and the evaluations of the leaders. It was a system of communication that had been effective for thousands of years and understood well by Jude and Joses.

Joses took his seat on the rock in the middle of his closest disciples (i.e. talmidim in Hebrew). There were about fifteen of them, and the rest of the gathering was split up into fifteen groups some distance from the main one. Then, Joses, speaking as Yeshua, began.

"Blessed are the poor, for theirs is the Kingdom of Heaven. Blessed are those who mourn, for they shall be comforted. Blessed are the meek[21], for they shall inherit land. Blessed are those who hunger and thirst for righteousness, for they shall be filled. Blessed are the merciful, for they will be shown mercy. Blessed are the pure in heart, for they shall see God. Blessed are the peacemakers, for they shall be called the sons of God. Blessed are those who are persecuted because they try to be righteous, for the Kingdom of Heaven is theirs. Blessed are you when people insult you and persecute you and lie about you because of your allegiance to HaShem. You are the salt of the land. But, if the salt looses its taste, how can it be made salty again? It is no longer good for anything except being thrown out for people to trample on. You are the light of the world. A town built on a hill cannot be hidden; likewise, when people light a lamp, they don't cover it up with a bowl but put it on a lamp stand so that it shines for everyone in the house. In the same way, let your light shine before the people, so that they may see the good things you do and praise HaShem. Now, go and take this message, and then return."

At that, the fifteen disciples got up and took the message to the separate groups. Kefa and Andrew leaned closer to Joses.

"You are ready to declare your Kingdom and say you will give the people land for their inheritances once the Kingdom is in place?" asked Kefa. Joses nodded his head affirmatively. "Then the message you send with Jochanan to Jorah's group is that if they do not support you, they will not receive a reward. This may be dangerous, brother. You call them by their codenames "poor" and "meek" as they are part of Damascus or your own order. They will see that you recognize them."

"They have done many good things, Kefa, but it is time that Jude and those with him, make a commitment we can rely upon. His methods in the mysteries should finally lead him to the truth despite his pride. His course will destroy Judea, otherwise.

"In what manner?" Kefa asked.

"He believes HaShem will support him even as he acts against HaShem's will, not waiting for the good order we propose. Let's see how it goes," Joses smiled as he turned his gaze from Kefa and looked towards Jorah. At that moment, Jorah gazed back towards Joses, obviously disturbed by what he was hearing.

"He has listened," Joses said with confidence. "Let's see how he takes the rest of it."

Kefa looked over to see Jorah tilting his head as if boarding on contentiousness with a slight squint to his eyes. Kefa felt uneasy, not sure what else Joses had in mind to say. At that moment, the messengers were returning to Joses for their next instruction. Joses, again acting as Yeshua, began as they sat down.

"Do not think that I have come to abolish the Torah or the Prophets. I have not come to abolish Torah but to do the Torah as an example to you that you may do the same. I tell you the truth, that until heaven and earth pass away, not so much as one yod (i.e. the tenth letter in the Hebrew alphabet which is also the smallest letter) or a stroke will pass from Torah. So whoever disobeys the least of these commandments of the Torah and teaches others to do so will be called the least in the Kingdom of Heaven.[22] And whosoever asks for anything in The Name of mine, shall receive it, for I tell you the truth, HaShem blesses all those who seek after Him. Do not give that which is holy to dogs, neither throw your pearls to pigs. Should you do so, be prepared for them to step on them and grind them with their feet in disrespect, and then turn upon you to attack you. Continue to ask, and the doors of the chambers will be opened to you. Seek for the truth and the mysteries, and you shall be brought to them. Treat others as you want them to treat you, for in this is the whole meaning of the Torah and the prophets."

The instruction went on for nearly two hours as Yeshua mixed Torah preaching with coded instructions to the resistance leaders of Galilee. He ended his words with a call and a warning.

"Therefore, whosoever hears my words and does them will be like a wise man who built his house on a rock. When the rain descended, and the floods came, and the winds blew, and beat upon the house, it did not fall because its foundation was built on rock, a sure place. Everyone who hears these sayings of mine and does them not shall be like a foolish man who built his house on sand. The rains fell, and the floods came, and the winds blew, and beat upon the house, and it fell. Its destruction was complete."

It was then that Jorah seemed to become edgy, and Kefa noticed that he did not have the same docile demeanor he had at the beginning of the instruction. Joses had just formally demanded that he be recognized as the only legitimate mashiach, and that all others needed to submit to him. This was obviously contrary to Jorah's allegiances to Jude.

"Where will Jude fall in with all this?" Kefa thought to himself. "Even with Jacob's support, Joses has not done what Jude has accomplished against the kittim despite his defeats. Even though Joses' experiences and wisdom seem so much greater, it is obvious Jorah is hesitating."

He did not approach Kefa as the meeting closed, but walked away with his companions toward Jerusalem.

Otherwise, Joses was pleased that he had effectively delivered his messages to the various units of the resistance, the several mystics, and the common people who had just come to listen. Furthermore, his method taught all levels of the Torah simultaneously to those present, each according to his own capacity and level of understanding. Having completed his intentions, Joses arose to leave, several of the new devotees to the Hechalot pressing him for answers to more of their questions. But, Kefa and Eleazer made way for Joses and he walked down the hill toward the shoreline where a small boat was waiting on the Sea of Galilee to return him home to Capernaum. The group around Kefa continued their efforts and Joses could see their sincerity as he turned back to look at them. He then motioned to Kefa to bring several of the more determined seekers to him.

"Men of Galilee," Joses, as Yeshua, hailed them as Kefa allowed them to approach, "You continue to knock and do not concede. Ask me what you seek."

One of the younger men spoke first. Joses did not recognize him from any earlier gatherings.

"Rabbi Yeshua, I want to be your student. I have studied the mysteries and seek further light and knowledge. All my belongings are in your hands. Only, I need a little time to take care of my family matters. We lost our father," the young man said.

"Do you understand what is meant by this-let the dead bury their dead?" asked Yeshua.

"Yes, rabbi. Those not seeking Torah and its mysteries are outside the community of the life. But, if the commandment is to love our neighbors, how less can I love those of my household? Therefore, do not cast me off, but give me this time, and I will return."

"I tell you the truth," Yeshua said in response, "Nothing can come before HaShem and His Torah. You have spoken truthfully, and you may return for further instruction as your circumstances permit. Kefa," Joses said to his brother, "See to it that the young man obtains what he needs."

Kefa nodded and pulled the young man aside to talk to him.

A man now approached whom Joses was sure he had seen before with the kittim. Obviously, this was a possible spy. His question seemed to confirm Joses' opinion of him. The Romans, the Herodians, and their sympathizers were always wary of preachers and constantly spied on Joses and others whenever they could.

"When will this Kingdom come, Yeshua?" the man asked.

"My Kingdom is not of this world," responded Yeshua in typical cryptic fashion.

"Is it a world of the spirit, after men are dead?" asked the man.

"As I told you, heaven and earth will pass away, but Torah will not. We lay up for ourselves treasures in the Kingdom of Heaven," Yeshua answered again.

But the man pressed on him harder.

"Who is the greatest in the Kingdom of Heaven?"

The man obviously expected Yeshua to name himself. But, instead, Yeshua called over a small child who was playing nearby.

"I tell you the truth, except you become as a little child, you shall not enter into the kingdom of heaven. Whosoever humbles himself as this little child, the same is the greatest in the Kingdom of Heaven," Yeshua said while stroking the young boy's hair.

Not quite satisfied, but not able to trap him, the man departed back towards those with whom he had traveled. Joses watched as the group descended the hill to the town.

At that moment, an older man spoke up.

"I seek to stand by you until this world passes away, Rabbi Yeshua" the man said confidently to Joses.

Joses recognized him from other gatherings and remembered that the man had always seemed to grasp the teachings. Furthermore, he always carried a sword, and Joses knew he had contributed significantly to the resistance when he was able to do so. Joses was about to respond to him when the man continued.

"The Kingdom of Heaven?" asked the man.

"As it is in this prayer, so it is," Yeshua responded and then began to pray aloud to his friends.

"Our Father who art in heaven, sacred is HaShem. Your kingdom come, your will be done, on earth as it is in heaven. Give us this day our food, and forgive us our shortcomings as we forgive those who have wronged us. And let us not be tested too hard, but deliver us from the tester, for the kingdom and the power and the glory are yours."

Yeshua looked back at the man. "The Kingdom is at hand, and HaShem's Will must be done on earth now.

"As you have said, he that receives the seed in good ground is he that hears the word and understands it. With me I bring fifty who abide with you in the word, Yeshua," the man said, nodding affirmatively with conviction.

Joses was impressed with his ability. It was obvious the man had studied long and had more than acquainted himself with the manner of parables, the story telling of the resistance to veil their plans. The man had just informed Joses that he had fifty men who were prepared to join the revolutionaries. Joses needed to test him further. He beckoned to him to step a little away from the others.

"The Kingdom of Heaven is like a man who sowed good seed, but while he slept, the enemy came in and sowed tares among the wheat," said Yeshua, staring intently into the man's eyes.

"Then," replied the man, "can he not gather up those tares and reject them?"

"But, if he cut down the tares, he may uproot the good fruit," said Yeshua. "So, we let the two grow together until the time of the harvest. Then, we gather only the wheat into the barn while the tares are bound and burned."

Joses had just told him that he would send a visitor to him to further inquire as to his commitments. However, Joses was nearly certain the man was of the best of intentions.

"Then, we will wait until the harvest," replied the man. "Blessed be HaShem.

"The servants will come to work in two days," replied Yeshua.

"We will honor the servants of the owner of the field," the man said as he bowed his head and departed.

In two days, Joses would send Eleazer or Kefa to him to further test his resolve. This secret method of gaining new additions to the resistance continued as an effective tool for recruitment under the noses of the Romans and their spy apparatus. No one could accuse Joses, or Jude when he did the same, of trying to incite people to rebel against Rome.

Another man approached Joses, one who was already a respected subordinate commander of the resistance and had already taken part in several operations against the kittim including the earlier rescue of Jude.

"The men need more weapons as the Romans have raided several of our supply stashes and taken them," the man said in an irritated but respectful tone.

Joses could not risk a raid on a Roman unit or an armory to supply the revolutionary forces. And, unfortunately, with all the trouble in Judea lately he had not been able to bring in the supplies offered to his emissaries by supporters outside of Palestine.

"If anyone has two cloaks, let him sell one and buy a sicar or a sword," Joses instructed him.

"Yes, that we will do," responded the man who then turned and walked toward town.

"Kefa," Joses called his brother who ran quickly to him. "We must send word to our supporters in Egypt, Syria, Cilicia, and all others abroad who can assist us in any manner possible. Arrange for the council of the 4000 and the council of the 5000 to meet us as quickly as possible."

"Yes, it will be done," answered Kefa who then returned to the few from the crowd who had not yet left.

The sun was now low on the horizon, casting a golden hue on the clouds. Having answered the questions of these few, Joses boarded the small boat that was rocking gently in the water.

"Are you going home, Rabbi?" asked one of the men who anticipated that Joses would want to immediately head north to Capernaum. "Not yet," replied Joses. "My oldest son is in Cana and should be near the shores of Genesarret[23] by morning. We will stop and can get him before we proceed to Capernaum."

"Of course," answered the man.

"Besides," continued Joses, "he is with the father of a particular young maiden with whom he seems to have a righteous fondness," he paused with a smile on his face and a look of satisfaction and joy in his eyes. "My time to arrange their betrothal has come, so the father needs to talk with me."

"Who is it?" asked the boatman, Jonathan, Joses' long friend and confidant, a loyal man who considered Joses the rightful king as well as a spiritual leader.

"A son of a noble who has managed to salvage his genealogy even after the Babylonian captivity and the chaos of everything since. The noble father is influential in Egypt among the Israelites there and is a mystic at On, as well. He is a great ally."

"Yes, but what is the girl's name, if I my ask?" Jonathan mildly continued his inquiry.

Joses closed his eyes as the boat turned and made its way north, a gentle breeze moving Joses' hair away from his face.

"Yedidah," he said. "She is the most worthy young maiden in all the world."

***

Jude and a band of Zealots were camped in the hills not far from Pella on the east of the Jordan River. Having been soundly defeated in Jerusalem in their attempt to unseat Pilate for his desecration of the Temple treasury, they began a recruiting campaign similar to Joses'. They had been moderately successful in only a few short days, but had not obtained the number of members they needed to cover their losses. Jacob, now the major voice at Damascus, had warned Jude during their meeting in Damascus after their visions not to allow the kittim any knowledge that may link the Community leadership with the resistance. Jude had agreed and kept his distance during the efforts to gain more support. Like Joses, he had been "preaching" around Judea and Perea using the same language as Joses to veil his true intentions.

The efforts of the two brothers to act as a single man named "Yeshua" was still very effective. The Romans and Herod's forces thought they were one and the same man. With the codes and parables, both brothers were keeping critical information out of Roman hands. And it appeared to Roman intelligence that this "Yeshua" was constantly traveling and could not possibly be any leader of the rebellion. He wouldn't have the time, and his manner of preaching seemed wholly non-political.

It was late afternoon when Jorah, the man spying on Joses in Tarichaeae, arrived in the camp and started talking to one of Jude's assistants, Laban. It was Laban who had sent Jorah on his mission to gather information on Joses.

"Sit down, Jorah. Tell me what you have learned," Laban said as motioned the three men with him to leave. He moved a leather water bottle and his blankets to allow Jorah more room so they could talk quietly.

"Here is some water, and some fruit," Laban offered him. "Refresh yourself as you have traveled quite far.

"Blessed is HaShem who provides this fruit of the earth and all that He has given me, Amen," Jorah prayed with uplifted hands. He then proceeded to eat and drink.

"Joses is speaking in terms that indicate he has already taken the right to the throne to himself. He speaks of dividing the land into inheritances. There is no doubt he is proceeding to strengthen his alliances in opposition to Jude," Jorah explained.

"Then, it is as we thought," responded Laban. I will report this to Jude."

Laban rose up and left Jorah to continue his meal. Jude was sitting only a few cubits away.

"May I sit with you?' Laban asked Jude.

Jude looked up and saw that Laban had left his guest. It was obvious this was of some importance.

"Please," Jude said as he gestured for Laban to take a seat. Once seated, Laban explained what he had just learned.

"Joses is recruiting in Galilee, and is talking of granting inheritances of land to those who support him," was all Laban said. It got Jude's attention.

"This will never end!" Jude said angrily. "Where is he now?"

"He is returning to Capernaum," answered Laban.

"It is time for me to visit him again," Jude said as he calmed himself. "We will go tomorrow to Capernaum. Go ahead of me and arrange for us to meet in a secure place," Jude instructed him.

Laban left before daybreak. He arrived in Capernaum and left word for Joses to meet Jude at a secure location near the water. It was difficult for the Romans to keep watch over all the fishing vessels, and it was an unlikely place, in the Roman view, for a meeting to discuss open sedition.

When Joses arrived in Capernaum, he found Jude there by the boats to meet him again. Standing next to Jude were Joses' son, Joseph, Yedidah, and Yedidah's father. Apparently, they had all converged at about the same time and were engaged in cordial conversation. As he left the boat, Joses waved at Jude and walked immediately past him.

"Give me just a few short minutes," he said to Jude in hushed tones.

Jude could see that Joses needed to have some words with his son and his companions. "The joy of family always comes first," Jude said in a good-natured tone.

"You are family, too," Joses quickly responded. "But, this man you see here with Joseph is likely soon to be his father-in-law," Joses quietly explained.

"By all means," Jude responded. "May HaShem bless you all," he said cheerfully and went to sit down with a few of his men who were casting pebbles into the water.

Joses smiled at Jude and then looked at his son, Joseph.

"My son, my son," Joses said to Joseph as he embraced him. The young man was nearly as tall as his father. Joses then turned to the man who was Yedidah's father after quickly giving her a reassuring smile. The young face blushed slightly as she smiled in return. The girl's features were as pure as Miriam's when she was the same age. Her light olive skin was perfectly framed with her light brown hair. Her eyes, though revealing some distress, were gleaming lights that seemed to dance all on their own. Joses recognized her as a most pure soul.

"Rabbi," the man said as Joses also embraced him. "May HaShem be always with you and bless you and your house."

"Likewise, Amram ben Kohath," Joses responded. "How is your father?"

"He is well and bids you the same," said Amram. "Your emissaries have been very informative, and we are presently proceeding back to Tarichaeae to be with family while we gather more information."

"And Joseph has had a chance to again see you and your daughter," said Joses as he motioned them to sit with him under a small structure used for shade. Joseph sat next to his father and Yedidah next to hers as Joses and Amram continued with some small talk. Yedidah could hardly look at Joseph now, and Joseph could only catch small glimpses of her when she would chance a quick peak around her father and produce a nervous smile. None of this went unnoticed by Joses or Amram.

"There is more, of course," Joses turned to the true topic at hand.

"Of course," Amram smiled with an expectation almost more evident than that of the two young people.

"It is fitting for me to ask for my son, Joseph, the hand of your daughter, Yedidah. Would you consent to a betrothal?" asked Joses as much to Amram as to Yedidah.

Amram turned to his daughter who was already nodding her head in the affirmative without realizing it, tears of joy filling her eyes. Amram laughed and embraced her. He then turned back to Joses and Joseph.

"There is obviously no hesitation to accept, and so it is done," answered Amram.

"May HaShem bless this holy union and forever bind our families," Joses said has he stood and helped Amram to his feet.

"I should be the one to stand before you," said Amram. Yedidah stood as well and now smiled even more happily at Joseph. "We will go on to Tarichaeae now and begin the preparations for the wedding," he continued. "Her mother will be very happy as will my father and the whole family.

"And, we will proceed to Capernaum. Send word when all is ready, our family will complete the hosting," responded Joses. He looked at Joseph and could see the immense joy erupting on his son's face. It was enough to bring a swell of emotion to Joses' heart. He embraced his son as Yedidah and Amram entered a boat not far from where they had been talking.

"As the sun rises today, so do our lives together," Amram said as the boat pulled away from shore.

Joseph watched with a mixture of sadness and anticipation at her departure.

"Your lives together have begun," Joses said to his son. "Enjoy this process and let the anticipation grow in you. Thank HaShem for this great blessing for she is the best for you."

"Thank you, father," Joseph said with tears now welling in his eyes.

"Go on home, son," Joses said to Joseph. "Inform your mother and the household to prepare for my arrival and also that my brother, Jude, may accompany me."

"Yes, father," the boy smiled and left, escorted by an older youth who was a dedicated Zealot and helped protect the family. Joses was now able to finally turn his attention to Jude. The two brothers approached each other, but it was obvious that neither was particularly happy to see the other.

"Joses," Jude was short and to the point, "you are interfering with our operations and leading astray those who seek the truth, and those who can stand for the strength of Israel and the glory of HaShem. You successfully divided the people, and by trickery in your dealings with me you have been successful in obtaining to your cause those dispersed in foreign lands while leaving me with only Perea and Judea."

"This was all according to your desires, my brother. Why are you angry? When a man starts his labor in the morning and agrees to work for a penny, it is not his concern if the master agrees to pay a penny to a worker who comes at noon. We agreed to these terms in a like manner," Joses explained.

Jude licked his lips, and slightly rolled his eyes, bringing them back to look at Joses.

"As I said in Emmaus, we are through," Jude's anger was barely under control. "I do not trust you anymore. And from now on, not only can you no longer keep a tenth of those you obtain in Galilee, but you may keep none at all. You must defer to Jacob and me, sending all your strength to Damascus. Do not force us into civil war. That is what you are bringing upon us with all your nonsense."

"My purpose is not to argue with you on these points," Joses explained. "As I told you in Emmaus, your methods will result in failure and the destruction of many, even our land and the Temple, of which you yourself are so fond of. My work is to prepare the people for the inevitable, strengthening Israel from without and within, that we may survive as a people, even elsewhere if we must."

"Treachery!" exclaimed Jude with disbelief. "Abandon the land of our fathers? What madness has gripped you? If nothing more proves your unworthiness, this does!" He rent his clothes, as did all those with him. "No more, brother. I now also claim all Galilee and those of our people dispersed in other lands. Any attempt by you to interfere with our efforts and you will meet the fate of Absalom[24]," Jude warned him.

"You, we, do not meet the prophetic profile of the Davidic Mashiach, Jude. Remember, we were born in Adar, not Tishrei. Why is it that you cannot see this? Why must we contend with one another?" Joses pointed out an old argument against their claims that he had come to grips with many years before during his meditations in On.

Jude was angered even more. He caught himself, however, and lowered his voice.

"Joses, you know well that was a minor point that the Council resolved. Why do you bring this up? It affects your stand, as well."

"I do not stand there," Joses responded.

Jude narrowed his eyes and slightly cocked his head, trying to understand what his brother had just told him. Didn't Jacob mention something about this? Jude thought it through as far as he cared to do. The issue was who should rule Israel? The claims should not matter, even if Joses wanted to call upon some heresy.

"The throne of David supersedes all others, even so say the prophets," Jude asserted.

"Only for those who refuse to see and hear," answered Joses. "Why do you fight against Joachanin's desire?" With that he turned and walked away, unwilling to answer to Jude in any other way. Likewise, Jude, and those with him, immediately headed south back towards Judea.

Joses remained in Capernaum for only a few short days. Convinced that time was running short for the unification of Israel, he decided that he should journey to Tyre and Sidon while Kefa and his assistants made their contacts in Ephesus, Alexandria, Tarsus, and Antioch. The purpose of his mission, as with that he commissioned Kefa, was to obtain stronger support for his position. But, as with Kefa, he found that with the disasters incurred by Jude in Jerusalem, support was dwindling for any kind of attempt to thwart Rome. Even in his hometown of Capernaum, he found that while the people hated the Roman occupation, they were now fearful of any attempt to assert any resistance.

"Indeed," Joses would often say, "The spirit is willing, but the flesh is weak."

His words to Jude resounded in his own mind. Jude's methods were inexorably leading to the destruction of everything they hoped to accomplish.

"What is the way?" Joses constantly asked himself.

***

While Joses was away at Tyre and Sidon, a Roman soldier raped Joanna, the daughter of Nicolaus the Samaritan and the wife of Eleazer. Devastated at such a humiliation, she lost all self-respect and even the will to live. She left home without explaining to anyone what had happened, wandering from one town to another until she reached Jerusalem. In her desperation and attempt to survive, she began several sexual liaisons. It was during one of these that Laban, the assistant of Jude, recognized her while she was with an unknown Jewish man. Laban knew Joses would soon come near Jerusalem, probably with his brother and bodyguard, Kefa. Eventually they would likely go to Damascus for visits with Jacob even if Joses and Jude were not on speaking terms. Laban conceived a plot to try and catch Joses in disobedience to the Torah. He wanted the recognition of Jude in deposing Joses.

As Laban predicted, Joses did make a journey to Judea a few months after his confrontation with Jude at the Sea of Galilee. He was with Kefa, and several of Laban's lookouts spotted them as they headed toward Damascus. It was just the right time for Laban's plans. He and several members of the Community watched Johanna when she was in the company of the man who they discovered to be Chuza, Herod's steward. However, Laban decided that her relationship with the ruling family would not interfere with the testing of Joses. When Joanna departed from Chuza's home, Laban and the members of the Community seized her and took her to the outskirts of Damascus to wait.

The next morning Joses and Kefa left Jerusalem and walked east toward Damascus. They were nearly there when they found a disturbance at the outskirts of the town. Moving closer, they could see a woman being confronted by a number of men wearing the customary white linen of the Zadokites of the Community who were pointing at her in the accusatory manner of the Jews. Upon a closer view, Joses and Kefa could see that the woman was Joanna. She had not been seen for weeks, and Eleazer had been sick over her disappearance.

Stepping into the middle of the crowd and placing himself next to Joanna, Joses addressed the men. "Brethren, brethren, what is the cause of this tribulation? What is the cause you have against this woman?"

The men all shouted, almost at once. "Joses ben Cleophas, you are no brother of ours. And this woman, your sister-in-law, is an adulteress! We caught her in the very act!" Joses showed little emotion, a mere furrow of the brow. He moved closer to Joanna and looked at her clothing that was now disheveled and dirty from her efforts to flee the group of men around her. He then examined the crowd, many of whom were already carrying stones with which to throw at her and kill her. He could find no sign of Jacob.

"Where is Jacob?" Joses asked the men.

"He is gone to meditate beyond the Jordan," answered Laban. "But, Joses, while she is a friend to you, you have no business interfering in the matters of the Law and we have the approval of the Council. We are fully initiated and have applied the Law as required in this case. The woman is worthy of death. Pick up a stone and stone her."

Joses could see that something did not seem to fit. "So," he began, "she was caught in the very act?"

"Yes, yes!" the men cried almost in unison. Laban answered more specifically, "The Law requires that she be stoned, Joses. But, what does the pretender to the throne of David say?" The mere manner of the question caused an anger to rise in Joses. It was obvious that this question was a trap to test his knowledge of the law of the Community and the Torah. He was still searching the crowd for his answer.

"Well!" cried Laban almost to the point of a scream. "What does the pretender say?"

Joses looked at Joanna who was now clinging to his garments, shielding her face from the men who were accusing her. He could see that she had been bruised and scratched from the forceful manner in which she had been seized. He again searched the crowd and could see that what he was searching for was not to be found.

"You men of Jerusalem and Damascus, do you know not that you have erred?" he asked, particularly singling out Laban. "Why do you disobey the Law yourselves?"

The crowd responded with a flurry of accusations, only one of which was totally heard by Joses. It was Laban. "You seek to council us according to the Law? You are in a tenuous position, Joses. You have failed the Law and you accuse us of the same?"

"Yes, indeed I do accuse you. All of you!" Joses was now agitated himself. "What is the meaning of the Torah in this manner?" he questioned Laban.

"To provide for the fidelity of marriage and the continuity of the seed of Israel!" responded Laban. He pointed at Joses and continued, "Something you have refused to do yourself by neglecting the requirements of dynastic marriage for the royal line!"

Joses again looked at the crowd, satisfied that he had the answer to the question in his mind. He heard Laban, again.

"Joses," Laban called to him, "What is the law in this matter? Or, are you going to dismiss it again? The Law requires that we stone this adulterous woman and put evil away from Israel. Where do you stand?"

Trying to put Joses into the position of defying the Torah was a trick that Joses recognized Laban was using to try to discredit him. But, Joses knew what he was doing and reached behind him to remove Joanna's hands from his garments. He placed her on her knees. The crowd cheered in anticipation while Joanna, crying and near total panic, tried to again cling to the hem of Joses' garment. The crowd raised the stones, preparing to pelt her body with them at the first command. Joanna's death was seconds away. Joses knelt down on one knee and began to write in the sand with his finger. The crowd, somewhat confused at this unanticipated action, watched almost in silence. Joses wrote a quote from the Torah (known as Leviticus 20: 10) that said, "The man who commits adultery with another man's wife, he who commits adultery with his neighbor's wife, the adulterer and the adulteress, shall surely be put to death." He then stood up.

Laban acknowledged him immediately, "Yes, yes that is the Law. Now, take a stone and join us in removing this blight from the people." Again the men began to raise their stones. But, Joses knelt and returned to his writing in the sand.

He wrote, "If the woman was caught in the very act, where is the man who should also be stoned?"

The crowd was stunned. Laban stepped back away from the scribble in the sand and lowered his stone, shaking his head as if trying to clear his mind. Joses had pointed out to them that they themselves had violated the law, for they had not brought the man for execution as well. At this point, Joses now stood to accuse them of their own violation of the Torah. "He who is without sin in this matter, let him cast the first stone," he said and returned to scribbling passages of Torah in the sand.

The men in the crowd looked at one another, at Joses, and at Laban. Laban stood with his stone in his hand at his side, looking at the message. As if he lost all strength to hold it, Laban's hand dropped the stone to the ground and he backed away, turning on his heel and returning to the town. The men of the crowd all began doing the same thing, until only Joses, Kefa, and Joanna were left. Joses was still writing passages of the Torah in the sand with his finger, when he looked up and found all the accusers had left. Kefa was marveling at Joses' command of the Torah, and his ability as a king to defend his people with it. Joanna, still sobbing, crawled over and again clenched the hem of Joses' garment, caressing his ankles with her hands, unable to speak any intelligible word. Joses reached down and said to her, "Joanna, where are your accusers?" Shaking, and barely able to see through her teary and swollen eyes, she took her head off his garment and looked around. Joses helped her to stand. "Your accusers could not find reason to condemn you. Neither do I condemn you. Go and live your life in obedience to the Torah from now on."

"Oh, Joses!" cried Joanna, "What is to become of me? What will you think of me?"

Joses backed away with his arms and hands upheld and looked into her eyes. She tried to turn away. His heart became heavy and he lowered his arms, allowing her to come closer to him. But, he would not touch her.

"Is it true?" he asked, searching her face for any sign of admission. She could not resist his earnest request, even if it broke his heart. "Yes, yes!" she cried, lowering her head and eyes and rending her clothes. "And I am also with child!"

Joses felt sickened and sorrowful for her and tears filled his eyes. He forced himself to back away from her as he told her, as Torah says, 'For whoever commits any of these abominations, the persons who commit them shall be cut off from among their people' (Leviticus 18:29). He then said to her, "Go forward and improve your life and forgive yourself this tragedy. But, sin no more. Considering the circumstances of all you have endured, you could go to your husband as he has the power to return you to himself."

Joses could see the hope return to Joanna's face.

"Kefa, go and find two stalwart men who will escort our sister to her home," Joses told Kefa as Joanna was trying to collect her thoughts.

During the hour that Kefa was gone, Joanna related all that had happened to her. Joses explained how Torah applied to such incidents, and again encouraged her to repent and submit herself to Eleazer. But, she reiterated that she could never bring herself to pollute his household. She desired to simply return to Jerusalem.

Kefa returned with two stalwart young men that would protect her until she arrived at her destination. Joses and Kefa, keeping themselves an arm's length away from her, bid her goodbye.

As Joanna returned to Jerusalem with her escort, Joses and Kefa went to a mikvah near the cliff face on the east of Damascus to wash themselves from the defilement. After completing the ritual bath to purify them, Kefa stayed in Damascus to await Jacob's arrival, while Joses made his way to Bethany to meet with his brother-in-law, Eleazer.

Eleazer knew that there was little hope that he could return Joanna to him. It was even more difficult for him to accept that Chuza, Herod's servant, had taken steps to make Joanna his wife. Joses asked Eleazer to return with him to Galilee and to spend more time in meditation, but Eleazer decided to stay in Bethany for the time being to try and heal his feelings and sense of loss. While being with Joses would be good for him, especially the frequent and deep meditations, he wanted time alone. Joses accepted his explanation and returned to Galilee.

At that moment back in Damascus, Reu, the Herodian spy, was closer than ever to getting what he wanted. The Community Council had called him to a test prior to his advancement.

"Reu, you have completed all the requirements so far," pronounced Jacob. "The Council has voted to accept you into fellowship."

Reu remained silent, absorbing the words with a feigned reverence and respect. He merely smiled and bowed his head slightly in pretended submission.

"Should you desire, you may now make offerings and they will be acceptable to us. What course do you want to take?" asked Jacob.

"All my possessions are the Community's for the use of the Poor and for the glory of HaShem and His Kingdom," Reu said as he raised his right hand to the square, his thumb extended in a sign of promise. "It is a substantial amount that I trust will show to my brethren my sincerity and concern for the kingdom and the Poor."

"Very well, Reu," stated Jude in his alias as Yeshua. "It has been my calling, as well as Jacob's, to teach the Community the rules of our order. We know, as do these here brethren of the Council, when it is obvious that a man seeks to dedicate himself. You have certainly demonstrated this to all here, and we witness it before HaShem. I must speak concerning my time with Reu," Yeshua continued, speaking to the Council members. "I first met him as he traveled Jerusalem with his master who is a leader in Jerusalem circles. Reu, at some discomfort to himself, ventured to seek our message and not depart from it. His persistence is admirable, even if it has taken much time due to the dangers involved surrounding the misunderstandings in Jerusalem of our devotions. Now, he brings himself to us, and delivers into HaShem's hands a substantial offering that will allow us to spend more time in the study and meditation of Torah. It is time, brother," Yeshua now spoke directly to Jacob, "that Reu receive the trust and friendship of this Community."

The men all nodded in agreement, including Jacob. Jacob saw in Reu, as did Yeshua, an important resource in new converts amongst the people attending the ruling Herodians. These people needed a quiet example, and Reu was most fitting. Or so it seemed. And as far as the resistance, it was possible he would become a source of important information concerning the Romans and Herodians if he kept his alliance with Damascus hidden.

After the council voted to accept Reu into fellowship, Jacob and Jude met each other at the corner of the hall.

"Indeed, this can mean a great deal to us in repairing our standing in Judea and replacing our losses," Jude said to Jacob.

"Your work has been steady and tried and found true," Jacob acknowledged. "HaShem blesses your efforts." But, Jacob was also concerned about Jude's lack of interest in Joses. "Have you spoken to our elder brother over your differences?" Jacob asked. He had a right, as the man standing in for the Teacher, to assess this fragile alliance and, more particularly, to encourage brotherly affection.

"It is obvious that you have recognized Joses' points, Jacob," began Jude, "but, can you not see that your own order here in Damascus sees otherwise, as should you? You do not insist on their understanding of Joses, yet you seem to require it of me. No! This issue has been settled before. The Community recognized me long before Joses' new interpretations. You, most of all, should see that his refusal to submit to the Community Rule disqualifies him."

Jacob pulled him aside even more.

"He does not argue with you any longer over the Davidic succession," Jacob pointed out.

"That is not the point!" Jude insisted. "The enmity of Ephraim and Judah has not departed, or else all Israel would be here in our lands, not spread all over the known world! Now, Joses even says that he sees the necessity of departing from the land of our fathers! That is treachery!"

Jacob did not want to go any further with Jude. The support Jude had throughout Palestine still outweighed that of Joses, and Jacob saw his own position as a point of conciliation, either now or later. Better let it drop for now, he thought. As it was, Jude had already walked away.

"Wait, brother, we must discuss Reu for a moment," he called quietly to Jude. Jude returned, obviously flustered.

"Go gently with Reu, but encourage him to supply us with as much information as possible. However, it is best not to show him our entire purposes," Jacob cautioned him. He did not feel entirely comfortable with a man with such close Herodian ties involved with the Community despite the apparent benefits.

"He sees us, and will see us, only as men of spiritual convictions," Jude assured him. "He will not realize he is supplying us with information. Besides, did not Herod think us and all Essenes honorable to him? So it continues."

"So it must," responded Jacob.

Jude was about to walk away when a thought occurred to him and he returned quickly to the side of his brother.

"Just to let you know," Jude said to Jacob, 'we have an operation planned against the newest member of the Jerusalem Sanhedrin. Not only has he defiled the Temple with his actions, but he is one of the main architects of the unjustified attacks on several of the villages in Judea where they were trying to capture those loyal to the resistance."

"Another assassination?" Jacob asked as his spirits sank. Jude nodded as Jacob continued. "Where will it stop? Yes, I know we are at war, but this will only bring more reprisals. Maybe there is another way."

"You are sounding more and more like Joses," Jude complained. But, he had too much respect for Jacob to denounce him outright. "Joses says there are other ways, but does not come forward with a plan. He says he is trying to obtain inspiration from HaShem on how to proceed. Does HaShem need to command us all the time to do what is right for Israel? The Torah says not to allow the heathen to rule over us, and not to allow the unclean to defile Israel. I, for one, take that seriously."

"I am sure you do the right thing," Jacob responded. He was not sure what else to say. He thought for a moment before he continued.

"Joses seems to be attempting a more general diplomatic solution. I am not sure exactly how that would help given the power and influence of Rome, but there is something to be said for cultivating alliances," Jacob pointed out.

"No! That is not the way," Jude strained to keep his voice down. "I told Joses the same thing I now tell you. HaShem had Gideon reduce his forces, and HaShem would certainly not permit Gideon to attach anyone but the most pure men to his army. Righteousness is the answer, not numbers."

"Well taken, brother," Jacob said. He touched Jude on the right shoulder and looked deep into his eyes. "Just keep in mind that it was Koresh, King of Persia, whom HaShem used to release our fathers from the Babylonian Captivity. Our fathers could not free themselves. Sometimes, HaShem uses other means for His own purposes."

Jude nodded, "Agreed. But, it was the Hasmonaeans who HaShem used to defeat the Seleucids, and we honor Hanukkah to commemorate that victory which set all Judea free of foreign rule. Likewise, we have sought to stand righteously, and a Mashiach has been promised us. We dare not doubt HaShem in this matter and wait dishonorably with that doubt."

Jude embraced his brother and then left. Jacob stood alone.

"Yes, my brother," Jacob said in a low voice to himself, "and pride and deceit then shortly destroyed the Hasmonaeans, and liberty was lost, again."

Jacob decided to enter meditation.

After several hours, Reu explained that he needed to return to Jerusalem to avoid anyone noticing his absence. However, the Community leaders were not overly concerned about anyone discovering his newfound understanding of Torah and his return to Jerusalem seemed no threat. There were many religious factions; Damascus was merely another one. The secret of their resistance activities remained intact, they were sure.

When Reu returned to Jerusalem, he went to his home first. Ensuring that no one had followed him, he waited until his time to report for work the next day. He met Amelaus first thing that morning and explained to him that he was in fellowship with the Community at Damascus. Amelaus then went to report the news to Caiaphas.

"Reu has succeeded in attaining a higher status in the Nozri[25] Community. He can still not positively identify any of these men having anything to do with the resistance," said Amelaus. "However, he has positively identified the leaders as a man named Jacob and another, Yeshua. Jacob apparently has replaced Joachanin the Immerser."

"Jacob?" repeated Caiaphas. "I wonder if it is the same man I had an encounter not long ago? Yes, he did not give me any indication that he was anything other than a Torah preacher. He never said anything contrary to Herod or Caesar. He seemed to actually encourage-can you believe it?—submission to us. What was that he said? Oh yes, 'They sit in Moses' seat, so do all they say to do, but do not do as they do.' Heh, what else could be more splendid?"

"Yes, that seems to be the situation," Amelaus agreed. "So, we still have no proof that these people are anything but piously observant of Torah and constantly in its service," Amelaus told Caiaphas.

"That may or may not be," Caiaphas said. "My instincts tell me that our troubles still arise from there. Have Reu continue his activities. As soon as we can offer the Romans evidence, they will move on it in confidence."

"Yes," Amelaus answered and departed.

Approximately one week later, Reu was delivering a message to one of the lower priests. As he was returning, he saw a group of six men he was sure he recognized as the same ones he saw traveling near Damascus the day he had received his fellowship. However, they were not wearing their white linens as they had before, if they were really the same men. He was surprised he even recognized them.

"My attention to detail must be getting better," he said to himself as he followed the men. But, he was wise enough not to assume more than he should. He continued to follow them from the shadows.

The men were obviously on a mission of some sort. They walked quickly and quietly, not talking much to themselves as people normally do as they travel. Also, Reu was sure that he saw small sicars under the cloaks of several of them. What could they be up to?

He got as close as he dared. Concealing himself behind an open door, he heard one of them men say something that made Reu even more suspicious. He strained to listen.

"The resistance in Galilee has many supplies and supporters in Tarichaeae..." Reu heard the oldest of the men say.

The men rounded the north wall of the city and entered the Damascus Gate. They split up as they approached the road to the Jaffa Gate, one heading east, one heading west while the four that were left continued on toward the area where the higher priests resided. Reu saw them stop just short of the southern steps of the Temple. They now seemed to enter into some sort of heated discussion as Jews often did when discussing different points of view. Reu noticed that the four who had spilt off were now in various positions in the area almost acting as lookouts. Then Reu saw him!

Binvi, a relative of Annas, Caiaphas' father-in-law and a supporter of Reu's work against the resistance, was walking toward the Temple steps with his new Herodian wife. He had divorced his first wife with whom he had been married many years and replaced her with this new young bride who also had just recently divorced so she could marry Binvi and increase her wealth. Reu knew he was well known for his contributions to Herod and for his collaboration with the Romans. Most notably, he had called for several attacks against towns falsely accused of rebel activity. In fact, the purpose of the raids was only to increase the wealth in his own pockets as he was paid for his "information."

It was obvious that the new wife was his reward for his contributions to the establishment, as was his new position in the Sanhedrin. For him to have attained a position in the Sanhedrin with such a history was an abomination, which everyone realized, except, of course, the Herodians and Caiaphas who assured his ascent. More importantly for Reu at this time, however, was that Binvi was a friend of Amelaus, Reu's master, and had contributed money to Reu's work of trying to discover the leaders of the resistance.

Normally Binvi had a small escort of guards, but for some reason he now did not. Strolling slowly, almost strutting to impress his new wife, he moved slowly toward the temple, obviously wanting to be seen by the people and admired by them. An older man with such a young beauty! What pride! What a testament of his virility and wealth!

The couple neared the stairs. Binvi's walk now slowed even

more to prepare to ascend to the Temple. Two of the men Reu had been watching came from behind Binvi; two more had begun to ascend the stairs ahead of Binvi and then suddenly turned and approached him from above.

Reu now understood what was happening! What should he do? He looked quickly to see where the attacker's companions were who had split off. He could see them watching the approaches to the area and apparently protecting escape routes. But, there was no time to warn anyone, and he did not want to reveal himself.

At that moment, he heard a woman's bloodcurdling scream. He turned back to look in the direction of the stairs.

"For the glory of HaShem and Israel!" one of the men from above Binvi was yelling after he had obviously plunged his sicar into Binvi's heart.

"Alleluia!" cried another man as he drove his dagger deep into Binvi's left side. This second assassin had ensured Binvi's death by running his blade up under the left arm at an angle, piercing the heart from the side and rear as he twisted the blade to lacerate the tissues. He knew his profession well.

Two of the other men had seized the woman, threatening her with a sicar, their intentions not clear.

As Binvi staggered and slumped to the ground, the assassins withdrew their weapons from his body. Then, the first assassin stood over the dying man, knelt beside him, and slit his throat from ear to ear, almost severing the head from the body.

At that moment, a contingent of Roman Soldiers and Herodian Guards were passing behind Reu and he saw them. Running to them in a panic, they drew their swords as if fearing attack. But, Reu yelled to them.

"Assassination! Sicarii! At the Temple steps!" he told them, pointing toward the Temple. The Romans could not understand his Aramaic, but the Herodian Guards quickly translated into Latin what he had said. The soldiers proceeded to the area just in time to see two men with blood splatters on them running towards a side street and two others moving away from a woman who was standing and weeping over the body of an older man that was lying on the steps of the Temple.

Covered with blood, the two assassins still managed to make it to the escape routes, the soldiers losing sight of them in the crowds. The lookouts simply disappeared. The two men who had held the woman and released her, were still yelling to the crowd that had just witnessed the murder.

"This man shamed Israel and had the righteous killed and their belongings brought to his own house! His woman is an adulteress, worthy of death. She lives only to testify of the vengeance of HaShem!" said one of them as they started to run away.

But, the speed of the Romans surprised them and was successful in cutting them off from their companions. A short fight ensued and the two men who had held the woman were captured while all the others escaped. The Herodian Guards attended to the victims while the Roman Soldiers conducted the prisoners to a Roman Officer. The Officer sent word to Pilate who commanded that they be tortured for information prior to their crucifixion.

True to their oaths, the Sicarii did not reveal anything of substance about themselves. No evidence of anything from Damascus was found, even though Reu's information about the men appearing to be from there was significant. The scourging went from beatings, to fire brands and poking with searing hot rods, to slowly skinning the men alive, removing body parts and feeding them to dogs. Still the Zealots refused to talk, choosing only silence even in the face of the excruciating pain and suffering. One died during the process of the torture, the loss of blood so extreme from the removal of several members of his body that his skin had turned white even before he died. But, in his delirium he did mention one word. Tarichaeae. This, Pilate latched onto. It was in Galilee, that hotbed of hotheads.

While Pilate had ordered the soldiers to torture them just short of the point of death, the soldiers had failed to show restraint. Pilate's anger against the soldier in charge was such that he had him flailed for his disobedience. Pilate had no compassion for the rebels, he was angry that he could not extract from the dead man more than just one word. The other rebel angered him for his refusal to divulge even a sound, though he was rendered but a shadow of a human being. For his own satisfaction, Pilate had both men crucified, the one dead and the other barely alive, outside the Dung Gate of Jerusalem for the vultures and the dogs to consume.

CHAPTER TEN

"Nechemyah and Jonathan were caught?" Jude could not believe that such a simple task as the assassination of Binvi could result in the loss of two more Zealots. How could it have gone so wrong? No one knew of Jude's plan other than the operatives and Jacob. "How close were the Romans? Didn't you keep a watch and plan to abort if our brethren were compromised?"

"We saw them nowhere near the Temple," lamented Mattathias ben Sabbas, one of the lookouts. "There were the usual crowds of people and some others watching from a distance, but they were not guards or Romans. And, our escape routes were wide open. The Romans caught them just after Nechemyah informed the crowd why Binvi was slain and the woman was spared. I saw no Roman but those on the watches at the Fortress."

"They were well away from us," Nathanael bar Talmai lamented. He had dealt one of the fatal blows to Binvi and then cut the collaborator's throat. "We discussed this on our return, Master, and we were in the clear. The lookouts were in their proper positions. All of us should have been able to escape. There was just one man..."

"There was one man who ran from one of the closer buildings just as Nathanael buried his blade into Binvi's heart," interrupted Arach ben Beeri, the other lookout. "The Romans and Herod's guards came from that way. But, I could not really say I recognized the man. And, he may have merely fled out of fear."

"Do we know what happened to them?" asked Taddai ben Netanyahu the other assassin who had stabbed Binvi in his left side.

"No, not yet," Jude answered and turned to look out of his

tent toward Jerusalem. He had left Damascus the night before the assassination and pitched his tent north of Jerusalem not far from the settlement of Choaza. He was always careful not to implicate Damascus, but he wanted to receive these reports directly. Setting up a different base each time kept the enemy unaware of the origins of the operations. The flock of sheep he kept with him, and some young boys to tend to them as shepherds, served as an effective deception.

"No one recognized you? No one followed you, there or back?" Jude asked after he had thought a moment. The men shrugged and shook their heads.

"You men are our most effective at eliminating our enemies," Jude said to Nathanael and Taddai. "You, Nathanael, are particularly without guile, a true Israelite. Neither of you have failed to do as you have promised. This is not your fault." He walked back from his tent door and stood next to them. "Neither Nechemyah nor Jonathan will talk. They will die with their knowledge." He stopped and took a deep sigh. "They are likely already hanging on a tree." Another sigh escaped his lips. "We kill one collaborator and traitor at the cost of two of our good men. This cannot go on." He looked away as if watching something far in the distance. "Go refresh yourselves and give me a few moments alone."

The men left and walked over to the shepherds for some water and olives.

Jude stood in the middle of his tent contemplating his difficulties. Why so many failures at such high costs? He could not understand why HaShem had not watched over them. NO! Don't question HaShem and His purposes. It's just the nature of war, perhaps? He again considered what Joses had told him. But, Jude could not see any other way. And he knew Joses had no better course of action. He looked back out the tent door towards these men who had sacrificed their own safety for the cause. He then looked at the two young boys he brought along to tend the sheep. He noticed how attentive they were, and how obedient and pure they seemed. They were sons of a man and woman from Choaza who were secret supporters of Jude. He had many such in Judea. Few in the countryside really contented themselves with Roman rule.

"What will happen to all of our young ones?" he whispered to himself as he watched them. For the first time, Jude considered that he may fail and that Judea, indeed all Israel, may be lost. "No, it cannot be!" he said aloud as he shook himself while holding on to one of the supporting poles of the tent. He was experiencing grief and self doubt. "The Teachers, the holy word, have all said that we must fight the war of the Sons of Light against the Sons of Darkness. It is the end times!"

But for a moment he considered again talking to Joses, then quickly dismissed the idea. Joses was a great mystic, and he had proven himself in minor battles, but he did not have the stomach for protracted struggle. Yet, could he be right? Could there be another way? Jude had succumbed to one of Joses' issues with him. Jude had discontinued the practice of forcibly circumcising goyim his followers found discussing Torah. He had realized that these forced conversions were no better than what the Hasmonaeans had done to the Edomite Herodians decades before. Unfortunately, the practice was common amongst the separatist revolutionaries Jude had no control over and who used it to instill fear alone, not for any singular holy purpose. The thought angered Jude, yet he put it aside. There were now more important matters. Pilate would not satisfy himself with the blood of Nechemyah and Jonathan. The kittim would soon strike back with a vengeance, and Jude wanted to make their efforts expensive for them.

***

Joses could now see the figure in flowing robes, his hair blowing in the gentle breeze and holding what appeared to be a Torah Scroll with his right arm. The man moved closer and closer through the bright light that filled the expanse all around him. At first he seemed uninterested, but then he approached and looked down upon Joses. A second figure suddenly moved in from the right and stood next to the first. They then offered their hands to Joses, the first reaching with his left hand, the other with his right.

"Avraham Aveinu," Joses said to the first man who had appeared in the light, a phrase that was simply, "Abraham, our Father."

The two men did not answer. Calmly, they reached down and grasped him under his arms and pulled him up onto the top of the building that was crumbling below him from a terrible catastrophe. Miraculously, the building was now gone, and Joses stood on top of a mountain, below him a parched and infertile valley. The men walked beside him and motioned for him to sit on the edge of a rock overlooking the panorama. Below him in the valley nothing moved. Nothing grew. There was no life, only desolation. Looking to his right, he saw a white stone about half a cubit in diameter, perfectly round and free of any blemish.

The second man who had appeared lifted the stone and gave it to Joses who held it with both hands. He could feel its glassy surface, smooth and almost velvety to the touch. It weighed almost nothing. In fact, he was not sure he could detect any weight at all. Father Abraham, still holding the Torah Scroll, then pointed to the valley. Joses understood. He held the stone out in front of him and pushed hard with his thumbs while pulling back with his fingers. The stone cracked open releasing a current of water that flowed down the mountain, watering the valley below him. At once, people appeared and began walking about and planting crops, playing with their children, and listening to readers of Torah. Joses looked up at the men standing beside him and saw that both were smiling to show their approval. Joses looked back to the valley, and continued reciting the Hebrew letter sequence he had started earlier.

"Hevay NuhevayNahavayGihev," he repeated as he breathed rhythmically while rocking his head.

Joses had been meditating for many hours in the seclusion of his home in Capernaum. Now long a master of Hechalot mysticism, he frequently purified himself in a mikvah containing ashes of a Red Heifer so that he could use the sacred names of HaShem to travel to the supernal chambers. He knew the names of the angels guarding these realms, thereby able to gain entry into the sacred places. He could descend into a Merkava vision and even go up to the Seventh

Chamber of Heaven and gaze through an Ispaklaria[26], usually the angel Anpiel who reflected the glory of the God.

But, he was also a master of another mystical system that used combinations of the Hebrew letters to obtain various visions and insights. It was in this system that he was now working.

Beside him, with a tallit over her head, was his wife, Miriam. While most mystics had a companion, even a senior master, to watch over them during their meditations, Joses was far ahead of his contemporaries by this time, and recognized as such even by the priests of On and the mystics of Bethshemesh. It was Miriam that Joses trusted the most, and he now conducted his meditations, contemplations and concentrations, almost exclusively with her as long as she was not in her time of the month and as long as she had purified herself in a mikvah. Furthermore, as his wife, she was the completion of the image, the female part that balanced him, the male.

As the Torah instructed, man was male and female. Indeed, to attain the highest heaven, the Seventh Supernal Chamber, one had to not be "male" or "female." To accomplish this mystery, the male and the female had to be united into one "man." For, as Joses understood it, Adam was in the image of God, male and female. All who arrived to the Seventh Chamber must be in the image of one, a man, with its component male and female parts. Miriam was his bishirtah, and he her bishirt. He was the yod and she was the hei, and together they formed Yah, a name of God, obtaining the right to again enter into the Divine Presence. For to see God, Joses recognized that you must be like Him.

As Joses' most trusted companion, indeed his wife, Miriam understood more about Joses than all the rest of his followers and disciples. She knew more about him than any of his brothers. Even Kefa sometimes had a difficult time accepting her place. While the obvious queen of the royal seed, her position went beyond that of most women. Her husband actually trusted her.

If anyone else had been able to look in on him at this moment, they would have seen a very odd sight that they would not understand unless they were initiated into the mysteries. He was seated on the floor, a tallit over his head and tefillin on his forehead and right arm. His head was between his legs and his arms extended to his sides, his hands with the palms up and in a slight cupping shape.

He had ascended through the chambers and found himself inside a building that was exquisitely decorated. There was no piece of furniture or tapestry out of place. Gold adorned the edges of the tables and even the fringes of the carpets. Embedded in the walls were the finest jewels that glistened in the light of the flickering flames of the candlesticks. But, his attention was inexplicably drawn to a window. As he looked outside through the window, he saw a stampede of wild animals, both clean and unclean, running towards the building. Suddenly, the building began to shake and the animals were breaking down the walls. Joses saw that his only escape was to try and climb on top of the building to avoid being crushed. Climbing steadily, he had almost reached the top but could not quite lift himself over the edge. It was then that he had seen the figures in the light, and the sight of the mountain and valley.

Having achieved this vision and message, he slightly altered the letter sequence he was repeating. The scene of the valley before him faded away as he ascended to the next chamber.

"Havay Nohavay Nahavay Gahav," he repeated over and over as he added a slightly circular motion to his head rocking and a slower breathing rate between the repetitions of the sequence. A brilliant blue colored light now arose around him and lifted him up from the mountain, carrying him west. A new and larger body of water appeared and he was moving quickly over it. As he watched, he saw a land of green rolling hills with lush vegetation appear before him. It was filled with many streams and mighty rivers flowing from the mountains and hills toward a great sea in the distance. On the shore of the sea he saw Miriam, his sons, his mother, and many members of his family smiling and happy. His oldest son, Joseph, was dressed in the robes of a king.

With the end of this vision, he changed the letter sequence again. This time, it was a significant change.

"AhaAheAhoAhiAhu, MaaMaeMaoMaiMau, TawaTaweTawoTawiTawu," he repeated over and over as he now moved his head from side to side in a perfect rhythm. He breathed in before each sequence and breathed out during it, not taking another breath until he began another sequence. As the previous vision faded, he now could see only a white veil. Time passed, but he did not know how long, neither did he care. The truth was all he wanted to see.

"AhaAheAhoAhiAhu, MaaMaeMaoMaiMau, TawaTaweTawoTawiTawu," he continued. He felt nothing but the letters. He thought of nothing but the letters. The letters were something. The letters were everything. The letters were nothing. Suddenly, without any conscious effort on his part, the letters began combining themselves in different sequences. He read them in his mind's eye, not consciously aware of their meaning, but merely pronouncing them as they presented their new forms.

"AhaMaaTawa, AheMaeTawe, AhoMaoTawo, AhiMaiTawi, AhuMauTawu," then, "TawuMauAhu, TawiMaiAhi, TawoMaoAho, TaweMaeAhe, TawaMaaAha," then, "AaMaTaAeMeTeAoMoToAiMi TiAuMuTu," on and on the sequences came. Joses lost all concept of himself. He was the letters. The letters were him.

Silence.

Miriam had been quietly meditating on her own as Joses proceeded through the chambers. But now she had come back. She had heard him in his whispers and when he changed the sequences or the rate of his breathing. But, now there was nothing. She was not sure if she should open her eyes. As she knew from experience, Joses' silence was not unusual as he entered the deepest visions. But, this one was different. The intensity of what she heard prior to his silence was as if he was speaking another language. It was foreign to her. Should she speak to him and ask him to return? She decided to wait.

Joses went to the first gate and the angel guarding it let him enter after he uttered the divine name for that gate. Then Joses proceeded in meditation to the second gate, where the angel allowed him to pass after he gave the next divine name. And so it went until he had arrived at the Gate to the Sixth Chamber. There, surrounded by many angels of fierce countenances and armed with swords, Joses uttered the Name that gave him entrance. Now, Katzpiel, one of the principle angels whose function was of destruction and annihilation should the seeker not correctly reveal the Name for that gate, still had his sword unsheathed as Joses moved slowly, and with great effort, towards the Gate of the Seventh Chamber. Katzpiel sheathed his sword and took up his bow that had been slung over his back. The bow was as of glistening, polished silver or glass, the arrows in his quiver translucent and bright as the sun upon a crystal. The mighty angel knocked an arrow and the arrowhead immediately burst into a bright, white flame. Katzpiel drew the arrow and fired it into the heavens.

As he moved forward and upward, Joses could see that the light had surrounded him; a wind had blown in from the west. Below him the light formed a chariot, and it lifted his spirit directly to the Gate of Heavenly Marble, the Gate of the Seventh Chamber, where he met Anpiel, the Angel of God's Face. Stepping from the chariot, Joses approached the guardian and gave the final Name for his journey. Anpiel nodded his head in satisfaction. The Angel opened the Chamber and the vision fell upon Joses.

Here was the Supernal Kingdom of Aravot. He placed himself just inside the Gate and went no further. He had come this far before when he was with Miriam and Martha during a meditation at Emmaus. Now, he looked to see in the short distance ahead of him a dark cloud, behind which, he knew, was the Supernal Throne. Joses remembered that HaShem hides behind the darkness. In the darkest parts of our souls is that veil of darkness behind which the revelation of HaShem resides. Joses wondered what the darkness was in him that he needed to confront so that the veil would part and he could then be pure enough to see clearly into the Supernal Heaven of Aravot and gaze upon the Throne of Glory.

Suddenly, before him appeared a Torah Scroll. Joses looked at it and found that it was opened to the first verse of Beresheit (Genesis).

Beresheit Bra Elohim ET Ha Shamaim ET Ha Eretz.

"In the beginning God Created the Heavens and the Earth."

As he watched, the sentence transformed. The words, although the same as he had always known them, then read differently because new vowels were placed between the consonants[27].

Beit Rashith Bra Elohim ET Ha Shemim ET Ha Eretz.

"The Place of Beginning created Gods, the Names, the First and Last, and the earth."

Joses looked in wonder.

Then, while the consonant letters still remained the same, the vowels changed again.

Bra Shith Bra El Him ET Ha Shamaim ET Ha Eretz.

"To set creation, God created a disturbance upon the waters and the earth."

Joses could see that there were literally endless meanings, all related and all true. Indeed, the Holy Language was an eternal language, a language of God.

Anpiel asked him, "What is it that you seek, seeing that The Holy One has shown you this great secret?"

Joses fell down on his knees and covered his head with his arms.

"Unclean are my lips that I cannot speak," he said as he trembled.

"Nevertheless," continued Anpiel, "you must ask for it to be given you."

Joses remembered that he must lose himself and separate his thoughts from his essence. He must seek to dispel any darkness in his own soul. Only then could he approach the Throne. He must ask what would be given him to ask, for he needed to be one, knowing the end from the beginning. He concentrated upon that other, which he was, and was not. He was not but nothingness. He was nothingness.

He knew the question. He knew the answer. He was the question. He was the answer.

Joses looked again at the Torah Scroll that had now rolled up to reveal only the first word.

BRASHITH

"Your answer to your question is in your hands," said Anpiel.

Joses gazed at the word and it started to unfold in its meanings before his eyes and in his mind. The letters divided themselves into words, and the letters of the words divided themselves again into words, and so it went on and on. Joses could not comprehend all that was being revealed to him, there was so much in this one word. If this all could be in Brashith, what did the thousands of letters and words of the Torah have in them? Joses realized that all creation could be contained in the Torah. The priests and mystics of On had taught him this truth, but the mystery of the method he had not fathomed, until now.

Next, Joses recognized an exchange of the letters of the word with words having the same numerical equivalent[28] appearing before him.

Brashith Rahi Elohim Sheyequebelo Yisrael Torah.

"In the beginning Elohim saw that Israel would accept the law."

Then, he saw the word Brashith connect to him, become one with him. It was almost as if the word and Joses were the same thing. As he gazed at it, he saw the many paths he could take, but none revealed how they would end. Apparently, that was up to him.

Suddenly, the Torah Scroll opened to the fourth word, which was also the sixth word; The door and the nail; The beginning and the end.

ET

Now this word connected to him. He became it, and it became him. He saw the depths of it, and the beauty of its message, one eternal round, the first and the last, the last is the first, and the first is the last.

Then the scroll was taken up into the Chamber.

"Surely I will do it," said a voice from the Chamber.

Joses came back to himself. The voice spoke again.

"Upon your works shall I restore the children to their mother, and the father shall rejoice in his posterity," said the Voice.

"Amen, Amen, Amen," Anpiel repeated.

"Deliver to him the two seals of ZHRRYAL[29] and the seal of Broniah," commanded the Voice.

Katzpiel, the Angel with the drawn sword and bow whom Joses had seen near the entrance to the Sixth Chamber, handed him the two seals of ZHRRYAL. They appeared as two bright crystals about the size of large olives, one emitting a dazzling blue light and the other a pure white light. As Joses took these in his right hand, the angel Dumiel stood in front of him with the seal of Broniah. Dumiel was a tall, but obviously humble being, not given to the extravagance of the lights, as were most of the others. His true station was not clear to Joses, but the seal this angel held was obviously of great importance. It was a clear white crystal that had no light emanating from it but which reflected the lights around it in such a way that it was almost as bright as the light from the Sun. As Joses reached for it with his left hand, Dumiel motioned for him to look inside of it. As Joses did so, he saw himself in the crystal. He fell to his knees.

"The seals enable you to pass the angels guarding the seven gates without any interrogation or interference. The seals of ZHRRYAL you must show to Katzpiel, and the seal of Broniah show to Dumiel, and they will announce you to the Seventh Gate and transport you upon the Merkava and bring you before Me," declared the Voice. Joses did not see it, but Katzpiel and Dumiel both bowed toward the unseen Throne to signify their obedience.

Joses finally looked up to see Anpiel standing before him with an outreached hand. Joses placed all the seals in his left hand and reached out for Anpiel's right hand with his own right hand.

The image of Anpiel faded as the vision closed and Joses heard the voice of Miriam pleading for him to return. She was touching him, the mere touch bringing him back from the Chamber, her voice reminding him of his life with her.

"Joses, come back, return to me, come back!" she continued

to plead, tears rolling down her cheeks. She was fearful that he had lost all desire to remain on earth with her. As he had meditated, she heard what sounded like a final breath and he fell over into a fetal position covering his head with his arms. Then, slowly, he had relaxed and rolled over onto his back. The vision had been so intense, that his spirit had no interest in maintaining control over his body. It was at that point that Miriam sensed the danger.

"Only go, and then return, my husband. You go, and then you must return!" she continued to plead as she shook him now to try to bring him back to the lower world. "Come back, Joses, come back!"

Joses could hear her cries, but he lingered on the image of Anpiel and the Voice from the Chamber. It was all still fresh in his mind. But, his love for Miriam finally took hold and brought him back. He slowly, and with great effort, lifted his hand and stroked her hair, lovingly, sensually.

"Oh, Joses, Joses! Miriam cried. "I thought I had lost you to HaShem. I am just not ready for that, not ready for that!" she sobbed and sobbed, taking his hand in hers and touching his hand to her face. The softness and warmth awakened in him the realization of his life he had yet to live.

"Miriam, my love for you is all more than it was before," Joses whispered to her. She bent down to better savor every word. "We are one, my love. Now and forevermore we are one." He kissed her softly on her cheek next to her ear, and squeezed her hip gently with his free hand as she had his other still pressed to her cheek.

Gaining more strength as the seconds ticked by, Joses finally raised himself to sit next to Miriam, still holding her closely with his arms. Her sobbing had subsided, but she kept her head buried in Joses' shoulder. He held her tighter to reassure her.

"Let's eat and drink a little something," he said to her. They stood up and walked out together to the adjacent room. On a small table were some loaves of bread, a small cruse of olive oil, and an urn of wine. They had shared some food prior to the meditation, as was the custom. Now, to gain strength and replenish their bodies after their spiritual quest, they would have a little more.

Miriam was now smiling, happy and relaxed. Joses smiled back at her and squeezed her hand as he kissed her often on the lips and cheeks. They almost felt like newlyweds, playful and loving.

After finishing the food and drink, the couple went outside. It was well after midnight, the stars bright with no moon to obscure them.

"I must tell you what transpired, Miriam," Joses said somewhat somberly. Miriam held him tighter. "I saw three visions. The first was a destruction of all that was around me, and then our father, Avraham, and another, I think his son Isaac, lifted me up and I was on a great mountain looking down into a valley that was without life. Isaac gave me a white stone and I broke it open, water gushing forth down the mountain watering the infertile valley. People then appeared and grew crops and tended their children."

He stopped and looked into Miriam's eyes. Then, as he held her close looking at her, he continued.

"Next, I saw that you and the children, indeed what appeared to be many of my family and friends, were away in a distant land of great bounty, free and happy."

Miriam noticed he did not include himself.

"And what of you, Joses?" asked Miriam.

He glanced at her for but a second and then went on to explain his third vision.

"A final vision came to me and a chariot of light took me to the Seventh Chamber where Anpiel greeted me as he has before," Joses began. "I saw the Torah and how just one word could explain worlds," Joses said, his eyes revealing his amazement.

"Apparently, HaShem will allow me to accept the Fathership of all Israel, as the chosen lineage of Joseph and Israel, Joses explained. "But, there is a disaster coming, and apparently we will not be able to avoid it. I must tell you now that you will depart this land of our inheritance, at least for some time, and will dwell in another land with our children. It is a land across the sea, lush and full of rivers and lakes, and streams. There our children will grow and obtain their birthrights."

Miriam looked troubled again. "Where are you in those visions, Joses?" she asked again.

"That was not something for me to see, and I can only proceed according to my hopes and what I know to be right. Perhaps my seeing you safe and sound shows that we are there together. But, I cannot know for sure. The great consolation is that I am assured of your safety and the safety of our children. Certainly, all of us live according to the will of HaShem. The message was that regardless of what I do, you and the children shall thrive in another land. We all know that this course I take is hazardous. It is sedition against Rome, even though we only seek our liberty. But, what was revealed to me is something about a transformation. Something we will do here, something I will do here. It is to inspire the hope of a renewed remembrance of mankind's origin and journey. It is a journey culminating in the defeat of those forces that seek to inhibit the heart and mind of man. For men to know HaShem, all tyranny over their minds must be removed, or else what rewards have they if all is forced upon them? So, I show the way, and if the nations do not stop their works to stifle the spirit of men, then HaShem will destroy them, and raise others. If they do the same, so it will go on until all nations are subdued and only HaShem's Kingdom will remain."

"But, Joses," Miriam interrupted, "men obtain liberty and then defile themselves, selling their freedom and those of their friends for money, favors, power. Can it ever be secured?"

"Its security lies in the heart of the individual. If it does not exist there, it exists nowhere. It must begin there, and we must ensure that it is planted in good ground," Joses responded. "And the king must be held responsible for securing those rights to the people. As Moses commanded, 'let your hearts always be toward monarchy and let no other form of government be over you' for the people have nothing to fear from a righteous king and can hold the wicked king accountable and pray to HaShem for his destruction."

Miriam thought for a moment. Her thoughts focused on the division between Joses and his twin brother. She also thought of Joses' visions.

"Joses, they are so true," she began. "You have done so much to bring the souls of the people to a higher level, even when destruction happens all around them, and you continue to do so. Your legacy will live on in your children. And," she paused, looking back at him, "departing to a distant land, is it really what we will do? Or is it symbolic?"

Joses knew what the implications were of fleeing the land of their inheritance. He tried to calm Miriam's concerns.

"For every dream or vision there are several interpretations, and each interpreter will see something different. Only after all has transpired will we know what the vision really meant," he said, trying to comfort her with a gentle embrace. "I tell you this, my wife, that should we depart our land, it is for the glory of HaShem. He has scattered Israel before when they would not heed His call or keep His commandments, perhaps there is some higher purpose this time should we be the ones to leave, us and the keepers of the Torah."

"You know, Joses," she said with tears again in her eyes, "Whatever you say, we will do. With your permission, I will make arrangements with your Uncle Joseph and others for any contingency. That should free you for whatever you must do here."

"My helpmeet, as always," Joses smiled and embraced her again. "Truly you are my bishirtah."

***

"We have them by the balls," Pilate laughed. "We have them fighting and killing each other. It is a glorious situation for us. If they kill off those of their own whom we place over them, it merely strengthens our position that they cannot govern themselves and that only Rome can protect them. If they allow those we appoint to stay in power, we emphasize how Rome's wisdom increases their security."

"You certainly understand how to control these vermin," said Viragus, a Roman Senator visiting Pilate in Caesarea. He was there to gather information for the Senate about the Emperor's operations in Palestine. It was obvious to him that Pilate had the right idea.

"It has come by years of experience, I assure you, Senator," responded Pilate. "I would have you go to Jerusalem to see for yourself, but it is admittedly a dangerous place, as is the Galilee. But, there is no doubt that Rome controls this country and we do with it as we will."

"The Sicarii?" Viragus asked.

"In their death throes," answered Pilate. "Oh, they flare up with a disturbance here and there, such as the recent assassination of a member of the Jerusalem Sanhedrin, but they cannot coordinate anything of any real danger."

"So, the trade routes remain secure and Caesar can look forward to a long time of tribute to the imperial treasury?" asked Viragus.

"Absolutely," responded Pilate with confidence.

"And this messianic hope, this king they long for?" asked the Senator.

"Every demented shepherd and blacksmith seems to want to step into the calling of the great star who will arise to defeat us," Pilate snickered. "I suppose they will continue with this vain hope, this remnant of the Hasmonaeans even long after we have departed this life. But, with each passing day, each passing year that this hope fails to save them, they fall more and more into our control. As you know, Senator, unrealized promises are so demoralizing."

"Have you uncovered the leadership of the resistance?" asked Viragus.

"We have several informants that are, even now, probing likely areas where these rogues are operating," said Pilate. "It is but a matter of time. They cannot remain anonymous forever. We will identify them, and crucify them in the sight of their precious Temple."

"They must eventually see that their perverse religion is a blight upon the civilized world," the Senator confidently asserted. "While Rome really does not care about their spiritual fetishes, it makes things so much easier when the gods are uniform throughout the empire. Eventually, we will win them over, one way or another. Substituting one belief for another over time is a good way to slowly change them, and they do not even realize it is happening."

"These people are not, as I am sure you recognize, anything like the peoples of other lands," Pilate explained. "Their traditions are kept sacred by a book and their sages have other traditions committed to memory. We have even taken control of their High Priesthood and their Temple, but we still see change coming slowly."

"Hence, the replacement of their sages with those of our own choosing is extremely important," responded Viragus. "We must re-educate the people."

"Precisely," said Pilate. "So, we have the multi-pronged approach. Caesar appoints men capable of effecting the needed changes to the people's most respected seats of power, and we track down and destroy those that offer alternatives. But, in practice, the vermin usually do this to themselves. One will say their way is right, and another will say his is correct, and they eventually wage war on each other. One dies and we crucify the other. Again, we use this to show the people that only our rule will bring them peace. This is all really ingenious."

"Do you think they will mount any large scale offensives anytime soon?" asked Viragus.

"Their feast day called the Passover is the time of their greatest gathering at Jerusalem," Pilate explained. "While the attitude of the mass of people at that time is unpredictable, historically they have not usually done more than minor demonstrations. They really do not like to disturb the importance they place on the celebration. That is coming up, shortly, and I really think we have nothing to worry about. The resistance is crumbling and ineffective, and we always increase the troop strength and security around the city. In fact, I will be in Jerusalem this Passover as will Herod. It is to show our 'goodwill' as well as to emphasize the omnipotence of Rome. They know their god has not had any power over the Emperor. Theirs is a lost cause, but let them have their religion. There is this one, I have not yet seen him, one they call 'Yeshua' who placates them with their religion. Such preaching appeases the people and eases their concern for their situation, hoping for a better life in the world to come. It really keeps the people from causing us any difficulty. It is as if the preaching keeps them at bay. It is good for Rome."

Pilate invited the Senator over to a window to take in the view and offer him some olives and grapes. Then, he continued.

"As far as the murder of Binvi, we had one of our informants witness the killing and he was certain that the perpetrators were some of the same men he had seen at the gathering of this man named Yeshua who was teaching Torah. However, he heard them discussing some information concerning supplies and supporters in a town at the south side of the Sea of Galilee, So, this was a Galilean action, I am certain of it. Our sources have long suspected this town south of the Sea of Galilee called Tarichaeae. The torture of the men captured after Binvi's assassination yielded only that one place. We will raze it soon."

Pilate moved closer to the window and looked outside, pointing to the baths. Viragus looked where Pilate was pointing and smiled. "So, what would Your Excellency like to do to relax before your return to Rome?" asked Pilate.

Viragus raised an eyebrow in expectation, "Did you mention something of women?"

"Ah, yes, women," teased Pilate. "I thought you would never ask. Let us go on over to the baths."

"I will ensure that your hospitality becomes legend with the Senate," Viragus said as the two men left together.

***

Joses was intent on spending more time meditating than on plans to kill kittim. Unlike Jude, he still believed that there must be a better way to defeat the Romans and expel them from all Palestine without the risks and uncertainties of open war. His meditations, however, became disturbed with his knowledge of Jude's loss of Nechemyah and Jonathan, two men who Joses had known quite well. Binvi, the treacherous collaborator, was removed from the stage, but there were always more to take the place of people like him. There were not so many like Nechemyah and Jonathan, and the numbers of the brave seemed to diminish every day. The desire for wealth and power drew Jews of questionable loyalty and

Herodians to the seats of power from all over the known world, not just Palestine. Caiaphas, himself, was from Egypt. But, fewer and fewer of the Jewish people had the courage to stand against them. Rome had been merciless in its retributions.

Joses continued his efforts to gain support from Jews in other lands, despite the dangers of discovery by the Romans. He used the same methods as he had used in the Galilee to conceal his true intentions, veiling his messages in parable and using his code name of Yeshua, as Jude was using it also, when addressing anyone but his closest supporters. His understanding and explanations of Torah, along with his diplomatic style and common sense, won him loyalty from the Jews of Egypt, Ephesus, Greece, and the Eddessenes. He continued to send members of his own Sanhedrin to these locations often. There was no lack of money for the cause. There was no lack of willingness to plead the cause before the supporter's respective rulers and men of means. Several times, well-connected Jews had even petitioned Caesar for redress and had succeeded. What Joses lacked was their willingness to return and provide numbers for their ranks. In the end, however, he could not blame them. Palestine was unstable, and it seemed unlikely anything but HaShem's intervention could change that.

His meditations had convinced him that diplomacy was a valuable tool. It was the real world, and the proper work could ensure more time. Sometimes, in fighting a disease, time could be almost as valuable as a victory. To prolong life enabled the physician more time to seek a cure, and he could oftentimes find it. So, reasoned Joses, his methods should prolong the life of his people until their prayers to HaShem caused Him to act in their behalf. Certainly, as Jude had said, these foreign powers ruling over Judea and Palestine were not lawful in HaShem's eyes. The question was, how long would it last? To this question, Joses still could not get an answer.

Kefa had arranged for a meeting with the representatives of Joses' Egyptian supporters. The meeting was held in Tyre to reduce the chances of discovery even though the gathering was quite small. Joses arrived with Miriam, Eleazer, Martha's son Jochanan, and several followers separately from Kefa and his Zealots to minimize suspicions. The meeting place was a small home not far from the shore of the Mediterranean. The purpose of the event was primarily to consolidate his support in Egypt and to receive a coded accounting of their numbers and military strength. But, Joses also planned his usual instruction and a declaration concerning his son, Joseph.

"My son, Joseph, is the heir to my kingdom," Joses declared to the gathering of the representatives of the 5000. This group was called the 5000, as the name was the code for the representatives from Egypt. In fact, there were only five representatives in attendance, three leaders of councils of fifty and two leaders of councils of 100. The designations depended upon their number and location. Kefa, Eleazer, Miriam, and many of Joses' supporters and followers from Galilee were there as well. "Should myself and my sons not be capable of completing our duties to HaShem and the people of Israel, look to my younger brother, Jacob, for whose sake heaven and earth came into existence." Joses had clearly set down the path of succession, as any good ruler would do.

"Heaven and earth came into existence for Jacob's sake?" asked a man when Kefa came near him.

"It is the thought of the mystics that each of us should look at creation as just for us," Kefa tried to explain. "In fact, the masters teach that we influence our own lives more than we realize. Jacob has shown his piety before HaShem better than any other man Joses has known. Joses respects Jacob, and is emphasizing his right to follow in Joses' footsteps."

"I see," responded the man. "The mystical life is the secret of the prophets, is it not?" he asked.

"Yes," answered Kefa. "It is the way of righteousness. HaShem wants our hearts, and our offerings and obedience are but the outward manifestations of the change in our hearts and minds. The mystical tradition began with our fathers, and passed down to Abraham. Moses carried it on to us, but Abraham had already given it to others, as well. For Israel, however, our duty and worship is to HaShem. The Torah is His commandment and instruction to us, Israel," answered Kefa. "We work within it."

"We offer you this food to strengthen and refresh yourselves before your journeys home," Joses said to the 5000 as several of Joses' followers brought out five loaves of bread, a vat of wine, a cruse of olive oil, and two fish which had been baked and deboned. The servers put the food in the center of the table and then reclined at a separate table with the rest of the people. Joses joined the representatives of the 5000 at their table so that he could discuss with them any further questions or offers they may have had.

"What is it that you need the most?" asked one of the men.

"Funds are always important," answered Joses.

"But, what do you need to buy?" asked another. "Money can pay for many things and provide sustenance. But, that alone cannot possibly win this struggle for you. What about weapons?"

"Liberty and freedom are never won without at least the threat of the sword," Joses said. "Surely, I must bring a sword before Israel can be free. But, I also know that if we live by the sword, many will die by it. It is as simple as cause and effect. Battle for battle's sake is bloodshed for the sake of bloodshed. That is short of the mark for the righteous. We must be wise in the choice of our battles, lest HaShem leave us totally to our own devices."

"So, you are not inclined to fight the kittim at every turn as your brother, Jude, is?" asked the man.

"As I pointed out," Joses paused to control a mild impatience, "we must choose our battles carefully. Our priorities must be targets we can defeat. We cannot stand against the military might of Rome. We must demoralize the enemy, but not suffer losses ourselves."

"But, Joses," interrupted another man, "I don't know exactly what you have in mind, but the kittim always punish many people, whole towns at times, for any action against them. How do you prevent that? A king must protect his people from slaughter. Remember the slaughter Pompey permitted against the priests of the Temple before he looted the sanctuary. And, of course, this criminal, Pilate, who dreams up ways to incite the people so he can kill and maim."

"Men come here for fortune and power. Those are the ones

upon whom we must concentrate our efforts. Jude had the right idea in killing Binvi, but we need to reach higher than that, using patience and stealth. If we position our forces appropriately, training them carefully, we can even take the operations to Rome itself. Small groups of men operating in Rome can cause such disruption that we become secondary. Start there, and then also destroy the representatives of Caesar here."

"In Rome?" one asked almost indignantly.

"There are ways we can accomplish this without exposing ourselves to them," said Joses, obviously annoyed at the man's attitude. "Part of this is diplomacy. We can work with our friends in Galatia, Armenia, and others as we are with you who are from Egypt. Rome will likely not withstand our ability to fight them off the battlefield.[30] We must control the place and the time, and take the fight to their land."

"Smaller, lighter forces, like the assassination teams but with more sophisticated missions," commented the first man as the others around the table listened.

"Yes, I believe it can be done," said Joses. "And, most importantly, we must raise the level of consciousness of our people. Our obedience to Torah, and our adherence to the sacred things surrounding it, will cause HaShem to notice and act in our behalf."

"How do you raise the level of the people?" asked another man.

"The Chief Priests and those in control of Jerusalem teach a form of worship, but deny the power of the Torah and HaShem's promises," Joses still spoke in mystical and spiritual terms even when engaging in diplomacy. "We must teach the people ourselves, freeing them from the constraints of the legalism that those in power use to weigh them down and keep them from realizing their own potential."

"Do you mean to deny the Oral Law?" asked one of the men, incredulously.

"Our traditions are sound," responded Joses, "as long as they are firmly founded in Torah. The secrets of Sinai were not left to the frailties of men's mouths and ears. The secrets are embedded in the language, the letters of Torah, and only from there can we extract meaningful interpretations. Mere judgments on matters based on consensus or a man's position defy the power of Torah."

"Then who determines it?" asked the man.

"HaShem commanded us not to add to or subtract from the words of the Law. Again," Joses restated his position, "the final word is in the letters. Arbitrary pronouncements are of no use. They are commandments of men, not HaShem."

"Then who determines them if not the rabbis or the priests?" asked the man again.

"How are men free when everything is dictated to them? Men of no understanding formed many of these laws even though they sat in high seats. Why is it that you left Judea?" Joses asked him.

"I see your point," responded the man.

"To the law and to the testimony!" Joses was quoting Yesha'Yahu (Isaiah). "If they speak not according to this it is because there is no light in them. Great are these words of Yesha'Yahu. To do otherwise, as those who rule from Jerusalem and are not even Jews, is to make our people worry about swallowing a gnat, and then they have them swallow a camel. These evil ones have carried us backwards, and we have lost the truth of Torah," Joses said. "We must restore Torah, and we must cast off the rule of Rome and any other people that seek to usurp our birthright. To answer your question, if we are to obey anyone's interpretation of Torah, let it be only those from whose mouths it is lawful to utter. The High Priests must be of the proper lineage and elected by the voice of the people, not imposed on us by foreign rulers."

"You are committed," the oldest of the councilors said. "We will take your message back with us."

Joses stood and all the rest did so as well.

"May HaShem bless you in your return to your homes," said Joses.

"Shalom," responded the senior man. "And, we have all left the tokens of our appreciation."

As the man stood up, Joses' son, Joseph, noticed that there were now two loaves of bread and two fish where the man had been standing. But, at the beginning of the meal, there had been only a total of five loaves and two fish. He puzzled over this for a moment and then saw that where each of the men had been sitting, there were several more loaves and more fish.

"Gather up what is left, son," Joses told him. "Ensure that the food remains in each basket as you find it and save it for Kefa and Andrew."

"Yes, father," Joseph said obediently, not understanding how all this food was left when he had seen the men eating. "But, how is this possible?" he asked his father.

"In good time it will be explained to you," responded Joses in typical kindness. "Remember to keep the baskets as they are."

Joseph began collecting the baskets and noticed that each one was different; some were different colors, some had different weaves. Each one was unique. But, the significance of it was lost on him. He simply did as his father directed him and gathered the baskets and placed them in the back room.

Kefa approached Joses as the men departed.

"Strong words, brother," he said to Joses.

"Why waste their time?" Joses said to him as he gave him a smile.

The two men exchanged only quick glances as a commotion outside disturbed their conversation. Suddenly, Eleazer rushed back into the room. He was out of breath and obviously grief stricken.

"Joses!" he hesitated, then caught his breath and slowly formed the words, "the Romans attacked Tarichaeae! Your son's..." he hesitated again.

Joses' mind raced! His son, Joseph was with him, but Joshua... No! No...he was left in Capernaum with Martha and Uncle Joseph. Surely he didn't go to Tarichaeae. And, mother...he tried to hold down the near panic as he tried to recall everyone's location.

"Your son Joseph's betrothed, Yedidah, was...killed."

Joses could only stare at Eleazer. Joseph and Yedidah had been betrothed now only for a few months. Being the daughter of such a fine family with strong ties to Bethshemesh and On had been so perfect. She had so reminded him of Miriam at a younger age, sweet, kind, beautiful...Most of all, Joseph loved her.

"Joses, did you...hear me?" asked Eleazer slowly. "The kittim destroyed our stores, and they randomly killed many in the town. Our strongest supporters they crucified. And...and, Yedidah..."

"Yes, I heard you my friend," Joses said sadly. He had to think for a moment.

Eleazer knew this was a blow. It was the first time a member of Joses' family had become a direct victim of kittim vengeance. He watched as Joses walked back into the room, then turned and walked quickly to the door to see the daylight. Joses composed himself, took a deep breath and sighed. Eleazer waited for him to speak. But at that moment, Miriam and Joseph also entered, the distress on their faces proof that they knew the worst.

"Father..." cried Joseph. Miriam was unable to speak at all. Joseph fell into his father's arms, stricken with grief. His sobs caused Joses' emotions to return to him again, tears welling in his eyes. Miriam stood alone, speechless, motionless, trying to pray, trying to cope. Joses reached over to her and embraced her at the same time he held Joseph.

After several moments, Joses knew it was time to act.

"If they struck Tarichaeae, they may have information that will lead them here or to Capernaum. It is time for us all to leave, right now. We should go to Emmaus until we know things are safe." Joses did not want to be insensitive, but the danger could be real.

"What about Joshua?" Miriam asked.

"Eleazer," Joses called almost at the same instant Miriam asked her question.

"Yes, Joses," Eleazer answered. Jochanan had just come to the door and stood next to the grieving family. He could say nothing and made no attempt to do so.

"Send word to my Uncle Joseph to have Joshua brought to Emmaus. As a member of the Jerusalem Sanhedrin, I doubt he will encounter any difficulty."

Eleazer shook his head and began to leave.

"What of her parents and family?" asked Joses.

Eleazer looked back and shook his head. "None survived."

"A retaliation for Benvi, no doubt," said Joses. "It was not our Galileans, but the Romans would probably not suspect Damascus. How did they tie our connections in Tarichaeae in any way to the assassination?" Then Joses answered his own question. "Treachery, a spy, or both."

***

"Eleazer and Kefa have totally withdrawn from the Way," said Laban to Jude. "They do only the bidding of Joses, no longer submitting themselves to the Teacher."

"What are you saying, Laban, that Jacob should cast them out as dead?" asked Jude.

"They are no different than any of the others, and if the Community Council stays its hand in the matter, they may think that the house of Cleophas protects its own," answered Laban.

"Is that what you are hearing?" Jude asked.

"Not only him," a familiar voice spoke from the side of the tent. It was Jacob. "Evil word from the north. Tarichaeae was destroyed a few days ago," said Jacob.

Jude was stunned. Even if Nechemyah or Jonathan had broken, why would they have said anything about Tarichaeae unless they were in delirium and merely trying to mislead their torturers?

"How bad is it?" asked Jude.

"We received word just now, and it looks like Joses' stores were all burned, and many of the men in the town crucified," Jacob stopped for a moment, took a breath, and then continued. "Joses' daughter-in-law was killed, as was her entire family."

The thought of it hung in Jude's mind. While the blessing that Damascus was spared did not escape him, he loathed any slaughter of the people. Even with his disagreements over the throne with Joses did not cause him any malice to his efforts at the resistance.

"Laban, send word to Joses for me that we offer our thoughts and prayers, and we will petition HaShem for vengeance," instructed Jude.

"Yes, master," replied Laban. "I will go immediately."

"Oh, and about Eleazer and Kefa, I will discuss it with Jacob," said Jude.

"As you wish," Laban saluted and departed.

"No need," interjected Jacob. "Despite my position in the Community and my understanding of Joses' mission, the Council has already cast out Eleazer. He is dead to us."

Jude was not particularly concerned. That was Joses' family, not his. But what of Kefa?

"And our brother, Kefa?" asked Jude.

"They are moving slowly," answered Jacob. "Kefa has been your liaison with Joses and he still partakes in the Community from time to time. They recognize all these things. But, Eleazer has not been seen here at all."

"Yes, I see," responded Jude now standing.

"Also," Jacob added, "the council has considered replacing Joachanin ben Zechariah soon. They believe he is dead, as they have heard nothing concerning him. They believe we cannot go on without a spiritual head."

"You?" asked Jude.

"Yes, and I told them that it is proper to wait on Joachanin as HaShem does not appear to have spoken definitively," Jacob said as he looked around him as if trying to find more words. "My grief in our Teacher's absence, and possible death, has not subsided."

"Nor mine. Nevertheless, brother, you are his successor," Jude said respectfully. "Who else is as righteous and pious as you? On who else has HaShem's light descended and made straight the Way?"

Jacob always hated hearing any words of praise. They made him uncomfortable. He was not a man caught up on himself, and he realized, deep inside, that he had erred extending his Nazarite oath in not marrying for life. Yet, that was his promise, and he could see no way around it, especially now that Joachanin had been gone so long, maybe even be dead. Even though Elazer had told him that

HaShem was leaving it in Jacob's hands, Jacob could not see through to break his oath. He would not enter the final chamber.

"I will do whatever HaShem directs the Council to support," Jacob said.

"And the throne?" Jude asked.

"You are demonstrating that you are the Mashiach been David," Jacob assured him. "But, Joses is the Mashiach ben Joseph, and this should not cause any conflict between you. Yet, the divide will not abate. So, I love you both. What else can I do?"

"Always wise, brother," Jude embraced him. "I may not always agree with you, but I can never find fault in you."

Jacob looked toward Jerusalem as he and Jude released their embrace.

"What will you do, now? Will you plan more attacks?" asked Jacob.

"We cannot look like we are weak, or that they can frighten us into doing nothing but accept their wickedness and debauchery, their killing of innocents," Jude said with a subtle anger. "The kittim and collaborators are not innocent men. They are evil, designing, hideous murderers and usurpers, profaning HaShem and His Holy Temple. If we do not take steps to remove them, will not HaShem take steps to remove us?"

"Is not the Temple already so defiled that perhaps HaShem will destroy it, anyway?" Jacob considered, his thoughts, words, which Jude heard.

"I will go to the Temple and clean it out myself," Jude swore. "If HaShem would do it, then He would expect His servants to do the same."

Jacob was startled.

"Alone? You cannot expect to do such a thing. It would take thousands," he pointed out.

"No. First we must expel the moneychangers and the merchants. Then, perhaps, the people will all assist us," said Jude.

"How will you do it?" asked Jacob.

"It is time the people hear my words concerning me. It is

dangerous, but the wrath of HaShem we do not want turned on us. Cannot we obtain some of our people here to announce me in Jerusalem? I could then enter with the multitude and drive the wicked from the Temple."

"Jude," Jacob spoke sternly, but quietly, "the kittim will see you as the leader of the revolt and have no doubts. They will take you in life or death. If alive, they will torture you and then crucify you. It cannot be the time for this."

"The people are losing hope. After the siege of Jerusalem years ago, it was difficult to gather the people to our cause. Now, with retaliation from the kittim against whole towns for the removal of just one traitor, the people fear even more, and have no heart. No, we cannot wait." Jude's determination was as strong as Jacob had ever seen. "Besides, the Mashiach ben David cannot fail. The prophecy says he will defeat his enemies and they will be subject to him. And from then on, the Torah shall go forth from Zion, and the word of the Lord from Jerusalem. How can we fail?"

"Indeed, the prophecy says the Mashiach cannot fail," said Jacob. But, he had a reservation in his heart that he dared not say. While the Mashiach ben David could not fail, the Mashiach ben Joseph would likely die in his attempt. And, the ben Joseph was to come before the ben David. But, Joses was the ben Joseph. Where could all this lead?

"Well, brother?" Jude called Jacob back from the innermost thoughts of his mind. "It is the time, is it not?"

"Let us take it to the Council," said Jacob.

"We should plan it just before the Passover to fulfill the prophecies," said Jude. "I will ride in on an ass and go straightway to the Temple. The people will follow. HaShem with us, we cannot fail. By Passover, Jerusalem will be redeemed."

"If it is to happen at all, that is when it will happen," said Jacob.

The brothers took the plan to the Community Council. It was not a long discussion. Everyone knew that the times were getting desperate. The Council approved the plan and agreed that the people should gather along the way to the gates of Jerusalem and honor Jude as the King of the Jews, the Son of David.

***

Joses and his family arrived intact at Emmaus. The journey had taken only a few days, and Joshua met them along the road with Uncle Joseph. After a short visit, Joseph of Arimathea went on to Jerusalem, as the Sanhedrin was to meet prior to the Passover. While Uncle Joseph subscribed to the earlier Passover celebrated by the Community and most mystics like Joses (i.e. the day before the popular Passover), he had to respect the responsibilities of his office. Being a member of Joses' Sanhedrin or Council of Seventy, and the Sanhedrin of Jerusalem, took up a great deal of his time.

They had heard that the problem at Tarichaeae had not developed further and that no one was looking for them in particular. The Romans could only control Jerusalem and Caesarea with any degree of consistency. In most of the rest of the country they could only use sporadic patrols, and these were usually not capable of any major operations. As a result, the people, and particularly the resistance, could move with relative ease. But, it was becoming more and more difficult as the Romans increased their power. For the time being, Joses and his family knew that to live their lives, they could not always be in fear.

"I will stay here for a few short days and then go on over to Bethany," Joses told his family. "Eleazer, you could go ahead and have your men prepare for our arrival there if you want. It is probably best to take the goods we have over there now, as we will not need them here. Miriam and the rest will follow behind you from a safe distance under Kefa's guard. Joseph and Joshua will remain with me."

"Done," said Eleazer in his usual good-natured tone. He would scout the way to Bethany and ensure there were no plans by the kittim to disrupt the people on their travels.

"I need a few days of meditation," Joses told his family. "Tonight, do not expect me, nor tomorrow."

His family and friends knew what he meant. Like most of the prophets and mystics, Joses usually conducted his deepest meditations around midnight. The rest of the day he spent in preparations and study.

He embraced Miriam, lingering for a moment as he whispered in her ear. Then, she put her lips to his ear.

"It is the time for us," she said. "I will see you afterwards."

Joses smiled. "I love you."

"I love you," she said with an affection Joses could barely allow to stand without another embrace. With that, she turned and walked to her home in Bethany accompanied by Martha and Eleazer.

Joses, Joseph, and Joshua watched her as she left towards the east and their home in Bethany. Once they were beyond hearing, Joses and his sons entered the home where Joses had his room for meditation. Meeting them there was a familiar face.

"Nehunia," Joses said to the man he had mentored now for many years. "You remember my son, Joseph?"

"Yes, of course, it is wonderful to see you again ben Joses," said Nehunia.

"My honor," the young man responded which brought smiles of appreciation from Nehunia and Joses.

"And this is my son, Joshua," Joses introduced his other son.

"Good to see you, Joshua," Nehunia greeted the boy.

"He is like you," Nehunia commented to Joses.

"Of course," Joses agreed, musing a little over the compliment.

"Joseph, of course, is my heir, and he needs to continue with us. Does that disturb you in any way?"

"Not at all. How can I hesitate when you began teaching me at my young age?" Nehunia chuckled. "It appears that the situation is getting more desperate, Rabbi. Have you decided to take any other action?" Nehunia wanted to address this quickly to avoid bringing up such distractions too close to meditation.

"Meditation holds the keys to solving our problems with the kittim and the collaborators," Joseph explained. "Yet, the violence does not end. Meditation does not preclude action. But, we must use it to try and discover what that action should be." He stopped speaking, but Nehunia remained silent. After a few moments, as they entered the home and stopped at the stairs to the upper room, Joses completed his thought.

"As Jacob, my brother, puts it, faith without works is dead. We must show that we are willing to sacrifice everything for the will of HaShem. That said; let us go find what His will is in the matter. But, even with all these things, the most important, my sons," he looked upon his two boys, "is to search out the secrets of HaShem and to see the purpose and meaning of your lives. Young men see a meaning and run towards it. But, as you age, this becomes more difficult, and you may lose sight of your life's meaning. Be patient, continue to meditate, and await the realization for it will come. Then, you can help others discover the purpose and meaning of their lives."

"Yedidah, father," young Joseph began, "so much of me was a part of her, even though we had not lived our lives together. The meaning of that?"

"One cannot give meaning to another, but each must discover it on their own," Joses explained. "It is all around you, and inside of you. Each moment has meaning, as do all the things that happen in and around us, even the appearance of a colorful butterfly," Joses pointed to the beautifully colored insect as it landed on a table in the house. He smiled and enjoyed the moment with his sons and Nehunia. "From time to time you will question the meaning of your life, and maybe of all life. Again, be patient and experience each day, each minute. Like now, live in this moment and enjoy this butterfly with us. One day, it will all come to you."

He looked over at Joseph, put his arm around him and pulled him closer in a partial embrace. "Yedidah will always be a part of you. Find the meaning of her manifestation in your life. It is there even though she appears to no longer be here. Your experiences are meaningful, even the ones that cause you pain. Just remember that all these things work together for you if you trust in HaShem. Remain patient and constantly seek for HaShem."

Joses then looked at his younger son, Joshua, and smiled lovingly at him. With a gentle hand, Joses guided him up the stairs with Joseph and Nehunia following. As they settled in the upper room, they entered a preliminary meditation together. After several minutes of giving thanks to HaShem for their safe passage to Emmaus, they again retired to the main floor and entered the hidden mikvah that was fed by the Dismas River next to the house. After purifying themselves, Joses then had Nehunia add ashes of a red heifer to the water for Joses' final washing. Joses completed the purification, and the two men then had a small amount of food and drink. Once they had completed the small meal, the men returned to the upper room.

The first meditation lasted until about an hour before midnight. It was then that Joses made a pronouncement concerning his sons.

"Nehunia, before we proceed, the impression comes to me to give my sons new names to conceal their identities as my code name, Yeshua, has done for me, and Jude for that matter.

Joseph, Joshua, and Nehunia understood.

"My son," he said to Joseph, "your new name shall be Jacob ben Zavdai, the son of the righteous covenant keeper of the way. Likewise, you, Joshua, shall be Yochanan ben Zavdai. You are my sons, but to protect you and to allow your meditations to arise to the chambers, you shall be the sons of thunder."

The boys seemed pleased.

"Very appropriate, Master," Nehunia nodded.

"That is well, be sure to inform your mother and Eleazer so they can make the proper changes under the appropriate circumstances," instructed Joses.

"Yes, father," the boys answered in unison.

"That should be enough for now. Nehunia will stay, you two can go and take your rest," Joses embraced them and lead them down the stairs.

Shortly, he returned and sat down next to Nehunia. He was obviously serious and reflective.

"I fear that the country and the people cannot be saved from the kittim," Joses said. "At least not without the proper guidance. Jude will certainly move ahead with more plans that will cause more death and destruction. His heart is right, but his methods have become unstable. Perhaps HaShem will accept me in exchange for the people."

Nehunia's brow furrowed and his mouth opened in surprise.

"What are you saying, master?" Nehunia asked.

"It is uncertain to me," Joses answered. "Let me refresh your memory of an incident in Torah. Remember when Moses was upon the mount receiving Torah and the people below corrupted themselves?"

"Yes. Rabbi," Nehunia was fully aware of the story.

"Moses asked that HaShem blot his name out of the Book of Life and that HaShem allow the people of Israel to live even as He was about to destroy them. And again, when King David numbered Israel, the people were struck with pestilence, and David, seeing his sin, asked HaShem to punish him in their stead."

"Rabbi..." Nehunia gasped, wide-eyed and unable to finish his sentence. The two men looked at each other for a long time.

"My sons will now be known by their new names to protect them. Miriam has made arrangements to flee the land should this not turn out according to my desires. The will of HaShem escapes me, but I do not know what else to do. Israel is lost, the Temple in Jerusalem defiled, and Shiloh nearly forgotten."

"You talk as if you already know," Nehunia said.

"Tonight I plead for Israel, and I will accept whatever HaShem sees fit to accomplish," said Joses. "Will you watch for me?"

This was Joses' request that Nehunia would not let him go so far as to receive the kiss of God and die.

"No sleep shall disturb my vigil, no sound go undetected, no shallowness of breath allowed to falter," said Nehunia. "I will ensure, HaShem help me, that you go and return."

"Then let us begin," Joses said as he began to stand.

The two men stood and bound tefillin to their foreheads and arms, then covered their heads with tallits and began reciting prayers. They thanked the Creator for all they had, for the water, the earth, their families, and each other. Then, they sat down, Nehunia just to the left and behind Joses. Joses concentrated and lowered his head between his knees. He then began repeating a number of divine names of HaShem 112 times.

After a little over two hours of meditation, Nehunia could tell Joses was beginning to enter the chambers. His rhythmic head motions and whispers of the divine names and letters were proceeding to the point where nothing else could remain in Joses' mind. All would be nothing, and in nothingness, Joses would be attached to HaShem.

Joses groaned.

He stood before the Angel Dehaviel and the Angel Tofhiel, the two main guardians of the Gate to the First Chamber. Joses brought forth his seals, the two seals of ZHRRYAL and the seal of Broniah. Immediately the Angels bowed and stepped backwards. Joses then looked to the west and saw a bright flaming arrow ascending to the heavens. Kaptziel had launched an arrow calling for the Chariot. The wind surrounded him as the light came from above his head and formed the Chariot underneath his spirit body. He continued to pronounce the divine names as he descended into the Chariot. It immediately lifted him upward, racing him towards the heavens. This was the Chariot of Elijah. He swiftly passed the other Angels guarding the way, watching them as they bowed before the seals Joses possessed. To show his respect and awe of HaShem, he continued to repeat the appropriate divine names.

Suddenly, he was before the gate of the Seventh Chamber, greeted by Anpiel, the same Archangel who guards the gate to the Seventh Chamber. Joses saw him as he had not seen him before. The Archangel was more regal and resplendent, a personage of supernal majesty. Anpiel stood before Joses, his crowns upon crowns on his head appearing so thick as to seem like foliage. His robes appeared to be of the finest white linen, with gold, blue, and red fringes. About his waist was a red sash, and he carried a Torah Scroll in one hand and a set of weighing scales in the other.

"Your bishirtah is not beside you," the Archangel said.

"But, I hold the Shekinah (i.e. the female aspect of God) in my heart during the period of her separation," responded Joses. Anpiel examined him and approved of what he saw.

"Seek, and you shall find. Knock, and it shall be opened," commanded Anpiel.

Joses said the divine name, and knocked three times on the gatepost. Suddenly, the gate appeared. It looked like a thick sheet of water, but he dared not say "water" for it was not. Here one could not lie or even be mistaken, and live. To lie in the Seventh Chamber was blasphemy. Joses knew the gate was made of heavenly marble, clear as crystal and appeared to flow like water. Anpiel opened it for him with no hesitation and accompanied Joses inside. There was nothing, only a bright light. There was no height, no depth, no beginning, no end. Only Anpiel standing now before Joses gave him any sense at all other than the hearing of the voice and the blinding light.

"What is wanted?" the Voice asked.

"Your servant, having passed through worlds true and faithful has come to speak to HaShem through the mirror of the Seventh Chamber," Joses said, again repeating the divine name.

"Enter," said the Voice. Joses took three steps to the right and stopped, Anpiel then stepped again in front of him.

Darkness.

No light, no beginning and no end. Not even the image of Anpiel stood before him. Joses prostrated himself and again repeated the divine names. Then he thought nothing.

The light reappeared and in it he saw a majestic palatial room with floors and walls that were also of the heavenly marble, clear and pure, beautiful, and defying all description.

The image of an Archangel appeared before him, Suriel, Prince of the Face. Joses again put his face to the floor.

"You seek upon you that which will free my people, Israel," said the Voice.

Joses could hardly find in himself the courage to think, much less to speak. He tried to move a toe, a finger, anything to ensure he had not succumbed. In his mind…was it his mind? He thought and formed his words. No words of idleness here.

"I am of unclean lips," is all he could say.

Another Archangel appeared beside him and touched his lips with a fiery coal. There was no sensation.

"Iniquity is not in you," said the Archangel, and took Joses by the hand to help him to his feet. Joses stood but did not open his eyes. "You have made the mark, not coming short of it, not going beyond it. Look and see."

Then Joses opened his eyes. Before him sat the Archangel Akhteriel, the mirror of God's Glory, on a high and exalted throne of intense white flame, the marble of the base and the chamber flowing endlessly around it. Akhteriel himself was brighter than the sun, flames and lightning from his personage filling the expanse of the chamber and beyond. Upon his head was a crown of pure light; his robes appeared to be made of brilliant diamonds. Everything about him was of a majesty Joses could never have imagined. Joses could see multitudes of angels surrounding the Throne and moving throughout the chamber.

"Your desire is granted," the Voice said.

Joses heard it with his entire being.

"Israel suffers for a wise purpose in Me," said the Voice. "You are Yeshua ben Yoseph. Babylon shall prosper but for a time, then your seed and all Israel shall see Mashiach ben David repent and put all enemies beneath his feet."

"Amen, Amen, Amen," came voices from everywhere, including Suriel and the Archangel with the fiery coal.

Suddenly, his Chariot of light was hurtling him downward and he felt an impact as he left the Chariot and returned to his earthly body.

Joses knew he was back, but he could not open his eyes or move. He lay motionless for a time, he knew not how long. Then, he heard Nehunia's voice.

"Return, Rabbi. It is time to return to your family and friends," he heard Nehunia repeating to him.

Joses slowly opened his eyes to see Nehunia sitting beside him. Joses smiled and nodded to Nehunia.

"The ransom will be paid," he said.

CHAPTER ELEVEN

Eleazer, Miriam and Martha arrived in Bethany without incident. They had no sooner settled into Miriam's home than they heard a knock at the door. Martha opened it to find a man's frame silhouetted against the brightness of the setting sun. With the light directly in her eyes, she could not immediately determine the man's features or identity.

"Martha," a familiar voice called her name, "is Eleazer here?"

It was Kefa. She smiled and completely opened the door, motioning for him to enter.

"Yes, we arrived just moments ago. Come in," she greeted him.

Eleazer, hearing Kefa's voice from the adjoining room, quickly joined him.

"Shalom," Eleazer saluted him. But, it was immediately obvious that Kefa was not here merely for a social visit.

"They have declared you dead in Damascus," Kefa told Eleazer.

"Why? I have not done anything to deserve this. If it is for following Joses' example, even Jacob has maintained Joses has a place, and what about you, Kefa?"

"Jacob could not stop it. The Council would have thought he was merely protecting his own interests," Kefa explained. "As for me, I have not separated from them the way they seem to think you have. But, I think the real reason was because Joses saved Joanna from the stoning and caused Laban and several of the Council to lose face."

Eleazer was surprised that Kefa even recognized the politics of it. Eleazer knew Kefa was a great man to have in a fight, but he also knew he often could not grasp the nuances of his own customs. In this particular situation, however, Eleazer was concerned more about his ability to help Joses. Being thrust out of the Community could damage that. Furthermore, his loss of Joanna still pained him even though there were many eligible maidens in Damascus where he now felt it was best to take a bride. He wanted to be very selective as few could stand in her stead. But, if the Council had removed him from the Community altogether, his future could be in serious jeopardy.

"I am sick," Eleazer said. "How could they have done this thing?"

As Kefa and Eleazer stood together and discussed the developments, Martha left the room to tell Miriam of the circumstances. She returned within less than a minute.

"Send word to Joses, Kefa," Martha told him. "Miriam has separated for her time of the month that came upon her as we traveled home, but this is her desire."

"Yes, I will send word to Joses that Eleazer is 'dead' according to the Teacher and the Council," said Kefa, and he hurried off to get messengers on their way.

They found Joses near Emmaus where he had gone to study and teach.

"Master, your brother and the Council at Damascus have declared your brother-in-law dead to them and have taken his goods for themselves which he consecrated to the Way. Your family asks that you return to comfort them and intercede for them in this matter," said the older young man.

Joses smiled and reflected on his words to Eleazer years before when Eleazer committed himself to the Way at the behest of Jude and Jacob. While the Way was, indeed, the most righteous and dedicated in Judea at the time, Joses had often warned Eleazer that they were far too regimented to allow true individual contemplation of HaShem. As such, they taught many things as doctrines of Torah that were actually the commandments of men, much as those in power in Jerusalem had done for many years under the establishment High Priests and the interpretations they gave based on their expansions of the Oral Law.

Joses knew then, as now, that the Torah had to be interpreted in every situation based upon its own content, literal and esoteric. All the levels of meaning needed to discover all truth were in the Torah. One need only understand the tools to extract those truths and be righteous enough to correctly administer them. And, most importantly, any changes or contradictions would prove the interpreter a fraud. To give oneself over to another in these most important issues of conscience was to try to defer one's own responsibility and try to ride on the other's coat tails to heaven. Teachers must teach, and all must obey the commandments, but aside from that, anything more was allowing men to have power over other men they had no right to judge.

"Did I not say that if you freed yourself from the stakes that others would put up for you that they would throw you out of their synagogues? So it has happened to Eleazer. Jacob should not have permitted this to happen, but it is likely he permitted it so my actions can be rendered for the glory of HaShem. Send my family word that my return is two days hence," he said as the young men listened carefully.

"We will do as you command," they said in unison and hurried back to Bethany.

Andrew spoke next as Joses stood and left the small home to look outside and breath some fresh air.

"Why is it that we men look to others for our own salvation rather than directly from HaShem? Why are we afraid to reach out on our own? Others should teach and guide, but never inflict their opinions on others," he said thoughtfully.

"That is very well said," Joses commented. "Unless a man can walk by his own light, he stumbles in others' darkness. It is best if he stumbles in his own darkness that he may understand to seek to walk in the light. But, even then, many deny the sun shining at noonday. Why do they do so? For the vain and evil purposes of men to bind the minds and hearts of others for their own gain."

Andrew looked at Joses and was fascinated by the depth of his understanding. Even now, after several years, Andrew could see Joses had no evil ambitions. He was a true king, and his concerns were to love HaShem and do His will, and to love his fellow man. Indeed, Joses had demonstrated these values all his life.

"Your words make me want to die with Eleazer," Andrew said. "Just so that I may hear your words, again, would I suffer the same. My progress in the mysteries has been slow, but you inspire me to reach out and try harder."

"Then there is nothing more that I can ask of you, or you to ask of yourself," responded Joses.

A tear crept into Andrew's eyes.

Joses placed a hand on Andrew's shoulder and turned to leave.

"Prepare for our departure. After my meditations tomorrow we will go to Bethany and restore all to Eleazer that he thinks he may have lost."

Two days passed after the message had been sent to Joses and he still had not arrived. Several of the brethren from the Community Council, led by Laban, had come to Bethany that morning to confiscate the rest of Eleazer's property which he had consecrated to the Community when he joined it many years ago, including his home, which he had given Joses and his family. But, Miriam and Martha were patient, as was Eleazer. They were confident that Joses knew what he was doing. Even though the Council members would not speak to Eleazer, considering him dead, they also waited for Joses because Jacob had commanded them not to complete their business until Joses could address them.

Finally, later on the second day, Joses arrived with several of his followers. Martha was the first to see them walking toward the home. Miriam remained in the house as was the custom considering her condition. She would only come out at the request of her husband.

"Joses!" Martha called to him as he approached. "We are so happy you have returned. Eleazer awaits your instructions. The men from the Community are here to take all away from him, and us."

"The true way of HaShem will show him that he has not

actually lost his life, but found it," said Joses. "And the same is for all men, first to the people of Israel, and then to the entire world. All may call upon HaShem, and He will answer them. No, dear Martha, the Community will not have Eleazer's belongings he has here, or his home which is also ours." He spoke loud enough so that the Community Elders could hear him.

Joses looked for Miriam, and Martha could see the question in his eyes.

"Miriam is in her separation," she explained as the group approached the house.

"Go in to her and ask her to come out. It will be alright," Joses said.

Martha quickly went into the home and told Miriam that Joses wanted her to come near to him. Miriam, gladdened that she may look upon her husband, immediately exited the house and stood near to him but not touching him.

"If you had been here, this may not have happened," Miriam said to Joses. "The Council seeks to not only keep all that Eleazer had in Damascus, but to take this also, our home, in payment for the apostasy they claim he committed."

"Call everyone here to me, Eleazer and the men of the Council as well," Joses told Andrew and Kefa.

The two men rushed off and returned a few moments later with everyone Joses had requested.

"We are not subject to you, Joses," said Laban of the Community Council. "These things are not your concern, but ours and your brother Jacob's, who officiate over HaShem's affairs on earth."

Joses smiled as he always did when confronted by men of such dedication to ignorance.

"As Joachanin ben Zechariah instructed you, my order is acceptable to HaShem even outside of the Way. Jacob knows this as well, as does Jude. Yet Jacob has sent you here to do your duty. Now, if Eleazer has, indeed, committed or omitted anything under the law, he is dead to you, and us. But, if he has not, then he stands to live in the presence of HaShem, and us," Joses said to them.

"The charge is that he has abandoned the Way and not lived the life," said Laban.

"Then under your rules, he can be cast out of the Community, and that is all," explained Joses. "But, to lose his belongings he consecrated, he must have also omitted or committed an act contrary to Torah. Jacob knows this as well. What is the charge?"

"He follows a man who says he can forgive sin," responded Laban.

"You refer to the occasion when Eleazer's Joanna was found in the act of adultery, and I asked how you could execute her contrary to the Torah requirement that the man also be stoned? Joses said to Laban, reviewing the circumstances for all to hear.

"Is that not forgiving sin?" asked Laban.

"And who committed the greater sin?" responded Joses. "A woman, or a man and priest under oath to execute HaShem's laws in faithfulness, piety, and righteousness?"

Joses was referring to Laban. As he had been all along, Laban was one of Jude's strongest supporters in the Community, and he had drawn many over to his radical efforts to ensure Jude's preeminence over Joses. But, even Jacob's reasoning had not been able to slow the tide against Joses. Jacob had obviously gone along with the Council only to allow a confrontation of Laban with Joses so that the Council could see, first hand, Joses' wisdom.

"Jacob says that you have the Ruach HaKodesh, earned by your deep meditations before HaShem," interjected Yitzak, one of the Councilmen. "Ultimate enlightenment from HaShem is gained only upon one's dedication to HaShem and submission to Him in all things, reflecting Him in all ways. Speak, Joses, that we may judge this situation."

"Why do you understand the secret codes, but not the secrets of life taught by the ancient sages and prophets?" asked Joses. "You have no right to offend these little ones. As you do to them, you do to me, for they are in my order. Do not be like the Herodians and their Pharisees, demanding blind obedience and loyalty. Show the way, and let HaShem be the judge of others. Again, aside from Eleazer assisting me, what sin has he committed?"

Yitzak looked at Laban and the other men of the Council. They seemed unable to counter what Joses had said. Yitzak whispered to Laban that Joses had reasoned them into a corner. Laban, knowing his limits, decided to back off once again.

"The Council voted that Eleazer was dead, and that was accepted by Jacob," Laban said almost with remorse.

"Do you know the secrets of the times of refreshing and the resurrection of the dead?" asked Joses to Laban and the Council members.

"We do," answered Laban. "But they cannot be uttered in the presence of the uninitiated."

"All here have been initiated. And if I do say them, now, to Eleazer, what would you do? You cannot condemn me, for you say I do not belong to your order, but my own. Yet, Joachanin, and Jacob, have accepted that my order is also acceptable to HaShem. So, what do you say?" asked Joses.

"You are not under our jurisdiction. You must do as your order commands," responded Laban.

"But the ordinance is the same. Will it have the same effect in your eyes?" asked Joses.

"The right use, righteousness, of any law is acceptable to those with understanding," Laban sighed. He knew he was not going to be able to stop what Joses had in mind.

Joses took Eleazer and pulled him close to him in a special embrace, placing his mouth to his ear and whispering to him the words of his return to life, a member of the Way.

"Now, then, go to Laban and Yitzak, and give them what I have given you," instructed Joses.

Eleazer walked over to Laban and repeated in his ear all that Joses had told him. As Eleazer spoke the words, Laban's eyes grew wider and wider with astonishment. One could almost hear him thinking "How does he know these things?" Eleazer then did the same in Yitzak's ear with the same result. The men nodded their heads in agreement.

"He is restored under the parameters of our own laws," said Laban. "And you, Joses, are wiser than we have given you credit for. We will leave in peace."

The men of the Community Council turned and walked back toward Damascus. When they arrived and explained all that had transpired to Jacob, he allowed the restitution to stand. Regardless of how Joses knew these secrets, whether from Joachanin or from On, the Community Council had to accept them. Eleazer had responded with the true words of restitution to the order. With no other charge against him, Eleazer had to be restored to his place, and considered "alive" to the Community once again.

Joses had won a great victory. And Jacob had allowed it to happen just as it did. The word of Joses' wisdom and knowledge would now spread quickly through the leaders of the Community.

***

"This Yeshua is the man, I am sure of it," said Caiaphas. He was meeting with the Sanhedrin to discuss the problems with the resistance and the many so-called spiritual leaders that were in Judea and Galilee. The worst problem, in his judgment, was this Yeshua who most certainly must be a Zealot and Sicarii as well.

"We must not be so hasty," said Nikdimon ben Gurion.

"I agree. If this is from HaShem, it will prosper," said Gamaliel, the senior sage, now slightly bent over with age, hoary white hair thinning on his head. "If not, it will die. It is best to let it run its course."

One member of the Sanhedrin, Joseph of Arimathea, sat quietly so that he could be sure to hear all that was being said.

"Enough!" yelled Caiaphas. "These men must be identified, especially this Yeshua, as he gives a false hope to the people. I tell you, if he continues in his present course, the Romans will come and take our seats of honor and power from us for our failure to control these pretenders!"

"There are so many by this name of Yeshua, how can we hope to get the right one?" asked another member.

Caiaphas did not want to tip his hand about his efforts to infiltrate the resistance. He realized there may be sympathizers in this governing body and he did not want to alert them. But, Pilate needed better information, and Caiaphas was hoping he might get some ideas from this governing council.

"All I am telling you," he said, "is that it is better that one man should die for the people rather than this whole nation perish because of the rebelliousness of an idiot and pretender. It is time that we kill any and all of these self-proclaimed saviors of the people. We are the ones chosen to handle these matters, and it is an offense for anyone else to do so," Caiaphas said as calmly as he could.

"So now there can be no open discourse on Torah as our people have so done throughout time?" asked Gamaliel, the only one strong enough to confront the High Priest. "Our religion encourages discourse and intense study, and yes, even debate. If we kill a man for teaching, where will the blood stop? Maybe not even before it reaches us! And as far as crimes, this man, or any like him, cannot be summarily killed without a trial and found guilty by this governing council. The exception, of course, is if Pilate discovers these men as true rebels. There it is required of us to turn such over to the Romans."

The entire room exploded in confusion as the men all began talking amongst each other. Caiaphas did not know what to do. He just let it go on for a few moments and let it slowly quiet down. When the noise level had finally dropped, he again spoke up.

"Yes, I understand what you have said, Gamaliel. In our zeal to protect our country, we should proceed cautiously so as not to trample even our own rights under our feet. But, mind you, that Rome is not so patient. I know, as I deal with it every day. Let's recess for now. We all need a rest."

The men again began talking amongst themselves as they slowly made their way out of the courtroom of the Temple. Caiaphas pulled aside his strongest supporters, Amelaus, Stephanus, and Bar Naaman.

"We need to more aggressively seek out and destroy this

Yeshua," Caiaphas said to them in a low voice. "While Amelaus is doing his part, I need you two to work with the few members of this council that still oppose me," he said to Stephanus and Bar Naaman. "Why is it that two or three out of seventy can cause so many problems?" he said referring to Nikdimon ben Gurion and Gamaliel.

"You made a point with them today, regardless of Gamaliel and Nikdimon," said Amelaus.

"And that was?" asked Caiaphas.

"You made them worry about themselves," responded Amelaus. "While most of these members are with us, they do not want to seem too harsh on the people. But, when you put it in such a way that they see their own livelihoods endangered, well, they will turn quickly to their real friend. That is you."

"Yes, you are right," Caiaphas said through his teeth. "They just are not realizing that quickly enough."

"We will find this Yeshua and have him eliminated, one way or the other," said Stephanus. "It may take some time, but we can get it going. Is your contact willing to help us with the one he sees?" he asked Amelaus.

"I think it wise to leave that one alone to Amelaus for now, as Pilate has his own hands in it," said Caiaphas. "Try to seek out all the others, especially that one from Galilee we keep hearing about."

"As you wish," responded Stephanus. "We will rid ourselves of anyone even remotely acting the part and claiming the name."

"You always were a help to your cousin Herod, weren't you?" Caiaphas asked rhetorically.

"Blood is thicker than water," replied Stephanus, a Herodian who had received his Roman name as part of an honor from Caesar. "But, loyalty and deference to you has made me the man I am today. We will pursue these Yeshuas and kill them one way or another.

"I should have used you long ago," Caiaphas said. "I really thought we would have been successful with our other plans before this," he grunted as he gave Amelaus a disapproving glance. The informant, Reu, had still not given them anything concrete. Contact with that Yeshua was fine, but it had yielded so little of substance. Stephanus had the right idea. Just eliminate anyone pretending to be any kind of Yeshua.

It was a new plan for a slaughter of innocents.

***

Even though the Passover time was fast approaching, Joses had an important meeting in Ptolemais, also known as Acre. The meeting was with the representatives of his supporters from Asia Minor, particularly Ephesus. They had traveled a great distance, and the choice of location was intended to avoid central Galilee and suspicion as much as possible. The meeting was in the port area and was disguised as a business venture for the shipment of wood. Joses' men had done an excellent job in arranging the meeting rooms and having various types of wood displayed just outside the main meeting area. The illusion worked well and disguised the true purpose of the gathering.

This particular group of supporters from Ephesus was given the code name of "the 4000" as they were not as numerous as those from Egypt. However, their support was just as needful and Joses treated them very well. He fed them the customary food signifying their status, seven loaves of bread and some fish to recognize them as part of his order at varying degrees.

As with the circumstances after the meal with the 5000 from Egypt, there was a great amount of food seemingly left over after the meal. His son, Joseph, again noticed this strange situation. Joses finally explained it to him.

"Your bewilderment is obvious, my son," Joses put his arm around his boy. "The number of the loaves of bread and fishes we served them is meant to convey a coded message of their priestly attainment. Also, the end result of these meetings is to inform me of any increase in the number of supporters, and those who can offer military assistance. Each man gives me a report by leaving a certain number of the fish and bread in his own colored basket. Each man, and his assigned color, is given a separate code. So, no one but me knows the end counts of the report. It is for our security. The more fish and loaves of bread left after the meal signifies the number of those supporting us. We will call upon them when it is time."

Joseph was still obviously confused. Joses continued to explain it to him.

"The strange increase in the amount of food was due to the fact that each representative brought his own fish and loaves to add as a coded message for me. For example, one man has an assigned code that a fish symbolizes twenty new supporters and a loaf depicts an additional ten supporters that could also be military combatants. The actual counts of member and troop strength are very important, the total number kept from even the members of the meeting. As a military necessity, no one but my closest leaders and I need to know this information. For their own safety, and ours, we never want even the possibility of being overheard discussing it. So, the counts were taken in the fish and loaf counts by my closest commanders and assistants so that no others could easily ascertain the actual numbers. It was a security precaution, as was the coded language in my discourse."

"I understand," responded Joseph. "You trust me so much, father."

"You and your brother are to carry on after me," Joses said, smiling assuringly at the young man. "This is for your training, as is everything I show to you."

After the meeting, Joses traveled east to Capernaum and boarded a ship on the Sea of Galilee to sail to Dalmanutha for a meeting with his subordinates he had left there. But, a group of supporters met him as he left the boat.

"The Sabbath starts tonight and we ask that you worship with us, Yeshua," asked one of the men whom Joses recognized as a Torah observant man by the name of ben Lanai. "Would you honor us and rest with us?"

Joses could see that the sun was nearly down and that the Sabbath was about to begin.

"Yes, we will observe the Sabbath together. Where do you wish us to go?" asked Joses.

"To my home. There you may rest yourselves and find everything in order," responded ben Lanai. He was telling Joses that the proper customs and cleanliness were observed in his home.

"Yes, we will accompany you," answered Joses.

After a short walk, they came upon a man by the name of Jairus who was one of the leaders of the local synagogue. He seemed quite distraught.

"Joses, Yeshua ben Joseph, may I tell you my grief?" he asked.

Joses was disturbed hat he would use Joses' name and his code name at the same time. This man had been a strong supporter and was usually careful as one of the men to know Joses so well. Obviously he was in some great deal of stress.

"What is it?" asked Joses.

"My little daughter is near the point of death. Will you please come and lay your hands upon her and use your knowledge of healing to help her?" Jairus asked, knowing that Joses had obtained training as a physician in On and in Emmaus. The Damascus Community also had a therapeutate, and many from there were also well trained in healing.

Just then, a messenger came from Jairus' home and it was obvious that he was upset.

"Jairus," the man began, lowering his head as he tried to open his mouth to speak.

"What is it?" Jairus asked impatiently. "What is it?"

"Your daughter has died," the man said and broke into tears.

"Don't despair yet," Joses said to Jairus. "There is a common fever now that can cause this sleep to fall over the sick. Let's go to her now and let me look at her."

With that, the men hurried off to the house. They arrived in just a few minutes. The family and friends were all gathered in the large main room, overcome with grief. Joses entered with his son Joseph, Kefa, and Jochanan, Martha's son, but asked ben Lanai to remain outside. Jairus fell into the arms of his wife and they cried on each other's necks. Joses gently touched Jairus on the shoulder.

"Where is the young girl?" Joses asked Jairus.

"I have her here, right here," he said motioning for Joses to come into an adjacent room. There, on the floor, was the young girl. Joses noticed that her face had the familiar pallor of many others who had had the fever. No one had been able to wake her, and that, combined with her color and shallow breathing, led them to believe she was dead. Joses knew it instantly from his experience.

"Your daughter is not dead," he said to Jairus. The fever she has caused her to go into a deep sleep. Go outside and tell all to leave the house, but you return and bring in your wife, a small bowl, and some wine," he told him. Joses could see the look of hope in Jairus eyes as he turned and left the room. Those who heard Joses make the remark started to laugh at him. Surely she was dead, what was the matter with this Yeshua? But, Jairus did as he had been instructed. He asked all the people to go outside the house and returned to the room with his wife. He handed a bowl and a cup of wine to Joses.

Joses removed a small pouch from his bag, opened it, and removed a little of what appeared to be a ground herb and placed it into the small bowl. He then poured in a little wine, stirring it gently until it was well mixed. He asked Jochanan to raise the girl's head and had Kefa place a tube into her mouth that he then pushed gently some distance down her throat. As Kefa held the tube in place, Joses was able to deliver some of the mixture directly into her stomach without getting any of it into her lungs. He then placed a small amount in her nostrils, and under her tongue.

"We now have but a little time to wait," Joses explained.

Within about twenty minutes, the girl began to stir. Joses looked under her eyelids and noticed that her color was returning to normal. Then, she coughed.

"Young lady," Joses said to her as he took her by the hand and gently pulled her up, "it's time to get up."

The girl opened her eyes slightly and coughed again. She sat up in her bed and her parents began to cry, but this time with joy.

"This fever can be dangerous if not treated in time," Joses told the parents. "Also, it seems to spread to others who come near to the sick. So, it is best to limit the number of people in the house. For all those who have been around her, give them a little of this as soon as possible," he said as he pointed to the contents of the bowl. "Here," Joses said to Kefa, Jochanan, and Joseph, "take a little of this and place it under your tongues." They did so as did Joses himself. He then handed the bowl to Jairus. "Do as we have done and place a little under your tongue and all those who have been here around her," said Joses.

The young girl looked up at her parents who then came to her side and embraced her and kissed her.

"Oh, our little one!" the mother said with tears streaming down her face. "Thank you, Yeshua, thank you," she said time and again.

"We cannot thank you enough," said Jairus, barely able to speak.

"You already have," Joses said in a comforting tone. He and his men then turned and left the house and met up again with ben Lenai.

"I heard what happened," said Lanai. "You have done a miracle, Yeshua."

"She was not dead, merely very ill. Now she will be fine," Joses explained.

They then went on to ben Lanai's home, arriving just as the sun went down below the horizon. The family and the guests began their Sabbath worship. During the meeting, ben Lenai asked Joses a question.

"How is it best for us to pray?" he asked.

"In this manner," Joses responded. "Our Father in Heaven, Sacred is your Holy Name and we say it only when it is proper to do so. May You restore Israel's kingdom, that Your commandments and righteousness may be seen in Israel by all nations, as it is in heaven. Commend to us that which we need today. Forgive us if we fall short of the mark, as we forgive others who fall short of our expectations. And, do not try us too hard, but deliver us from hard testing. Amen."

"That was wonderful, said ben Lanai.

"Anyone who prays in The Name, HaShem, will be given what he asks," said Joses. "There is no other name given for the salvation of men."

***

Back in Damascus, Jude found out that Joses had given the words of life to Eleazer who was then able to keep his status in the Community. Jude was extremely angry that Joses could get away with such things, and he was even upset with Jacob. He went to see Jacob at his tent.

"Is not the Council the final word?" Jude asked his brother, trying to show him the respect he so deserved. "How can Joses' mere understanding of these secrets overrule the Council and you?"

"It is the law, Jude. We have no right to keep HaShem from giving these things to others. That is out of our hands," explained Jacob. "These things are meant for righteousness. There has been no loss of righteousness in any of this. If Joses misused the words of power, or if he or Eleazer had broken the Torah, we would have a stand against them. But, they have not done so."

"The Community Rule outlines these infractions," Jude said as calmly as he could. "How can we allow anyone to use them against us?"

Jacob could see he was not getting through to Jude. "What are you going to do?" He asked Jude.

"You will know when it is time," Jude said as he turned and left.

Jude called a meeting of his closest supporters. They met in the Meeting Hall even though Jude wanted to keep the plan quiet as long as possible. What he had in mind would require many people, and he decided to go ahead even if Jacob, or anyone else, discovered his intentions.

"What we need is an event, a monumental event that will

excite the people and bring about their demand that you assume the leadership of all the people and the nation," said Laban.

"Yes, and why not now? Why not bring Jude into Jerusalem as the Mashiach ben David that he is?" rhetorically asked Jude's oldest son, Jacob. "We have been wrong not to trust HaShem, and take the proper steps without being commanded to do so. We know what is right. We must do HaShem's will and seize the moment!"

"The Temple must be cleansed, Jude," said Mattathias ben Sabbas. "We have fought so long and so hard for this. If we can but gain entry and secure it, and then have Jacob purify it..."

"Yes, I see what you are all saying," Jude responded. "I agree with you. I just wanted to hear it from your own hearts and mouths. It is time. The time is right, and all has been brought to this time and place for the glory of HaShem and Israel."

"We can gather all of our people and meet outside Jerusalem. There, with our people honoring you and HaShem, more and more of the people around the countryside and in Jerusalem will see you," said Laban, almost shaking with pride. They will praise HaShem and His Mashiach ben David. It has to work, as HaShem is with us. And when is the right time, if not now?"

"The prophecy calls for me to ride a donkey into the city," Jude thought out loud. "Obtain a donkey from a local farmer along the road and make sure it will be there when I arrive," he commanded. "I will ride the donkey into the city while you encourage the people to gather. Ensure all of our Nazarenes are armed and ready to fight. But, HaShem will be our true strength. We will take the Temple and stop this outrageous crime of Pilate stealing our people's offerings to HaShem. And, we will prepare the Temple for cleansing, that HaShem's presence may again abide there. It should take no longer than three days to cleanse and purify the Temple of all the impurities that have happened there. Then, we will re-institute the commandments of HaShem properly."

"Amen," said Laban.

"Praise to HaShem and His Mashiach!" others said in unison.

As Jude and his men finalized their plans, Ivraham, one of the older men of the Council, overheard them. While it was obvious Jude intended for this to be no secret, it was also obvious to Ivraham that someone must inform Jacob. He immediately departed to do just that.

***

Joses returned to Capernaum to teach and to evaluate potential Nazarenes. As he was talking in a market, a Roman Centurion approached with his soldiers. Joses was certain that this signaled a very dangerous situation. He had heard that the High Priest had put out an edict that anyone named Yeshua may be arrested, possibly even assassinated. But, he did not think the Romans would be involved in that. Perhaps they knew something else. The best thing, Joses thought, was just to remain calm.

The Centurion gestured to his soldiers a command that signaled for them to wait, and then he approached Joses alone. The soldiers obeyed the command and kept a distance of thirty cubits.

"You are the teacher called Yeshua, are you not?" asked the Centurion in a strong Aramaic.

"Yes," answered Joses. He was cautious, but not alarmed or frightened. HaShem was always in his heart and mind. He usually saw himself as something apart from the being in this body, looking at that person, that body, in a detached sort of way.

"I have no interest in becoming part of your people," the man explained. "But, it seems to me that the old idea that every nation and land has a separate god is nonsense. I have heard you talk. You do not give honor to any god but yours. Now, my feeling is that all the world has one god."

"For you that is Caesar?" asked Joses.

"I am a free man, a Roman, but of Greek birth," answered the Centurion. While I have, indeed, taken the oath to Caesar, I do not believe him to be an incarnation of any deity. I am for Rome, not Caesar."

"You are what we call a gentile, goyim, not of the seed of Abraham, Isaac, and Jacob," explained Joses. "As far as our religion, only we are bound to all of its commandments. You are not. You follow what we call the Noachic laws, simply to treat your fellow man as you would want to be treated. But, the Israelites must do Torah. You can convert..."

"No, I really do not have any desire to do so," interrupted the Roman.

"Then you, as all men from all nations, kindreds, tongues, and peoples, may call upon HaShem and receive His assistance," explained Joses. "That is a gift to all mankind. But, it is Israel's calling to do Torah, and to pray for the nations of the world that HaShem may bless them. The blessings flow from HaShem through Torah and Israel to the nations. As such, my mission is only to my own people. But, as I said, you, as a creation of HaShem, may feel free to always call upon Him, and He will answer you in His own time and way."

"You are not Greek?" asked the Centurion.

"Truth from HaShem has been sent all over the earth," said Joses. "It is HaShem's right to hide a thing, and the honor of men to search them out. This is how we grow. Torah has all secrets, all knowledge, but the world is for our education. The world was made just for you...and him," he pointed to one of his men, "and for her," he said gesturing to a woman carrying a water pot. "We create our own world in HaShem's creation. Yes, feel joy that you may call upon Him and He will answer you,"

"And what does this, HaShem...What is His Name?" asked the Centurion. "All gods have a name."

"We call Him, HaShem, meaning THE NAME, to stand in for His real Name. That way, we do not repeat it irreverently or in vain. It is written and spoken in our language under certain circumstances, but we do not violate its sacredness. Here it is in our language." Joses showed him a section of Torah Scroll where the Name was written. "Do not try to pronounce it as this is not proper under these circumstances."

"I will keep His Name before my eyes, and I will pray to Him who is known as HaShem," said the Centurion.

"He will listen," Joses repeated, "as He does to all who truly worship Him."

"You have said well, Yeshua," the Centurion nodded to him. "May HaShem bless you." With that, the Centurion departed. Joses' followers finally started breathing again.

Joses, his son Joseph, and Jochanan, left the group as the Centurion went away. They returned to their home where Miriam and her sister, Martha, were waiting. As they neared their home, two men in white linen, obviously from Damascus, were standing outside the door. Joses knew that these Nazarite Essenes would not enter his home without him there.

"Hail, men, how long have you waited?" Joses tried to set them at ease as he could see they were warm and somewhat uncomfortable.

"We are here with a message from your brother, Jacob," said the taller of the two. "He sends word that your twin brother is planning to enter Jerusalem three days from now, just before Passover, to take the Temple and announce himself the Mashiach ben David."

***

Jude arrived outside of Jerusalem just before noon. Laban had obtained a donkey from a local farmer to ensure that Jude fit the description of the Mashiach ben David as explained in the prophetic books about the Mashiach's triumphal entry into Jerusalem. Jude sat upon the donkey and began riding it towards the city while his men, led by Laban, encouraged the people to welcome him as the Mashiach ben David and place palm branches on the ground before him.

As Jude rode along the narrow road, Laban and his men worked the people into almost a frenzy. The excitement brought more and more people to the road to see what was happening. As they got caught up in the excitement, many of them began to take off their clothes and place them on the ground before Jude. The excitement grew more and more as the people began to believe that this was, in fact, some significant event.

"Hosanna to ben David: Blessed is he that comes by HaShem to rule on David's throne; Hosanna in the highest!" yelled Laban as loud as he could. The people in the crowd began to take up the pronouncement and recited it almost in unison.

Hosanna to ben David: Blessed is he that comes by HaShem to rule on David's throne; Hosanna in the highest!" the crowd became deafening.

"Hosanna to HaShem and to his Mashiach!" cried some.

Jude and his men were astounded! They had done the right thing. The people were ready for the Mashiach ben David and Jude would fill the requirements. Surely, HaShem was with him. He had done everything the prophets had said the Mashiach would do with one exception. And, he would, no doubt, free the people from Rome and return the Temple to those who had the right to it. His thoughts turned to meditation so as not to allow himself to become too concerned about this adoration for the people. Indeed, this was HaShem's hour of glory.

"Remember HaShem, remember His Torah," admonished Jude as he approached the city gate. Ahead he could see that more people were already gathering to greet his arrival. It was obvious they had heard and seen what was going on and wanted to be a part of it.

Laban and the other men with him who had accompanied Jude were now yelling again to the crowd.

"Yeshua Ha Mashiach! Yeshua ben David!" they yelled.

The crowd also began to repeat this and the clamor and the noise continued to arise. People began to strike cymbals, drums, and even blow horns as Jude proceeded.

As he entered the gate, many more who had gathered began to chant and to lay down their garments before him. But then, suddenly, Jude also noticed that many of the people were obviously hurrying away from the crowd or not coming close to it at all. Some hid their faces as they rushed away, and now even some Romans were taking notice. Still, Jude continued on to the Temple.

Everything was going well until the Romans began to form in small phalanxes at different points along the route to ensure that the mob was channeled away from the important parts of the city where the affluent lived as well as the Roman and Herodian nobles. As the crowd approached the Temple, the Temple Guards and the High Priest's guards took up positions ready to defend their positions. The people began to see these military movements, and many started to break off from the main group and disappear down the side streets where there were no soldiers. In light of the recent massacres at Tiberias and Tarichaeae, with thousands of Jews lost, the crowd was losing its confidence.

At the Temple, Jude dismounted the donkey and ascended the steps to where the moneychangers and the merchants located themselves.

"This house is holy, a house of prayer, and you have polluted it and made it a den of thieves!" Jude yelled as he began to overturn the tables of the merchants. Many tried to fight back, but Laban and his men, as well as a number of the crowd, protected Jude from any serious confrontations. Bolstered by his success, Jude continued on. He took a whip from a table of a merchant and began cracking it at those who resisted his commands to leave. He struck several with the whip who refused to move and then chased them down the stairs.

The Temple Guards were now closing in, as were the Roman soldiers from the city streets and a contingent from the Antonia Fortress. Jude knew that his time was now or never. Despite the excitement of the crowd and the apparent enthusiasm for him that they had been exhibiting, fewer and fewer were standing by or taking part in his efforts. As the soldiers closed ranks, more and more of the people stood or ran away.

"Listen to me! Listen!" he yelled to the crowd. "Today HaShem delivers you from the hands of the kittim!"

Several of the Chief Priests had heard enough.

"By what authority do you suppose to do these things?" asked one of the priests who was obviously a Herodian.

Jude ignored his question, but spoke to him and the other

priests who had gathered to stand between Jude and the rest of the Temple.

"Do you not hear what the people are saying, even the children? Out of the mouth of babes and sucklings have you perfected praise," he said to them, quoting a messianic verse from holy writings. "The sign to you is that I will restore this Temple to its proper purity in three days. And you will no longer be able to allow the kittim to use the sacred treasure for their own purposes, like Pilate's aqueduct! Now, stand aside!"

Jude called upon HaShem in a prayer in his heart and began to move toward the area of the altar. The crowd was now smaller than it had been, and they did not have the numbers to penetrate the line of priests and guards who blocked the way. Some of the guards had already drawn their weapons and slashed members of the crowd.

Jude kept pushing, but he could not break through the line. He looked over toward the porticoes of the Temple and saw that the Roman soldiers were now moving forward to his position in their formations. At this sight, more and more of the people began to flee the area to avoid any mayhem upon them.

"Are you the ben David?" the senior priest yelled his question to him.

You have said it!" answered Jude.

"You are Yeshua, aren't you?" the priest demanded, as the line pushed back the demonstrators.

"Yes, that is the truth!" responded Jude.

"That is a tall claim, Yeshua," the priest said angrily. "But there is more to it than words. You will need to prove it!"

The priest was a member of the Herodian family, but he understood the requirements for the Mashiach ben David. He must conquer all his foes, and establish a free and independent nation of Israel, restore the throne of David, and not fail.

"Again I tell you, you have destroyed this Temple by your impurities, but I can restore it to its original purity in three days and HaShem will return to it!" cried Jude.

Now the Romans were upon them, pushing the line of

demonstrators and supporters back. The Romans then joined ranks with the Temple Guards and began moving toward Jude to take him.

"I am losing ground!" he said to himself. "HaShem, give us Your strength to defeat the kittim and return Your house to Yourself!"

But, the Romans kept coming. The time for a possible escape was nearly past. Where was HaShem?

There were now several members of the crowd lying wounded on the ground. Jude and his men had not yet been hurt or captured, but their time had run out. As had happened before, Jude needed to retreat and flee the city. There was nothing else he could do. He left what remained of the crowd he had gathered at the Temple and ran through a number of streets and alleys to escape the soldiers who remained in their formations. The Roman patrols throughout the city failed to see him and his men as they made good their escape. They were sure that no one could have followed them.

They were wrong.

CHAPTER TWELVE

Jude had returned to Damascus from Jerusalem. His attack on the priests and the money exchangers as 'Yeshua, the Mashiach ben David' had not generated the immediate following he had hoped. As disappointing as that realization was, he also detested the fact that no one seemed particularly concerned about the continuing use of the Temple Treasury to fund Pilate's aqueduct. Having confronted the Herodians and the establishment Pharisees and Priests in the Court of the Gentiles, he had rushed away. Changing his garments several times in the city while he quickly moved enabled him, as usual, to avoid anyone following him.

Anyone except Joses, who had been watching him from the time he entered the city until he left through the Gate of the Essenes. Joses made good time and arrived at Damascus well ahead of his twin brother. He went to Jacob's tent to wait for Jude to arrive. He and Jacob did not wait long. Jude came to Jacob's tent immediately after washing himself and once again changing his clothes.

"Greetings, my brother, may the blessings of HaShem be upon you," Jacob said to Jude as he stopped at the door of the tent. "Come in and rest yourself."

Jude stooped slightly to clear his head past the door and was surprised to see Joses sitting next to Jacob.

"Joses!" Jude said in surprise. He let out a long breath. "What brings you to Damascus and Jacob's tent?"

"I followed you after your entry into Jerusalem and your attack on the exchangers and merchants at the Temple," said Joses.

"Joses wanted to ensure that no one followed you that could track you back here," Jacob tried to explain.

"I don't need Joses' help to do that," Jude said with a slight hint of displeasure.

"No, your skills are excellent, and your men well trained," Joses said. "The only real problem was that you did not see me."

"Why should I have been looking for you?" Jude asked, his impatience showing.

"The people are too weak to do anything more," said Joses, deliberately not answering his question, "The people want to expel the kittim, but they have lost hope. The occupation has gone on for too long, and the methods of the kittim too severe for them to overcome."

Jude was beginning to think that Joses was right. But, he could just not let Joses hear the words.

"Jacob, I realize you have a respect for Joses' claim as the Mashiach ben Joseph, and that you do not see it as a threat to the Throne of David," Jude explained, trying to calm his initial anger. "But, this is confusing to the people, or it will be when this is explained to them."

"There will be no explanation to them," Joses said. "This is not an issue they need to choose, though a small number have embraced it. Even when they call me 'Son of David,' just as they do you, it is not something for their eyes or ears. You can, and should remain as you wish, to be the Son of David. All that is required is that you do the demonstration."

"I suppose you will do the demonstration of the ben Joseph?" Jude asked sarcastically.

Joses did not answer him.

"Do you know what that is?" Jacob asked Jude.

Jude tried to suppress his frustration.

"I do not wish to see my brother, any brother, any Jew, any Israelite, die at the hands of the kittim," Jude said. "But, Joses' position divides the people. They need one standard at a time."

"And you are the Mashiach ben David?" asked Joses.

Jude looked at him as if he were mad. "You were born with the crimson thread, and went about your life in opposition to its requirements. I took your place out of necessity. I was the rightful heir when you abrogated your birthright. Even the Community Council recognized that." He stopped for a moment, and Joses and Jacob allowed him to gather his thoughts. Then, he continued. "Why ask me about what you no longer seek? You now claim the position of the Ben Joseph."

"And the two callings are not the same. There should be no enmity between us," said Joses.

"They cannot exist at the same time!" Jude insisted.

"Correct," said Jacob.

Jude stared at both of them. He was not sure what Jacob meant, and he really did not want to ask.

"Look, Joses' brother-in-law, Eleazer, was pronounced dead, and you, Jacob, let it stand," Jude was trying to grip the situation. "You are the righteous one. We all recognize this."

Joses nodded his head in agreement. "Eleazer's removal was merely a revenge for my refutation against the Council and Laban regarding Joanna," Joses commented, but without much emotion. "I sincerely trust you had nothing to do with that."

"Eleazer was in no danger, for Joses' ordinances are as authentic as that of the Community Council of Twelve, or mine," explained Jacob. "Joses remedied the loss of Eleazer's position in the Way by raising him more fully into his own order. Joses reprimanded the Council, and they recanted."

Joses reprimanded the Council? What? How could that be?

"I brought the Council to Joses the day he raised him," Jacob continued. "They no longer see him as an opponent."

Jude was stunned again. He had been so busy trying to give life to the resistance that he had not known of the recent events.

"As for me," Joses carefully interjected, "the Temple in Jerusalem is defiled, and I do not see that anything done there has any validity. I look to Shiloh, not Jerusalem.[31] The first house of HaShem was a Tabernacle in the wilderness, as it was in Shiloh. There the Ark was kept. The Ark was HaShem's presence and it was HaShem we worshipped. We did not worship an idol of stone,

Temple or otherwise. We were, and are, to perform the Torah, with or without a Temple. Do you not remember why the Temple was first built? It was to be the house for HaShem's Presence, the Ark of the Covenant. Yet, the Ark has not been seen for hundreds of years. Why do you insist that the Temple holds the key to our relationship with HaShem? What is the body without the spirit? Do we not bury the body when the spirit is gone?"

Jude became more incensed the longer he listened. He was about to rise in anger, but Jacob waved him to remain seated. Jacob's motions convinced him to remain calm. Joses continued.

"Should you desire to prepare the Temple for HaShem's blessings, that HaShem may return the Ark to its tabernacle, then there may be a purpose to honor it. But, then again, the Ark's proper place is in Shiloh where Moses' sons originally kept it. Judah removed the Ark; our own King David of Judah took it upon himself to remove the Ark from its home of antiquity and placed it in Jerusalem for safekeeping. Safekeeping? Cannot HaShem fight His own battles? Anyway, the house that Solomon built was to house the Ark. Our enemies destroyed the Temple and took the Ark because of our folly. After the captivity, our people returned and built another Temple. But, there was no Ark. Then, this pretender, Herod, enlarges the Temple. For what? To house the Ark? No, for the Ark is gone. No, he built it for the people...for his priests...for his own glory. He had no honor with HaShem. He was not even the rightful heir of the Throne or of Israel. Most certainly he had no right to administer HaShem's house. How can you deny this?" Joses was calm, but firm and relentless. Jude remained silent.

"However, you were right to tell the Herodians and their collaborators that even though they have destroyed the Temple, in three days of purification you could have it again acceptable to HaShem, and His Ark. Of course, they will not allow it, neither will they stop the sacrifices for the kittim, or prevent Pilate from obtaining the Temple Money for his projects like the aqueduct. But, if you were successful in cleansing the Temple, then Jacob could do the Yom Kippur Atonements there in the Holy of Holies as the Torah commands him, or continue his prayers in the desert, as he sees fit. That is his duty, and never should he stop. Again, perhaps HaShem will return the Ark. Admittedly, at the very least, we would have a place of purity to conduct our ordinances and prayers as you have argued. But, our hearts must be sufficiently pure first. The problem is that your recent activities there did nothing to purify that place. What you have done is endangered our efforts to surprise the enemy. Caiaphas and Pilate surely took notice and are making every effort to infiltrate and identify us. You may have made their efforts much easier for them."

Jude felt deflated. But, he was also a man of reason. He had to admit that his work had not gained him, or the resistance, any major advantages. He let out a long breath and hung his head.

"What do you have in mind?" he asked Joses.

Jacob smiled.

"We cannot hope to defeat the kittim in open battle, or by assassinating those of little power and authority. HaShem holds the leaders responsible. They are the ones that should pay, not the people, and not even the men of mere wealth or lower positions. Why not the men of wealth? Because such men with mere wealth are nothing but the pawns of the truly powerful. We must not waste our efforts. We must attack the head. If we must spill blood, it must be that which is most guilty. And, with them desecrating the Temple and stealing the Temple Treasury for their own gain, we have a righteous reason for our actions and a purpose to solidify the people to our cause."

"That will not end the retaliations which so demoralize our people, Joses," said Jude. "In fact, it may increase them. Whom are you talking about, anyway?"

"We are speaking of Herod, Caiaphas, and Pilate," Joses explained.

Jude, shaking his head in disbelief, immediately sat down where he had been standing.

"What are you talking about?" Jude asked. "They are the most protected men in Judea."

"Yes," Joses agreed. "However, at Passover they are all in Jerusalem greatly easing the problem of making a strike against them. Even though their guards are increased, we can penetrate their defenses with three concentrated efforts since they are our only objectives. Besides, seizing them will bring a halt to the theft of the corban[32] and allow the cleansing of the Temple you so desire to accomplish. If it is done quickly, HaShem may bless our efforts as he did for Joshua when he circled Jericho with the Ark to destroy the walls and defeat their enemy within. HaShem's people and the chosen lineage will again administer in the Temple, its treasures again in the hands of HaShem. Is this not what you have always desired?"

"Caiaphas in his home, Pilate in the Fortress, and Herod in his palace," Jacob commented before Jude could answer. "Only Caiaphas will have one change, the Temple. Otherwise, their places are known and fixed.

Jude shook his head, "Joses, do you desire death at the hands of the kittim?"

Joses did not answer. The two brothers looked at each other. There was a long silence. Jacob sat quietly.

"My desire is to do the will of HaShem," Joses finally said. "The removal of the kittim from our lands is a part of that will. This plan has a chance for success, as they will not consider that we would attempt such a bold action. It is a step to a better position of negotiation, and it may make the price of occupation too high for them. A soldier is nothing to Caesar, as he will allow thousands to die. His aristocracy is his weakness. They are his real support."

Jude had the most intense feeling that Joses had not really answered his question. Furthermore, he had written Joses off before. To entertain his ideas seemed weak and ridiculous. But, these new plans had his attention. His own, unfortunately, had been found lacking.

"How do you see it unfolding?" asked Jude.

"We have fooled the kittim into thinking we are one and the same person," Joses began. "Both of us should bring our forces to

Jerusalem under the cover of the people coming for Passover. We will divide the forces on the east and place unarmed men inside the city. The kittim will believe that if anything is going to occur, it will happen before Passover begins. They think the people will not disturb their celebration. They will not think it will be after the celebration if no one stirs up the people with inflaming oratory. And we won't. They will also believe the people too tired to do anything after the Passover, especially days later. With no stirrings among the people before or during the Passover, Pilate and Caiaphas will think there is no cause for concern. They let down their guard, and then we make the three-pronged assault on the second day of the week to take all three of them, and no others. Our priests will then enter the Temple under Jacob's direction and begin the purifications so that in three days we may offer sacrifice. We can then prepare for Yom Kippur."

"Why did you mention our duality? I see it of no effect here?" asked Jude.

"I will depart toward Galilee after our own Passover on the first day of the week and ensure that my departure is noticed," explained Joses. "You will stay in Jerusalem and conduct the operation."

Joses is not going to take any credit? Joses will not lead the people, but only be a planner and diversion? Is this what he is willing to do? Jude was full of questions.

"So, we will both be in Jerusalem for the celebration of the Community Passover, celebrate the regular Passover, and then you will make a very obvious departure that will draw attention to you and away from us," Jude repeated the plan to be sure he understood it. "Then our forces need to be controlled from the Mount of Olives and Mount Scopus. We can place a flag system there for our leaders to watch for signals. The central command post should be in Gethsemane," Jude was reasoning out loud. "Once you have departed, we pass weapons over the wall to those inside, and with three spearheads, enter the city from different directions but each close to their final objective." Jude stopped and thought a moment. "You know, it just may work."

"Then we are agreed?" asked Joses.

Jude held his words until he stood up and brushed the dust off his robes.

"Agreed," Jude said. "I have a man who is very reliable, and he has ties to the Herodians. I believe I can use him to plant the information that I will be going to Galilee after the Passover to do more preaching."

"You are sure he is trustworthy?" asked Joses. "Someone, as you know, identified my operations in Tarichaeae."

"This man has never known our entire system. But, he has progressed in his studies and piety," explained Jude. "All I need tell him is that I am going to Galilee. What could he make of that even if he did suspect anything?"

Joses nodded in agreement. The men shook hands and embraced. Joses headed back to Bethany and Jude went to his family in Damascus. Jacob resumed his meditations.

The next day, Jude, as Yeshua the Rabbi, met with several new proselytes and several Zealot resistance leaders disguised as shepherds, in a small home in Jericho. The Zealots were only known to each other, the regular attendees to the meeting not even usually aware of their dual roles. This was the best way to communicate to the resistance throughout the countryside. The mystical practice of keeping something hidden by placing it in another form before everyone's eyes continued its effectiveness. Jude had sent word for Reu to come to the meeting as well.

"Brethren, this is a day of rejoicing," Jude, as Yeshua, began. "The Passover quickly approaches and we need to complete our preparations. The Kingdom of Heaven is at hand." Jude was giving his Zealots the code for preparation of military action. "HaShem desires us to purify our minds and our hearts, cleave to righteousness and shun evil. We must remove evil from Israel and from ourselves, and make straight the path of the Holy One of Israel."

"Yeshua," called one of the men, "what is the Kingdom of Heaven like?"

Reu was all ears.

"The Kingdom of Heaven is like a mustard seed," explained Yeshua. "A man took it and planted it in his field. Indeed, it is the least of all seeds. But, when it is grown, it is the greatest of all herbs. It becomes a tree and even the birds of the air come and lodge in its branches."

The parable had two levels of meaning. To the uninitiated, the story explained how the love of HaShem begins small and then grows big in a man's heart. To the initiated, like 'the Kingdom of Heaven is at hand,' the message was that the tree is ready to grow, expel the kittim, and begin Israel's time of deliverance. Yeshua continued with another parable to dull the ears of those who he did not want to understand the message, and further explaining what his strategy would entail for his leaders.

"It is also like leaven, which a woman took, and hid three measures of meal, leavening the whole."

Three hidden forces were going to be needed. The leaders had their orders and would meet Jude later to hear the details.

Yeshua taught from the Torah to complete the meeting and to deliver something of worth to every person present. As the meeting ended, he explained he would be gone to Galilee immediately after the Passover. Reu was surprised. As the group split up, he noticed several men enter a small room in the building. Reu secreted himself outside the door of the side room where the men, all of apparent standing, were talking in hushed tones.

"Jude intends to enter the city after the Passover and take Pilate, Caiaphas, and Herod hostage, or kill them in the attempt," said one voice.

"Jude? Did he say the name Jude?" Reu thought to himself. "Who could that be?"

"How soon do we need to report on the number of our available men?" asked another.

"Planning is well underway, so get these to me as soon as possible," said the first voice.

The men then exited the room and Yeshua stopped one of them.

"Laban, we will gather the sheep at noon tomorrow," said Yeshua. "Also, would you please have Reu see me before he leaves."

"Yes, Rabbi, I will make the arrangements," answered Laban and walked on out of the building while Yeshua proceeded back to the place in the building where the first meeting had finished moments before. Reu left his position from behind the door and quickly moved over to the main door while Yeshua was examining a document. Reu then acted as if he had just re-entered.

"Rabbi, may I disturb you?" he asked Yeshua.

"Ah, Laban found you already," said Yeshua.

"No, Rabbi, I just came back to ask you a few questions, if that is alright?" Reu was careful not to do anything to raise suspicion. But, he needed to get at least one necessary piece of information-if he could get it and survive.

"Of course," answered Yeshua. "Come on over and let us talk."

Reu walked closer.

"Your words seem to be from HaShem Himself," he praised.

"Pray only that HaShem guides me in all things," Yeshua answered. He then drew in a deep breath and exhaled slowly. "The first day of the week after the Passover I plan to go again to Galilee. I will not see you for sometime."

Reu was sure he had understood the code delivered to the others. While still not fully initiated, his close association had revealed many of the hints of things to him. Now this information, to him, that Yeshua would not be around after the Passover seemed to be a subterfuge. Was Yeshua using him? The only question was, why? Also, dare he ask him if he was indeed the man who beat the exchangers at the temple? It was now or never.

"I will miss you but will look forward to your return. What will you do there? He asked.

"I will go there to preach Torah to those who did not see it important enough to come to Jerusalem for Passover."

"A wise thing to do. I have one burning question though. It is difficult to ask, but please understand my concern. It seems that if this was you, it could be some trouble."

Jude anticipated the question as many had identified him as the man at the Temple cleaning. Joses had been right, thus the necessity for his apparent departure.

"Were you the man who scourged the priests and merchants at the Temple?" asked Reu.

Joses was right, indeed. Apparently Reu may have seen him at the time and it was best not to deny it.

"Yes, Reu, that was me," responded Yeshua. "After all this time, you finally know. Keep it to yourself. My purpose is merely to ensure that Torah and the Temple rites are done correctly. You see this, don't you?"

"I do," answered Reu. "But, I am a little confused as I thought I heard one of the brethren call you by the name of Jude. What does this mean?" Reu was taking a leap that could be dangerous, but he was willing as he knew the money Pilate might pay him for the information could be very high.

Jude now studied him for a moment. How could anyone have been so careless, and how did he miss the mistake? Yet, Reu had always been faithful, giving much to the brethren and giving them such reliable information for so long. Jude decided to confide in him.

"How you have heard it means it was meant for your ears. Man has not revealed this to you, but HaShem," explained Jude. "Yes, my name from birth has been Jude, and Yeshua is but my calling. As with my strict adherence to the Torah, you see how this name is so important to emphasize all that is done?"

"Again, I do, Rabbi. I feel so very blessed to have this knowledge of my friend and teacher," said Reu so sincerely that any suspicion Jude may have been entertaining vanished with the words Reu spoke.

"Then, please ensure that your master knows I will not be there to cause any trouble. I will leave afterwards and depart north to Galilee. Perhaps, then, your master will tell others and they will have no concerns." Reu nodded in agreement. "Now, as far our topic today, do you feel more edified?" asked Jude.

"Much more," responded Reu. "I return to my home with gladness in my heart. I only lament that you will be gone after Passover. I will await your return."

"May HaShem bless you and your family," said Jude.

"And may HaShem grant you peace," said Reu as he left for Jerusalem, his intention actually to report to Amelaus.

***

"So, it appears they have some grand plan to seize myself, Herod, and you, Caiaphas?" Pilate looked serious. Suddenly, he roared with laughter, obviously finding the whole idea ludicrous. "Who would have dreamed up this ridiculous plan other than a desperate bunch of thugs? You cannot be seriously worried about this?" Pilate asked, barely able to restrain his amusement.

The Roman and Caiaphas were meeting Amelaus in the Antonia Fortress. The Sicarii never seemed to come close to it, an appropriate place to discuss their plans.

"The leader seems to be this Yeshua or Jude fellow," Caiaphas said. "He is the man we have occasionally seen and heard so much about who preaches Torah in the city and the countryside. I should have known it was a cover. So, this is the man who rode into Jerusalem on the ass as if he were the Mashiach! Then it was he who also whipped and beat the priests and the merchants and money exchangers in the Temple to try and stir up the people to support him. He defies your use of the Corban for the aqueduct so desperately needed here. I have smelled this vermin and his plans all along. And as far as taking it seriously, yes, your Excellency, desperate men are like caged animals! You also know that."

Pilate could only grin and take a sip of wine. The warning from Caiaphas did not even make him move in his seat. He was totally unconcerned.

"There are still some unanswered details," Amelaus interjected. "May I speak freely?" he deferred to Pilate.

"Absolutely," Pilate assured him.

"While they plan to conduct this operation around Passover,

they will not violate the day the Essenes observe it with their special calendar, nor the orthodox day set in the regular calendar as observed by everyone else," explained Amelaus. "These two days are merely a day apart this year, one following the other. Therefore, they will need to wait until the conclusion of the Sabbath the day after the orthodox Passover. This means we should not expect any activity until evening after the Sabbath, and it likely will not occur until the next morning."

"You have really thought this through," Pilate said as he leaned forward in his chair, quite impressed with the Herodian. "But, you fail to consider the amount of soldiers and guards we have at this time. The siege of Jerusalem under Sabinus many years ago resulted from weaknesses we have since corrected. Any attempt to take either or all three of us will result in the immediate deaths of the perpetrators. It would be suicide!" Pilate sat back in his chair and smugly took another sip of wine.

"Suicide is a small price to pay for those who believe they go straight to heaven for their sacrifice," Caiaphas wryly commented. "As I said, these are fanatics! They believe their god will save them. They are not like the common people who have been beaten into submission, or the noble and wealthy classes who have their lives of leisure. These men live only for their deaths. And they want to take us with them. Your, Excellency, do not underestimate them." Caiaphas circled a table in the center of the room and took a chair, sitting down and then wiping his brow.

Pilate looked at Caiaphas and tried to laugh at him again. But, it now seemed a little bit more difficult.

"We could just take him and crucify him the next time he shows himself," said Pilate. "Or, we could toy with him a bit. Let them fall into a trap and take many more of his followers with him. That would be much more effective, sending a strong message to the rest of the people."

"It seems none do anything without instructions from the leaders. I think we should let them come to us. Reu will be meeting with them again," Amelaus said. "They have greatly increased their trust in him. I am certain we will find out what we need to know to counter anything they do. He will take us to where the leader is the night before Passover."

Reu will point him out and we will arrest him with hardly a fight, then parade him to the people as the cause of their troubles," said Caiaphas.

Pilate nodded his head. "That is why we have used this insider," Pilate lifted his cup and waved it at Caiaphas. "It is obvious we have the upper hand, and we control the time and place. As soon as Herod arrives prior to the celebration, we will meet again and ensure we use the information we have to plan several courses of action. I tell you, they will not succeed."

Pilate took another drink from his cup and waited for a response. But, it was obvious Caiaphas was not convinced. What would encourage him? Maybe they should bait the resistance to make them come out in the open as they had before.

"Why don't you go ahead and execute your Immerser?" Pilate asked Caiaphas. "Have Herod find something against him in your law and execute him. Beheading isn't it?"

"Strangulation, beheading, or stoning for blasphemers," Caiaphas said with some interest. How long had he wanted to rid himself of his archrival? The idea sounded delicious. "I am sure Herod will come up with an adequate reason as long as you agree to let him go through with it."

***

"It seems your people have forgotten about you, old friend," Herod was trying to intimidate Joachanin who now stood before him in chains at his throne room inside the Fortress of Machaeros. "Our plan has worked quite well. Out of sight, out of mind." Herod looked over at his wife, Herodias[33], laughed, and waited for Joachanin to answer him.

Joachanin refused to look at him or say any word.

"You know," Herod continued, "we have not changed in any single way because of your preaching. The old religion is gone; the old prophets were not all right. HaShem approves of our changes that are really nothing but the new way. Your accusations against us are groundless and extreme. HaShem has not punished us; He punishes you for your vile lies and distortions. Look at you, a pitiful excuse for a man."

Still Joachanin said nothing, but he did look up and smile at Herod. It was as if he said, "Oh, you think so." The act put fear in Herod's heart. This man still had the ability to unnerve him.

"Pilate and Caiaphas agree with me that it is time for us to part, you and I," said Herod. "You are the violator of the Law and the Torah, seeking to shame the leaders of HaShem's Kingdom and the Temple, trying to force us to return to matters long dead. Things have changed. HaShem has changed. You have committed blasphemy against HaShem, lied about His anointed ones, and nearly caused the Romans to take away our place and nation because you have oftentimes incited the people, as do your followers now."

Herod called his niece, Salome, his wife Herodias' daughter by his brother, over to him. She stood by Herod and looked at Joachanin with no pity.

"What should we do with him?" Herod asked her.

"He insults God's anointed ones," she responded. "Is that not blasphemy, questioning the leaders HaShem has placed over the people? Is that not questioning HaShem?" She ran over to her mother. "What should I say?"

Herodias did not hesitate, "Ask for his head."

Salome turned back to Herod. "Take off his head!"

Herod half nodded, half shrugged. He then took a drink from his wine cup and wiped his lips. He still half feared Joachanin, even though he stood before him in chains. How would the people react once Herod killed him? So what?

"The punishment for blasphemy is stoning, my dear," explained Herod. "Yet, he has committed other crimes."

"I think we should have his head, so does mother," responded Salome.

"As you wish, my dear. I would give you anything," he said

to Salome and looked at Herodias who was nodding in agreement. "Blasphemy, lying, deceit are all punishable by us," said Herod to Joachanin. "The Romans permit us to execute our laws on all accounts except where theirs take precedence. And in this case, we can pronounce judgment upon you. So, tell me, are you the Mashiach ben David?"

Joachanin would not answer him.

"The Sanhedrin and Caiaphas have agreed that I have the power to order your death by beheading!" Herod said angrily.

Still Joachanin was silent.

"Take him away!" commanded Herod. "Bring only his head back to me."

Herodias and Salome wickedly giggled. Salome taunted Joachanin by dancing in front of him.

Joachanin would not look at her. His only thoughts were the words of Torah he repeated in his mind.

***

"Joachanin's body was found outside Herod's fortress at Machaeros," Eleazer told Joses in the main room of Joses' home in Bethany. "Herod beheaded him and left his body unburied for the birds and wild animals. The head was missing and could not be found."

It was not enough for Herod to kill him; he had to defile him, Joses thought as he arose from his seat where he had been reading from one of his many mystical texts. It did not surprise him that Herod would do all in his power to humiliate Joachanin and refuse him a proper burial. It was fortunate enough that the family would have the body without the head.

"Is my Aunt Elizabeth aware of this?" asked Joses.

"Not to my knowledge," responded Eleazer.

"How about his wife and son?"

"The same," said Eleazer. "They want nothing to do with any of us, it seems."

"That task shall be mine," Joses said solemnly.

Joses had long feared Joachanin's death at the hands of the kittim or Herod as the only eventuality. Despite their desires, the resistance in Galilee did not have the ability to mount any kind of rescue against the fortresses of Herod. The lines of communication and the distances prohibited any concerted and coordinated effort. Joses felt a twinge of isolation, even here in his home in Bethany.

"Have word sent to Jude and Jacob," Joses told him. "The timing seems strange. Why incite the people prior to the Passover? You would think that they would not want to cause any anger as the masses of the people descend on Jerusalem. It's like they are taunting us. Do they know something?"

"How could they?" asked Eleazer.

"There are several indications that there is an informer amongst us or Jude's closest associates," Joses pointed out. "We had the attack on Tarichaeae, the capture of Nechemyah and Jonathan, and now this to provoke us. There just seems to be too many coincidences." Joses stopped again to think.

"Should I go ahead and send word?" asked Eleazer.

"By all means, yes," Joses said, as he nodded and rubbed his chin with his right hand, still pondering his own question. He was actually surprised that Joachanin had stayed alive as long as he had. "Also," continued Joses, "instead of going with us to Jerusalem, I need you to go to Galilee and prepare for assisting us from there. It is best to have my most trustworthy commander watch the north. While your skills will be missed in Jerusalem, we need to avoid the problems Jude had with the Roman Legions to the north many years ago."

"Yes, Joses," responded Eleazer, "I understand."

As Eleazer left to instruct the messengers, send them to Damascus, and then proceed to Galilee, Joses considered his own fate and that of his family. Should he send Miriam and the boys away immediately? While he had finally been successful in getting Jude to see that his methods were not gaining them any ground, he was also unsure that his own plan of trying to concentrate on the seats of power would win in the end. He was still waiting for the inspiration, the answer from HaShem that would ensure the gathering of all Israel and the expulsion of the Romans. Despite the seeming clarity of his visions, the actual event escaped him. The windows of heaven had not opened to that point. He did not doubt; he just did not know the end. So it is for man. And as far as Miriam, she would do whatever Joses requested of her. Yet, maybe this was not the proper time.

He walked outside and looked at the clear blue sky contrasted against the mild greens and the light browns of the land around him. Several children were playing on the hill just to the south of his home, their mothers standing not far away discussing the common topics for the preparation of Passover. He could faintly hear them talking of cleaning their homes and removing all leaven from inside their houses, even selling that which they had. These were his people, and most of them were trying to do the right things. All they needed was the proper leadership, not those seeking their own glory, but those willing to bring all to a higher level of understanding and awareness. That was, in fact, the true meaning of the deliverance from Egypt that was accomplished by HaShem through Moses nearly 1500 years before. It meant the dividing of the light from the dark and the separation of the upper waters from the lower waters. It was a deeper mystery, but one Joses could not openly discuss except with selected individuals. It would be considered heresy by those unfamiliar with Israel's true history or those uninitiated in the deeper levels of meaning in Torah.

The end truth, however, was that HaShem would thrash the nations for the burdens and injustices they inflicted on the people. The rulers were the ones truly responsible for the evils in the world. While one man may injure a few, a nation could wreak horrible destruction upon thousands, even innumerable people. Where much is given, much is expected. The rulers had not taken their stewardships seriously for any but themselves. Instead of using their power to raise men to new levels of intelligence and awareness, they used it to increase their own treasuries or just to have control over the minds of the people. Joses wanted to change all that. Israel was supposed to be the nation that would be the great example. But, even they had squandered it, and now the kittim were securely controlling most of the known world, poisoning the minds of men.

It must be time for change, a return, a restoration. It must be the time for a resurrection of ancient understandings. Certainly, Joses thought, HaShem would not wait much longer.

***

The crowds were beginning to gather in and around Jerusalem as the Passover approached. The masses of pilgrims flooded the city and the countryside and the amount of housing space for the sojourners diminished. If the travelers had no one to stay with in or around the city, they camped in the hills and valleys. This was typical for the celebration. There were so many people that no one could possibly have discerned the movements of the resistance forces as they mingled in the crowds inside the city and in the hills to the east. On the day of the assault, the Zealots in the city would receive their arms from their comrades by having the weapons hoisted up on ropes over the south wall. This they would do as the celebration came to a close and the guards were less alert.

With the plans set and the gathering of forces proceeding as scheduled, Joses and Miriam, Kefa, and Jacob, along with other close relatives and friends planned on celebrating the Community Passover at the Jerusalem home of Nikdimon ben Gurion so that they could properly observe the Passover but still be in a better position to conduct the operations. While ben Gurion was a secret member of the Community and understood the earlier celebration observed by the mystics, he did not have any certain information regarding the times and dates of any resistance military activities. This was a safeguard as he was a member of the Jerusalem Sanhedrin overseen by the High Priest Caiaphas, and he did not need to know details in case he came under suspicion.

While Joses and his followers were at the home of ben Gurion, Jude was hastily concluding his part of the plan and positioning his people. His son, Jacob, and another young man assisted him in many of the details and served as his messengers to the dispersed zealots. Any changes in orders as well as important updates were sent through Jude's son. They also took time to occasionally discuss Torah with various men as they walked around Jerusalem, thus further veiling their activities.

Jude and his family would celebrate Passover at the home of a relative to his wife so that no one would see him and Joses together, a disastrous possibility that could undermine the entire plan. It would not be until after the Community Passover meal that the two leaders and their closest followers would meet in the Garden of Gethsemane. But, Jude did have one more important task to complete and he called for Reu. Reu met him by the water pool on the north side of the Temple. Although the Antonia Fortress overlooked the pool, it was of little concern to the Romans because they could plainly observe the area and the people used it solely for healing and cleansing. As such, the meeting would draw little attention, and Jude could conceal himself in the crowds. Should escape become an issue, there was a city gate adjacent to the pool that led directly to the eastern hills.

"Yeshua, my master and king," Reu said in a low tone, almost a whisper, "what are your commands?"

Jude sat with him at the edge of the pool, two of Jude's bodyguards sitting on either side of them to ensure that it remained a private conversation.

"This is the most important mission you have yet received," Jude began. "As a member of the Herodian household, I want you to go to your master and tell him that you know who the man is who claims to be the Son of David and that he is amassing a following in Samaria."

"If I say this, they will immediately think of you," Reu responded in as concerned a voice as he could put on. He was now concerned that his own true purposes would not be discovered, and he needed to ensure that this was not some secret test of his loyalty. Could the resistance have discovered that the Romans were onto them and that he was actually an informant? These thoughts flooded his mind as he hurriedly added, "Whatever you command will be done, but why would they believe you to be in Samaria and not here in Jerusalem at the Passover?"

"Tell them that I was rejected by the people and that I have gone to the Samaritans. They will think me nothing but a man of light-mindedness, seeking only vain ambitions of no consequence. A simpleton," explained Jude.

"Very well, master," said Reu. "Do you still want me in Gethsemane? I can gather many who will support you."

"We can certainly use all the men we can get," said Jude. "But, I think not at this point. We have those whom I have chosen. It is too late for anyone who may choose me; I do not have the time to test them as to their loyalties or their degree of commitment to HaShem. So, go and do only as I have commanded. Report to me as soon as you have delivered the message and get word to me. You will then go to Gethsemane and wait there until I find you."

Reu nodded and excused himself. He made his way to Amelaus as Jude had instructed, but for very different reasons. Upon his report to him, Amelaus then took him to Caiaphas to report of this attempted new subterfuge. Again, they met in the Antonia Fortress.

"Jude has asked Reu to lead us to believe he will now be in Samaria, even during the Passover" Caiaphas explained to Pilate.

"Why would he think we would believe such a thing after all his efforts in and about Judea?" Pilate asked shaking his head in doubt. "Is it possible they know Reu is really our man?"

"Not likely," interjected Amelaus. "We must look at this from the rebel's point of view. His stunt at the Temple did not gather to him the support he obviously and desperately needed. Yet, he has enough forces to conduct this operation after the Passover. His show at the Temple may have been a ruse to lead us to believe he cannot command a large base of support, thereby leading us to believe, as he would like it, that he has gone to raise followers among the Samaritans and is now no immediate threat. Furthermore, he told

Reu to meet him today in Gethsemane to report to him of his success in delivering this message. We could seize him then."

"Crafty," said Pilate as he arose from his seat and walked over to Caiaphas. "We must accommodate their plans."

"What do you mean?" asked Caiaphas.

"I want you to send a number of your guards north to Samaria, and I will send a century with them. Let it be known that we are looking for a fugitive. It is not necessary to name him, as the rebels will take it that we have swallowed their bait," explained Pilate.

"That could be dangerous, your Excellency, as we are really not sure of the strength of the forces that plan to accomplish this mission against you, Herod and myself," objected Caiaphas. "We may need the security. Why not get him this afternoon?"

"I want this on our terms. We will strike the night before the Passover as we have agreed. With their plans set for after the Passover, they will not have consolidated their abilities so early," said Pilate as he walked confidently across the room and looked out over Jerusalem. Your guards and the century need not even go that far. As soon as we have arrested the culprits, they can return."

Caiaphas nodded and smiled. "The trap is set. Very well done, Reu."

"Always at your service," Reu replied. "What should I do now?"

"Send word to this rebel that you have told his story to your master and that you have heard that some of our forces are soon to be dispatched to Samaria," Pilate ordered. "You will be with our troops for the arrest and point out this traitor to the unit commander," Pilate continued. "After dark on the night before Passover, I will send a Cohort reinforced with a number of Caiaphas' guards to seize this pretender, this maleficent leader of the Sicarii, and kill whomever stands in our way. This dreamer will be caught off guard. We will then crucify him. Commander, prepare your men," he said to the Roman Cohort Commander who stood in the corner of the room. "Tonight we will have their blood and spread it upon the gates of the city. Some Passover this will be."

"As you command," said the officer. "Hail, Caesar!"

"Hail, Caesar!" responded Pilate.

"We will now depart and do as you have commanded," said Amelaus as he and Reu bowed and left the room.

"This is the end of this mashiach," Pilate vowed to Caiaphas.

"So be it," Caiaphas agreed.

As Reu and Amelaus reached the street, Reu immediately went to find Jude in Gethsemane. There were so many people already gathering on the hills that Reu knew he could not possibly find Jude. He waited by the Golden Gate of the city just down from the garden. It was not long before Jude's representatives came to him.

"Follow us, Reu," commanded the taller one. They took him up the hill and circled several times. Finally, Jude walked toward them from the shadows of a tree as the sun was starting to set.

"What have you accomplished, brother?" asked Jude.

"All that you commanded of me," responded Reu. "I have heard that many Romans and many of the High Priest's guards are preparing to leave for Samaria in search of you."

"Very good, HaShem bless you," said Jude. He then turned to his son, Jacob. "Deliver the messages to all that the kittim have taken the bait and our time has come. Tell them to prepare to execute our plans."

The young men nodded and ran off to instruct Joses and others of the success of Jude's disinformation to the Romans.

"You have earned a place to stand among the sons of light," Jude said to Reu. "Very well done. We will take you to the next level of instruction as soon as we have secured the Temple."

"How can one so lowly as me thank you and HaShem?" asked Reu.

"You already have," said Jude. "Now, go and prepare for your Passover. After your duties to HaShem, return here and join us."

"Yes, thank you," said Reu.

"Follow me," said Jude. "I, too, must go and observe the Passover."

Reu followed Jude and his guards down the hill. They parted

just outside the Golden Gate. As Jude walked off to attend his Passover meal, Reu rushed back to Amelaus. Tonight he would lead the Romans to Jude and tomorrow he would be a rich man.

***

Night had now fallen in Jerusalem and Joses and Jude completed their respective Passover meals. As agreed, they met in Gethsemane to discuss Torah and to finalize any last parts of their plan. Gethsemane still had many quiet garden areas even with the many people who had come for the celebration. It was a place the brothers thought the Romans and the Herodians would not consider as a staging area since any real military operation would be difficult to mount, especially with the many people now camping there. Joses and Jude discussed their plans with Jacob and several members of the Community Council. The only point of contention, the one that mattered most, remained the issue of the crimson thread.

"A divided house cannot stand," Joses explained to the gathering. "I cannot forsake my birthright, and even Joachanin agreed. There is, however, no point of contention between us," he said, motioning to Jude. "Our demonstrations will prove our respective rights and obligations. Only when that is done, can there no longer be any doubt as to whether we are as we say we are."

"I see no point of issue at the moment, brother, since you do not question my position as the Mashiach ben David," Jude again emphasized in hushed tones to avoid any possibility of someone outside their small gathering from hearing. "As you said, our demonstration is at hand."

At that moment, Reu arrived and sat down just outside the main group. He had been allowed to pass the guards under Jude's instructions. As Reu watched and listened, he saw Joses and compared him to Jude. Even in the dim light, what a resemblance! Brothers? What did this mean? His thoughts raced even as he carefully remembered the route they had taken to arrive here so he could bring the Romans later.

"Let this agony be gone from us," Joses asked the group. "Give us strength so that we can do HaShem's will without impediment. We need to concentrate on our plans. At present, these override all other issues."

"It is set. On Monday the Temple will be ours, and the leaders of the kittim will be in our hands. Praise HaShem," said Jude to Joses and those with him. "All Israel can rest."

With the tension released for the moment, the men began to think of other things.

"That is well," said Joses. "We have yet a little to do for our joy this day to be complete. Would you like to join us?" he asked Jude.

Jude looked and could see that Jacob and Kefa were obviously ready to involve themselves in some additional spiritual ceremonies as they had their tallits and kepas ready. Most obviously, Jacob and Joses' son, Joseph, were in white linen robes preparatory to some additional special ordinances. Jude merely made note of it. As long as Joses supported the resistance in ending kittim control of the Temple, he did not now care what other things he did. However, it was now Jacob with whom he found some disappointment.

"Do as you must," Jude said in as civil a tone as he could. "This is, indeed, a joyous Passover. The liberation of our people and HaShem's Temple is at hand."

Joses and those with him continued on their way up the hill to a quiet spot where few people had yet gathered. Jude watched them as they sat down and began their discussion. He then went on to attend to his own concerns. He wanted to ensure that the forces he had were properly dispersed in what would appear to searching eyes to be unorganized groups on the hills and throughout the area. He made sure that they intermingled with the pilgrims who were already there for the orthodox Passover celebration that was to begin the next evening.

He designated as a control post the area of a depression between two hilltops, Mount Scopus on the north and the Mount of Olives on the south. He also planned observation posts on the Mount of Olives and the southeast side of the city and Mount Scopus on the northeast. Finally, he checked the system of flags that he would use for communication along with his runners to ensure timely and accurate information and dissemination of commands. He planned to wait until after Passover to make all the posts operational so as to avoid any premature suspicions. After his check, he would settle for the night and inspect everything again tomorrow.

He did not notice that Reu had disappeared.

Up in the quiet grove where Joses and those with him had gone, Jacob, still in his white linen robe, asked Joses more questions about his own spiritual journey.

"And what of the secret and sacred ordinances of On?" he asked. "Can we discuss those here?"

Kefa and Joses' son, Joseph, nodded in agreement. Young Joseph was also still in his white linen clothing while Kefa was his usual disheveled self. But, their appearances were not altogether inappropriate for only Jacob and Joseph would receive any further initiations this night while Kefa would act as a watch.

"There is meaning to your lives that is greater than expelling the kittim," Joses began. "We must imitate the attributes of HaShem if we are to grow and reflect Him, reflecting nothing but HaShem. The first of these is forbearance in the face of evil and patience in enduring evil so that we do not return evil when it is done to us. We must constantly seek for the right in all we do, the right use of all things for the glory of HaShem."

The men sat in silence listening to this great mystic.

"Forgive others that the evil that has been suffered is erased. Be aware of your neighbor and refuse anger, seeking the higher good. Become mercy and recall only the good qualities of those that torment you, and eliminate all traces of vengefulness. Give no thought to your suffering which others inflict on you, and remember only the good. Show compassion for those who are suffering, even those who do not do the will of HaShem. Cling to the truth and be not afraid to show mercy beyond the Torah. In assisting the wicked to improve without judging them will lift you and them and all of creation. Treat all men as children of HaShem, even those not of the House of Israel. Pray for all these attributes to come to you and demonstrate them in your lives. Once you have bound these to yourselves, you may take not only yourself to HaShem, but all the worlds as well."

"Then, we are to submit ourselves to the evil of the kittim?" asked Kefa.

"It is that which is in your heart to which this applies," responded Joses. "HaShem expects us to stand for the truth and defend it, but have no evil in your hearts against those you seek to repel, for they must eventually learn these lessons as well. And who better to learn them from than those they thought to vanquish? But even more importantly, look into the evil in your own heart. That part which is the darkest in you is like the smoke behind which HaShem conceals himself. Bring the darkness out into the light and examine it, understand it, do not run to hide it, then purge it, and the Glory of HaShem will be revealed and in you will be His reflection."

"Can a man fight with strength and without passion against his enemy?" asked Kefa who seemed to be having the most trouble understanding what Joses was saying.

"Remember, to return to others the evil that is in their hearts is to destroy yourself and to slow down the rising of all creation," Joses explained. "Defend your family, your friends, and your land, but do so with no hatred towards those who suffer from the work of your hands. Afterwards, show them an increase of love, and show them all good things by your own example."

"Can one man's acts truly receive the notice of HaShem for the good of all peoples and nations?" asked Jacob. "Can the prayer asking HaShem to bless the seventy nations and the pleading for the atonement at Yom Kippur truly bring all creation to a higher level?"

"If no other than one being at a time," responded Joses. "For them to imitate HaShem's attributes and eventually attain to that level, they must see the example in you. We must be the Hand of HaShem, just as the Torah commands. Be as wise as serpents but as harmless as doves. And remember, no greater love has any man than to lay down his life for others. But, this will not find the evil ones without guilt in HaShem's eyes."

Jacob pondered what he had heard and then asked another question.

"Are any others outside of Israel in possession of the secrets?" he asked.

"Shem had many sons," responded Joses. "Abraham was but one of his posterity. Yet, in our father Abraham, was the example to all of us. Who knows what others HaShem has chosen? But, what Abraham received, he imparted to others whom he found worthy. Moses brought the sacred words from Egypt where they had been safeguarded for centuries and revealed them to those directed to him by HaShem. The righteousness of a man, true right use of all things, will bring to him piety and wisdom until he emulates HaShem to such a degree that the man becomes like HaShem. Then, HaShem cannot hide himself from him, as they are near to one another."

"What, then, will he become?" asked Jacob.

"A ben Adam and ben Abbas," answered Joses, "an adopted son of HaShem, a son of the Father."

At that, Joses stood up.

"To approach HaShem one must practice the right use of all things and then meditate upon the letters and words of Torah until you reach the divine names. From there, all things will be shown to you. Arise, my brother," he said to Jacob.

Jacob stood and faced Joses.

"To you falls the succession of the Mashiach ben Joseph should I go away. You, in turn, shall again replace the mantle onto my son, Joseph, when he reaches his time of age."

"Then I am to lead Damascus as the Teacher and High Priest, and the nation of Israel?" asked Jacob.

"You are my successor until my son attains to his time," Joses said again.

"What about Joachanin's heir?" asked Jacob.

"That seems to have taken care of itself," answered Joses.

"Are you going away, Joses?" asked Jacob. Kefa became alarmed as well and young Joseph could only recite his father's words to himself, trying to understand.

"This is all to ensure the continuity of our order," said Joses. "And in all things, council with Miriam."

Jacob understood his instructions.

"Now, watch for me as I go into meditation, that I may not receive the kiss of HaShem and depart from you," Joses instructed.

The men gathered closer together, donning their tallits, tefillin, and phylacteries in preparation for meditation. Jacob took the position closest to Joses to watch so that he could go and return. With a few initial recitations of the sacred names, Joses was off in a vision as the men watched over him. The meditation went on for so long, that the food they had eaten earlier in the evening, combined with the lateness of the hour, began to bring upon them the need for sleep. Jacob saw that Kefa and Joseph had slipped into unconsciousness, but did not believe he would allow himself to do the same. Joses continued his meditation, and then came back on his own. When he removed the tallit from his head, he saw that all three men whom he had asked to watch for him had fallen asleep.

"Jacob, Kefa, Joseph," he quietly roused them. "Wake up so that I may continue."

The men startled awake to find Joses smiling.

"The spirit is willing, but the flesh is weak," he said chuckling slightly. "Remain with me just an hour and it will be done," he asked them.

The men agreed and Joses returned to his meditation. As he recited the words, however, the rhythm caused first Kefa, then Joseph, and finally a weary Jacob to again fall asleep. Joses was on his own.

The Merkava had taken him to the seventh gate and there he stood with Anpiel who motioned him to enter. After passing through the clear marble gate and the columns of the inner courts, Joses found himself once again standing before the Throne of Glory. There, before him, sat Akhteriel, the reflection of HaShem. But, he heard no words from the Throne, only the continual rushing of wind that normally precedes the entry into the vision. The lack of any instruction and the absence of any assurances left him to his own thoughts. The situation rose almost to a level of confusion in his soul. What was happening? What steps should he now expect to take?

Suddenly, he was hurled back into the garden. He slowly opened his eyes, not sure of how the vision had so abruptly ended. He could see that his companions were asleep, but that, in and of itself, should not have caused HaShem to send him away. He could see no reason for the interruption. Then, he heard something. What was that noise? Was there a disturbance at the entrance to the garden?

"You are under arrest!" the voice of a Roman, no doubt.

A Roman Cohort with a few soldiers from Caiaphas' guards had entered the Garden and confronted several of the Zealots. The Zealots had tried to cover up who they were, many just continuing to mingle with the crowds. But, the soldiers had reached the location of Jude and it was obvious he had been caught by surprise. Joses arose and awoke the other three with him, and then hurried to the point of the tumult.

As they ran to the lower part of the garden, they could hear the sounds of battle. Men were yelling and the sharp, ringing of metal striking against metal pierced the cool night air. Through the trees, Joses could now see a desperate struggle. Jude and his men were heavily engaged in combat with Roman soldiers. Several of Jude's men lay wounded, or worse, on the ground. Jude himself had just run a Roman through with his sicar and taken the man's sword. Joses saw Jude run another Roman through with the sword he had just taken from his dead companion, the man's face wrenching in the agony of the pain. Jude spared no skill in dispatching his adversaries.

As the battle grew and intensified with more and more men from both sides joining the mayhem, Joses stood motionless for but a second to determine where he should place himself in the fight. His pause was just in time to see Reu pointing out Jude to some other Romans that were just then deploying their soldiers into the combat. This larger, more concentrated Roman force immediately seized Jude and slew his guards when they tried to protect him.

Realizing the danger, more Zealots began to engage the Romans until the entire Garden of Gethsemane was engulfed in riotous killing. All military order seemed to vanish from both sides in the darkness as opposing groups of men faced each other randomly about the garden as opportunity or fate presented to them, and they fell upon each other in murderous rage. Most of the Jews in and around the garden fled, as they wanted no part in the cause of either side and were only there for the Passover. But, others more inclined joined the Zealots in their desperate struggle.

It was all out of control. Joses watched as Reu fled the most severe fighting, running almost directly in front of him. The two men looked at each other for but a second, and then Reu continued his flight from the bloodshed. Joses turned to try and ascertain the extent of the battle and could see only more fighting erupting all around him in a chaotic manner that convinced him there was no chance of rallying a command. While Kefa had already joined in the melee, killing several of Caiaphas' guards and wounding a Roman, Joses realized it was now a rout and there seemed little chance to bring together meaningful forces to repel the attack as the Romans had concentrated their forces immediately in Jude's and Joses' vicinity. As he looked toward the city, it was obvious that the line of torches from Jerusalem to Gethsemane were more Roman reinforcements.

Just then, Joses saw his son, Joseph, seized by a Herodian Guard. Joses struck the guard with a sicar, blood immediately flowing from the guard's right arm. As Joseph tried to pull away from the soldier's grip, his linen robe caught in the man's belt and tore. In the struggle to free himself, Joseph's robe completely came off his body and Joseph ran away almost naked but for his loincloth.

Joses also saw his own chance to escape, but was too concerned for all the others. He made his way to where the fighting sounded the worst as other Zealots began to flee. He could see torches almost completely surrounding his position and any other avenues of escape were quickly disappearing. He turned around and headed straight for Kefa's location where he could see him struggling to fight off several Romans who had wrestled him to the ground. The Romans overcame Kefa, but did not kill him. They dragged him roughly over to where Jude was held and threw him to the ground. There, beside Kefa and Jude, were two severely wounded Zealots.

Joses could see that they had been surprised and the fight was lost. He could possibly still escape, but that would seal the fate of his brothers, and, possibly, the end of the resistance. He hesitated but a moment realizing that he was the only chance for the salvation of their lives. He laid down his sicar, raised his arms and hands, and stepped forward toward the Roman Commander and the High Priest's Guards.

CHAPTER THIRTEEN

Jude was pushed to the forefront, a blade in his back to encourage his cooperation.

"Which one of you is the leader, the so-called Mashiach ben David?" demanded the Roman Commander. Joses, seeing the danger to his friends and ever ready to protect others at all costs, stepped forward. Jude was horrified. The commander could see the resemblance in the two men; they were nearly identical in appearance.

"Are you the man, or is this the leader?" the commander demanded of Joses, simultaneously forcing Jude to stand beside him for the comparison.

"I am the one you seek," Joses stated with authority. "Release him as he is just my younger brother. I am the heir of the Throne of Israel you seek."

"You are this Son of David we hear so much about?" asked the Roman again.

"As you have said," responded Joses, not agreeing with the Roman but allowing the accusation to stand. It would protect all the rest, especially Jude.

Jude recalled Joses' words from just a short time before where he had said no greater love has a man than to give his life for his brother. Suddenly, he thought of his own sons. He looked around to see if there was any sign of them. Perhaps they were dead? Maybe, HaShem willing, they had escaped. His thoughts returned to the predicament facing him as the Roman Commander grabbed his face.

"You two look very similar to me," the Roman said as he again studied the two men, finally releasing the hold he had on Jude's face.

"I cannot be sure that I have the right man unless I have both of you. You hardly look like a king," he grunted at Joses and then sneered, "I think we should rid the world of all the Jews, but especially anyone from the line of your King David. Take them away."

Even in the dim light of the night, the brethren could see the color on Jude's face go pale as the soldiers moved forward to take Joses and bind him. Jude's lifelong rivalry with Joses now seemed to him entirely needless and selfish. He also now realized that it was possible someone had tricked him into revealing the meeting to the Herodians.

Kefa, ever ready to defend the leaders and seeing a possible opportunity to free Jude and Joses, drew his sword and attacked one of the guards from the High Priest nearest to Joses, cutting his left ear. At that moment, a skirmish began amongst the soldiers and some of the Zealots closest to Kefa. Jude was forcibly taken by a guard and placed behind the commander of the Roman Cohort, but their attention was diverted just long enough for Jude to flee into the darkness. The brethren yelled for Jude to run quickly as they engaged part of the guard force immediately surrounding them. It was enough for Jude to escape.

"Kefa, put away your sword," commanded Joses, relieved that Joseph and Jude both appeared to have successfully escaped. "Those who draw it here will die by it. We are outnumbered. The Romans can do anything they want with the lot of us. It is best that they take me than our whole cause should perish. I could call now and have all the reinforcements we need, but it is not wise. I will submit." He then turned to the Roman Officer. "Let them all go. It is me you want."

The Roman stared at him, unsure of the cause of Joses' peaceful submission. But, his command of the men was surly proof that this was the one he should have arrested, anyway.

"It is me you want, let the rest go," Joses repeated. Joses looked at Kefa and nodded. Kefa and a number of the zealots also fled into the darkness, with Romans in hot pursuit. But, they did not know Gethsemane as well as the Zealots, and Kefa escaped.

The two other Zealots who had been wounded in the skirmish were arrested and bound, as well. They had killed a Roman soldier on the lower part of Gethsemane in their effort to provide a path of escape for the leaders. In the process, they themselves were grievously wounded. Samuel and Benjamin were beaten during the arrest almost to the end of their lives. Samuel's nose and shoulder were broken, and several of his fingers on his right hand had been severed by a Roman blade. Benjamin was bleeding profusely from a gash in his left side that had almost penetrated to his heart. He had also been struck around the eyes and ears, which resulted in his left eye protruding from its socket and blood draining from his left ear. Both men were forced to walk. When they could not do so, the Romans had the High Priest's guards drag them by their bonds.

As Joses and the two wounded Jews were led away, the rest of the Zealots continued their flight. Most left Jerusalem entirely, but a few remained in the area of Jerusalem to warn others and to try to determine what the resistance should do now that Joses was in Roman custody. The news spread through the Zealot community like wildfire that Joses would be crucified as an enemy of Caesar. The Romans administered crucifixion only to those they saw as political outlaws and revolutionaries who attempted to stand in the way of Roman power by supporting the messianic hope of a new King for Israel.

Once at a safe distance, Jacob turned to Nathanael bar Talmai and told him to hurry to Miriam's home and inform her of the developments. All the royal line was now in danger. Joses' family needed to get the message quickly so they could prepare for a possible escape with the children from Judea. Jacob then went to a supporter's house to obtain some clothing.

As the Romans escorted Joses and the two captured Zealots back to the city, many of the people wandering about could see what was happening and the curious followed them from a safe distance into Jerusalem. Some of the Zealots mingled with the other people. But, they realized that there was no hope of freeing the captives from the bonds of the Roman Cohort. Any Zealot reinforcements to the short battle in Gethsemane would have had to react long before this moment, and Joses had prevented any chance of that. As the men followed they could hear Caiaphas' guards discussing the arrest with the Roman Commander, and Annas, the father-in-law of Caiaphas, the High Priest. The Roman agreed to allow them to take Joses to Caiaphas' palace first so that the Herodian Pharisees and Sadducees could make an official statement opposing Joses, thus making it appear that Rome would honor the Jewish leadership in order to quell any further disturbances.

Caiaphas allowed the accusations to flow from the Chief Priests. Only Nikdimon ben Gurion was in Joses' favor. He dissented and maintained that the accusations were based on false information and the fact that the Sanhedrin was not to meet at nighttime or away from the proper area of the Temple. Furthermore, not all of the required members were present, Gamaliel being one of those absent. However, Caiaphas set the arguments in favor of Joses aside and condemned Joses as a pretender and magician, accusing him of endangering the place and nation of the Jews by claiming the right to the throne of David that Herod had occupied. The entire Sanhedrin, with only Nikdimon ben Gurion dissenting, voiced their approval. Caiaphas then had the guards take Joses to Herod Antipas.

***

After his narrow escape from Gethsemane, Joseph ran to his home in Bethany, stopping only long enough to obtain a sackcloth with which to cover himself. As he burst into the front door he informed his mother Miriam of the outcome of the battle at Gethsemane and the arrest of Joses. She knew this was eventually going to happen as she and Joses had planned for the possibility, but she had always prayed that it would somehow fail to occur. She embraced her son and kissed him while walking with him to the boys' room where the younger son, Joshua lay asleep. She kissed both her sons lovingly and longingly upon their cheeks. Here were the children given her by Joses, and they were the future of the promised line. She must protect them at all costs.

Awakening Joshua, she told him to dress and instructed Joseph to change into some different clothes. She then handed them over to Salome, Joses' sister. Miriam's sister, Martha, had already gathered her necessities and had arrived at Miriam's home to assist in anything that was needed. All the women had a sense of mission and urgency, even while quietly discussing the developments so as not to alarm the children.

Just then, Nathanael bar Talmai came to the door with his warning from Jacob. He was surprised to see that the household was already in motion. He was grateful that the young Joseph had brought word so quickly. He excused himself and hurried on toward Damascus.

Martha began to cry, shaking almost uncontrollably at the prospects now confronting them. Miriam, while also almost to the point of panic, managed to calm herself and reminded Martha that they needed to act quickly and move the children to safety as quickly as possible. Miriam also knew that it was important to notify Joses' mother, Miryam, and sent a messenger to get her.

***

As planned, Herod was in Jerusalem at the time and it was fortuitous for Caiaphas to have him there to begin the judgment in the Roman realms of power. By obtaining Herod's condemnation, the first rung in Roman administration would be satisfied. Herod took the opportunity as a sport, humiliating and accusing Joses. But Joses would not even acknowledge him, because Joses would not recognize Herod as a rightful ruler of the Jews. Unable to get a response from Joses, Herod had him delivered to Pilate, with the accusation that Joses claimed to be the sole King of the Jews in defiance of Roman authority.

Just as the guards were about to bring Joses before Pilate, Amelaus reached Caiaphas and informed him of Reu's report of two brothers in the resistance. Caiaphas realized that the twin brothers had effectively used their likeness to confuse everyone, including the common people. Caiaphas then prepared himself to go see Pilate with the Chief Priests and report of this sedition against Rome and the two brothers leading it.

Joses was quickly brought before Pilate at the Antonia Fortress and stood before him in silence. Despite his predicament, Joses did not seem to show any emotion, typical of the Sicarii. Pilate took one look at Joses and turned to his Centurion. The Centurion recognized Joses and remarked how similar he appeared to Jude, one of the leaders of the Sicarii, corroborating the story from Amelaus and Reu. The reason for the difficulty in breaking the resistance was now obvious to Pilate and he interrogated Joses as to his claim to being the King of the Jews and his ties to the Sicarii. Joses refused to answer him. Pilate continued to question him, demanding to know if Joses was indeed the heir to King David's throne, or if it was Jude, who had escaped. Finally, Pilate lost control and let his uncontrolled anger flow as he demanded to know if Joses was the King of the Jews, Joses merely answered, "You have said it."

Caiaphas then arrived with the Chief Priests and told Pilate that Joses should be the one crucified, that Jude, also known as Yeshua bar Abbas, or simply Barabbas, could be located again later. Together with Pilate, they formulated a plan where they could intimate Jude as a traitor to the resistance and a tool in the capture of Joses. The disinformation would confuse the followers of the rebellion and a full-scale revolt could be avoided. In fact, the rift created by the suggestion that Jude betrayed his brothers would further erode the resistance. Pilate agreed to their plan and then turned to Joses.

"Joses ben Cleophas, you claim to be Mashiach ben David, the heir to the supposed royal line of your fabled King David. This has caused us a great deal of trouble. Rome has allowed this chicanery and deception, this challenge to its Emperor, to go on for too long. Also, the charges against you include an act of violence against one of Herod's soldiers who was attempting to effect an arrest in the name of the Emperor. You almost killed the man. This is sedition, and criminal activity, as well. Before I sentence you, do you have anything to say?"

Joses looked at him and did not answer.

"By the gods, man, I have the power to crucify you! What do you want to say? Let me hear you say something in your defense. Beg me to spare you."

Joses still did not answer. The Herodian Priests were getting agitated with him and wanted this over, now.

"Crucify him!" they shouted, almost in unison. "He has taught the people not to pay taxes to Caesar and not to bow to the Emperor, claiming that no man should bow to another, only to his God. He claims to be the King of the Jews, even all Israel. He has taken a Nazarite vow and will not obey Caesar. This is against Caesar."

"Is this true?" Pilate smugly queried Joses. "I have heard it from my officers and now from your countrymen. What do you say?"

Joses finally answered, "They are not my countrymen, but vile and deceitful usurpers. Again, you have said it."

"Done," said Pilate. "I sentence you to be crucified. Take him away. Exact a price from every piece of his flesh and scourge him mercilessly. Are their any others with him?"

The Centurion replied that two others had been arrested in Gethsemane and that they had killed Roman soldiers.

"Crucify them with him," commanded Pilate. To further the plan of disinformation, Pilate then spoke to the assembly of Jews on the outside of the hall. "I have released the brother of this traitor, the one known as Jude or Barabbas who has benefited Rome with the knowledge of this man now in our custody."

The crowd, many of whom were secret followers of the resistance, was shocked. Those who had been loyal to the resistance spread the word of Jude's betrayal of Joses. Shock and disbelief spread throughout the Zealots and the Community, but the evidence seemed to speak for itself. Even Jude's strongest supporters began to believe the lie. It seemed to them that Jude's jealous mistrust of Joses might have actually caused him to go against his own brother. The effect planned by Pilate was beginning.

As the Roman soldiers prepared to take Joses away, members of the crowd excitedly talked about what had happened. The

Chief Priests, keeping to themselves and seeing the fruits of their subterfuge, were satisfied that Judea and the Herodian interests were secure. They prepared to depart when Pilate spoke again.

"On his tree", Pilate spat, "Place a sign that says the 'Yeshua the Nazarite, King of the Jews' and write it in Hebrew, Greek, and Latin. It will tell all who hear of it what the might of Rome will do to the likes of these false claimers and dissenters."

The Chief Priests were not sure it should go that far. They feared it might give the impression that Rome recognized any legitimacy at all to Joses' claims and to the revolution. "Your Excellency," they begged, "Do not put this inscription upon his tree, as it will only incite the people. Consider writing, 'He claims to be the King of the Jews' and then all will know of his charade."

But Pilate was adamant. He wanted to crush everything, every hope, and every conceivable purpose these traitors to Caesar and the Empire might hold as important. "What I have decreed, I have decreed," he stated so certainly that the priests knew that they should not counter again. But, Pilate went further.

"What about the children of this Joses? Where are they?"

No one knew what to answer. The priests looked at each other, realizing that they had not followed through as completely as they should have. "We do not know, your Excellency, but we can find out and report to your officers."

"Yes, do that. It is time to put a total end to this whole line of pretenders." He turned to the Commander of the Cohort and barked at him. "Once they are found, have them placed in bonds and brought to me, or killed if they resist."

Joses' heart, already heavy with the realization of his impending doom and that his efforts to protect the revolution and its leaders was a gamble, now became more concerned about the danger to his family and the fact that he may never see them again. The thought produced in him an overwhelming anxiety and grief. He thought about his sweet wife and his adorable children. He longed for the company of his family and the serenity that had so long escaped him. He knew that Miriam and his friends would follow through on the plans to thwart Pilate's intentions against the bloodline. But, hearing it from Pilate's mouth, with such disregard for the lives of his family, bore upon him an anguish he had not yet known. He could give his own life for his friends, but the thought of the destruction of those he loved so much caused a quaking in him that penetrated his very soul. Wisely, he kept his silence, quietly shedding tears of grief and hope. He did not have to worry. Even while the Romans led Joses away in bonds, Miriam was already moving the children to safety with the help of a Zealot guard. Their whereabouts would never come to Roman attention.

***

Jacob could not control the well of emotion and despair that filled his whole body. He was sick, almost to the point of death. What would he do now? Standing in the position as Opposition High Priest in Joachanin's absence, he knew he was a marked man, but such a title was not cause for Rome's wrath. He did not directly challenge Caesar's rule. No, something else gripped him in his liver and bowels. He had so long challenged Joses and believed him to be a buffoon, not serious about the Torah or his duties as prescribed in the Manual of Discipline as pertaining to a Davidic King, that he felt partially responsible for what was now happening. Indeed, Jude was long encouraged by Jacob, so much so that even when Jacob began to support Joses, Jude could not see it.

But, Jude would not betray his own brother, would he? Jacob put it from his mind. All he could think of was that he could now see that Joses had been doing the requirements for his proper heirship all along and recognized his wisdom. He realized Joses' position as that of the father of Israel, greater even than King David's throne in its scope and responsibility. Joses, by right, was the heir to the birthright of Joseph, the son of Jacob, the same who was sold by his brethren into slavery in Egypt. Even then, it was Joseph's brother, Judah, who formulated the plan. That was nearly 1500 years ago. How odd that this was all so similar.

Now, as a replay of history and Torah, Joses was given over to the Romans, the Egypt of his day. But, Jacob knew it would be far worse. They would kill Joses. The teaching Jacob had received from Joses in the last few days had been more than revealing and brought new understanding to him. He realized Joses was willing to sacrifice himself for his brethren and the revolution. He could have escaped. Why didn't he? Jacob could not reconcile his pain, and his concern turned momentarily to Kefa. What could he be doing?

After having escaped Gethsemane, Kefa had tried to work his way back to the area of Joses' trial in an attempt to find out the proceedings. Several of the guards and workers of the High Priest had seen Kefa and accused him of being one of Joses' men. Apparently, despite the obvious, Kefa had denied the accusation several times. But, he had heard the accusations against Jude. It seemed to Kefa that the impossible must be true. Jude must have betrayed Joses, and there was plenty of evidence to support it. He must find him. Now, no one was sure where Kefa had gone.

Jochanan was concerned for his mother, Martha, and his other family members. While he wanted to remain within a short distance of Joses, he also knew of the danger his family and friends faced. Jacob agreed that Jochanan should go with haste to assist his mother and Joses' family. He thought that maybe Kefa had come to his senses and gone to assist in the protection of Joses' family, as he should have done immediately upon Joses' arrest. Jacob asked Jochanan to get a report back to him as soon as possible. At that, Jacob proceeded to Damascus by the Dead Sea to notify his supporters there of the developments of the last few hours. Despite the fact that it was Passover, the one recognized by the Zealots, not the establishment Pharisees and Sadducees who bent the law to fit Roman customs, Jacob knew he had to act. He realized he should not have anyone travel more than the law allowed, but, as Joses had often said, there was a spirit to the law that was indeed the most important. He sent a messenger to Damascus.

***

The soldiers delivered Joses to the prison and handed him over to the guards for the scourge that was to prepare Joses for his death by crucifixion. They removed his white linen garment and his loincloth, leaving him entirely naked and exposed. They derided him for his circumcision and pridefully revealed their own genitals to him with taunts of, "We are real men." The soldiers took great pleasure in this taunt, which was now always included in the treatment of Zealot prisoners in retaliation for the forced circumcisions inflicted on many of their own by the Sicarii. Joses turned his face away, but they then repeatedly spat on him, all the while striking him across the face and body with their hands and with rods. They mocked him, begging him to resist them, screaming their personal hatred for him. In fact, they so fiercely hated the Sicarii and the revolutionaries as a result of all the recent activities by the resistance that they took their rage out on this one man more than they had any previously known to them. Each one of them, seven in all, had lost a friend to the Sicarii uprisings, and they took their turns inflicting ferocious blows and scathing insults.

Joses was bleeding from his nose, ears, and mouth when they chained him to a stake. After throwing a pot of cold water on him to ensure he was conscious, then they took turns beating him with the whip that had pieces of sharp bone attached to the ends. Each strike tore more flesh from Joses' body, the pain searing him and detaching him from all else life had to offer. While gasping for breath and wanting to scream at every lash, he found he was unable to make a sound since the blows to his throat in the first beating had damaged his voice, and the silence of his screams all the more terrified him. Other than prayers to HaShem, all that filled his mind was that he would never again speak to his loved ones. The grief of his hopeless condition overwhelmed him, and he wept again for his friends and family, especially his children.

***

While the scourging continued, the Sanhedrin met to evaluate the direction of the events. Caiaphas was certain that the revolution would now suffer a major blow and that with Joses out of the way, and Jacob merely acting as the High Priest at Damascus by the Dead Sea, all danger to their power would dissolve. Having Jude appearing to have betrayed Joses and receive payment for his cooperation guaranteed that he would never replace his brother Joses as the Mashiach ben David. In fact, Caiaphas laughed at the prospect that no one in the movement would ever trust Jude again and may even seek his life.

Kefa, who had already heard the story of Jude's betrayal and believed it might be true, was at that moment undertaking that very act. He had tracked Jude and found him. Unable to contain his own guilt at denying his attachment to Joses and the revolution, his only thought was to exact revenge against this brother he felt was responsible for the tragedy. He lay in wait as Jude approached the hill west of Jerusalem.

Jude was distraught himself. He had abandoned his brethren, especially Joses. At the beginning he felt Joses was not worthy of the throne, but now he saw that Joses would do anything to further the revolution and protect the movement. He now recognized Joses' position. In that moment, a curved blade was at his throat, pressing against his left ear and cutting his flesh.

"You traitor!" bellowed Kefa. "How could you have done this? He is our brother and despite your disagreements, he has as valid a right as you."

Not knowing of the lies stated of him, Jude tried to defend himself. "Kefa, no I did nothing, I just trusted someone I should not have," Jude's words were muffled by the lack of air he could gather in his lungs. Kefa held him tight around his chest and the blade was further impeding his airway. "Let me explain."

"There is nothing to explain," cried Kefa. "You have disgraced the family and the revolution. The Romans and the Herodians have pitted us all against each other. What hope is left now but to avenge Joses for your betrayal, Barabbas? NO, you have no right to that name!"

Jude was unsure he could make his case before losing

consciousness from lack of air, even though Kefa had not yet run the blade into his throat to the spine that would cut his jugulars in the process.

"My dedication to all we have stood for speaks across the years! I have betrayed no one!" cried Jude, forcing the air out of his lungs only with a near superhuman effort. Taking a slow, but deep breath against the force being applied by Kefa, he continued, "What else should I have done? It was my opportunity to escape."

Kefa eased up on his hold. He wanted to hear what this was all about. It suddenly dawned on him that Jude's escape was not easily accomplished.

Jude, breathing easier, slowly pulled away from Kefa. "What is going on? Why are you so angry with me? I have betrayed no one!"

Kefa explained the story then spreading that Jude was a traitor. Jude was beside himself. Who could have betrayed them? His thoughts turned to Reu, and he then realized the Romans and the Herodians had skillfully used him. He rent his clothes and hoarsely wailed; almost wheezing from the pressure Kefa had placed on his throat.

"It was all a way to discredit us, to end the support of the people," he slowly choked out the words. "Once Joses had taken the lead in the movement, their attention was diverted from me. They realized, as I do now, that Joses is the rightful heir. But they want all of those in the Davidic line. Don't you see?" Jude had not understood Joses' full position as it had been hidden from him because of his rivalry. Now, with all seemingly lost, he sat down on the ground and held his head. "Kefa, we were never able to duplicate our earlier successes. Everything we have done is undone. The kittim took advantage of our weakness and exploited it. Even with all our efforts to secure our plans, it took only one infiltrator to destroy us. My greed, my pride took me too far and I did not listen to the whispers of HaShem."

Kefa released Jude. He could not disbelieve his brother. Besides, what was done was done and it was time to get Joses' family to safety.

"Barabbas, Joses does not claim the Davidic Throne. He has been explaining that for a very long time. He is the Mashiach ben Joseph. He has not had any conflict with you since he came to this understanding. You know that." Kefa moved away and looked toward the west. "There is nothing to stop you from your birthright. If all you say is true, and it seems so to me, then you have not disgraced us. How to convince others will be another story. I suppose," he turned back to Jude, "that it is as Joses has said. If you do the demonstration, then you are who you say you are. There is nothing yet that can stop you if it is to be."

He left Jude on the road and hurried to the appointed rendezvous with the family of Joses. Jude watched him and was amazed at how knowledgeable and self-assured Kefa had become. As he watched his brother head west, he returned to the thoughts of the lost glory of Israel. Where would HaShem take him? For the first time in his life he felt despair, and there was no one to comfort him. He lay prostrate on the ground and wept.

***

The guard threw Joses to the right, causing his arms, which were held by the chain, to feel as if they would tear from their sockets. Joses had been beaten so severely that the stone floor beneath him was covered with blood and pieces of flesh. His blood, forming pools at his feet, caused him to slip and lose what little balance he had left as it mixed with the dust from the stones and caked between his toes. The guard released the binds from his hands and Joses fell to the ground as another kicked him in his left side to turn him over onto his back. They picked him up under his armpits and sat him down on a small stool, placing a purple robe over him. The fabric clung to his open wounds. Another scourger, who had been working on a crown made from thorns, jammed the wicked device far down onto his head, the thorns penetrating deep into the scalp. Despite the pain of the beatings, this new torture awakened a horrible agony as the small daggers stung his flesh and scraped the bones beneath it. A wave of new blood filled Joses' eyes and soaked his shoulders as the wounds bled profusely. Every new torture was designed to force the sufferer to experience a new pain as the old waxed away.

"There, now," the head guard laughed. "and here is your kingly scepter," he said as he placed a reed in Joses' right hand. "You are properly attired as the great king of the Jews." They all laughed and derided him, striking him constantly and spitting in his face. One of them struck Joses in his groin and he dropped the reed and fell to the ground. He could no longer see the Romans clearly, barely perceiving them only as shapes and shadows. He tried to pray and call upon HaShem for strength, the pain making the effort almost of no effect. He silently relegated himself to his death.

The soldiers then stood him up and removed the robe, which tore new wounds as it peeled off the developing scabs. At the same time, one of them again pulled at his genitals and mocked the circumcision of his foreskin. He recoiled at the violation, but was immediately forced toward the gate with a shove on his back. He again fell to the ground, striking his head on the stone floor. They carried the crossbeam for his crucifixion to him and placed it across his shoulders, fastening it to him with a rope. Then, they forced him to stand with the terrible weight burdening his already weak body and biting his damaged flesh. Despite his disorientation and inability to think clearly, he knew he was on his way to Golgotha where the Romans performed special executions. As he looked around through bloody vision, he could see that Samuel and Benjamin were also near him, carrying their crossbeams for their execution. They would die together. He also noticed that one of the guards was carrying the white linen garment and other pieces of his apparel he had been wearing before they took it from him at the scourging. The thought crossed his mind that it was spared the stain of his blood.

The streets were nearly deserted even though it was now well after sunrise. Word had spread of the action in Gethsemane and the arrest of the Sicarii leader causing most of the people to fear an overwhelming Roman reprisal. They stayed indoors, trying their best not to look suspicious or like they were in any way connected with the revolutionaries. Only a few dared come close enough to get a glimpse of the condemned men as they struggled along the streets with their burdens.

"You scum!" a rich Herodian yelled as Joses passed. "You Sicarii filth! Murderer!" The man turned to the few people who were watching from their homes or from the alleys. "He is the cause of all our grief. He killed my son. And he has probably killed many of your sons!" said the man, referring to the many battles the Sicarii had conducted with the Roman and Herodian forces over the years.

Joses was able to carry the crossbeam only a few more paces before he fell. He was too weak from the scourging to carry the heavy burden. Now, several of the more affluent citizens, mostly Herodian sympathizers and collaborators, were gathering to look at this man they knew only as "Yeshua." They began talking amongst themselves, pointing at Joses and then spitting at him or hurling various verbal insults. Joses could only lay still. To hurry the condemned along, a guard took a man from the crowd named Simon who was a servant of one of the Herodians and ordered him to carry the crossbeam for Joses. As Simon lifted the crossbeam, Joses could see a number of common people, especially some women, bewailing and lamenting him.

"Oh, Yehoshua ben Joseph, what are we to do? What will become of us?"

Another next to her cried, "Oh Son of David, why have you not saved yourself and us?" There was still so much confusion, and rightly so.

Joses stood up and the guards pushed him forward. But, he stopped, looked at the women, and simply stated, "Weep not for me, but yourselves, for I failed to free you. But do not blame HaShem, for He is Great and will provide a way again.

Immediately a guard kicked him to the ground to silence him. To ensure that the growing crowd would not get out of control, a large escort secured the way on to Golgotha so that no one could again interfere with the executions.

***

Miriam, Joses' mother Miryam, and Salome had just been joined by Jochanan and they had all placed the children and important possessions with a group of supporters who would transport them to a ship waiting in the Mediterranean offered by Joseph of Arimathea. Kefa, who had also just arrived to assist them in the escape, begged them to depart. But, the women told him they wanted to return to Jerusalem to see after the fate of their beloved Joses.

"No, you must not go back to Jerusalem! Don't you understand that Rome is now ready to destroy Joses' family as well as him? This is insane," argued Kefa.

Miriam would not consent to Kefa's argument. "Our children are secure and we have the need to be as near to Joses as possible. He has been our life! How can we leave him now, even at the end of his life?" She was now succumbing to the grief she had been suppressing for the last many hours since the news of the arrest. Salome and Miryam, Joses' sister and mother, were also sobbing now. The duties they had consigned themselves to in order to protect the royal children now accomplished, all of their emotions turned upon them and fed their grief.

Martha, unlike herself, was now the quiet one, pondering her plight and that of Joses' family. She looked at Miriam, the inquisitive and daring wife of Joses with whom she had felt some competition, and witnessed a welling of devotion rising in her toward this woman who had so selflessly dedicated her life to the career of her husband. She wanted to be more like her, even though she knew she could never be the mother of the chosen line as Miriam was. Having been given more to the requirements of domestic duties, Martha had never fully appreciated Miriam's understanding of the philosophies of the kingdom—until now.

"Miriam," Martha began, "I will stay with the children to

ensure their safety. That should free all of you to go. I will follow the instructions you have left with Kefa should the need arise."

"Oh, Martha!" cried Miriam, "What have I done to deserve such love from you?"

"And us?" cried Salome and Miryam, Joses' mother.

Martha, sobbing yet clear in her response cried, "We have the honor of our wonderful Joses to uphold. He binds us all together, and we have bound ourselves to him in an unbreakable covenant. I am so privileged to be here, and with you wonderful women. But, go now, and see to our Joses and I will continue the preparations. I do not think I could bear the pain of the sight of Joses and his condition now. I will do better to be mindful of the duties required here. You know, Joses always said we should attend to our natural talents and use them for the good of all."

The women embraced each other, realizing that all they had stood for together was now what they cherished and prized the most. It was the defining moment of their lives, and they were all steadfastly dedicated to the cause of the royal patriarchal line and to Joses. They also knew they may never see each other again should the Romans identify them. So those proceeding back to Jerusalem used precautions and all set veils upon themselves to hide their faces. Martha and Kefa stayed with the children and provisions as the other women and Jochanan departed for Jerusalem.

***

Joses was now approaching the crest of the hill of Golgotha. It was a desolate place, designed by Rome to be a metaphor for those who stood against the empire. No one was permitted on the top but the soldiers engaged in the duties of the execution and those who were to be the victims. The location was high enough that it could be seen from some distance away.

The soldiers took the crossbeam from Simon and threw it to the ground, at the same time ordering him to depart the site. They then pushed Joses down and dragged his naked body across the stony ground to the upright stake. It was, however, his nakedness that continued most to inflict him with torment. The executioners placed the crossbeam beneath his head and tied his arms anew to it.

Though he could not see clearly, he realized that two soldiers were approaching him from each side carrying a hammer and several iron spikes. He was too weak to resist as several soldiers held his arms to the beam as the rusted, dark brown spikes were driven through his wrists below the joint, crushing the nerves and causing a new pain that swept Joses into a bitter agony that made death seem paltry. His arms and chest convulsed, the contractions searing his sanity and yet not sufficient to bring on unconsciousness or death. His fingers and hands burned and ached with uncontrollable distortion. He kicked his legs and tore at his arm sockets in his attempts to flee the pain. Again, his actions were dictated not by reason or hope, but involuntary efforts of his body to escape the pain.

To ensure their work, the soldiers then took two smaller spikes and drove them through the palms of Joses' hands. It was an order from Pilate to inflict a special insult to the self-professed mashiach. They then used a set of ropes and pulleys to lift the beam to which Joses was nailed and place it on the upright that had been sunk in the ground earlier.

The weight of his body caused the wounds in his wrists to feel as if they were tearing apart the very joints and muscles, and he could not breathe. Someone grabbed his feet and an unbearable pain filled his right foot and leg as he felt bones and sinews separate and shatter as a piercing blow thrust a spike through his foot at the instep. Then again as the right foot was placed over the left and the spike hammered through the instep of his left foot and into the upright. The tendons in his feet and calves contracted violently, but he could now push himself up for a needed breath.

He opened his eyes and looked down at his bare body exposed to the world, broken, bleeding, humiliated and suffering. He could not entirely fathom why he had permitted himself to suffer such torture. Then, faintly through the bloody strands of hair blowing across his face and the blood trickling into his eyes, he could make out the forms of three women in the distance. He would never again be as close as this to those he loved and cherished.

"For HaShem and Israel," is all he could think. Had not HaShem agreed to accept Joses' death in exchange for Israel's salvation, the kingdom brought forth through Joses' heirs? Yes, this was the path. It was, wasn't it?

The sight of Joses hanging broken and bloodied on the crossbeam and stake was more than any of the women could endure. Each sought some solace in the embrace of the others. It was fruitless. Jochanan, watching Joses die a cursed and ignominious death, could find no comfort even in the company of Joses' mother, and he could not find the strength to speak any words. Any possible comfort was transcended by the horror of the sight that was before them. Their unbridled grief and terror could only be matched by the sufferings Joses was experiencing himself. They watched as the Roman executioners lifted up two more of Joses' followers for crucifixion next to him, one on either side. They could no longer recognize any of them except Joses, and that only because of their long and intimate attachments to him. The hopes and dreams of a new world were in complete shambles.

Jochanan held Joses' mother, Miryam, to his small shoulder and took the right hand of Joses' wife, Miriam, into his. He doubted everything at this moment, but he knew that these women, and the family, were really all that mattered. It was time to get them out of the land, and he dutifully pressed them to leave. But, Miriam and Salome would stay to attend to the burial, even at the peril of their lives. So, Jochanan took Joses' mother, Miryam, and left.

Salome and Miriam were shortly joined by Joseph of Arimathea who had already made arrangements with Pilate to obtain the body of Joses for burial so that it would not remain on the tree through Passover. The three of them looked over at the site of the crucifixion, now in the fading light caused by the approach of an afternoon storm. None of them spoke a word.

Then, Miriam saw Joanna. She was horrified that she would be here at this moment, defiling Joses with her presence. But, the thought quickly faded as Miriam considered how Joses had protected her according to the law. She motioned to Joanna with her right hand, and Joanna bowed her head to her in respect. Miriam could see Joanna's eyes filled with tears, red and swollen. Now was not the time to speak, however. Both women turned their eyes back toward Golgotha.

***

The thoughts of Joses were eerily similar to those of Jochanan. He startled himself out of his delirium. "HaShem has promised, but when will it be?" he asked himself, realizing that he did not know the answer. "When will it be?" he asked. "When will it be?"

He tried to enter into a meditation, even in the pain and the humiliation, knowing his death was approaching. He recited sacred letters and words in his mind and with his lips over and over, trying to visualize the chamber, trying to obtain an assurance, a comfort.

Nothing.

He raised himself up on his feet to try and gain a deeper breath, the nail through his feet grinding on the bones causing an excruciating pain. He whispered out the words again, and tried to move his head from side to side in a respectful, rhythmic manner to empty his mind of all but the thought of HaShem.

But, he received no answer. Now a panic rose in him above and beyond the pain and fear of death. He had found his answers in his meditations, but he could not receive any comfort now. Why? Why, at the moment of his submission could he receive nothing? The promise—what of the promise?

"When shall these things come to pass?" he asked.

Nothing. He was alone.

"My God, My God, why have you forsaken me?" he cried aloud with what little breath he could summon. "HaShem cannot abandon me!" he cried to himself. "All of this, all we have tried to do. My family, my children, my brethren, my nation-will they survive?" He had lived a life of selfless service to his people. He had tried to defend them against the invaders from Rome, the usurpers of Herod, the false religions of the heathen gentiles, and the fanaticism of religious zealots who used the Torah beyond the mark of its spirit. He had tried to teach them as a father teaches his children. He had tried to fulfill his mission to be the Mashiach ben Joseph, the birthright son of Israel, to bring them back, as many as would come, to HaShem.

In short, he tried to raise their consciousness and see the kingdom of God within them, and raising all of creation as well. He did it all for the love of his brethren and most of all for his love for HaShem.

"I thirst," he said without realizing it. A soldier close by him brought a sponge soaked in vinegar and placed it in his mouth. It was sour, but wet. The taste reminded him of the purpose and meaning of his life, as he saw it. He was to stand for the people at all costs, even his own discomfort and peril. HaShem had made an oath; Joses could do nothing more than live and die for it. It was the calling of the Righteous King, the true Father of his people. He was to give the bread of life to those suffering famine, as Joseph had done in Egypt so many centuries before.

But, the bread from Joses was his willingness to sacrifice himself that a new consciousness would be born in the world, the light of individual liberty. He trusted that he might return as was promised in the Torah at the end of days, being born again at another time and place as the mystics of Bethshemesh foretold. Would he then be the Davidic King, indeed freeing Israel of all oppressors and bringing in a new age to the world? A resurrection, or a remembrance of himself and his past, would be the key to his success.

Resolved, and comforted by the realization that he had lived as he desired, Joses wanted to completely lose consciousness to rid himself of the pain the crucifixion brought upon his body. His desire seemed to slowly accommodate him as the afternoon sun hid its light in the clouds of an approaching storm. He looked through his dimming eyes as his executioners cast lots to see who would win his white linen robe. Then, he felt an indescribable thump and pain in his chest, like he had been hit with a spear. It was all he could do to summon another breath; the pressure bearing down so hard that only a small amount of air entered his mouth. In agony and barely conscious, he looked over at a stream of red blood dripping from his right arm. It looked like he would die as he was born, true to his birthright with a crimson thread around his wrist.

He looked away and simply groaned in a low tone with his final breath, "It is finished."

CHAPTER FOURTEEN

Evening was descending and, as the Passover recognized by most of the Jews was about to begin, Pilate had agreed to order the guards to break the legs of the criminals so that they would die quickly. One Roman took a large beam and broke Benjamin's legs, and then Samuel's. The men, already near death as a result of their serious injuries and no longer able to hold themselves up, immediately began to suffocate. The soldier with the beam then approached Joses. He was about to do the same when it appeared to him that the man was already dead. Joses had arrived at the place of execution almost dead from his scourging, anyway. It was no surprise that the additional extremes of the crucifixion would kill him so fast.

For some unknown reason, the Roman did not feel it advantageous to break the legs of a corpse. He threw down the beam and took a lance, driving it deep into Joses' side, up into his heart. He turned away, satisfied that his work was done. Once the other two criminals were obviously dead, the soldiers made their way from Golgotha and headed toward the city. Joseph of Arimathea had arranged for the body and none of the Romans, not even Pilate, thought it of any concern that Joses' immediate family would risk exposure at the site of the execution.

Joseph of Arimathea, Miriam, Joses' sister Salome, and a physician from the Damascus Therapeutate, along with several others, arrived at the base of the stakes. Working quickly, they pulled the nails from Joses' feet, the one wrist and then the other. Joses' body was lowered carefully by the use of a large linen cloth. The wounds from the scourging and the crucifixion were massive. Even if he had survived the crucifixion he would have succumbed to the injuries and infections already taking hold upon his weakened body. There had been that remote hope that they could revive him. But, as the physician examined him and tried to administer resuscitation, it was obvious that nothing could bring Joses back. He was dead. Miriam held him and cried, her heart wrenching for him, and she tore her garment in her grief.

Back in Jerusalem, Jacob had paused to speak to a group of Jews and members of the Community assembled together about him as he descended the steps of the Temple where he had gone to meditate and pray. Jacob stopped and looked around as the people began to press closer to him. They were all asking him what should be done about the cruelty of the Herodians and the Romans in killing Joses. While constantly assailing their opponents, Jacob could not escape the guilt he felt personally. He also could see that the crowd felt no culpability of their own. He stopped and stood motionless in thought. The people, seeing him in such a state, quieted themselves, anticipating his words. After a few moments of reflection, Jacob looked up and examined the faces of the people about him.

"Hear me out, Oh brothers of ours, House of Israel! Lo, it says, 'When a corpse is found, and your elders and judges go forth and measure. Now as it is to us-whither and whence shall we measure? To the sanctuary? Or to the courtyard?"

The sharpness and truth of his words penetrated every soul there. Some began to weep; others groaned and sat upon the ground, rending and ripping their clothes in the customary fashion of the Jews, all realizing their mistakes in not supporting Joses and yet understanding that he sacrificed himself to ensure their protection and mission. What Jacob was quoting was a requirement from Devarim (Deuteronomy 21:1-9) that when a body is found, and murder is suspected, the elders of the cities about it measure to find their distance from it. The town closest to it must take the responsibility for the crime. Jacob was saying that he and everyone else had failed Joses.

Miriam and Salome prepared Joses' body for burial. The execution of Joses on the day of the Community's recognized

Passover, with its accompanying Sabbath the next day, made the entire ordeal even more agonizing and repulsive. Despite strict rules against such situations, the group had no other choice but to carry on. They, with the assistance of Joseph, the physician, Nikdimon ben Gurion and Jochanan, carried Joses in a litter to a temporary burial place as night was approaching and there was not time to complete any other necessary requirements.

The body was prepared with several spices and cleaning substances to ensure that it would be well enough preserved until they could later complete the burial ritual. They would then transport the body to the permanent burial tomb prepared by Joseph. The place was not far from the tombs in Hebron of Jacob and Joseph, the Hebrew Patriarchs. Joses' body was placed in the temporary crypt and the stone rolled into place. The party would return immediately on the morning after their Sabbath ended the next night to complete the preparation and transport the body to Hebron.

The night after the completion of the Community's Sabbath, Jacob and several of Joses' followers discussed how they should proceed. The Community Elders now fully recognized what Joses had actually stood for and accomplished. Jacob, for certain, would be his successor, not only because of his position as the Teacher of Righteousness, but because Jacob recognized the declaration by Joses that Jacob would stand in his place at his death. This act would require a vote by the assembled councils, however, and that would be weeks away. But, in the meantime, they laid out the general particulars of administration. Jacob would take over Joses' position but work from Damascus and Jerusalem. Kefa would continue his efforts with the Diaspora Jews that Joses had him contact, as well as all of Galilee and Samaria. They believed they could be successful in the resistance and would start planning after the family of Joses was safely out of Judea. Also of importance was what to do with the body of Joses. To leave it near Jerusalem would allow the Romans and Herodians to desecrate it or not allow it to be moved to its appropriate burial site in Hebron with the Patriarchs of old.

Also, there were several severely extremist Zealots who could not allow the Community brethren to fail to act. They, also, had an interest in ensuring that the Romans and the Herodians did not display the body of Joses. Furthermore, with their desire for Zealot martyrs, they needed an example of a resurrection to life of the great leader, so that those not normally willing to die may sacrifice themselves for the chance at a resurrection. These, likely, would attempt to remove the body as well.

Despite the difficulties, the burial party of Miriam, Salome, Arimathea, and Jochanan decided to wait another day as they did not want to be seen as if they were violating the regularly recognized orthodox Sabbath. It would not be wise to be accused of violating the Torah, especially with tensions as high as they now were with the Herodian administration. So, they waited and agreed to return to complete their duties and finish preparing Joses' body nearly three days after Joses' crucifixion. For Miriam, Joses' body would need to remain where it was for another day, until the first day of the week. As the children and Martha were safe on the ship ready to sail, Miriam decided to stay with Salome, Jochanan and family near Jerusalem so she could return to the sepulcher on the first day of the week.

On the morning of the first day of the week, just before sunrise, Miriam and the burial party went to the tomb under the cover of darkness so as to hinder detection of their activities. However, when they entered the tomb, they were startled to find two men dressed in white linen garments, the same type worn by those of the more extreme Zealots, who appeared to be finishing some tasks and were preparing to leave. Most distressing was that Joses' body was gone!

"Where have you taken him!" demanded Miriam. "What have you done with him?"

The men looked at each other and Miriam could detect that they had a full knowledge of what had happened. She pressed them further, now Salome and Jochanan also demanding answers.

"He is not here," one of the men said as he pointed out of the sepulcher. "He has gone to Galilee."

"Gone to Galilee?" asked Jochanan rhetorically. His anger

swelled in him and he placed his hand on his sicar. "You are not going to use this for your own purposes. We know very well who would use his death to gain more followers against Rome. But, these things cannot work. Even Joses said that. He would not approve of your methods nor sanction your cause. His body belongs to his family, and to HaShem. Return it to us or prepare to meet the dust."

The two men backed away out of the tomb and ran. Jochanan started to pursue them, but he realized he could not leave Miriam, Salome and the elderly Joseph of Arimathea alone. He watched as the men disappeared over the next rise and out of sight. He returned quickly to Miriam's side.

Miriam was bereft. After all Joses and she had gone through, now she was to be robbed of the very last right of a wife and queen. Despondently, she turned and left the tomb and motioned for the others to follow her. They all hurried to a home not far away where several of the followers of Joses were just arising from their sleep.

"He is gone!" Miriam said to the group as she burst into the main room.

"What do you mean, he is gone?" asked Kefa who had returned to Jerusalem after sending the family off to the coast under guard. He saw that she was beside herself.

"Joses, he is not in the tomb," Miriam said with a sudden resolve. It came to her that her duties were over as far as the burial was concerned. She needed to get to the ship and ensure the escape and survival of the rest of the family, especially the children. "He has gone to Galilee," she said softly. She turned to Salome and Jochanan, and then back to Kefa. "We are leaving for the ship. It is time for us to depart. Will you do all you can for my husband?"

"The tomb is empty?" Kefa asked her as she walked out the door.

"He is gone," answered Miriam. "Go see for yourself."

Kefa immediately started towards the area of the temporary tomb. Nathanael bar Talmai followed closely behind him.

"I told you that they would take the body and claim HaShem

resurrected him so others would fight on," Nathanael bar Talmai said as he followed Kefa out the door.

"Go to the ship and wait for me," Kefa called to Miriam. "I need to see for myself and then I can assist in helping you to depart."

Miriam waved to him as he started to run. She walked out the door and headed west to the waiting vessel.

Jochanan did not follow Miriam out the door.

"Are you coming, Jochanan?" asked Miriam.

"It seems as though my place is here, to do whatever is in my power," answered Jochanan. "What is important is that father's heirs remain free. Let me remain and do as is needed. It is what HaShem would want me to do."

"But, your mother needs you," answered Miriam. "Go to her, and discuss it with her before you make your final decision."

"Tell my mother that her son loves her. Tell her, that it is father's business that concerns me. If possible, we will meet again later," Jochanan was adamant. Miriam could see his desires.

"Very well," Miriam said to him. "Your father would be proud of you, and you will certainly lend a great deal to the resistance and to Israel. May we meet again in the mansions of HaShem. Please let Eleazer know all that has transpired and that we have left as planned." Miriam hugged him and then turned and walked westward.

Miriam, Salome, and Joseph of Arimathea began their journey to ensure the survival of Joses' heirs. Their sailboat was on the shore of the Mediterranean Sea, less than a day's journey from Jerusalem. Awaiting them were Martha, Joses' mother Miryam, and Joses' children. Word was already circulating that Caiaphas had sent his guards to find any members of the immediate family. In all likelihood, Herod would see to it that, as Galileans, they would be executed for some charge of sedition against Rome and, as with the Hasmonaeans, eliminated from all affairs in Palestine. It would be up to those who were staying behind to carry on the resistance until Joses' sons could stand in their father's place. As the family knew, Rome would answer that resistance with more violence. Jude, Jacob, Kefa, Eleazer and Jochanan would carry on the fight.

But what none of them knew was that Caesar was already designing a strategy he would soon employ. It was a plan even darker and more sinister than violence. The Emperor was preparing a scheme of diabolic proportions to change the religion and hopes of the Jews that would also subdue their will to resist. The war with Caesar was only beginning.

As the ship made way from the coast of Judea and sailed west, the voyagers all gathered on the back of the deck to bid farewell. Miriam looked back at her homeland, now slowly drawing away into the distance. True to what Joses had told her, HaShem was again sending the holy seed into the world for His own purposes. Miriam understood her duties and she would impart her knowledge to her sons and guide them in attaining the gifts of their father. She looked at her oldest, Joseph, who was now so like Joses when she met him for the first time. Joshua, too, was looking more mature at this moment than any boy his age should. Together they would be the key to the renewal of Israel. The boys arose and stood by their mother. As they faced the land to the east, the wind from the sea blew their hair in their eyes, partially obscuring their vision.

Then, as if Joses' spirit voice instructed them, they all turned at the same time to look out over the Mediterranean to the west, the shifting wind blowing their hair away from their faces. Their vision was now clear.

Neither Rome, Herod nor Caiaphas ever imagined that they would leave their beloved country. The thought never occurred to them that the family would depart the land of their birth and heritage to seek a new land for the lost King, the heir of the crimson thread.

GLOSSARY

bat—daughter in Hebrew

ben—son in Hebrew. The Aramaic equivalent, often used, is "bar."

breaker of the matrix—the firstborn of a woman, and if male, the heir. If twins are born, the firstborn receives a crimson thread to ensure identification of birthright.

bishirt/bishirtah-masculine counterpart/counterpart. Sometimes referred to, under special circumstances, as soulmate.

Century—a Roman Army unit consisting of 100 soldiers.

Cohort—a Roman Army unit consisting of 300-600 soldiers.

corban—money offerings to the Temple treasury.

cubit—a measurement equal to about 18 inches.

furlong—a measurement of about 201 meters or 220 yards.

HaMashiach—Literally, the Messiah. However, the concept of a messiah in Israel was not as Christianity presents it today. It simply meant a "king in waiting" or "crown prince" or "anointed one" idea. Once that messiah became a king, he was no longer a messiah. King David, for instance, was a messiah before he became King of Israel. In Israelite tradition there are two major promised messiahs. The first is actually the Messiah ben Joseph, a descendent of the patriarch's son Joseph who was sold into slavery and sent to Egypt by his brothers. This messiah was to act as the family heir over all Israel and it was understood that he would die in the course of his mission. The second was the Messiah ben David, or Davidic King, as foretold principally by Daniel and the later prophets. He would arise to re-establish Israel and conquer all of HaShem's enemies and would not suffer defeat. Today, the person we call Jesus Christ is the one commonly believed to have held this position. But, as the story explains, this was not, and is not the case. There is also the Mashiach ben Aaron, or priestly messiah, the position John the Baptist sought to fulfill.

HaShem—literally, The Name, meaning the name of God, specifically the Tetragrammaton. It is used so as not to pronounce God's true name or appellations irreverently.

hechalot/hekhalot—the name of the Jewish mystical system before it became kabbalah.

hitbodedut—Hebrew for meditation.

kabbalah—literally, "to receive." A system involving practical, meditative, and theoretical aspects to gain enlightenment.

kepa—a small cap.

kittim—a code name for foreign invaders. At this point in history, the Romans.

Legion—a Roman Army unit made up of sixty centuries (6000 soldiers).

Maniple—a Roman term for a small unit of soldiers (5-20) particularly suitable for special tasks.

merkava—also known as "Workings of the Merkava." This is the ultimate experience sought by the prophets using the meditative techniques of the hekhalot. A meditative chariot of light is formed with which one ascends to the upper chambers. There, through the visions of angels or "Ispaklaria," "mirrors and lenses," one views God. It also refers to the mystery of Ezekiel's vision.

mikvah—a ritual bath for immersion for purification. Usually a kind of cistern through which water can flow, and sometimes nothing more than a stream or river, such as the Jordan River.

Moreh ha Tzedeq—the Teacher of Righteousness. Also called Rabbi Tzedeq.

Nazarite—Numbers 6:1-27 explains it. A person who takes a vow of specific separation (separation means holiness, being one and the same, the Hebrew word being kodesh).

Passover—the day commemorating the exodus from Egypt.

Pax Romana—Latin meaning Roman Peace. To achieve it, a nation or people had to submit to Rome's rule.

Pentecost—in Christianity, the day commemorating the

descent of the Holy Spirit on the Apostles which was the 50th day after Easter. However, it was actually the Jewish Festival of Shavuot, and the Apostles would have been together to celebrate it. See Shavuot below.

Ruach HaKodesh—literally the "Holy Breath of God." A point reached during meditationwhere the individual ascends to the spiritual realm. It is the Hebraic term for the Holy Spirit or, more properly, ultimate enlightenment.

Shavuot—Feast of Weeks. It is celebrated seven weeks after Passover. It was the day commemorating the giving of the Torah and thanksgiving for the grain harvest.

sicar—a small blade larger than a dagger which had a curved shape similar to Arab blades.

Sicarii—one of the Roman names for the Zealot groups of the Jews fighting to free their nation. The name came from their habit of carrying concealed weapons, particularly the sicar.

tallit—a four cornered prayer shawl with tzitzit attached.

tefillin—also known as phylacteries, these are two boxes with Torah verses from Deuteronomy and Exodus in them. One is attached to the forehead, the other to the arm and hand.

Tetragrammaton—the four letter name of God corresponding to the letters YHVH in English. It is never pronounced, except once a year by the High Priest in the Holy of Holies of the Temple.

Torah—the first five books of the Old Testament.

tzitzit—ritual fringes attached to a four-cornered garment, usually a tallit, to remind the wearer of the commandments.

The Way—another term for the life and duties of the group of ascetics at Damascus or Qumran. It involved strict discipline, observance of Torah in all its aspects, and obedience. By following it, one could reach piety and get closer to God.

Zealots—a group that arose around the time of the Census of Cyrenius and the Roman tax with the express purpose of fighting Roman rule. A name for all those of the Jews who were strong for the Torah and willing to fight for it. In Hebrew the word for Zealot is Kannaim which is often mistranslated as Cananite.

BIBLIOGRAPHY AND SOURCE MATERIALS

Atwill, Joseph; Caesar's Messiah; Ulysses Press, Berkeley, CA: 2005.

Baigent, Leigh, & Lincoln; Holy Blood, Holy Grail; Dell Publishing, NY: 1983

Eisenman, Robert; James the Brother of Jesus; Penguin Books, NY, NY: 1997

Eisenman, Robert; The Dead Sea Scrolls and the First Christians; Castle Books, Edison, NJ: 2004

Eisenman & Wise; The Dead Sea Scrolls Uncovered; Barnes & Noble, NY: 1992

Epstein, Perle; Kabbalah; Barnes & Noble, NY; 1978

Frankl, Viktor E.; The Will To Meaning; Meridian, Penguin Group, NY; 1970

Gardner, Laurence; Bloodline of the Holy Grail; Element Books, Rockport, MA; 1996

Gaster, Theodor; The Dead Sea Scriptures; Anchor Press; Garden City, NY; 1976

Jaynes, Julian; The Origin of Consciousness in the Breakdown of the Bicameral Mind;

Mariner Books, New York; 1990

Josephus; Antiquities of the Jews; Kregel Publications, Grand Rapids, Michigan; 1978

Josephus; Against Apion; Kregel Publications, Grand Rapids, Michigan; 1978

Josephus; Wars of the Jews; Kregel Publications, Grand Rapids, Michigan; 1978

Kaplan, Aryeh; Meditation and Kabbalah; Samuel Weiser, York Beach, Maine; 1982

Klinghoffer, David; Why The Jews Rejected Jesus; Doubleday, NY; 2005

Knight & Lomas; The Hiram Key; Barnes & Noble, NY; 1998

Matt, Daniel C.; The Essential Kabbalah; Harper Collins, San Francisco, CA; 1996

Old and New Testaments

Sefer Yetzirah

Stern, David; Complete Jewish Bible; Jewish New Testament Publications, Inc., Clarksville, MD; 1998

Stern, David; Jewish New Testament Commentary; Jewish New Testament Publications,

Inc., MD; 1992

The Talmud

Telushkin, Joseph: Jewish Literacy; William Morrow and Company, Inc.; NY; 1991

BIOGRAPHY OF ROYSTON POTTER

Royston Potter was born in Washington, D.C. and raised in Hyattsville, Maryland. He holds a Bachelor of Science degree in Law and Justice Administration and is a graduate of the United States Army Command and General Staff College. As a commissioned officer in the United States Army, he completed assignments in the Military Police and Military Intelligence fields.

Having always had an abiding interest in historical and spiritual matters, he studied several disciplines and religions for many years. The last ten years, since 1995, he spent almost entirely in the Hebrew language and its esoteric meanings as presented in the mystical aspects of Judaism, known as Kabbalah.

He brings to the reader a new approach to history and the roots of religious expression, redefining the origins of the western world. His insights reflected in this book are directly related to his personal studies and his military experiences.

He now resides in Evanston, Wyoming with his beloved wife.

ENDNOTES

(Endnotes)

[1] The name coined by Frankl for the method of enabling one to find meaning in life. See the bibliography on Frankl's The Will To Meaning.

[2] Knight and Lomas; The Hiram Key; page 193.

[3] A Hebrew name for God used out of respect to symbolize the four letter name or Tetragrammaton, YHVH, commonly referred to in modern times as Jehovah.

[4] For further study on this issue, see the following: Genesis 49:10; Joshua 18:1-10; Judges 18:31; Judges 20:27; 1 Samuel 1:3, 24; 1 Samuel 3:3; 1 Samuel 14; 3; 1 Samuel 22: 16-23; 2 Samuel 6; Psalms 78: 60-72; Isaiah 11:13; Jeremiah 7:12, 14.

[5] Jeremiah 31:9

[6] Exodus 13:2; Exodus 22:29; Numbers 18:15-16

[7] Exodus 13:15

[8] If a man progressed in his initiations at Damascus while he demonstrated his righteousness and dedication to Torah, he would eventually reach the highest levels of the Community Way and be declared a Son of God. The appellation was never intended to denote a true lineage, but a spiritual adoption because of one's worthiness.

[9] A covered walkway around the roof of the courtyard.

[10] See footnote #4, Chapter 1.

[11] Also known as Bethshemesh or Emmaus.

[12] Kaptziel is an armed angel. Metatron is one of the Angels who speak for HaShem and has immense power. HaShem says of this Angel, "He has my Name in him."

[13] The Three Nets of Belial are the evils of riches, fornication, and pollution of the Temple.

[14] Pronounced Pardes, also known in English as paradise. It is a Hebrew acronym for the levels of meaning of Torah.

[15] This was a system fully developed several centuries later by Rabbi Abraham Abulafia. Joses is merely experimenting here.

[16] Meaning "My Lord."

[17] 2 Maccabees 7:1-42.

[18] See Glossary. Literally, the breath of God, also known as the Holy Spirit. A feminine part of God.

[19] Merkava is a chariot, in the Hechalot a mystical chariot of light used to transport the spirit body to the Seventh level.

[20] A prayer shawl.

[21] "Poor" and "Meek," among other such appellations, were codes for initiates or members of the Community at Damascus, or, as here, Joses' initiates. See bibliography for works by Eisenman.

[22] See translation of David Stern, Complete Jewish Bible, pp.1227-1228. and compare to King James.

[23] Another name for Galilee.

[24] Absalom was King David's son who attempted to usurp his father's throne. See 2 Sam 18.

[25] Nozri continued as the Hebrew name for what are now called "Christians."

[26] Literally a lens or mirror through which you look to see an image, not the actual thing, which in this case would be God.

[27] Original Biblical Hebrew was written only with the 22 Hebrew consonants with no spaces between the letters. Vowels were added as tradition noted and the sages agreed. In fact, the language had more than one meaning, and new vowels substantially changed the level of meaning. Joses is now seeing a different level of meaning.

[28] In Hebrew, the letters of the alphabet are also the number system. Words having the same or relevant meanings, or other important associations, have the same numerical value.

[29] ZHRRYAL is one of the secret code names of HaShem.

[30] Historically, this likely actually happened during the reign of the Roman Emperor Nero when the Zealots (Sicarii) successfully

burned Rome. Nero blamed "Christians", but they were not known by that name. The "Christians" at that time were known as Nozri, and they were the Zealots or Sicarii as we have shown. So, Joses' plans were eventually put into effect.

[31] See Footnote #4, Chapter 1.

[32] Corban is the money donated by the people to the Temple Treasury.

[33] See Mark 6. The basis for Joạchanin's denunciations of this Herod revolved around him marrying his brother's wife, Herodias. This would have been lawful if his brother had died and had no children. But, Salome had been born.